Outstanding praise for M.V. Byrne and *Meet Isabel Puddles*!

"I was very happy to meet Isabel Puddles and I'm sure readers will enjoy making her acquaintance, too. M.V. Byrne's small-town sleuth with a big heart sees the *possible* in impossible, whether she's cooking up a delicious pot roast or solving a devious crime."
—Leslie Meier, author of *Easter Bonnet Murder*

"A charming debut, captivating cast, and many spells of laugh-out-loud humor."
—*Kirkus Reviews*

"When you meet the delightfully witty and no-nonsense Isabel Puddles, you'll never want her to leave."
—Lee Hollis, author of *Poppy Harmon and the Backstabbing Bachelor*

"Fans of Garrison Keillor's tales of Lake Wobegon will be enchanted."
—*Publishers Weekly*

"I've met Isabel Puddles and I love her. She's a smart, funny AARPster who can whip up a mean pot roast while solving a diabolical murder. I eagerly turned the pages of this charming, action-packed whodunit. What a fun read!"
—Laura Levine, author of *Murder Gets a Makeover*

Books by M.V. Byrne

MEET ISABEL PUDDLES

ISABEL PUDDLES INVESTIGATES

ISABEL PUDDLES ABROAD

Published by Kensington Publishing Corp.

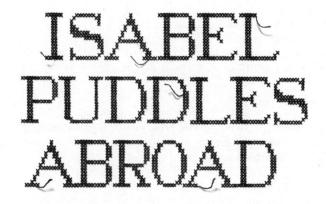

ISABEL PUDDLES ABROAD

M.V BYRNE

KENSINGTON PUBLISHING CORP.

www.kensingtonbooks.com

KENSINGTON BOOKS are published by
Kensington Publishing Corp.
119 West 40th Street
New York, NY 10018

All Kensington titles, imprints, and distributed lines are available at special quantity discounts for bulk purchases for sales promotion, premiums, fund-raising, educational, or institutional use.

This book is a work of fiction. Names, characters, businesses, organizations, places, events, and incidents either are the product of the author's imagination or are used fictitiously. Any resemblance to actual persons, living or dead, events, or locales is entirely coincidental.

To the extent that the image or images on the cover of this book depict a person or persons, such person or persons are merely models, and are not intended to portray any character or characters featured in the book.

Special book excerpts or customized printings can also be created to fit specific needs. For details, write or phone the office of the Kensington Sales Manager: Kensington Publishing Corp., 119 West 40th Street, New York, NY 10018. Attn. Sales Department. Phone: 1-800-221-2647.

The K and Teapot logo is a trademark of Kensington Publishing Corp.

ISBN: 978-1-4967-2836-4 (ebook)

ISBN: 978-1-4967-2835-7

First Kensington Trade Paperback Printing: December 2022

10 9 8 7 6 5 4 3 2 1

Printed in the United States of America

For Uncle R.J. with love and admiration for a life well lived . . . And to Roberta, Jennifer, Christopher, Rachel, and Ryan, who continue to teach me the importance of family, unconditional love, and the value (and necessity) of laughter.

Chapter 1

The first day of spring arrived in Isabel Puddles's hometown of Gull Harbor, Michigan, with about a foot of snow on the ground and more on the way. But that wasn't unusual. The weather along Lake Michigan didn't pay much attention to the calendar, so Isabel never bothered putting her warm clothes away until she got her first mosquito bite. Only then could she be sure summer had arrived.

Easter Sunday was approaching, so she was meeting her best friend, Frances, for breakfast at their usual breakfast haunt, the Land's End, to discuss the menu for Easter dinner, although Isabel didn't see that there was much to discuss. It's Easter. You bake a ham, scallop some potatoes, devil some eggs, and call it a day, as far as she was concerned. But Frances had called the night before to say she wanted to "shake things up a little this year," which made Isabel more than a little nervous. Frances had a true talent for baking, but cooking was, to be kind, a challenge. Unfortunately, her limited abilities on that front didn't stop her from experimenting with dishes and techniques some trained chefs might shy away from. And when she did, things could go very Lucy Ricardo, very quickly. Her husband, Hank, was about as meat-and-potatoes as a man could be, so his wife's forays into gourmet cooking were completely lost on him. In fact, he once accused her of deliberately sabotaging her overly ambitious culinary endeavors just so he would have to take her out to dinner after yet another of her epic fails. Knowing Frances as she did, Isabel thought Hank might be on to something with that theory.

When it came to holiday menus, Isabel Puddles was a traditionalist. Forgoing ham at Easter was tantamount to skipping turkey on Thanksgiving. Frances's pending Easter dinner "shake-up" brought back memories of the Thanksgiving her cousin Freddie decided he was going to "shake things up a little," too, and deep-fry the turkey. Carol, his wife, begged him not to do it, but Freddie was on a mission. He had seen it on some cooking show and was sure it was going to revolutionize turkey preparation forever. Because it was a cold and rainy afternoon, he set up the operation in the garage, and in less than an hour he had nearly set the garage and the house on fire and turned a perfectly good turkey into something resembling a large charcoal briquette with legs. Luckily Carol had anticipated some such catastrophe and secretly put another bird in the oven, so Thanksgiving dinner proceeded as planned, although Freddie had to eat a little crow with his turkey that year.

All Frances would say about the reasoning behind *her* plan for a shake-up was that she felt ham was overdone and that it was time to try something "new and different." Again, not words you want to hear coming out of Frances Spitler's mouth when the topic is meal planning. Isabel didn't want to rain on her Easter parade, but she planned to lobby pretty hard to keep things simple and keep ham on the menu.

When she was a girl, Isabel and her father drove out to Billy Bartles's farm every year on Good Friday to pick up one of his succulent, maple-smoked hams for Easter dinner. She continued that tradition with her own kids until one year she went out to the Bartles farm to pick up her ham and made eye contact with one of his hogs on her way out to the smokehouse. Ham was off the menu that year, and she convinced her late husband, Carl, and the kids—Carly and Charlie—that going to Pizza Hut for Easter dinner would be a nice change of pace.

A months-long pork moratorium in the Puddles household followed, involving a lot of turkey bacon for breakfast and fish for dinner. Charlie, a member of his high school debate team and a serious bacon enthusiast, finally called his mother out on what he referred to as *selective reasoning.* "We're still killing and eating what were once living creatures. Fish, turkey, a pig . . . Can you please explain the difference?" he said sadly while holding up a limp piece of turkey bacon.

"Fish and turkeys don't have eyelashes. Once you've had Wilbur the pig bat his eyes at you on your way to pick up his cousin's maple-smoked rump, it changes things," Charlie's mother responded in her defense.

By the following Easter her disturbing encounter at the farm had faded from memory, at least somewhat, but she did start having Mr. Bartles deliver his Easter hams to the Puddles household on Good Fridays to avoid any future guilt-provoking barnyard run-ins.

Mr. Bartles was long dead, and those maple-smoked hams were a thing of the past, but Isabel was adamant that a baked ham should still be the cornerstone of any Easter dinner, this year and every year, so she walked into the Land's End that morning determined to steer Frances away from a potential culinary calamity. But it turned out her Easter menu was not top of mind for Frances, who remained hidden behind her newspaper until Isabel sat down, and she collapsed the paper into her lap. "Harold Stover's dead."

Whenever she picked up the morning newspaper, Frances turned to the obituaries the way some people might turn to the comics, and with about the same level of enthusiasm. She had somehow managed to turn longevity into a competition, and she liked to know where she stood at all times.

"What do you mean, he's *dead*?" a shocked Isabel asked.

"I mean he's no longer *living*," Frances clarified.

"But I just saw him at the bank a few days ago," Isabel said, still stunned by the news. "We said hello and had a nice chat. He looked the picture of health!"

"Well that picture faded," Frances said casually.

"But how?"

"Doesn't say."

"Had to be something very sudden. We would have heard if he'd been ill." Isabel shook her head sadly. Harold Stover owned a local flooring company and was a well-known businessman in Kentwater County. He and Isabel had been in tenth-grade algebra together.

Kayla arrived with coffee, flipped Isabel's cup over onto its saucer and began to pour. "Morning, Izzy . . . So do you think Harold's wife did him in?"

Isabel's jaw dropped open. "Where in the world did you come up with *that*?" She then followed Kayla's eyes across the table to Frances. "Are you spreading that ridiculous rumor around, Frances Spitler?"

"Have you *met* that woman? She's as cold as they come. And, according to my sources, she's having an affair with one of Harold's employees," Frances offered, as though cold-blooded premeditated murder were a foregone conclusion.

"She's not my *favorite* person," Isabel admitted. "I did see her reduce a bag boy at the Kroger to tears recently because he gave her paper when she asked for plastic. But that doesn't make her a murderer. You really shouldn't be making such wild accusations with no basis in fact."

"Can't let facts get in the way of a good story," Frances replied with a chuckle.

"You shouldn't be making light of his death either. Poor Harold," Isabel scolded.

"He used to come in here from time to time. Such a nice man," Kayla said sadly.

Isabel was ready to lighten the mood. "Can we please talk about something more pleasant, like maybe the menu for Easter dinner? Wasn't that the plan? Now, I assume I'm bringing my usual deviled eggs and banana pudding for dessert?"

Frances reached into her purse and pulled out a paper clipping. "Yes, please. And here's what I want to do for our main course."

Isabel took out her reading glasses and reached for the clipping. "Pheasant à l'orange? Seriously, Frances?"

"Hank shot six of them last season and they've been out in my garage deep freezer ever since. I think out of respect for the birds the least we can do is eat them, don't you?"

"I agree with the sentiment. If you're somebody who gets their kicks out of shooting such beautiful birds you should either eat them or give them to somebody who will. But not for Easter dinner."

"Why not? Too fancy? Maybe it's time those hayseed in-laws of mine stepped outside the box."

"Depends what they're stepping *into*, Frances. How many are coming for dinner?"

"Oh, I don't know. Ten? Maybe twelve this year? They keep reproducing."

Isabel took a breath and shrugged. "I've never cooked pheasant. Or eaten it, for that matter. But they aren't very big. With only six birds, that's going to make for a very light supper."

"Perfect! Then maybe they won't want to come back next year!"

"I'm not going to tell you what to make for dinner, Frances. You're the hostess. I'm just a guest. But if you don't mind, I'd like to bring along a ham for backup."

"Not exactly a vote of confidence, but suit yourself, Iz," Frances replied as she snatched back the clipping.

After the breakfast rush was over, Kayla sat down with her two favorite customers and a freshly baked cinnamon roll, a Land's End specialty. They all immediately began to pick at it, and after a bit of local news and gossip in between bites, Isabel decided it was time to make an important announcement. "*So*, girls . . . you remember my English friend, Teddy?" They both smiled and nodded. "And you remember he invited me to come and visit him in England?"

Frances was all ears. "And?"

"*And* I've decided to take him up on it. I'm going to jolly old England!" She let her big news settle while she tore off another piece of cinnamon roll, dunked it in her coffee, and popped it into her mouth.

"By *yourself*?" Frances asked with alarm.

"Yes, by myself. Teddy said he'll pick me up at the airport and give me the grand tour of London, then we'll drive to his country house in Cornwall."

"Where's Cornwall?" Kayla asked.

"It's in the southwest part of England. It's supposed to be absolutely gorgeous, especially in the spring."

Frances looked concerned, which Isabel found puzzling. "What's wrong? You're the one who's been promoting this relationship with Teddy. Which by the way is nothing more than a lovely friendship and I have every expectation will remain so. And if you'll remember, you're the one who introduced us in the first place, Frances! I thought you'd be happy to hear I was going."

Kayla was quick to chime in. "Well, *I'm* happy you're going, Isabel. I think it's very exciting! I'd love to see where Harry Potter's from!" Isabel was pretty sure Kayla knew Harry Potter was a fictional character, but not a hundred percent.

True to form, Frances had already formulated a strong

opinion about Isabel's trip abroad. "I do approve of you getting better acquainted with Teddy, but here in Gull Harbor, not off in some foreign country you know nothing about!"

"I do speak the language, Frances." Isabel found her concern touching, but also slightly annoying.

"And what do we really know about this Teddy character anyway?" Frances said as she began building her case against the trip.

"Oh, here we go . . . You mean other than him being a well-known mystery writer who is so devoted to the memory of his late wife that he wears her wedding band on a chain around his neck, has two corgis named Fred and Ginger, and loves to garden? I think we can safely assume he is not the reincarnation of Jack the Ripper."

"Ha! How do we know *how* his wife died? And who knows what he might have in store for *you* after he gets you alone in his *country house*."

"I don't think *country house* requires air quotes, Frances. It's a house he owns in the country and has for many years. I've seen pictures. It's like something out of a storybook. I'll be staying in the guest cottage, just FYI, *and* I'll be staying in a hotel, alone, while we're in London. I can assure you there is nothing untoward afoot. And I'm disappointed in you for suggesting that there would be. Teddy is a perfect gentleman."

Kayla was still eager to show her support for Isabel's trip. "I only met Teddy the one time. Same day as you did, Isabel, but I thought he was absolutely charming."

Frances shook her head. "The best ones are always charming."

Isabel was almost afraid to ask. "The best what?"

"Serial killers . . . Let's just hope tulip bulbs aren't the only things he has buried in that garden of his."

"Oh, for the love of—"

"And Ted Bundy was quite the gentleman. And a real

charmer too, by the way. The man wrote poetry!" Frances was on a roll.

Isabel rolled her eyes and took a sip of coffee. "You are too much."

"I'm worried about you, Iz, that's all! You're my dearest friend in the world and I don't think it's a good idea for you to go gallivanting off to Europe all by yourself." Frances stopped to take a breath. "I think I should probably go with you."

Isabel laughed. "I'm too old to gallivant, Frances. I don't think my knees could handle it. And you're sweet to be concerned, but you needn't be. I'm a big girl. And, not to be rude, but you weren't invited."

"Have you told Carly and Charlie their mother is off to a country she's never been to, to meet a man she barely knows, to stay in his *country house*?" Again with the air quotes.

"Yes. And they are fully supportive. Charlie's handling my travel arrangements, and Carly's helping me pick out a new travel wardrobe online."

Frances let out a heavy sigh of defeat. "It just feels so far away."

"It *is* far away, Frances. But it's not like I'm being dropped into the middle of the Amazon rain forest. It's England. It's where my great-grandfather Peabody came from!"

"Well, I can see you've made up your mind, so I guess I'll just drop it." Isabel knew that was highly unlikely. "I still think I should chaperone, but I'm certainly not one to pry into your business."

Isabel barely avoided a coffee spit take. Frances had been prying into her business since kindergarten and showed no signs of letting up. "Yes, that's one thing I've always loved about you, Frances. You're so good about minding your own business."

Frances ignored the remark. "When do you plan on leaving? And how long will you be gone?"

"I'll be gone the first two weeks of May. I told Freddie I'd be back in time to help him get ready for our Memorial Day sale."

"And the dogs?" Frances asked, searching for a hitch in the plan.

"Ginny and Grady are coming to stay at the lake and dog-sit for me. And they're taking me to the airport. So everything is squared away." Ginny was Isabel's cousin, and Grady, once the Kentwater County sheriff, was her new husband.

The front door jingled. Isabel, Frances, and Kayla all turned to look and were immediately stunned into silence. Harold Stover and his wife had just walked in the door. Harold smiled and waved. "Yes, ladies, it's me! I'm still on the right side of the dirt!" Nobody said a word. "They've got a new fella doing the obits down at the *Gazette*. He had me mixed up with ol' Harold Stater, who passed a day or two ago."

"Oh, no." Isabel said sadly. "Harry Stater died? He was such a lovely man. That's a shame."

"Sorry to disappoint you, Isabel!" Harold laughed as he pulled a chair out for his wife, who seemed quite disinterested in the conversation.

Frances leaned forward and whispered to Isabel. "You want to see disappointed, take a look at the wife."

Isabel smiled at Harold. "That's not what I meant, Harold. I'm thrilled you're still alive. But poor Harry Stater."

"Well, he was ninety-seven. It gets a lot of 'em, Iz," Harold said as he casually opened the menu.

After Isabel and Frances finished their breakfast, they paid their checks, waved goodbye to Kayla, and congratulated Harold on their way out for still being alive.

"And where are you off to now, Mrs. Spitler?" Isabel asked, as she opened her tote bag and began fishing for her keys.

"I've got to take my mother-in-law grocery shopping," Frances answered with a noticeable lack of enthusiasm.

"Well, that's very nice of you," Isabel replied, still digging for her keys.

"I didn't volunteer. I'd rather be put to death. But Hank seems to think we need to keep the old gal fed. And what about you, Mrs. Puddles?"

"I'm off to the hardware," Isabel replied after finally locating her keys. Isabel was still working part-time at her cousin Freddie's hardware store, which was less a job than it was a family tradition. She'd been working at the store on and off since high school; first for her uncle Handy, and now for his son, Freddie, who was more like a brother to her. "I'll catch up with you later, Frances," Isabel said as she climbed into her van, then yelled back, "and be nice to your mother-in-law, Frances! Someone's going to have to keep you fed in your old age too!" Frances just rolled her eyes and waved her off.

Although she still had her office above the store—one that Freddie was nice enough to redo for her when she received her private investigator's license—today the Isabel Puddles Private Investigation Agency was pretty much defunct. All that was left to do was scratch the lettering off the frosted-glass door. After successfully closing the Bachmeier case, Isabel had decided, in a moment of clarity, that private investigating was not a career path she wanted to travel any longer. And although she had been encouraged to go back to college after solving the Jonasson murder case to pursue a degree in criminal justice, she had officially stepped off that path too. Yes, she did seem to have a flair for solving crimes, and murders did seem to be her sweet spot, but she had come to find it all just too depressing. Waiting around for a murder to solve seemed like a pretty ghoulish way to earn a living.

When Isabel and her late husband, Carl, went away to college together, just out of high school, her plan was to study literature and get her teaching degree. But that plan was put on hold when Carly came along. And after Charlie was born, the plan was never re-implemented. It may have taken a while, but after a few decades she was finally back on track. Today she was taking classes online and pursuing a degree in literary studies at Michigan State, the university she had gone to those first two years. No more classes in bullet-wound analysis or crime-scene technology or blood-spatter patterns or looking at gruesome photographs of murder victims. Although she did find her criminal psychology classes interesting, Isabel now felt she knew everything she needed or wanted to know about the criminal mind.

The moment she made the final decision to leave the criminal justice program, Isabel felt a tremendous sense of relief, but she was still determined to complete her college degree. So in only a matter of weeks she was a student again, and was now studying something that left her feeling happy and hopeful about human nature, instead of disheartened and disillusioned about how evil people could sometimes be.

The world of literature—English and American, mostly— had always been a passion for her. Reading classic literary works provided her with a window into history, another passion of hers, and it exposed her to a whole world outside Gull Harbor without her ever needing a passport. But Isabel Puddles was a woman who knew her limits. Many of the other "great works"—in her mind, a subjective term if ever there was one—left her scratching her head. Her decision to take an ancient literature class was a particular disaster. Bring up Homer and *The Iliad* or *The Odyssey*, and she practically broke into hives. After slogging through as much of it as she could endure, and understanding none of it, she finally dropped the class. "I'm not a quitter," she told her kids in their weekly phone chat, "but I'm not a masochist either."

Carly supported her mother's decision to drop the class and reminded her about the time she had supported *her* when she walked out of tenth-grade biology after refusing to dissect a frog. Charlie then took his mother back to her unwillingness to support *his* efforts to drop eleventh-grade shop class when the curriculum turned to fixing automobile transmissions. "The likelihood of me ever fixing a transmission was about the same as Carly ever having to do emergency surgery on a frog. I thought it was a pretty egregious double standard at the time, and I still do today."

Isabel laughed. "You're absolutely right. I was being selfish, and I'm sorry for that. I just remember thinking at the time that having a kid who could fix a transmission would be a lot handier than having one who could extract a frog's liver. But I do think it's time to let it go, honey."

Chapter 2

When Teddy's last letter arrived, gently reminding Isabel that his invitation to visit him was still standing, she happened to have just completed a literary history class on eighteenth-century English writers. It had to be a sign, she told herself. So before talking herself out of it, and before Frances caught the scent and talked her out of it, she immediately wrote Teddy back, thanked him for his gracious invitation, and accepted.

The whole time the letter sat in her mailbox with the red flag up, alerting her mailman, Barney, that she had outgoing mail, she wrestled with her decision. More than once when she looked out her kitchen window and saw the flag still up, she stopped herself from running out and grabbing it. But after leashing up Jackpot and Corky to take them for a lunchtime walk, she opened the front door to see that the red flag was down. Barney had come and gone, and Isabel Puddles was going abroad.

One of her lifetime dreams—to visit England—was about to come true, and she could hardly believe it. From that day forward she teetered between excitement and anxiousness. This was the most adventurous thing Isabel had ever done in her life, and she was doing it alone. But Teddy would be waiting for her at the other end, so she knew she was in good hands.

When she walked into the hardware, Isabel found Cousin Freddie in a particularly chatty mood while ringing up a customer she didn't recognize. After quietly walking behind the counter and grabbing her red apron, she pulled it over her head, tied it up, and got busy with her ritual straightening of the counter while waiting for Freddie to finish the transaction. "Who was that?" she asked after the front door closed behind the man.

"I have no idea," Freddie answered with an odd lilt in his voice, closing the cash register drawer with a flourish. "How are you today, Cousin?" Freddie asked, grabbing her in a bear hug.

After he released her, Isabel looked up at him somewhat suspiciously. "Why are *you* in such a good mood today, Freddie? I've never seen you so excited about selling a pair of fifteen-dollar garden sheers."

"Oh, it's not that! Although fifteen bucks is better than a kick in the teeth. I'll *tell* you why I'm so excited. I just found out Frank has appendicitis! He's going in for surgery in a couple days and he'll be laid up for the next month or two! *Three,* knowing Frank!"

Isabel was taken aback by her normally kindhearted cousin's callousness regarding the illness of the stock boy who had worked for him for two decades. Despite Frank's never coming close to attaining the status of being "a keeper" in her opinion, Freddie continued to keep him. But that was a personnel matter, so she stayed out of it. She knew Freddie must have his reasons for keeping him around, although, again, in her view there were plenty more reasons not to. Frank was lazy, grumpy, showed zero initiative, and did nothing unless he was asked, and he usually had to be asked twice. And when he finally did do it, he never did it very well, so Isabel or Freddie would end up having to redo it. Freddie once grumbled, "It's like having a milk cow in the barn you have to feed every day but it never gives you any milk." Isabel thought it was a pretty apt analogy. But what bugged her most about Frank was the man's chronic negativity. Make a passing comment to him about what a beautiful sunny day it was, and twenty seconds later you'd be talking about some uncle of his losing an ear to skin cancer. Still, whatever her personal feelings were, she would never wish serious illness and major surgery on him.

"That's not even the *best* part!" Freddie continued gleefully.

"Good *Lord*, Freddie! Listen to yourself! What, are his kidneys failing too? Is that what has you so giddy?"

"Oh, Isabel, stop being ridiculous," Freddie chuckled. "No! Not five minutes after I got off the phone with Frank's mother, who called to share this terrible news—"

"The term *terrible news* is not, as a rule, accompanied by an ear-to-ear grin!" Isabel scolded.

Freddie took a breath. "As I was saying, not five minutes later, who do you think called, but Andy! He wants to come back to work for the summer!"

Andy was the college student and stock clerk extraordinaire who had worked at the store the summer before. Not that Frank needed anybody to make him look bad, because he did a pretty great job of that himself, but Andy hammered the final nail into *that* coffin. Andy knew right where to find that hammer and nail too, whereas Frank still wouldn't be able to tell you what aisle hammers *or* nails were on after twenty years. He could, however, rattle off about a dozen different spots within the store and in lawn and garden where you could hide out and take a nap.

Isabel couldn't help herself. She smiled. "Well, it's not like appendicitis is a death sentence. Pretty simple surgery, really. And he could probably do with a nice long convalescence."

Freddie laughed and clapped his hands together. "I would think Memorial Day weekend through Labor Day weekend would be sufficient, wouldn't you, Iz?"

"That sounds about right," she agreed. "Don't want to rush these things." Having Andy back in the store for the summer would make her life a whole lot easier, and she adored the boy, so this was indeed a happy development.

Business was slow, so Isabel left early to go home and continue her packing. The closer she got to her departure date, the more nervous she was getting about her first trip outside the United States, and so were her dogs, Jackpot and Corky. They knew some serious change was coming, and they were not happy about it. That morning she made the mistake of leaving her half-packed suitcase out on her bed, returning to find they had expressed their opinion about her upcoming trip by pulling everything out, piling it in the middle of the floor, and then, based on the amount of fur she found, napping on it.

Isabel looked at her empty suitcase on the bed and felt a pang of embarrassment. She'd had the old hard-case American Tourister for at least twenty years and it was in pretty ratty condition. The color was hard to call but it looked like it was trying to be yellow, which was likely just another sign of age. It was time to upgrade. She called Frances to see if she wanted to go shopping, knowing she would say yes, because Frances lived to shop, in fact she counted it as exercise. And the way she shopped, it was.

After Frances picked her up, and because she never missed an opportunity of late to try to convince Isabel to change her mind about the trip, she regaled her with a story she claimed to have heard on the news about a lonely American widow who flew to Amsterdam to meet a man she had been corresponding with online. Two weeks later she was found dead, floating in a canal. It was Frances's version of a helpful cautionary tale. But at breakfast the next morning she had to update the story, and with some measure of disappointment. It seems the woman had not in fact been murdered by her new Dutch lover but had tripped into the canal trying on a pair of newly purchased wooden clogs. "Clop, clop, clop, splash!" Frances laughed. Ghoulish, inappropriate jokes were Frances Spitler's specialty, and she never missed an opportunity.

Easter dinner came and went, and Frances, thankfully, had dropped the whole pheasant idea and decided to stick with ham. They did, however, plan to prepare the pheasant for what would be Isabel's last Sunday dinner before leaving for England. Freddie and Carol, Ginny and Grady, Frances and Hank, and Isabel, all sat down to a beautiful dinner of roasted pheasant with a cherry-and-balsamic sauce she had prepared, and an assortment of delicious sides prepared by her guests, mindful that Isabel had too much on her plate to spend the whole day in the kitchen.

As they sat down to enjoy the homemade cheesecake Frances brought for dessert, Isabel looked around the table and was suddenly reminded of her singleness, and felt a pang of loneliness, which was unusual for her. After a twenty-three-year marriage that started out as promising and ended up as tolerable, becoming a truly independent woman—albeit by way of widowhood—was something she was not only proud of but also something she had grown quite used to. She had never really experienced true independence before. Isabel would freely admit to having been fairly sheltered growing up as an only child with two wonderfully devoted parents who showered her with love and attention. And although there were many times she felt completely alone in her marriage to Carl, technically she wasn't. But tonight she found herself wondering what it would be like to be part of a couple again.

Ginny and Grady seemed very happy together, and if they weren't, Isabel would have heard about it, but they were still newlyweds. She and Carl were happy once too. Freddie and Carol had been together since junior high and were as devoted to each other as any couple Isabel had ever known. When it came to Frances and Hank? Well, theirs was a marriage that had its ups and downs—and Isabel had been through all of them—but there was no doubt the love was still there.

Isabel even went on to wonder if perhaps, even subconsciously, her trip to England was more about spending time with Teddy than it was about visiting the United Kingdom. But she quickly shook that notion out of her head. For one thing, Teddy had given her no indication that he was interested in anything beyond a friendship. If romance was on his mind, he was doing a good job of hiding it. And how would a romance between them work anyway, with them living on opposite sides of the Atlantic? No, it was silly to even ponder. Isabel was merely going to spend time with a new friend who lived in a country that had captured her imagination when she first saw *Mary Poppins* and *My Fair Lady* as a little girl. She had never stopped imagining what it would be like to visit, and now it was actually happening.

After her guests left, Isabel made a cup of chamomile tea and sat down with her knitting. When the phone rang, she knew it was the kids. They almost always called on Sundays after dinnertime, and they had some way by which they could call their mother together, and then all three of them could talk. It was always the highlight of her week. They had recently talked about some means by which they could talk and *see* one another at the same time, but Isabel told them she would need some time to ease into that. There were limits to her embrace of modern technology, and in her mind, that was something Jane Jetson might do, but not Isabel Puddles.

Carly began with inquiries about the new clothes they had picked out for her trip. Had everything arrived? Did everything fit? "Yes, honey, everything has arrived, and, yes, it all fits. But it feels so, I don't know, too sophisticated for me maybe?"

"Mom, you're traveling to one of the world's most sophisticated cities. You don't want to look like some frumpy American tourist with no taste."

"Well, I like to think I do have *taste*, but I *am* a frumpy American tourist. And it's not like I'll be having tea with the queen. And, by the way, she's a little on the frumpy side too, so I'm in good company."

"She's the queen, Mom. She gets to be frumpy. You don't have that luxury," Carly said in her usual matter-of-fact way.

"Well, I've got everything packed, and I appreciate all the effort you put into helping me shop, I really do, but I'm packing my duck boots, my big sweaters, and my mom jeans for Cornwall. I understand it can get chilly there so close to the sea."

"You do you, Mom," Carly replied, slightly exasperated.

Now it was Charlie's turn to enter the fray. "First of all, you aren't *frumpy*, Mom."

"Thank you, honey."

"I'd say you're more *dowdy*," he added.

Isabel laughed. "Is that a step above or below frumpy?"

"I think it goes drab, frumpy, dowdy. But Carly's right. You have to bring your fashion A game because I've booked you into a very fancy hotel. It's called the Tottenham. I stayed there on my last visit to London. It's very near Buckingham Palace. Maybe you can drop in on Her Majesty."

"I thought we agreed on something modest. I don't want you spending that kind of money on a hotel, Charlie. Isn't there a—"

"Please don't say Holiday Inn," Charlie interrupted. She wasn't. She was going to say Motel 6. Charlie continued. "Carly and I are splitting it and I got a good deal. You deserve it, Mom. It's your first trip abroad! Just enjoy being pampered a little. And steal the soap and shampoo if it makes you feel better. That's what I do. I don't have a bottle of shampoo, conditioner, shower gel, or lotion in my bathroom that's over two inches tall. Like mother, like son."

After hanging up with the kids, she went back to her knitting and quickly got lost in thought. It had finally sunk in. The trip of a lifetime was now less than a week away. Isabel Puddles was going to England. Her only wish now was that her kids were going with her. But she would have Teddy there to greet her and give her that grand tour of London he had promised her before going on to Cornwall. Isabel looked over at Jackpot and Corky lying on the sofa staring at her with sad eyes. They definitely knew she was leaving, but how? She was convinced dogs were smarter and more emotional than people could ever imagine or, in many cases, could ever measure up to.

Chapter 3

The big day had finally arrived, and Isabel was up at five o'clock feeling just as excited as she was as a kid on Christmas morning. Ginny and Grady would be there at seven o'clock to take her to the airport, so the clock was ticking. After coffee, a breakfast of oatmeal, and a quick walk with the dogs, Isabel went into her bedroom and finished packing while Jackpot and Corky watched her with doleful eyes. She was already feeling guilty enough, so she tried to avoid looking at them. After she zipped up her new suitcase, they jumped off the bed and slowly followed her as she wheeled it into the foyer. She then called them over to the sofa so they could all sit and have a final cuddle before she had to leave. She finally leaned over and kissed them both on the tops of their heads, and to help placate her guilt, went to the kitchen to get them a couple of treats. When she looked out the kitchen window, she saw Ginny and Grady pull into the driveway. She paused and took a deep breath. This was it. Isabel's journey was about to begin.

Isabel Puddles was not a woman who enjoyed flying. It made her very anxious. Actually, it wasn't a fear of flying, it was more a fear of crashing, but she always found a way to work through her anxiety. Small planes were what really made her nervous, and her flight to Chicago was on a small regional jet, which wasn't great news, but at least it was a jet. She always figured pilots would have a harder time keeping propeller planes in the air than they would jets, although she had absolutely nothing to base this judgment on.

It was a beautiful spring day, and her flight across Lake Michigan, calm and glistening white under the sun, went by so fast, her nerves never had time to get the better of her. Before she knew it, she was on the ground at Chicago O'Hare. Leg one of her journey down. Now if she could navigate her way through this gigantic airport and find her way to the gate, leg two would soon be underway. With a three-hour layover she was pretty sure she could pull it off, but for a woman from Gull Harbor, Michigan, whose biggest navigational challenge was Fourth of July weekend traffic, she was not entirely convinced there wouldn't be complications.

As it turned out, she had nothing to be worried about. She found her way to the international terminal and then to her gate with ease. When she saw LONDON on the sign above the gate agent's desk, she could hardly believe that in just a matter of hours—eight, to be exact—she would be in England. There were still ninety minutes before the flight boarded, so she pulled out her book and thought she'd read for a while, but instead her attention was drawn to the parade of people passing before her. Isabel couldn't remember ever seeing so many people in one place; people of every ethnicity, every age, every style of clothes, and virtually every walk of life. Some were rushing through the crowd looking intensely serious, some even looking panicked, while others floated happily along smiling and chatting and appearing completely carefree.

A handsome, dark-skinned woman about Isabel's age, with jet-black hair and a streak of gray running through it, wearing a beautiful sari in dazzling golds, reds, and oranges, sat down across from her and smiled. Isabel smiled back and couldn't resist complimenting her. "That's the most exquisite sari I have ever seen. It reminds me of autumn in Michigan."

"How funny you say that! That's exactly why I bought it. You're from Michigan, I gather?" the woman asked with a lovely English accent.

"I am. From Gull Harbor. Just across the Big Lake."

"I've been to Gull Harbor. Charming little town. My husband and I have a home in Harbor Springs. I adore Michigan. What takes you to London?"

"I've been dying to go for as long as I can remember. I can't believe it's finally happening."

"And you're traveling alone?"

"Only to get there. I have a friend who's invited me over. He's picking me up at the airport."

Suddenly a voice came over the loudspeaker. "If London passenger Isabel Puddles is here at the gate, please come to the desk for a message. Isabel Puddles, please see the gate agent."

Isabel looked concerned. "Uh-oh. That's me." Things had been going so smoothly. Could this be the first snag? She approached the young man at the desk cautiously, but his friendly, disarming smile immediately put her mind at ease. If he *was* about to deliver bad news, he had a very peculiar sense of humor. "I'm Isabel Puddles," she said quietly.

"Oh, hello! First of all, I'm in *love* with your name. It's fabulous. And I have a message for you to"—he looked down at the piece of paper—"to call Elizabeth Mansfield, Teddy's daughter, at this number before you board your London flight." He handed her the slip of paper with Elizabeth's phone number.

Isabel's heart sank. Had something terrible happened to Teddy? After all that had transpired over the past couple years of her life, her worldview had dramatically changed, so she was already preparing for bad news. Instead of being the cockeyed optimist she had always been, Isabel's mindset these days was more hope for the best and prepare for the worst. Her mind was racing as she went back to her seat. The woman in the sari could tell something was amiss. "Is everything all right?"

"I'm not sure, but I hope so. Excuse me. I have to make a phone call."

Isabel walked across to an empty gate where she could sit quietly and call Elizabeth. Her hands were shaking as she took out her cell phone and dialed the number.

"Isabel, hello, it's Elizabeth! I'm so glad I caught you. . . . Nothing's wrong, so nothing to worry about!" Isabel breathed a sigh of relief and her heart returned to its proper place. "It's just that Dad's hit a little bump in regard to picking you up at Heathrow tomorrow morning. You see he's teaching a class in mystery writing at a uni near our place in Cornwall, and just this morning he realized he had his dates wrong. Classes start *tomorrow*, not a *week* from tomorrow. Poor man hasn't been in the right place at the right time since my mum died, bless him. He's driving back to Cornwall as we speak. He feels terrible, Isabel, and he wanted you to know he promises you'll do London together before your return. As far as picking you up at Heathrow, Dad hired a car for you. After you go through customs, look for somebody holding a placard with your name. They'll take you to your hotel and Dad will call you a little later to talk about getting you to Cornwall next."

Elizabeth was a fast talker, and that was a lot of information to process. Isabel tried to play it cool, but this was not exactly a happy development. She had been feeling safe and secure knowing Teddy was waiting on the other end, but now her safety net had been yanked away. She was feeling disappointed too, because she was really looking forward to seeing Teddy. "Well, that's too bad, but of course I understand. Tell your dad everything's fine and I'll talk to him later."

"I know arriving in London alone for the first time may

feel a bit daunting," Elizabeth replied, "but I *am* talking to
the woman who's solved two murders and nearly been murdered herself, so I'm not too terribly worried about you. I do
feel awful that we've buggered up the welcoming committee,
though."

Isabel laughed. "It will be an adventure, but I think I'll
manage," she assured her. "But tell Teddy I'll expect a rain
check on that grand London tour."

"I know he'll be delighted. Do have a safe flight and have
a lovely time in London, Isabel. I think you're going to fall
in love!"

"Thank you, Elizabeth." Isabel slipped her phone back
into her tote. Fall in love? Fall in love with London? Or did
she mean fall in love with her dad? Had to be London, she told
herself, then suddenly felt silly. Whatever Elizabeth meant or
didn't mean, it was a ridiculous thing to ruminate over.

The woman in the beautiful autumnal sari was reading a
book when Isabel came back and sat down. She hated appearing nosy, but anytime she saw somebody reading a book she
tried to find a discreet way to see what it was he or she was
reading. This time, before she could see the cover, the woman
closed it, plopped it down in her lap, and looked across at Isabel with a concerned smile. "I hope everything's all right?"

"Yes. Fine. It's just that my friend's not going to be able to
pick me up, so he hired a car to collect me, which seems like
an unnecessary expense. I could have taken the . . . oh, what
do you call your underground train?"

The woman looked alarmed. "The Tube?" she shook her
head. "I would hate for that to be your first impression of
London. A car service is far more civilized. Well, I'm glad
everything is okay." The woman went back to reading her
book, but left it in her lap, so Isabel still couldn't see the jacket
cover. Her curiosity, as usual, finally got the better of her.

"What are you reading, if you don't mind my asking?"

The woman smiled and held up the book for her to see. "It's the first in the new Archie Cavendish series. He's one of my favorite mystery writers. Do you know him?" Isabel did indeed know him. Archie Cavendish was Teddy Mansfield's nom de plume.

Isabel was stumped for a moment. She didn't want to sound like a braggadocio and tell her that he was the friend she was going to visit, but she didn't see any reason to lie either. "I do know him, yes. I just loved his Detective Waverly series."

"Oh, I did too. . . . Big fan. I just started this new series but it looks very promising. It's about a former Chicago detective. An African American woman fighting police corruption. Great character! The imagination it must take for an English gentleman to write a character like this. It's rather amazing."

Isabel remained tight-lipped about the new series, even though Teddy had told her about his new character soon after he had begun writing the book. Of course she was very anxious to read the new book herself, but she was waiting for the signed copy Teddy promised to give her after she arrived.

After boarding, Isabel and the woman in the sari found themselves sitting in the middle row of seats, but on opposite aisles. "Oh, hello again," Isabel said to her, fastening her seat belt.

The woman smiled. "Hopefully these middle seats will remain unoccupied so we can have a nice chat about our friend Archie Cavendish. . . . I'm Runa, by the way, and I already know you're Isabel."

Isabel reached over to shake hands. "Pleasure to meet you, Runa . . . And what takes *you* to London?"

"I live here in Chicago, but I'm from London originally. I'm going back for a wedding."

Isabel was intrigued with Runa. She had never met anybody of South Asian descent. But then, given the demographics of Kentwater County, she hadn't known many people who were not of English, Irish, Dutch, or Scandinavian decent. On Charlie's last visit home, he had remarked that the last time he saw so many white people in one place, it was in a line to buy tickets for a Neil Diamond concert.

The middle seats did remain empty, so Isabel and Runa were able to continue their friendly chat. With her innate but subtle interrogation style, Isabel learned that Runa was a pediatrician who was married to a cardiologist, and that their marriage had been arranged by their parents. This was interesting. When Isabel first heard about arranged marriages, in whatever culture, she thought the concept sounded pretty archaic. She imagined, although it was pure conjecture, that couples whose marriages had been arranged had most likely seen less than ideal outcomes, and others who were doomed to a lifetime of misery. But, looking back at her marriage to Carl, Isabel wondered if maybe her parents might have come up with a better option, so who was she to judge?

Runa went on to say that when she and her future husband first met, it was love at first sight for them both, so she considered herself very lucky. "Well, he was the luckier," she said with a smile. Her sister, she added, had drawn the short straw with her marriage. "Quite literally! My sister towers over her husband. But he's a lovely man. There just isn't much *of* him," she said, along with her wonderfully infectious laugh. Runa and her husband had three children; two of them were in medical school, and the youngest was an actor. "He'd seen and heard enough about medicine growing up, he told us. But now he's playing a doctor on a soap opera!" Isabel joined Runa in another hearty laugh.

The two women carried on chatting through the meal service and toasted their new friendship over a glass of red wine. After a dinner of something that resembled chicken served over rice and another glass of red wine, Isabel dozed off. When she woke up, Runa was fast asleep. Now she was wide awake and with nobody to talk to. She checked the in-flight entertainment menu of the monitor in front of her—after she finally figured out how it worked—and was thrilled to see that *My Fair Lady* and *Mary Poppins* were two of the movies available. What luck! And she had more than enough time to watch them both.

Two movies and another nap later, Isabel woke up to the pilot's announcement that they were beginning their descent into London Heathrow. She couldn't believe how quickly the flight had gone by. Now she was starting to feel her nerves again. At that very moment, as if Runa could sense her am-bivalence at what lay ahead, she leaned over and asked her where in London she was staying. Isabel had to think a mo-ment. "Oh . . . It's called the Tottenham. My son picked it out."

"Very nice hotel. Off Hyde Park and near the palace. You know, I'm going to be around there tomorrow. Perhaps we could meet for tea?"

Isabel jumped at the opportunity to have tea in London with a new friend. "I would love that!"

After clearing customs and collecting their luggage, Isabel and Runa said their goodbyes and agreed on a time to meet the next day in the lobby of the Tottenham Hotel. Isabel then spotted a nice-looking young man in a dark suit holding a sign that said PUDDLES. The next thing she knew, Isabel was sitting in the backseat of a large black sedan on her way into London.

Chapter 4

Isabel entered the lobby of the Tottenham Hotel and was overwhelmed after taking only a few steps in. It was the most elegant interior she had ever seen in person, and the people milling about were just as elegant. But she had never felt more out of her element either. It was a little like being the only guest at a costume party not wearing a costume, or vice versa. The fact that she was wearing her favorite canary-yellow velour tracksuit didn't help matters. Carly had warned her against it after asking her mother what she intended to wear on the flight. She wasn't thrilled with the answer. "So you're going after kind of a Tweety Bird meets mall-walker vibe, Mom?"

"Whatever happened to Tweety Bird, I wonder?" Isabel asked nobody in particular before answering Carly's question. "Is being comfortable a vibe? Because if it is, that's exactly the vibe I'm going after. I'd wear my flannel nightgown and my fuzzy slippers if I could get away with it." So that ended that conversation. Carly knew a lost cause when she saw one.

A bellman dressed in formal black attire, complete with tails, had been waiting at the hotel entrance when Isabel's black sedan pulled up. The bellman opened Isabel's door and bowed, or more like dipped his head, before offering his hand to help her out of the car. "Welcome to the Tottenham Hotel, ma'am."

"Thank you. I'm very happy to be here." Isabel leaned back into the car to thank her driver, then smiled at the bellman again, who wore a name tag that read BERNARD. He was an older gentleman—older, as in he might have been working there since the hotel was built in the '60s . . . the 1860s. Bernard lifted her bags, barely, and managed to get them onto a brass luggage cart, then slowly escorted her to the front desk. Isabel had to fight the urge to help him push the cart.

"Good morning, Mrs. Puddles. Welcome to the Tottenham. You're very welcome," said a distinguished-looking clerk with a bald head and beautifully manicured goatee standing behind the desk. Isabel was immediately puzzled; for one, because she hadn't yet said "thank you," so "you're welcome" seemed a bit premature, *and* because how did he know who she was already? The clerk could tell she was curious. "Your driver called to tell us you would be arriving."

"Oh, I thought maybe you were clairvoyant," Isabel said, feeling the need to say something.

The clerk politely smiled to acknowledge her effort to engage, and at the same time picked up her accent. "Ah . . . American. And how are things in the colonies? Are you still enjoying your independence?" the clerk asked with a faint chuckle.

Isabel couldn't tell at first if he was being clever or a little snide, but she settled on clever. "I think we have more than just the thirteen now. I'd have to check. But, yes, it seems to be working out for the most part," Isabel replied.

"I see you're here with us for two nights," the clerk continued, "And Mr. Charles Peabody has prepaid your room, and any incidentals will be billed to his credit card."

"That's my son, Charlie. Well, Charles. He goes by Charles *Peabody* now—Peabody's my maiden name. He thought Peabody was more professional. I think it was probably smart. Puddles is a rather unusual name. They called him 'mud puddles' in school, which he hated. Charlie's an architect in San Francisco now. And a Buddhist." As soon as she finished talking, she wondered why on earth she had just prattled on like that. Was it nerves? Jet lag? She laughed nervously. "I guess that's more information than you really needed, wasn't it."

The clerk smiled almost sympathetically as he gave her jogging suit the quick side eye. "Not at all, Mrs. Puddles. If I ever find myself in San Francisco in need of a Buddhist architect, I know just whom to call." He tapped an antique bell on the desk, and Bernard instantly appeared. "Bernard will show you to your room. I hope you have a delightful stay with us, Mrs. Puddles."

Isabel thanked him and headed for the elevator. She still wasn't sure if he was trying to be nice or making fun of her. She settled on trying to be nice. When they reached her floor and got off the elevator, Isabel again had to stop herself from helping Bernard pull the luggage cart along the thickly carpeted hallway, which seemed to take forever. But he had plenty to say along the way, presumably about the hotel, but his accent was so thick she barely understood a word of it, so she just smiled and nodded politely, which Bernard seemed fine with, if he even noticed at all.

After tugging her suitcases off the cart in the hallway and wrestling them into her room, Bernard gave her a tour of the room and pointed out the amenities in a roughly five-minute script he seemed to be following in his head. Isabel understood hardly anything of it. When he finally wrapped up, she thanked him and tipped him with a five-pound note. But because she had yet to work out the exchange rate, she wasn't sure whether she had just overtipped him or undertipped him. Bernard tilted his head to her again and closed the door behind him.

A gorgeous arrangement of flowers was sitting on an antique mahogany table waiting to greet her. She walked over to see if the flowers were even real and then saw a card. They were from Teddy with a note apologizing for not being able to be there in person. She looked out the window and across the busy street to a row of large trees bordering a park that she assumed to be Hyde Park. She finally sat down on the edge of the canopy bed and took in more of the beautifully appointed room, done in various shades of light blues and greens with silver accents. She had closed her eyes and laid her head back for less than a minute when the phone rang. Had it not rung, she would have been fast asleep. It was Teddy.

Professor Mansfield was on his way to class, so the conversation was short, but Isabel was happy to hear Teddy's voice again. He had arranged for her to take a train the day after tomorrow from London to Penzance in Cornwall, where he would pick her up. The front desk had her ticket, and the same driver who had collected her at the airport would be picking her up at the hotel at ten a.m. sharp to take her to Paddington Station. Isabel thanked him for making sure she was feeling comfortable in his absence and said goodbye.

Isabel laid her head back and closed her eyes. Just as she was about to doze off the phone rang again. It was Carly and Charlie checking in to make sure she had arrived safely. She explained what had happened with Teddy, which concerned them at first, but she quickly assuaged their fears and convinced them their mother was doing just fine. Carly did have one more pressing concern, though. "Did you wear your jogging suit on the plane, Mom?"

"Yes, I did. And can I just tell you how comfortable I was on that flight?"

"Was it the bright yellow one?" Charlie asked.

"Yes."

"Taxi!" Charlie chirped, making his sister laugh.

Isabel could almost see Carly shaking her head. "Okay, now I want you to fold it up and put it at the very bottom of your suitcase and leave it there."

"Unless you're jogging along the Thames, then break it out again," Charlie added.

"Why? So it will be easier to find my body?"

"Why must you always go to that dark place, Mother?" Charlie asked with a sigh. "I'm so glad you're out of the murder business."

After a little more lively conversation about the trip, her new friend Runa, and how fabulous the hotel was, Isabel thanked them for calling and got up off the bed. Having traveled to Europe before, they had both advised her not to nap, no matter how tempting, but instead stay awake until her usual bedtime. It was the best way to reset her body clock and ward off jet lag, they told her. Isabel had of course never experienced jet lag, but she didn't imagine it could be as bad as her kids and others had warned her. But as directed, she freshened up, put on one of her new outfits—nothing fancy, brown slacks and a sweater in brown and beige. She had to admit that when she put it on and walked through the lobby this time, she did have more of a lilt in her step. Even the desk clerk gave her an approving nod as she walked through the lobby, past Bernard, still alive, and through the revolving doors into the warm embrace of London on a beautiful spring afternoon.

Isabel imagined her first impressions of London were something like how Dorothy must have felt when she landed in Munchkinland minus the dead witch and all the little people. She couldn't quite believe she was there after having dreamed about it for so long. Her heart skipped a beat when she saw her first red double-decker bus while riding into the city, and for the rest of the day it was one skipped beat after another. Teddy had suggested she take a bus tour, so the concierge directed her to a nearby bus stop where she could catch it. She bought a ticket with a gaggle of other tourists and climbed right to the open-air top of a double-decker tour bus and found a seat at the front. Although she had assumed her first tour of London would be with Teddy, she decided to treat this one as an introductory course. Teddy's tour would be the advanced course.

The bus tour took her past Parliament, Big Ben, Westminster Abbey, St. Paul's Cathedral, the Tower of London, Tower Bridge, Trafalgar Square, the National Gallery, countless statues and fountains, pristine gardens, elegant architecture everywhere she looked, and finally, the main event, Buckingham Palace. There she felt an actual lump in her throat when she saw the palace guards at the gate who looked like living breathing nutcrackers with their tall, furry bearskin hats and smart red uniforms. Above the palace flew the Royal Standard, which, according to the tour guide meant the "sovereign was in residence," or in Isabel's vernacular, "the queen was home." Isabel had been infatuated with Queen Elizabeth all her life and couldn't believe that the grand old lady was knocking around somewhere inside that enormous palace at that very moment. Or maybe she was walking her corgis in the garden. What a thrill it would be to actually catch a glimpse of her while visiting London, Isabel thought, but she knew it was not likely to happen.

Everywhere Isabel looked, it was as if a series of postcards were coming to life before her very eyes, and she was in the center of them all. But what struck her most about London was the sense of being so completely steeped in history. The only big city she had ever visited that rivaled London in size was Chicago. And although she always enjoyed those visits, and did appreciate everything the city had to offer, there was no real sense of history. There had been that big fire, a lot of gangster shoot-outs, compliments of Al Capone, and then of course there was Oprah Winfrey. And that was about it. But from the moment she arrived in London, Isabel felt as if she were breathing in history for a change instead of simply reading about it.

The Londoners themselves also fascinated her. Carly was right about the sophistication with which many of them dressed, at least in this part of the city. But in such proximity to Buckingham Palace, and with the "sovereign in residence," it made sense to Isabel that one should look one's best in case the queen happened to look out the window to check on her subjects. But, wardrobe aside, it was more the way Londoners carried themselves that she found so intriguing. They weren't haughty, the way many of the Gull Harbor summer people could be, but instead appeared composed and quietly confident. As far as Isabel was concerned, if you were a Londoner, you could get away with being a bit haughty if you wanted to. It was London, after all. But if you were from suburban Detroit, it was a lot harder to pull off.

After the bus tour ended, Isabel walked and walked, taking in as much of London as she could until sheer exhaustion finally forced her to get a taxi back to the hotel. With the help of some coffee, she managed to stay awake until about nine o'clock, then fell into a deep coma-like sleep until just before nine o'clock the next morning. Although she had slept the clock around, she was still groggy. Maybe there *was* something to this jet lag thing. She was famished too, having skipped dinner the night before, so she called room service and ordered coffee and a scone, then pulled the drapes and stood at the window, watching London coming to life.

After coffee, Isabel took her book down to the lobby, where she pretended to read while covertly people watching instead. Her tea date with Runa wasn't until two o'clock, when she would meet her in the lobby, so she had some time to kill.

When Runa arrived at exactly two o'clock, Isabel almost didn't recognize her. She was no longer wearing her sari but instead wearing a smart cream-colored pantsuit and what looked like some very expensive shoes. It was the kind of outfit her friend Beverly Atwater would wear, and Runa looked beautiful in it. Isabel was glad she had changed into another of her new outfits, another slack-and-sweater set Carly picked out for her in navy and white.

They decided to have tea at the hotel since it turned out the Tottenham was famous for its afternoon tea, and because she was a guest, a table had already been reserved for her. The atmosphere in the "tearoom" was so refined and so chic, Isabel couldn't help thinking how radically different this was from the Land's End, where she congregated with her friends. But for these chic-looking women who were gradually filling the room to the soothing sound of a harpist—friends meeting to chat, maybe gossip a little, and just enjoy each other's company over some tea—it seemed to serve the same purpose. But she could only imagine how different the conversations in the Tottenham tearoom were from those at the Land's End. Not likely anybody in this room was asking around to see who might be in the market for a used snowplow, or if they knew anybody who could rebuild a carburetor on an outboard motor, or asking pointers on how best to keep raccoons from getting into your garbage cans.

Tea included a sumptuous array of finger sandwiches, petit fours, and macaroons displayed on a three-tiered porcelain platter, which seemed to float to the table in the hands of a waitress wearing some sort of period smock with a white bonnet. She softly asked them for their tea preference, and Isabel and Runa agreed on Earl Grey for the caffeine. The tea was poured out of a beautiful hand-painted porcelain teapot into delicate-looking matching cups. Very fancy. Isabel couldn't remember the last time she had tea that it didn't involve a tea bag and a chipped mug.

Isabel and Runa picked up right where they left off on the flight, talking about their families, Runa's life in Chicago compared with her life in London, summers in Michigan, Runa's work as a pediatrician, and Isabel's decision to go back to college, which Runa found inspirational. Not that she was embarrassed in the slightest about her job at Freddie's hardware store, but Isabel was pretty sure "I work in a hardware store" was a sentence that had never been uttered in that room, so she kept it to herself.

A cool and cloudy London morning had turned into a beautifully sunny afternoon, so after their tea they took a stroll through Hyde Park. To Isabel's delight, Runa was a fountain of fun facts and other bits of British trivia.

"You know the queen technically owns Hyde Park. *And* Kensington Gardens. And Trafalgar Square was where the palace stables were once located, so she owns it too." But it was the next piece of trivia Runa shared as they walked around the Round Pond near Kensington Palace—filled with ducks and geese and swans—that really got Isabel's attention. In fact, she wasn't quite sure she believed it at first. "You see all these swans? The queen, or whoever the sovereign is at the time, owns all of them, not just the ones here, but all the swans in the United Kingdom. Well, the vast majority of them. As I understand it, all the swans in open water anywhere in the UK belong to the crown."

"Why only the swans? Why not the geese or the ducks?" Isabel asked.

"That's a good question, Isabel, but one I do not have an answer to. I also know that killing one of the queen's swans is a crime."

"But ducks and geese are fair game? Doesn't seem fair." Isabel couldn't quite wrap her head around this. "And how do they tell the queen's swans apart from the others?"

"Another good question for which I have no answer, but they must have a way. Maybe they stamp them with the royal seal. They also do a count every year of all the swans in England and Wales to see how many swans the queen actually owns. It's called the Swan Upping, and it lasts several days. I've never been."

"Swan Upping? Hmm. How curious. Does she own any other wildlife?"

"I know it all seems rather silly and strange. But it gets stranger. Her Majesty also owns all the porpoises, dolphins, whales, and sturgeon swimming within something like three miles off the coast of the entire United Kingdom. And if you accidentally catch one in your nets, you're obligated to offer it to the queen—or, again, whoever the sovereign happens to be at the time—as a gesture."

"I can't imagine dragging a dead sturgeon into Buckingham Palace would be a gesture Her Majesty would welcome," Isabel offered, and they both chuckled at the idea of it. She didn't yet realize that her crash course on the ways, and sometimes the peculiarities, of the British people was only just beginning.

When it was time to say goodbye, Isabel and Runa agreed to meet in Michigan in the summer. Isabel invited Runa and her husband to her Fourth of July barbecue, and promised to make the trip north to see Runa in Harbor Springs in August. Isabel was delighted to have made a new friend. That didn't happen very often at her age, especially living in such a small town. Not because she wasn't open to it, but because she knew everybody, and was already friends with anybody in town she cared to be friends with.

In meeting Runa, Isabel was kind of amazed that two

women from such diverse backgrounds had clicked so naturally and comfortably. That, she concluded, was why traveling, and being open to meeting different people from different backgrounds was important. She wished she could have done more of it in her life, but between raising a family, and working, and the expense of traveling, she really hadn't ventured out into the world at all. She hoped she could do more of it in the future, and preferably while she could still get around under her own steam.

After finding out that Teddy had not been able to make it to meet her in London, Carly and Charlie had arranged a surprise waiting for her when she got back to the hotel. They had the concierge book her a seat that evening to see *The Mousetrap*, one of Agatha Christie's most famous works, and the longest-running play in the history of London theater. She was ecstatic. The theater, like traveling, was not a big part of Isabel's life either. High school productions of *The Sound of Music*, in which Carly played one of the von Trapp kids, and *Oklahoma!*, in which Charlie played one of the dancing cowboys, was pretty much the extent of her live theater experience, unless you counted going to the Ice Capades with her parents as a girl—*Winnie the Pooh on Ice*—or the Grand Rapids Ballet company's performance of *The Nutcracker*.

Isabel was enthralled by the play. She would never brag about it, but she figured out pretty early on who the murderer was. The theater manager came onstage after the play to ask the audience to make a solemn pledge not to spoil it for others who might attend by divulging to anybody the murderer's identity. Isabel of course wouldn't dream of it. Plus, because she was slowly accepting the reality that her memory was not quite as sharp as it used to be, she knew there was a good chance she would forget anyway.

Chapter 5

Isabel was up bright and early on her third day in London and took a stroll through Hyde Park again—wearing her bright yellow velour jogging suit, which she would not mention to Carly—and then got ready to catch the train to Cornwall. Her train ticket was waiting for her with the concierge—Teddy had reserved a window seat in first class—and the driver was there at ten o'clock, as promised, to take her to the station.

Paddington Station was an enormous, cavernous building, bustling with travelers. Yes, it was a bit daunting, but Isabel felt she was getting the hang of traveling alone in London now, so after giving her luggage to the porter, she managed to find her way to the right platform, board the coach, and find her seat.

Once the train reached the countryside, Isabel felt an unusual sensation of calm. She was transfixed by the shifting, lush green panorama unfolding outside her window. As far as the eye could see, the rolling fields looked like a bright green rug that had been bunched up on the floor. Beautiful spring wildflowers were in bloom everywhere. Splashes of yellow, purple, orange, and blue dotted the pastures, and like so many cotton balls strewn across the meadows, hundreds of sheep and lambs could be seen grazing in one parcel of land, and dozens of cows in another.

The rambling farmhouses, stone barns, and thatched-roof cottages—all so quaint and picturesque, they looked as if they had been painted rather than built—mesmerized her, and the occasional manor house ignited her imagination. It was a landscape that was as foreign to her as it could possibly be, but for some reason it didn't *feel* foreign. Maybe, Isabel thought, this was the result of so many years of reading English writers, or her affinity for British films and television shows. Or, what if this odd familiarity with this country landscape was somehow programmed into her DNA by way of Chester Peabody? Could it literally be in her blood? That seemed pretty far-fetched and a bit too *sciency*, so the romantic in her settled on the idea that she had lived in the English countryside in another life. But whatever the reason, it did feel more as if she were coming home after a long absence than seeing it all for the first time. It was a strange feeling but a comforting one.

Not only did the landscape captivate her, but so did the names of the stops along the way: Hayes and Harlington, Maidenhead, Twyford, Thatcham, change here for Bradford-on-Avon, Bath, and Filton, continuing on to Dawlish Warren and Newton Abbot. Isabel loved that the Brits were not shy about naming their towns with such pomp and flourish. Kalamazoo was about as exotic as it got in Michigan. The train itself was also impressive. She had traveled by Amtrak many times over the years, but there was never any question you were aboard a behemoth of a train, chugging and rocking and clacking along the tracks, powered by a diesel locomotive billowing clouds of exhaust. Whipping along through this bucolic landscape on a sleek electric train, though, was like gliding on air. Isabel didn't want to miss anything, so she fought the gentle motion of the train that wanted to lull her to sleep—as best she could, anyway. But she was still feeling the jet lag, so the trip turned into a five-hour sightseeing excursion with intermittent napping.

Isabel was both happy and relieved to see Teddy standing on the platform with his smiling face when she got off the train in Penzance. Teddy Mansfield, aka Archie Cavendish, looked every bit the English country gentleman, and he was just as ruggedly handsome as she remembered him. Teddy had thick, longish gray hair and a healthy, ruddy complexion. And behind his gold, wire-rimmed glasses were sparkling, slightly mischievous blue eyes. It was a sunny but cool spring day, so he was wearing a green tweed sport coat worn over a darker green sweater and a brown plaid cap, but it was what he was wearing below that really caught her eye—a wool kilt in a bright yellow-and-black plaid. He walked over with his arms extended and gave her a warm hug, and then, quite unexpectedly, a kiss on the cheek.

"Welcome to Cornwall, Isabel."

"Thank you, Teddy. I'm thrilled to be here. And I have to say you look very fetching in your kilt."

"It's a Cornwall tartan. It belonged to my father, but I trot it out for special occasions, like picking up my dear American friend at the train station." Teddy commandeered Isabel's luggage and steered her toward the parking lot and over to his beautifully kept red vintage sedan.

"What a beautiful car, Teddy . . . What kind is it?"

"It's a 1979 Jaguar. First and only new car I ever bought, right after my first bestseller. I call her the Iron Lady, named after Mrs. Thatcher, who was elected prime minister that same year. I never voted for her, but I did admire her pluck. And this old gal has plenty of pluck too. More than two hundred thousand miles and still going strong, which is more than I can say for myself!" Teddy laughed and opened the Iron Lady's trunk—or the boot, as he called it—then went around and opened the door for Isabel, reminding her of what impeccable manners Teddy had.

"And how was your train journey, Isabel?" Teddy asked as he started up the Iron Lady and pulled out of the station's parking lot.

"It was lovely. The countryside was absolutely beautiful. . . . I still can't believe I'm here, Teddy."

"I can't quite believe it either. But I'm very pleased you've hopped the pond to pay us a visit. I'm so sorry I was unable to meet you in London as planned."

Isabel reached over and patted him on the arm. "It's quite all right, Teddy. I made a new friend on the flight over. Her name is Runa, but I'm afraid I'll never be able to say her beautiful Indian last name. She's a pediatrician from Chicago, but originally from London. We had tea together at the hotel yesterday and then we had a lovely stroll through Hyde Park and walked past Kensington Palace. It was a very British afternoon. Did you know the queen owns all the swans in the United Kingdom?"

"The queen owns *everything*," Teddy replied with a chuckle.

Isabel laughed. "Runa and her husband have a summer home in Michigan, so they're coming to my Fourth of July barbecue this summer. I hope you'll be there this year as well?"

"I do not intend to miss it this year. I've already made my sister, Matilde, commit to looking after Fred and Ginger for all of July, and Elizabeth and the children plan to be in Gull Harbor most of the summer. My dear daughter and son-in-law bought me what they call a 'tiny house' for Christmas. They're going to have it placed in the back of their property in a little stand of trees so I'll have a quiet retreat to work in while I'm there. It's going to be delivered in June. I'm quite excited."

"What a wonderful gift. Then it looks like I'll be seeing more of you this summer."

"Perhaps more than you'd like." Teddy smiled and winked at her.

"I can't imagine that's possible," Isabel replied, smiling in return. "Oh, and guess what? Runa was reading your latest book when I met her at the gate waiting for our flight. She's a big Archie Cavendish fan."

"Obviously a woman of discriminating taste," Teddy offered dryly.

"Obviously . . . I didn't let on that we were friends, so imagine her surprise when the two of you meet at my barbecue! Won't that be fun?"

Driving the short distance from Penzance to Mousehole (pronounced Mow-zul, she learned, after chatting with the conductor on the train, who couldn't figure out at first where this American woman thought she was going), Isabel was mesmerized by the lush, rustic scenery and sweeping vistas of the English Channel along Cliff Road. Occasionally her attention was diverted by oncoming traffic when she cringed and stepped on her imaginary brakes to avoid an imaginary head-on collision with cars coming at her on the wrong side of the road. This opposite-side-of-the-road driving was going to take a lot more getting used to. More than once during her short time in London, she had come close to becoming a taxi driver's hood ornament while attempting to cross the street. Once she was grabbed by her jacket and yanked back by a young man talking on his cell phone, just as a delivery van nearly grazed her coming from the left when she was looking to her right. After catching her breath, she managed to yell a thank-you to him as he crossed. He turned back and smiled and waved nonchalantly, probably never even letting on to whomever he was talking to that he had just saved the life of a confused middle-aged woman from Michigan. After that near-death experience, she stood at every street corner, looking as if she were watching a tennis match before finally finding the courage to cross.

As they turned off Cliff Road and onto a narrow road lined with hedges, Teddy pointed out Mousehole in the distance. Isabel was dazzled by the quaint-looking seaside village. "It looks absolutely charming," she said to Teddy. "I read that Dylan Thomas once called it the most beautiful village in England."

"Brilliant poet, but a hopeless alcoholic, so I'm not sure how much credence we can give that assessment. It is a charming little hamlet, though, and I do love it. I've been coming here all my life. We'll have a stroll into the village after our tea and I'll show you the sights. Maybe we'll take Fred and Ginger with us."

"I'm very anxious to meet Fred and Ginger," she said as she stared back at Mousehole.

"You'll get along swimmingly, you three. It's Tuppence, my housekeeper, whom you may find to be a bit of a challenge."

This caught Isabel's attention. She looked back at Teddy. "Oh? How so?"

"Tuppence can be—how shall I say it?—a bit rough around the edges. I'm guessing you'll be the first American she will have ever met, so she'll either be on her very best behavior or she'll be as temperamental as the hind leg of a donkey. But don't take it personally. She's not much better with me. My late wife, Fiona, is the one who hired her despite my preference for another candidate we'd interviewed. Tuppence later found out she wasn't my first choice and she's never forgiven me for it. And it's been twenty-five years. *My* candidate of choice was hired by a family down the lane and ended up making off with the family's silver and jewelry belonging to the lady of the house. Tuppence has never let me forget about that either."

Isabel laughed. "She sounds like a character. I'm sure we'll get along just fine."

"If anybody can charm her, Isabel, I'm sure it will be you. Fred and Ginger have never warmed up to her, or her to them. They completely ignore her, which can be quite amusing, because if there's one thing Tuppence hates, it's being ignored. Of course, she has a personality which makes that rather difficult."

Isabel was beginning to strategize about how best to manage the approaching Tuppence challenge when the Iron Lady turned into Teddy's gravel driveway and they slowly crunched their way up to the house. A plaque on the stone wall next to the front gate read: PEMBROKE COTTAGE. It was pretty big to be called a cottage, at least by Michigan standards, but even more enchanting than the photographs Teddy had sent her. Pembroke Cottage, which was well over one hundred years old, was made of white stucco with timber framing, had a steep slate roof, tall brick chimneys on either end, and English ivy intermingling with light purple wisteria climbing all over it. Surrounding the house was a perfectly imperfect garden full of wildflowers bordered by low boxwood hedges. And in the center of it all, a large weeping willow tree. It was the sort of place Isabel had seen in countless English period pieces, photographs, or Beatrix Potter illustrations, but never imagined she would ever see the inside of such a place.

After Teddy parked the car, Isabel got out and turned around to see a patchwork of meadows and pastures populated by grazing sheep, a smattering of old stone farmhouses, outbuildings, and low stone walls standing between Pembroke Cottage and the cliffs overlooking an even more sweeping vista of the English Channel. Teddy pulled Isabel's bags out of the boot, then looked back at the view and noticed the sea was getting choppy, and gray clouds were gathering on the horizon. "Looks like we may have some foul weather coming our way. I suppose we better get a fire built."

"Way ahead of you, Lordship!" came a gravelly voice from the other side of the car. When Teddy closed the lid to the boot, there she stood—a short, rotund, red-cheeked lady about Isabel's age, give or take, with curly gray hair, wearing an apron over a long brown wool coat and holding an armload of firewood. "It's colder than a ditch digger's bottom in that house! Hello, Mrs. Puddles. I'm Tuppence. Lovely to meet you. I've heard so much about you."

"The pleasure is all mine, Tuppence. I've heard a lot about you as well. And please call me Isabel."

"Welcome to Pembroke Cottage, Isabel. Hopefully you'll not need to solve any murders while you're on holiday in Mousehole! Did His Lordship tell you there was a murder in this very house eighty-some years ago?"

Teddy shook his head. "Mere rumors, Tuppence, and you know it. And is that any way to welcome our guest?" He turned to Isabel. "There was some speculation at the time that the lord of the manor may have been poisoned by his wife, but it was never proven, and she was never charged with the crime. Tuppence, of course, is sure she killed him and that the place is haunted by the man's ghost."

"His name was Duncan McCray. He was a Scotsman. His Lordship doesn't believe in ghosts, but I do, and I've felt a presence in the kitchen from time to time. It's like a rush of cold air that just comes out of nowhere."

"Which strangely enough coincides with her opening the refrigerator," Teddy added, giving Isabel a wink.

Tuppence ignored him. "*And* I've heard bagpipes."

Teddy looked at his houseguest reassuringly. "She's being ridiculous. I can promise you, Pembroke Cottage is not haunted. Although I have every expectation that Tuppence will come back to haunt the place if she goes before me."

"Not likely, Lordship! My mum lived to ninety-eight and my gran to ninety-nine. You may as well get used to me!"

"I've spent twenty-five years getting used to you!" Teddy laughed and turned to Isabel. "By the way, she calls me Lordship only because she knows it annoys me. My wife bought me a lord's title for a few hundred quid as an anniversary gift one year. You can do that in the UK. I bought her the accompanying ladyship title the next year. Tuppence never called us anything but Lord and Lady Mansfield after that. . . . It's all rather silly."

"I hope you're feeling peckish after your trip, Isabel!" Tuppence yelled on her way to the front door. "I've whipped up a batch of my orange-rhubarb scones for you, and I've put the kettle on. Oh, and the duke and duchess are still at the groomers, Lordship. They'll be ready at four! I was happy to see the back of them today, I can tell you. We were not getting along at all well this morning."

"When have you *ever* gotten along?" he said to her.

Tuppence laughed and opened the front door by banging her rear end against it. "Do I look bothered! They've got more attitude than Her Majesty's corgis, that pair. Cheeky monkeys they are. I've got the guest cottage all ready for you, Isabel. And a fire built in there for you as well!"

"Thank you, Tuppence. That's very kind of you." Tuppence slammed the door behind her with her foot. Isabel smiled at Teddy. "She's perfectly charming, Teddy. You had me worried there for a minute."

Teddy scowled and shook his head. "Don't fall for it. She's a wily one. I've never seen her so friendly. It's rather disconcerting." Teddy thought things over for a moment. "Or maybe she's taken up drink. She's been spending a fair amount of time with my sister, Matilde, who has developed quite a cordial relationship with gin and tonics of late, ever since she retired."

Isabel remembered Elizabeth talking about her aunt's fondness for gin, but it wasn't a conversation she was at all anxious to embark upon. Alcohol, and any excessive use of it, was a tricky subject for Isabel. She enjoyed a glass of wine or two now and again, so Isabel Puddles was no Carrie Nation. And there had been a few evenings when she and Frances or Ginny may have been overserved at a party or while out for dinner. And still other times the three of them had been known to empty a box of wine, but those nights always ended with a sleepover at Isabel's, since driving home afterward was out of the question. But, as a rule, Isabel shied away from people who drank too much. It wasn't necessarily a judgment, it was just her preference to be around people whose personalities remained consistent and were not prone to wild, alcohol-induced swings. Her late husband, Carl, had been a beer drinker for years, but he never drank excessively; a few beers watching a football game, a pitcher with his buddies on bowling night, or maybe a couple while sitting out on the dock in the summer. But for whatever reason, not long after the kids left for college, Isabel noticed a definite uptick in Carl's beer consumption, and it wasn't pretty. Thankfully the kids never saw that side of their father, but their mother saw plenty of it.

When Carl had one too many—which happened one too many times for Isabel—he went from a fairly quiet, mild-tempered, some would and did say, "boring" man, to a loud man with a bad temper who was often looking for a fight. It was jarring and sometimes even frightening. So when it happened, she usually found a reason to leave the house and not return until she was sure he had gone to sleep, which meant spending plenty of evenings at Frances's or Ginny's watching movies during those years. Isabel had always tried to avoid conflict in her marriage, even over minor things, but she had never in her life been around anybody with a "drinking prob-lem," so she wasn't sure how to deal with it other than to leave him alone. Her resentment toward him slowly grew, though. She didn't think it was fair—and it wasn't—that she should feel the need to leave the home she grew up in because her husband was a Budweiser-swilling jerk.

By then they were sleeping in separate bedrooms, so when she finally came home, he was either passed out in bed or on the couch, so they wouldn't see each other again until break-fast, where there was never any mention of his behavior the night before. Isabel told herself time and again that if Carl's problem continued, or worsened, she would have no choice but to issue him an ultimatum: either knock off the drinking or move out. She had discussed the issue with Frances numer-ous times, and with Freddie and Ginny as well. They all sup-ported her decision to give him the heave-ho if he didn't clean up his act, but she kept hoping he would stop on his own. But Carl conveniently died before she needed to kick him out. And it's worth mentioning he died with a can of Budweiser in his hand. Frances had never really been a fan of Carl, even before he became a problem drinker, so when Isabel called and broke the news to her that he had just collapsed on the garage floor and died of a massive coronary, the first words out of her mouth were, "Problem solved." That seemed a bit harsh to the newly widowed Isabel, but she knew Frances was never one to mince words, no matter what the situation.

So, given her own unpleasant history with drinkers, and Teddy's reference to his sister's "cordial relationship with gin and tonics," Isabel's growing apprehension about meeting Matilde was well founded. But she was going to reserve judg-ment until they were introduced. The last thing she wanted to do was make an enemy of Teddy's sister.

Chapter 6

Pembroke Cottage was as charming inside as it was on the outside. The large living room had an enormous stone fireplace with a fire already crackling when they stepped inside. A vaulted ceiling with wooden crossbeams gave the room a sense of space, and the old wood shutters that hung along a row of a half dozen beveled glass windows let in just the right amount of light. The room was filled with comfortable-looking overstuffed vintage furniture, antique tables, and stained-glass lamps. Large oil paintings of seascapes and landscapes in ornate gold frames hung along the dark green fabric-covered walls. A large antique model of a nineteenth-century ship with triple masts at full sail sitting on a carved library table at the center of the room caught Isabel's eye. She walked over for a closer look, and Teddy joined her. She looked up with a coy smile. "I'm sorry, Teddy . . . I've already begun snooping around."

"No apology necessary. Your snooping instincts have served you well, Mrs. Puddles, so please, snoop away."

"This is quite an impressive ship," she said, leaning in to examine the model more closely.

"That's the *Marchioness of Bristol*. She ran aground over

on the west coast of Cornwall in 1847, just south of Wales. She was carrying thirteen hundred tons of timber from Quebec to London and had just sailed over from Cork where she was dry-docked for repairs after having run aground there as well."

"Well, that's bad luck," Isabel offered.

"Or, I'm sorry to say, complete incompetence. The captain who ran her aground—twice—was my great-great-grandfather. I think it was about that time the Mansfield family decided the sea was perhaps not our calling."

"Oh, dear . . . Were there any souls lost?"

"Only his . . . eventually. The crew all survived. But Captain Mansfield came ashore after the wreck with his head hung in shame and crawled into a pub in Mousehole. When he got word, unsurprisingly, that the shipping company he sailed for had decided they would rather have a captain who did not make a habit of running ships aground, he bought a piece of land outside the village, had a cottage built, and then proceeded to drink himself to death. Well, in a way. He passed out one night with a lit cigar in one hand and a whiskey in the other. In a thatched-roof cottage that's the sort of thing you want to avoid doing. So he burned the place to the ground with himself in it."

Isabel cringed. "Oh, that's awful. Poor man."

"Luckily his wife and two sons were away, or I wouldn't be standing before you. The land sat empty for decades until my grandfather eventually built a new cottage on it, which then became our family's summer home. My sister, Matilde, lives there now. It's just down the way. Thankfully she doesn't smoke, or history could quite easily repeat itself, given her, as I mentioned, increasingly intimate relationship with gin and tonics."

"Yes, you mentioned she enjoyed a cocktail or two."

"I think we're well past two by now. She hasn't yet taken

to hiding bottles in the lampshades, at least not that I know of, but it may well come to that if we stay this course. I think the poor girl is just feeling a bit lost since she retired."

"Retired from what?" Isabel asked as she went back to examining the ship.

"Matilde owned a dress shop in Mayfair for many years and did quite well. Camilla Parker Bowles, now the duchess of Cornwall, was one of her regular customers, along with other women of a similar station in British society. Matilde always had a posh air about her, so they got on well."

"Why did she retire? Sounds like business was good."

"It's still a bit of a puzzle. I think something may have happened in her life or business she didn't want me to know about. And I didn't pry. I discouraged her from selling because I couldn't imagine what she would do instead. She's only sixty years old. But she's a stubborn one. So of course she ignored me and went ahead and closed the shop and sold the building. I believe there's a Sunglass Hut there now. But it's been over a year since she moved here full-time and she has yet to find a constructive way to fill her days."

"Was Matilde never married?" Isabel asked, feeling increasingly sorry for Teddy's sister, and now increasingly nervous about meeting her.

"She was engaged twice, but I don't believe she was in love with either of them. First time in her early twenties—there's a bit of a story there—and again in her forties when an elderly earl, I've forgotten his formal title, but he was a cousin of Mrs. Parker Bowles, became absolutely besotted with her. He used to come in with Camilla and shop. He was relentless in his pursuit, or as relentless as an eighty-year-old man can be, so she finally agreed to marry him. But I think it was the allure of becoming a countess that finally tipped the scales in the earl's favor."

"Who broke off the engagement? Matilde or the earl?"

"God broke it off. The earl dropped dead right there in Matilde's store. It was most unfortunate. Both for Matilde and for the earl. Not great for business, either, because he died in the middle of her autumn fashion show."

"Well, that's all very sad. . . . So poor Matilde has never been in love?"

"My sister is a tough nut to crack, but she hasn't always been so, what's the word? Rigid, perhaps? She was quite lovely as a young girl, really. And I happen to know she was *madly* in love with a boy here in Mousehole when she was seventeen or eighteen. But that didn't turn out well, either, I'm afraid."

"Oh, dear," Isabel said, trying not to reveal her curiosity about how this next story was going to unfold.

"Hugo was his name. Quite a handsome chap. Excellent cricket player. But my mother and father did not approve. They were quite conservative, you see, and a bit snobbish. And when I say *a bit*, I mean *very*. They objected to the boy merely because he was the son of a butcher, and his mother was a seamstress. Perfectly lovely people, as I remember. But Mum and Dad refused to let her see him once they caught wind of how serious it was getting. She did, of course. They carried on secretly until my parents eventually found out. I can still remember the row that followed, and Matilde telling them she and Hugo intended to marry, which was not *quite* true because he hadn't formally proposed, but they had been talking about it. It was also not the thing to say to my parents because they then took action."

"This doesn't sound good. I'm almost afraid to ask. . . . What happened to Hugo?"

"Mum and Dad sent Matilde off to Paris to study for a year. They told her if she still had feelings for Hugo when she returned, they would not stand in the way of a marriage. But it was a trick. And she fell for it. They had no intention of that marriage ever happening. I don't know if it was *completely* diabolical, because I'd like to think they genuinely believed after a year in Paris she would forget about the butcher's son and the problem would be solved. But when she returned from Paris, and with her feelings for Hugo stronger than ever, she discovered he was engaged to someone else."

"Oh, no . . . That's heartbreaking."

"It really was a shame. I do think Hugo truly loved Matilde. But he knew my parents, and they were formidable. They were also not shy about sharing their displeasure over the relationship with him. He knew they would never accept him, so I think poor Hugo finally just gave up the fight . . . and gave up Matilde."

"Poor Matilde . . . She must have been crushed."

"Gutted . . . absolutely gutted."

"So who did Hugo get engaged to?" Isabel was feeling even worse for Matilde now.

"A very pretty local girl named Hyacinth, the daughter of a sheep farmer. She was also Matilde's best friend. Well, best *summer* friend."

"My goodness. It gets even sadder."

"*And* more interesting . . . A year or so later, Matilde was finally over Hugo, or at least appeared to be, so she got engaged to a lad from Oxford called Raleigh Leyland of British Leyland automobile manufacturers. Mum and Dad were naturally over the moon about it until Matilde broke the news that she had discovered he was a cross-dresser, so she was going to call off the engagement. How she discovered this remained a mystery. My mother discouraged her from doing anything rash, and instead encouraged her to look at the advantages. The most obvious of course being that she would be marrying into a very wealthy and prominent industrial family, which was the next best thing to marrying royalty in Mum's opinion. And two, she could double her wardrobe."

Isabel couldn't help laughing. "So what happened?"

"Matilde ignored my mother and called off the engagement, but amicably. Mum and Dad were most unhappy about it."

Naturally Isabel was curious to know more about Matilde's story, but she thought it was probably best to move on for now. She turned and looked into a dark study tucked into an alcove off the living room. "Well, that's a cozy little study you have there, Teddy."

"It's my favorite room in the house. Do come in." Teddy led Isabel into his wood-paneled inner sanctum and switched on a lamp. An impressive collection of books lined shelf after shelf of a floor-to-ceiling bookcase behind a large antique desk where Teddy's computer was set up. Next to the desk sat a well-worn leather chair and an ottoman with an antique side table, and upon it, a handsome brass lamp. Beside the lamp was an elegantly framed photograph. Isabel of course knew exactly who it was.

"May I?" she asked. Teddy nodded and smiled. Isabel picked up the photograph and looked at the picture of the woman admiringly. "Fiona was certainly a beautiful woman. What a wonderful smile."

"A smile that lit up any room. And an absolutely contagious laugh. I can still hear her laugh." Isabel carefully set Fiona back down on the table. "I know it's a bit silly," Teddy began, somewhat self-consciously, "but I sometimes read to her when I'm sitting there with a book and come across a passage I think she'd enjoy. Sometimes, if *I've* written a passage I'm not quite sure about, I'll read that to her too. And I know this will sound mad, but I feel she somehow either guides me through a rewrite or provides me with a sense that it's fine as written . . . Do you think I'm crazy?"

"Not in the least . . . I think it's lovely. I take it Fiona was a reader?"

"Fiona loved to read. She loved real literature—English

and American writers—and she loved the French classics. She was fluent in French. She also read a lot of historical nonfiction and biographies. She was most definitely my intellectual superior! I think she read my books merely so as not to hurt my feelings, although she claimed she enjoyed them. But what else could she say, really?"

"How did you two meet?" Isabel loved a good falling-in-love story.

"We met at the library in our second year at the University of Bath. Love at first sight for me, but it took her a while to come around."

Isabel smiled. "You must still miss her very much."

"I miss her every day. . . . But to be fair, over the years, the loss I have felt, and still *do* feel, has been shored up a little bit anyway by a feeling of immense gratitude that I was lucky enough to have somebody so wonderful as a partner in life for so long."

Isabel was touched by Teddy's love and devotion to his wife's memory. "That's a beautiful sentiment, Teddy. And I'm sure she felt the same way about you."

Teddy seemed to want to avoid getting too sentimental. "Oh, she was not nearly as lucky as I was, bless her. Patience of a saint on top of everything else!" Teddy clapped his hands together. He was ready to move on. "What in the world is holding up our tea?"

And just as if she had been waiting for her cue, a voice already familiar to Isabel called out from the other room. "Tea's on, Your Lordship!" Teddy rolled his eyes and led Isabel into the dining room, where Tuppence had set the table with a silver tea service and a plate of homemade scones. Teddy pulled out a chair for Isabel and came around to sit just as Tuppence walked out with another silver tray. "I've got some fresh Cornish clotted cream and some homemade orange marmalade here." Tuppence looked at Teddy. "Shall I be mother, Lordship?"

"Putting it on a bit thick today, aren't you? And aren't you *always* mother?" Teddy smiled at Isabel, who, from her expression, looked as if she might be in need of an explanation. "'Shall I be mother' is a very old British expression which simply means, 'shall I pour the tea?'" Teddy looked at Tuppence and smiled. "It's a term used mostly by the elderly."

"Well, then, I don't know where that puts you, Lordship, given that I'm ten years your junior! I expect Mother will be cutting your meat for you before too long!" Teddy ignored the remark and reached for a scone while Tuppence poured the tea. "Do you take milk, Isabel?"

Isabel was trying to figure out if this prickly banter between Teddy and his housekeeper was all in good fun or if there was some level of animosity lurking beneath it. Whatever the case, she was determined to steer well clear of it. "Yes, please. Just a splash. Your scones look out of this world, Tuppence."

"Well, let's hope they taste that way," she said as she poured a splash of milk into Isabel's cup. "I hope the judges at the bake-off next week agree. I do believe this is the year I'm going to take home the Golden Rolling Pin! Don't you feel it's my time, Your Lordship?" she asked Teddy, passing the plate of scones to Isabel, then lifting the lids off the porcelain pots of clotted cream and marmalade.

"Well, it would be nice for a change. Your second-place moping is a bit trying." Tuppence left the room without comment. Teddy leaned in toward Isabel and spoke in a much quieter voice, "She's come in second for five years straight. Outdone—or out-baked, rather—by her baking nemesis, Hyacinth Amesbury, who has been on quite a winning streak. She doesn't handle second place at all well."

"Is this the same Hyacinth whom Hugo got engaged to?" Isabel asked, as if she were familiar with all the players at this point.

Teddy nodded, "The very same."

The plot was thickening, and Isabel was becoming even more intrigued with this decades-old Cornish love triangle. Teddy knew Isabel well enough by now to know she was hoping for more. "Matilde didn't speak to her for years, but eventually they rehabilitated their friendship. Well, somewhat. They're still prickly with each other and fall out constantly over all manner of things."

"I can see why that would have created some turmoil." Isabel stirred her tea but she was waiting for Teddy to start on his scone before she did . . . and the wait was killing her.

"I don't think I mentioned that Hyacinth eventually broke off the engagement with Hugo, but by then Matilde was engaged to her Oxford cross-dresser. Hugo disappeared after being jilted and joined the Royal Navy or the French Foreign Legion or something."

"And what about Hyacinth? Did she eventually marry?"

"She married a fairly well-to-do appliance store owner from Penzance. But he died years ago. Hyacinth is a tricky one straight across the board. I've never liked her nor have I ever trusted her. Tuppence doesn't, either. She's convinced Hyacinth is cheating, which I certainly wouldn't put past her. Although I don't see how one cheats their way to victory in a scone bake-off."

Tuppence came back into the dining room having heard the tail end of the conversation. "I don't know how she does it, either, but I intend to get to the bottom of it if she wins again this year. I happen to know that my rhubarb scone recipe is going to be, hands down, the favorite of the lead judge—Raul Bollywood *himself* from *The Old Blighty Bake-Off.*"

"And where does this confidence come from?" Teddy asked.

Tuppence was only too happy to share. "Because I read in an interview that Mr. Bollywood's beloved nan—you know his mother's from Manchester—anyway, his nan used to bake rhubarb scones for him when he was a boy, and he said it's one of his fondest childhood memories. He said a rhubarb scone takes him right back to his nan's kitchen. I'm including just a hint of orange zest in my recipe to brighten it up a bit too."

"That sounds like a delicious pairing, Tuppence. Is that what *these* are?" Isabel asked, pointing to the plate of scones and hoping it might prompt her host to start eating his.

"Yours is, but His Lordship doesn't like me getting experimental with his scones, so I always bake a batch of raisin for him."

"What is it you say in America, Isabel? If it ain't broke, don't fix it?" Teddy offered in his defense. "But, Tuppence my dear, I do think Hyacinth Amesbury could use a lesson in humility, so I hope your rhubarb scones do the trick. It's high time her reign as Mousehole's queen of scones comes to an end!"

"Thank you, Lordship. I don't think she'll give up the crown without a fight, but that's what she's got coming this year. . . . More tea, Isabel?" Tuppence didn't wait for an answer and poured anyway, then returned to the kitchen, mumbling to herself.

Teddy looked across the table at Isabel with raised eyebrows. "These are the sort of pressing issues we face here in Cornwall these days. . . . Aren't you going to eat your scone?"

Finally! Isabel laughed. "I was waiting for you!" She immediately pulled her scone apart and reached for the clotted cream. "I just love clotted cream," she said as she spooned out one and then two globs and plopped them on each half of her still slightly warm scone. "My Grandmother Peabody used to bake scones. She had an old Peabody family recipe. And from time to time she'd make clotted cream too, but as I recall it took quite some time."

Isabel was generously spreading the cream onto each half of her scone with her knife when she suddenly realized Teddy was looking across the table at her with some concern. "I should mention there is another pressing issue we face here in Cornwall, Isabel."

She stopped spreading. "One that involves clotted cream?"

"Strangely enough, yes. There is a bit of a rivalry between Cornwall and Devon—which is the county to the west— regarding how to, shall we say, *embellish* one's scone." Teddy could see that his guest was once again sufficiently puzzled. "You see, in Cornwall we put our jam on the scone first, and then top it with the cream. In Devon they do it the other way around. I don't want to see you falling out with Tuppence over this after you've gotten off to such a good start. She's very much a traditionalist, and Cornish to the bone. If she sees you going clotted cream first on one of her scones, she will not let it go without comment."

"I certainly don't want to start any trouble, but I have to say my instinct is to go with the Devon approach. That's also how my grandmother served them, *but* when in Cornwall"— Isabel scraped off the cream onto her plate and reached for the marmalade—"do as the Cornish do!"

"I'm with you if I'm being honest, Isabel. It just makes more sense, doesn't it? The cream provides a nice solid base for the jam. Putting the jam on first makes for a rather unstable foundation for the cream in my view. But between Fiona, my daughter, Elizabeth, and that one out there in the kitchen—the Cornwall method remains the only acceptable way to accessorize a scone in this house. Anything else is heresy. Eventually I caved to the pressure and gave up my independence."

Isabel slathered enough marmalade on each half to hide any sign of the remaining cream, then scooped up the cream and topped them off. There was no sign that a crime had ever been committed. Tuppence looked at Isabel's plate approvingly when she came back in to pour more tea. "I'm happy to see that the Americans know how to eat their scones!"

Isabel laughed, then proceeded to take a bite. She was transported. "Tuppence, this is, hands down, the most delicious scone I have ever tasted in my life! I don't see how you could not take first place in any bake-off with this scone!" She took another bite. "Not only do the rhubarb and the orange zest work beautifully together, but the texture is perfection." Isabel was in awe. "I don't know how you do it."

"Scones are not all that complicated. But I have a few tricks I'm happy to teach you. I've been baking them since I was a little girl. I pulled a chair up to the kitchen counter and made them nearly every morning while me mum and dad were out tending the stock."

"I would love to learn. I haven't had very good luck with scones, I'm afraid." Isabel was the first to admit her skills as a baker were limited to pies. And one of her greatest misadventures involved baking, or trying to bake, scones.

Isabel's great-grandfather, Chester Peabody, emigrated from England to Michigan around 1900, so there had always been a strong British influence in her family. His wife, Zelda, although of Dutch descent, had the scone recipe passed down to her from Chester's mother, which she then passed down to Isabel's grandmother, Hazel. One of Isabel's fondest childhood memories was sitting in her grandmother's kitchen drinking chamomile tea, just the two of them, while they waited for Grandmother Hazel's cherry scones to come out of the oven. When they did, and after waiting a torturous fifteen minutes for them to cool, her grandmother would take a jar of her homemade clotted cream out of the fridge, if she had it, along with whatever homemade jam she had on hand, and the ritual of high tea would begin. In the spring and summer they would have their tea in Grandmother Hazel's backyard rose garden. In the fall and winter, the oven would keep them toasty warm in the kitchen.

But unlike most of the old family recipes, Great-Grandmother Zelda's mother-in-law's scone recipe had never been written down or, if it had, it had been lost long ago. Because drinking tea—Earl Grey in the afternoons, and chamomile in the evenings—was a daily ritual for Isabel, she had never stopped longing for her grandmother's sweet, fluffy, buttery cherry scones to go with her tea. So one rainy day she threw caution to the wind and decided to try to replicate the recipe. It did not go well. Whether she had overmixed or overbaked was unclear, but the end result was a scone that looked like, and had the texture of, a hockey puck. It also tasted a lot like how she imagined a hockey puck might taste if it was slathered with clotted cream and jam. They were, in a word, inedible.

She broke one in half and set it down in front of the dogs. Not even Jackpot and Corky—who were not exactly known for their sophisticated palates, considering that grass and bark chips were two of their favorite snacks—were remotely interested. They each had a sniff of their half of the unappealing foreign object on the floor in front of them and then looked up at her as if to say, "What are you trying to pull here?" To their credit, they did take a nibble, but then looked up at Isabel again with a look she interpreted as utter disappointment before leaving the room.

After her epic scone fail, Isabel washed up, put her baking supplies away, and made a pact with herself, her grandmother, and her dogs that she would never attempt to bake another scone. And she never did.

Chapter 7

After their tea, Teddy showed Isabel out to the lovely little guesthouse where she would be staying; it looked like a scaled-down version of the main house but was covered almost entirely by climbing white roses. Teddy opened the door and placed her bags just inside the foyer, then stepped back. Isabel knew this was him being the consummate gentleman, and probably not thinking it was proper to go inside with her, given that it was essentially just a large bedroom.

She was still feeling the effects of jet lag now almost four days after arriving in the UK, and because Fred and Ginger wouldn't be ready to be picked up at the groomers for a while, she asked Teddy if he would mind if she rested up a little. He was quick to approve and began to pull the door shut, then remembered he had forgotten to mention that Matilde was coming for dinner. "Oh, wonderful. I'm excited to meet her," Isabel said convincingly, despite it not being remotely true. In fact the news created almost enough anxiety to prevent her from falling asleep as she lay down and imagined various unpleasant scenarios. But the jet lag won, and she was soon fast asleep.

An hour or so later, Isabel woke to the sound of voices.

Tuppence was having a conversation in the backyard with somebody who she instinctively knew must be Matilde. Was it dinnertime already?

"Well? What do you think of her? This Puddles woman," Matilde asked.

"I think she's lovely. Seems like a very nice woman," answered Tuppence.

"Well, I guess I'll decide that for myself tonight. Where are they now?"

"The groomer called to say the duke and duchess were ready just as I was headed out to the shops. I reckon they drove down together to pick them up."

Just as the "Puddles woman" was about to make some sort of noise to indicate she was in fact in the guesthouse, Matilde began to speak again. Isabel couldn't resist eavesdropping, knowing she probably shouldn't. She didn't want to form a negative opinion without even having met her. But she also couldn't resist sneaking over and peeking through the curtains to have a look at her.

Matilde was a handsome woman, and Isabel could see the family resemblance. She was tall, refined looking, with a nice figure, and dressed as if she were on her way to a fox hunt. All that was missing was a riding crop. But Isabel could already tell that Matilde's tongue could serve a similar function.

"Why do you think she's come? Do you suppose she's trying to get Teddy to the altar?"

Isabel could feel her cheeks flushing. Who did this woman think she was? Who did she think *Isabel* was? She made sure she was adequately concealed behind the curtain and kept watching and listening.

"I think they're just good friends," Tuppence replied. She'd been picking herbs with her back to Matilde, then suddenly turned around, looking a little annoyed. "But what would be so wrong with Mr. Mansfield finding love and marrying again? Mrs. Mansfield's been gone over ten years now. And she made him promise before she passed that he would go on living, *and* that she approved of him falling in love again. I knew if it ever happened, it would take a very long time, but after ten years I think maybe the time has come. I think it would be just grand!"

"But to an *American*? It's bad enough my niece married one. Do we really want another one in our midst? I can't imagine Fiona would have approved of his marrying an American either."

Tuppence got a peculiar look on her face. "What's wrong with Americans? George Clooney's American, and I'd marry him over any man in Cornwall! And so would you, I reckon!"

"Don't be absurd. I'm just saying, how do we know she's not just looking for a rich husband?" Matilde said with a sneer in her voice. Isabel was fuming. Matilde was not only questioning her character but was now disparaging her country too. "And when Teddy finally does fall off the branch, she'd clean up quite nicely, wouldn't she. And probably move back to America with his money. And where would that leave you?"

"Don't drag me into this, thank you very much! I don't have time for this nonsense, Matilde. You've concocted this whole thing in your head and you've never even met her. I don't see any reason at all to think Isabel is here to trap your brother into marriage, or make off with the inheritance I'm assuming some of which will go to you. Maybe it's *your* motives we should be questioning here?"

Matilde was incensed. "Are you questioning my integrity, Tuppence?"

"You're questioning Isabel's integrity. What's the difference?"

"Because you've known me for, what, forty years?"

"Exactly," Tuppence responded without skipping a beat.

"My *only* concern is what's best for my brother," Matilde said with not a hint of sincerity. Tuppence had known Matilde too long and too well to buy into that claptrap. She knew very well that Matilde's primary concern in life was herself. "I mean what do we really know about Isabel Puddles?"

"From what I've heard from Mr. Mansfield, Isabel is a widow with two grown children, both apparently very successful, she's devoted to her family and friends and the community she's lived in all her life, *and* she's quite a well-respected private investigator. She single-handedly solved a big murder case not long ago and became quite famous for it. Mr. Mansfield read about her in the newspaper."

"Yes, yes . . . I've heard *all* about her murder-solving prowess. But that doesn't mean she hasn't got an agenda with my brother. I'd still like to know more."

"What else would you like to know about her? Birth sign? Blood type? Shoe size? My advice to you, Matilde, is to stop overthinking this and give her a fair chance. What they have going, right now at least, is nothing more than a lovely friendship. And I think it's brilliant."

"You do know that Americans are notoriously sneaky."

"I don't think they have the patent on sneaky. She's the first American I've ever met, and I find her to be very open and honest, which I find quite refreshing." Tuppence gave Matilde a look. "I trust my instincts. . . . And she raved about my scones."

"Well, there you have it! No wonder you're so taken with her!"

"Don't be ridiculous. It just shows that aside from being a very nice woman, she's also a gracious guest who happens to have very good taste. Now, this is a welcome-to-Cornwall supper I'm preparing for her this evening, so it would be lovely if you could adjust your attitude to fit the theme."

Matilde was clearly not happy about the dressing-down

she was getting from her brother's housekeeper, but it was obvious Tuppence could not have cared less. And Isabel was loving it. Teddy had already explained to her that he considered Tuppence family, and that she had always been free to speak her mind in the Mansfield house, and did so on a fairly regular basis.

Tuppence was finally done with Matilde. "Now, if you'll excuse me, I've got pasties in the oven and I'm making a banoffee pie for tonight's pudding, so I need to get back to the kitchen. Now if you—"

"Good afternoon, ladies! It's turned into quite a glorious day, wouldn't you say?" Teddy called out as he stepped out onto the brick patio with Fred and Ginger flanking him. Neither dog made any effort to greet Tuppence or Matilde.

Tuppence smiled and raised her eyebrows at Matilde. "Well, look who's got a little extra spring in their step today." Then to Teddy. "Afternoon, Your Lordship! Yes, it has indeed turned into a delightful day!" Tuppence looked behind him. "Where's Isabel?"

"I assume she's still napping," Teddy offered as he sat down at the patio table and began sorting through his mail.

Tuppence's eyes widened. She looked at Matilde's frozen expression, then under her breath, "I hope she's a sound sleeper, because you really stepped in it."

"You told me she had gone with Teddy," Matilde quietly fumed, her face still frozen.

"I said I *reckoned* they had gone together. Looks like I reckoned wrong."

"What are you two whispering about?" Teddy asked as he opened another piece of mail.

"Oh, nothing, Lordship! Just talking about the menu for this evening."

"What are we having?"

"I'm making a Newlyn crab soup, beef pasties, chicken

curry pasties, sautéed broad beans, and a banoffee pie for pudding."

"Sounds like a right Cornish feast! But can we not have supper too early tonight, please? As soon as Isabel gets up, I want to walk down to the village with the dogs and show her around a bit. Can we plan on seven thirty?"

"Seven thirty it is, Lordship! Will that suit you, Matilde?" Then, whispering to her, "Or will you still be trying to get your foot out of your mouth?"

Matilde glared at a smiling Tuppence. "Seven thirty will be fine."

After hearing Teddy's voice, Isabel decided it was time to make an appearance. And safer now too, after hearing his sister sharpening her claws in the garden she wasn't sure what she was dealing with. So after freshening up and fixing her hair, she opened the door and stepped outside, looking as though she didn't have a care in the world. But underneath, Isabel was not happy.

"Good afternoon, Mrs. Puddles!" Teddy called from the patio, obviously happy to see her looking rested and refreshed. "Did you have a nice nap?"

"I slept like a log. I can't believe I'm still feeling the jet lag. But then I haven't left my own time zone in years, so I'm not surprised my body is a little confused."

Even happier to see her than Teddy were Fred and Ginger, who immediately ran over to say hello. Isabel crouched down, did a quick chassis check to figure out who was who, and began to scratch their heads as she introduced herself. "Hello, Fred. Hello, Ginger. I'm Isabel. I've been very anxious to meet you two. Yes, I have. Aren't you two beautiful? And you're so soft and smell so nice." Isabel had no control over her "doggie voice," as she called it. Whenever interacting with dogs, her own included, it just came out. She knew it probably sounded silly, especially to people without dogs, but the dogs always seemed to respond, so she never thought twice about it. Not even in front of her new nemesis, Matilde.

After a few kisses on the cheek from them both, Isabel stood up and faced Matilde with a smile she hoped didn't read as forced despite its being completely forced. It had been no mistake that she introduced herself to Fred and Ginger before she did Matilde. "And I've been very anxious to meet you as well, Matilde. I'm Isabel." Isabel walked over and shook her hand firmly, on purpose, but still not letting on that anything was wrong.

Matilde's expression after Isabel introduced herself was hard to pinpoint. She looked slightly contrite, because she still didn't know if Isabel had overheard the disparaging remarks she had just made about her. But she was still looking suspicious of who this American interloper was. Then in her phoniest, former-owner-of-a-dress-shop-catering-to-upper-crust-of-British-society-women voice, she smiled and replied, "I'm absolutely *delighted* to meet you, Isabel. I'm Matilde Mansfield, Teddy's sister. You're every bit as lovely as I expected you to be."

Boy, this woman could really lay it on thick when she wanted to, Isabel said to herself. "Likewise, Matilde," she replied, slightly distracted by Fred and Ginger, who were repeatedly jumping up on her—no easy task for a corgi—and looking for attention. Isabel crouched down to pet them again. "They're just adorable, Teddy!" she yelled to him.

"Well, they have certainly taken a liking to you, Isabel. I think they sense who the dog lovers are . . . and who they are *not*." He fake-smiled at Tuppence and Matilde, who were both looking quite annoyed at being so blatantly slighted by two corgis who had known them both for years.

Isabel walked over and joined Teddy at the table with Fred and Ginger right on her heels. Both of them lay down at her feet and were napping in no time.

"I'm beginning to feel a bit dejected," Teddy said, staring down sadly at his beloved dogs. Then, looking over at Tuppence and Matilde, "I can't imagine how *you* two must feel."

"Well, the feeling's mutual! I'm sure I've got bigger things to worry about in this life than whether or not those two dogs like me!" Tuppence said defiantly as she picked a stem of rosemary off the bush a little more aggressively than she probably needed to.

"Apparently they like Americans. . . . Not *everybody* does," Isabel said, deliberately not looking at Matilde. "But then they *are* named after the most beloved dancing team in Hollywood history."

"These two are not exactly light on their feet," Teddy said with a chuckle, "but they do love to walk. Shall we take a stroll into the village?"

"That sounds delightful." Isabel stood up, joined by Fred and Ginger, then waved goodbye to Tuppence and Matilde. "Ta-ta, ladies!"

Ta-ta? *Where did that come from?* Isabel said to herself. Must be the UK was already rubbing off on her.

There was no denying that, regrettably, she and Teddy's sister had gotten off to a rocky start, but Isabel was going to play it smart. She might even try to have some fun with it. *Keep your friends close but your enemies closer,* was an adage she had heard more than once, but it had never really resonated with her because Isabel Puddles had no enemies. Not unless one counted the murderers she had helped put into prison recently. But it looked like she had already made one in Cornwall, and she had been there only a few hours. What she had found touching, though, amid Matilde's spewing of unfounded accusations, was hearing Tuppence defending her, having no idea that Isabel could hear them. Now she knew she had a friend and ally in Tuppence.

Whatever Matilde thought of her didn't really matter. At least that's what she told herself. But in reality it did matter, because Isabel was not somebody who was used to having her character casually thrown into question like that. It really irked her. And she didn't care for her America bashing either. But she was less angry than she was hurt. However, she did intend to make it clear to Matilde, if it became necessary, that *this* American was not going to be bullied, at least not without consequence.

Chapter 8

The threatening clouds that had been gathering over the channel earlier in the day had failed to come ashore. What started out as a gloomy day turned into a beautiful spring afternoon. "The Cornish gods have smiled upon you, Isabel. Cornwall always looks its best in the sun. But that's really true of all of Great Britain," Teddy said.

"It's stunning. More beautiful than I ever imagined, Teddy." The fact that she was really there was still sinking in. The stroll into the village was peaceful and picturesque, and Isabel had all but forgotten about the unfortunate incident with Matilde earlier. Or at least she was trying to. It was just too lovely a day to be bothered with such petty nonsense.

Teddy was as interesting and colorful in person as he was in his letters, regaling her with stories of his childhood in both London and in Cornwall. Isabel, who was holding Fred's leash while Teddy held Ginger's, was impressed with how well behaved they were. They heeled and walked with a perfect gait, as though they were being shown at the Westminster Dog Show. Isabel had never really trained Jackpot or Corky to heel on walks, or to do anything she asked of them once they were outdoors. They were very well-behaved dogs inside, but the minute they got outside, all bets were off. Their senses just seemed to overwhelm them, and they went a little berserk. Not so with Fred and Ginger. They were both models of English propriety.

The view of the water was indeed spectacular, but Isabel was most intrigued with all the houses and cottages they passed on their way down the gradually declining narrow road that wound into the village. All the homes and cottages had charming, often elegant names. Apparently, it was a common thing to do in Cornwall. There was Thimble Cottage, the Magpie Nest, Pippins Cottage, Windermere House, Fox Hollow, and her favorite—both the cottage and the name—Squirrel's Leap Cottage.

People in Michigan named their cottages too, but they weren't usually as quaint. Over on the Big Lake there was the Hodge Podge Lodge and the Shore Thing. Isabel's mother had named their home on Gull Lake Poplar Bluff, which was not exactly a stretch, since it sat on a bluff surrounded by poplar trees. Then there was the Wander Inn—predictable. Knotty and Nice—silly, but cute. Sillier still was her personal favorite—Dock Holiday, owned by her dentist. She also remembered a cottage across the lake called the Stumble Inn, which certainly didn't paint a proud picture of the owners.

"You see that stone cottage on the other side of this field? The one with the thatched roof?" Teddy asked. Isabel squinted and nodded. "That's our old family summer cottage, where Matilde now lives. You can't get a very good look at it from here, but we'll go by there on another walk."

"Does it have a name?" Given what she had heard about Matilde's penchant for gin, the Stumble Inn might be perfect for her too.

"Well, it's not very original, but as an homage to the unlucky Captain Clive Mansfield—who burned the original cottage to the ground—we call it the Captain's Cottage. Now you see that rather run-down old Tudor home up that lane? That's Amesbury Acreage, also known as the Cuckoo's Nest, because there resides the woman whose name you've already heard mentioned more than once today, Hyacinth Amesbury, who seems to get more and more cuckoo every year. She lives there with her son, Alby, who is somewhere around thirty-five years old by now, I would guess, has never left home, and is, to be kind, a few bricks short." Isabel looked puzzled. Teddy clarified. "He's a nutter. Completely harmless, though. He does work for me around the house and in the garden from time to time. You'll likely meet him at some point. And there'll be no getting around meeting Hyacinth. I'm sure she's already heard from my sister that I have a houseguest from America. That's big news in this little hamlet. That is when scone recipes aren't top of mind."

"So you say Matilde and Hyacinth are still good friends? Despite what happened all those years ago?"

"I suppose it all depends on your definition of 'good friends.' In the summers they were inseparable when they were girls. And we came down through the year for weekends quite frequently too, so they more or less grew up together. These days they seem to go from one kerfuffle to the next. But I think when you've known somebody for as long as those two have—over fifty years—you're just used to them being in your life, whether you like it or not. Hyacinth is not the easiest person to get along with, but then neither is my sister, so in that regard they're rather kindred spirits."

After they reached Mousehole, Teddy took Isabel over to sit down on his favorite bench along the boardwalk overlooking the cozy little harbor. She wondered if he and Fiona used to sit there together. After a little more chitchat about their present surroundings, Isabel realized she had not asked Teddy about his new teaching position.

"It's only two afternoons a week, and I have just fourteen

students. But they're a lively group of kids, all of them aspiring writers. Some I must say show some real talent. But there are a few others who I hope will develop other interests, bless them, as I don't believe writing is a calling they should answer. I've seen Tuppence write more interesting grocery lists. But it's not my place to crush their dreams. . . . Life will take care of that."

"That's an unhappy thought, Teddy. Couldn't you maybe find a gentler way to coax them in a different direction before life crushes their dreams? Maybe encourage them to think about a *new* dream?"

"Well, that sounds lovely, but when it comes right down to it, who am I to judge? My evaluation of their work is just one man's opinion. I may have the Cornish Ernest Hemingway in my class and I'm too daft to realize it. I just think it best not to interfere with whatever path they may have put themselves on, personal or professional."

"Hemingway's story didn't end well," Isabel added, quickly realizing it was not the least bit apropos to their conversation. She was relieved when Teddy waved at someone he knew along the boardwalk so they could move on.

"That gentleman walking toward us is Nigel Plumbottom. And, yes, that *is* his real name. Mr. Plumbottom is in fact the former mayor of Mousehole." Teddy sprang up when Mr. Plumbottom reached the bench and they shook hands. "Nigel, may I present Isabel Puddles. She's just arrived from America and will be gracing us with her presence for the next couple of weeks."

Nigel Plumbottom was a large man, not in height but more so in width. Before he even opened his mouth, Isabel was completely taken with him. Mr. Plumbottom was probably somewhere in his sixties, impeccably dressed in a gray suit, a red vest, and a bright yellow patterned tie with a matching pocket square. He had wisps of gray hair growing out of his bald head, reminding Isabel of a Chia Pet she once had that she did not have great success with. Mr. Plumbottom had a happy face with red cheeks, eyebrows so long they looked as if he had combed them out, and a mustache that matched them.

Mr. Plumbottom looked over the rims of his wire-framed spectacles and gently took Isabel's hand, then cupped his other hand over it. "I'm absolutely enchanted to make your acquaintance, Mrs. Puddles. I did hear through the grapevine that Teddy was expecting a houseguest from America, but I never expected her to be quite as fetching as you, my dear."

Isabel knew he was full of it, but she was charmed and flattered just the same. "That's very kind of you to say, Mr. Plumbottom. I'm very pleased to make your acquaintance too."

"Please call me Nigel."

"If you'll call me Isabel. This is a lovely little village, Nigel. And I understand you were once the mayor?"

"I was indeed. For—what was it, Teddy—twelve years? But I finally decided politics was not on the cards for me any longer, so I retired. And when I say I retired, what I really mean to say is that I was voted out of office. So I suppose it's more accurate to say I was retired by the citizens of this community, the people whom I served loyally and honorably for more than a decade. But no point in harboring any resentment over it."

"No, you seem to have done a cracking good job of letting it go, Nigel," Teddy said with a straight face. Nigel was oblivious, and continued. "I'm quite enjoying my retirement. I putter in my garden part-time and I have a little antique shop in my converted garage. That's where I do my puttering when it rains. So I've gone from politics to puttering. Perhaps I should take up pottery next!" Nigel laughed at his own odd alliteration joke. "You must come by and visit, Isabel. Do you like antiques? I see you're enjoying the company of Teddy, so I suppose the answer is yes." Nigel laughed.

Teddy scoffed. "Ha! I'm still a vintage classic. You, my friend, have crossed the threshold into antique, and now on your way to artifact."

Nigel laughed. "Touché, Teddy. I should know better than to get into a jousting match with a writer!"

Isabel was about to tell him about her antique booth at the Antique Barn back home when a car with an unusual horn honked from the street. She turned to see a dark green vintage Rolls-Royce parked at the curb. Isabel was not a car person per se, but this was one gorgeous car. She had seen ones like it in countless movies and TV shows, but she had never seen one up close. A burly man with a stern-looking face wearing a chauffeur's cap was sitting behind the wheel. He honked again. "Oh, there's Tiegan. I must be going, I'm afraid."

"I see you're still driving the Margaret Mobile, Nigel." He turned to Isabel. "That Rolls-Royce has royal provenance. It is rumored—by Nigel, so one must consider the source—to have once belonged to Princess Margaret."

"It has the cigarette burns in the upholstery and the carpeting to prove it! *And* it still smells of Chanel No. Five and gin," Nigel proclaimed, defending his car's provenance. "I don't take it out much, as you know, Teddy, but I'm afraid Tiegan ran into the back of a street sweeper in my Mercedes yesterday, so it's in for repairs . . . again. Well, I'm off! Hope to see you at the shop, Isabel. Do have Teddy bring you around!"

And with that, former Mousehole mayor Nigel Plumbottom was off. Teddy watched him leave with a smile. "Look," he said to Isabel. She turned again to see Nigel's chauffeur squeezing out from behind the steering wheel to get out and open the rear door for his boss. Nigel said nothing to him as he slowly settled into the backseat. The chauffeur closed the door and squeezed back into the driver's seat. "Care to guess who that is?" Teddy asked.

"I assume that's his chauffeur. I believe he called him Tiegan?"

"Yes, that's Tiegan. Who happens to be not only Nigel's chauffeur but also his sister."

"Wait. What? I just assumed she was a man!" Isabel raised her eyebrows and shrugged. "Well, you shouldn't just *assume* things these days. I've learned that . . . And if I forget, I have my kids to remind me of it."

"I would guess anybody who doesn't know her *would* assume she's a man . . . Tiegan may too. She's an odd bird, that one. Rather a loner. She lives in an apartment in a building Nigel owns in the village. And apparently has a bevy of cats. Poor woman has lived here in Mousehole all her life but doesn't seem to have *any* friends. And she rarely talks to anybody. Perhaps she talks to her cats."

"That's very sad. I feel bad for anybody who's that shut off from the world," Isabel said sympathetically.

"Oh, and I failed to mention she's the worst driver in the village, which begs the question: why, then, does she work as a chauffeur? So far as I know, being a threat to the safety and well-being of pedestrians and other drivers is *not* part of a chauffeur's job description. She's an absolute menace. If you're a local, and you see Tiegan coming down the street, you either stand in place or pull over and let her pass. . . . I don't think she sees well. I call her Mr. Magoo."

Isabel laughed and watched the Rolls-Royce pull away. "Is she—"

"A lesbian? Nobody knows. And in this village, nobody cares one way or the other."

"Well, I'm happy to hear that. I don't care either. But that's not what I was going to ask. What I was going to *ask* was—is she older or younger than her brother?"

"I haven't any idea."

Isabel was probably overthinking things, but she couldn't help being curious about these two eccentric siblings. "I was an only child, so I don't really have a frame of reference, but I can't imagine it's very common, *or* very healthy, for one sibling to work as a servant for another sibling. It just doesn't feel right."

"I see your point, but that's for Nigel and Tiegan to work out. Staying out of other people's business is a tradition in this village. All we have to concern ourselves with as far as Tiegan goes is trying not to let her run us over."

The sound of screeching brakes suddenly caught their attention. Teddy and Isabel both craned their necks toward the street to see a man picking his bike up off the ground and yelling at the driver of a dark green vintage Rolls-Royce.

Teddy shook his head. "Looks like another near miss. One of these days her luck is going to run out. Or somebody else's will." Teddy stood up and reached for Isabel's hand. "Shall we? I want to show you around the village a little before we sojourn home."

Walking through the narrow, Old World–feeling streets of Mousehole, Isabel was captivated by the architecture, the shops, the people—just the whole mood of the place enthralled her. It was as quaint and charming as she had always imagined an English seaside village would be. Strolling through Mousehole was a very different sort of feeling from walking through the streets of London. Of course she was thrilled to be there. Visiting London was a lifelong dream come to fruition, and she was completely in awe of the city in all its majesty. But Isabel Puddles was not a city person, so London was also a daunting and sometimes unnerving experience. And her abject fear of being flattened by a red double-decker bus while crossing the street never left her either. But Mousehole was comforting. It felt familiar to her in a strange way. Tourist season had not yet begun, so she was grateful to be seeing Mousehole now. She knew how much Gull Harbor changed in the summer months once the tourists and the summer people arrived, so she imagined Mousehole became a very different place in the summer as well.

"Mousehole is a very different place in the summer," Teddy said, as if reading Isabel's mind.

She smiled. "What sort of tourists visit?"

"We get throngs of Londoners here, but a smattering of tourists from the Continent too. And the occasional Canadian or American. But we're rather off the beaten path, and we can only accommodate so many, so it's not as bad as, say, Penzance, which has a bit of a carnival atmosphere in the summers. Generally speaking, all of Cornwall is popular with the well-heeled London set, many of whom keep second homes here."

"Like you."

"Yes, I suppose, like me. But as far as *well-heeled,* I'm not certain I'd make the grade. Remember that shoe repair shop we passed?" Isabel nodded. "I've had the shoes I'm wearing now for twenty or more years, and I've had them re-heeled there at least a half dozen times. London's well-heeled crowd and the re-heeled crowd don't tend to mix."

Teddy and Isabel were laughing and rounding the next corner when Fred and Ginger suddenly began to lunge and bark at a young man in a uniform walking toward them. He was tall, slender, and pale, and had a lightly whiskered chin that looked more like part of his neck. With his shirt sleeves rolled up, Isabel could see his tattoos. She couldn't make out what they were, but didn't care to, as she took a rather dim view of tattoos. As far as the young man's overall appearance, Isabel was not someone who would ever be so cruel as to disparage a person's looks, but even she would have to admit this particular young man was not a looker. It wasn't his looks that bothered her, though, it was his presence she found unappealing. There was something almost menacing about him. Fred and Ginger were obviously way ahead of her in that assessment.

Teddy grabbed Fred's leash from Isabel and yanked both dogs back firmly while the young man flattened himself against the building to avoid the wrath of the killer corgis. "Down!" Teddy scolded, giving them a couple more firm yanks with their leashes until they started to calm down. "Good afternoon, Bobby. Sorry about these two. I'm afraid they've forgotten their manners today."

"Afternoon, Mr. Mansfield. No worries. They've never liked me. Most dogs don't. Comes with the territory, I guess." The young man gave Teddy a salute and continued on his way, keeping his eyes on Fred and Ginger until he was safely away. "See ya round, Mr. Mansfield."

After he was out of earshot, Teddy handed Fred's leash back to Isabel and explained that Bobby Blackburn worked for the Royal Mail and he was their postman. "Third generation," he continued. "His father was a lovely man, and I have a vague recollection of his grandfather, who was so revered they named a street after him. But the Blackburn charm didn't quite carry over to this generation. Bobby is not the postman you want to have a friendly chat with at your mailbox. He's more the postman you peek out the window to make sure he's gone before you go out to get your mail."

Isabel concurred. "I'm not one to make rash judgments, but there was something about him I just didn't like."

"Most of us don't. But we do like to get our mail, so we tolerate him. He's known as rather a troublemaker. Always has been. And a face that looks like a dropped pie." Isabel couldn't help but laugh at that one. She was thoroughly enjoying all the new British slang words and phrases she was learning.

They had almost made it back to Pembroke Cottage when

a car approached. "Oh, dear," Teddy said as he steered them all off onto the shoulder. "First Bobby Blackburn and now Hyacinth. And it looks like she's got Alby with her. Boy, you're meeting all the kooks in the village today."

The small white car pulled over to the shoulder and tooted its horn. Hyacinth rolled down her window and Teddy walked over. "Hello, Hyacinth," he said as he leaned down to wave at her passenger. "Hello, Alby." Alby was wearing headphones and staring straight ahead, apparently not in the mood to be social. But he did manage to turn and give Teddy a noncommittal wave. Teddy gently steered Isabel over to the car door. "Hyacinth, I'd like to introduce you to my friend Isabel."

Hyacinth was a handsome woman of sixty or so with gray hair, wearing a bright flower-print dress, a wide-brimmed straw gardening hat, and a large pair of sunglasses, which she pulled down onto the bridge of her nose before putting out her hand. "Oh, yes, I've heard all about you. Welcome to Mousehole, Isabel. I do apologize for the state you've found me in, but my son, Alby, and I have just returned from the gardening center. Spring planting time, you know. I do hope you're enjoying your visit to our modest little hamlet."

"Thank you, Hyacinth. I'm already enjoying my visit immensely. You're very lucky to call a place as beautiful as this home."

"I could not agree more. You must come by for tea. Will you bring Isabel around for tea, Teddy? And you can try my scones. It's a new recipe I've come up with that I'm afraid is destined for yet another first place in our little scone bake-off on Saturday. I'm starting to feel a little guilty about taking first place so many times in a row." There was no way Teddy was taking a swing at that hornet's nest, although it was tempting. "And can you believe Raul Bollywood is judging?" Teddy had no reason not to believe it because he had no idea who that was. "I just hope your Tuppence can handle another second-place showing, Teddy. But I can't imagine she isn't used to it by now though, poor dear."

Teddy decided he needed to take a swing after all in defense of his loyal housekeeper. "You're certainly very confident, Hyacinth. But I wouldn't count your scones before they're baked. Tuppence may just surprise you this year."

Hyacinth smiled sympathetically. "Oh, bless her heart."

"What kind of scones are you baking this year, Hyacinth?" Teddy asked innocently, hoping to gather some intelligence for Tuppence.

"Cheeky! Wouldn't you like to know? You'll just have to wait until Saturday to find out. But I'll make sure I put some aside for you, so you'll have a chance to experience what a real scone tastes like. All right, well, we're off. Say goodbye, Alby." Alby grunted something like a goodbye. His mother shrugged. "That's as much as you'll get. It's like living with the village idiot. He's his father's son, that's for sure. I think!" Hyacinth cackled and hit the gas. "Cheerio!"

"So *that's* Hyacinth. Charming."

"Yes, she has all the charm of a death-row prison matron."

Isabel had to agree. "And I certainly can see why Tuppence wants to beat her so badly if she flaunts her wins around like that."

"She has always felt like she has something to prove. It's rather silly because nobody cares," Teddy said dismissively. "We all think she's mad."

The minute they walked in the door, Tuppence yelled out from the kitchen, "Your sister canceled, Lordship! Says she has another one of her migraines!"

Isabel was awash in relief but tried not to show it. Teddy seemed indifferent. "Matilde's been having migraines for as long as I can remember, but they only seem to come up when she wants to get out of something she doesn't want to do." He quickly revised for Isabel. "I didn't mean having dinner with *you* is something she doesn't want to do." *Oh, yes it is*, Isabel said to herself.

After the fabulous Cornish feast Tuppence had prepared in Isabel's honor, and her outrageously delicious banoffee pie, made with bananas and toffee, hence the name, Teddy had schoolwork to attend to, so he retired to his study. Tuppence, who lived just down the road, went home, and Fred and Ginger were already fast asleep in their beds next to the fire.

Isabel was happy to call it an early night. She was anxious to climb into bed and start reading *Wuthering Heights* again. But no more than ten pages in, right about where Mr. Lockwood first comes to visit Wuthering Heights and spots a pile of dead rabbits in Heathcliff's living room—a grim image that, unhappily, had always stuck with her—her jet lag kicked in again and she fell sound asleep with her reading glasses on, the bedside lamp on, and *Wuthering Heights* collapsed on her chest.

Chapter 9

After awakening from a restful eight hours of sleep, hopeful that she may have finally licked the jet lag, Isabel dressed and went into the main house, where she found Tuppence busy in the kitchen. "Good morning, Tuppence."

"Well, there she is! Good morning to you, Isabel. Now, do you fancy coffee or tea to start your engine in the morning?"

"Coffee if you have it?"

"Oh, yes. Mr. M. loves his coffee in the morning. I've got some scones right out of the oven for you too."

"That sounds wonderful. . . . And where are Fred and Ginger this morning?"

"They go to class with Mr. M. And I can tell you those are my favorite days of the week. I have all three of them out of my hair for the whole day!" she said with a lighthearted laugh.

Isabel sat down at the kitchen table. She wasn't used to being waited on unless it was Kayla at the Land's End, but she knew better than to go poking around in Tuppence's kitchen. Before she knew it, she had hot coffee and another delicious scone with pots of clotted cream and jam sitting in front of

her. She made sure Tuppence saw her preparing her scone using the Cornish method.

"Mr. M. tells me you ran into Hyacinth on your way back
from the village last evening," Tuppence said, sitting down at
the table with her. "Mad as a box of frogs that one is. Did she
have that nutter of a son with her?"

Isabel was pretty sure the term *nutter* wasn't exactly PC,
but she couldn't hold back a smile. "Alby? Am I getting his
name right?"

"Alby, correct. Didn't he remind you a little of Harry
Potter? If Harry had a drug problem? And that mother of
his? Lord Voldemort in a bad wig and orthopedic shoes, only
meaner. Poor boy never really had a chance."

"Yes, Alby was with her, but he didn't have much to say."

"Count your blessings!" Tuppence huffed. "He's trapped
me more than once right here in this kitchen, going on and
on and on about absolutely nothing! His mother's son, that
one is. I've always said there was something dodgy about him.
I wish Mr. M. wouldn't hire him but he feels sorry for the
lad. I've told him I don't feel safe alone here with him. I said
if you come home and find me dead on the kitchen floor one
day, he's either murdered me or he's bored me to death! So
what did Hyacinth have to say for herself? Did she mention
the bake-off?"

Isabel hesitated. "Well . . . she did say she was pretty sure
of having the winning scone recipe again this year."

"Ha!"

"I told Teddy I could certainly see why you wanted to
beat her, given the way she brags about her past wins."

"She's a bloody braggart that one is. You'd think she invented scones! I know they say that *hate*'s a strong word, but
I wish I knew a stronger one to tell you how I feel about
Hyacinth Amesbury. She's been a right pain in my arse—
excuse my French—since I was a girl. Her and my older sister,

Euphemia, were friends back in secondary school. High and mighty Hyacinth, I called her. For a girl whose father raised hogs and a mother who tended chickens and sold eggs in the front yard, she packed a lot of attitude. Her mum and dad were lovely people, but she was awful to them. She was an only child. Unusual for a farm family, but I'm sure they didn't want to risk having another one like that. Boy, she was mean. Teased me endlessly for being chubby. Had me in tears nearly every day. Well, I *was* chubby! Still am! But no cause to remind a wee girl of it every day. She even named one of their new piglets Tuppence."

"That's horrible! I'm so sorry you had to go through that. Nothing worse than a bully, especially at that age. . . . So this isn't just about scones, is it?"

"No, it is not! This is about finally putting that old cow in her place! But I've got her right where I want her this year." They heard the front door open. "It's Matilde. She never knocks."

Matilde swept into the kitchen and unwrapped a beautiful pastel plaid cashmere cape before tossing it over one of the kitchen chairs. Isabel had by now determined that her clothes were much nicer than the woman wearing them. "Good morning, Isabel. Tuppence. How is everybody this morning?" She didn't bother waiting for an answer. "Isabel, I do want to apologize for having to cancel dinner last night on such short notice. And to you as well, Tuppence. These migraines come out of nowhere and they just leave me shattered." Tuppence rolled her eyes behind Matilde's back. "I trust Tuppence pulled out all the stops for you last night."

"All the stops and then some. It was one of the most delicious meals I've ever had. And no need to apologize. We had a marvelous time just the three of us." The subtext there was obvious: *You* were *not* missed.

"Well, I'm elated to hear it." The subtext there was also obvious: she couldn't have cared less.

"We were just talking about your dear friend Hyacinth," Tuppence told her with a healthy dose of sarcasm.

"*Dear* friend may be overstating it just a bit. We currently are not speaking to one another, and I for one would be quite happy if we never spoke again."

"And what are you two on about this time?" Tuppence asked with undisguised disinterest.

"I'd rather not waste time talking about it. May I have a cup of tea, please, Tuppence?" Matilde sat down at the table across from Isabel and forced a smile. "I trust you had a pleasant night's sleep?"

"Yes, I did, thank you, Matilde." Isabel wondered if she was attempting some damage control, assuming her less-than-flattering commentary yesterday *had* been overheard. "So, Isabel . . . I understand—oh, what did Teddy tell me?—was it your *great*-grandfather who immigrated to the States from England?"

"Yes, that's right . . . Chester Peabody. My father's grandfather. I never knew him but I understand he was quite a character."

"When I first saw you, I said to myself that you *must* have some English blood in you with such a charming demeanor."

Unfortunately Isabel could not return the compliment. And, boy, "charming demeanor" was certainly a far cry from yesterday's assessment of her as a gold digger trying to trap her brother into marriage. If there was one thing Isabel Puddles couldn't stand, it was a phony, and as far as she was concerned, Matilde Mansfield was about as phony as they came.

"And what part of our fair kingdom did Chester Peabody hail from?" Matilde asked, as if she cared.

"If I remember correctly, he came from Yorkshire."

Tuppence's face dropped as she put a cup of tea down in front of Matilde. "Even the mention of Yorkshire gives me chills."

Naturally, Isabel was puzzled by this comment. "Why is that, Tuppence?"

"Here we go," Matilde mumbled as she raised her cup to her lips.

Tuppence hesitated, then lowered her voice. "Have you ever heard of the Yorkshire Ripper, Isabel?"

"No, I can't say as I have. I've heard of *Jack* the Ripper, of course, and Yorkshire *pudding*, but never the Yorkshire Ripper."

Tuppence's voice became very somber. "Serial killer. A real monster, he was. Murdered thirteen young women in Yorkshire, two were in Manchester, I think. Started back in the 1970s."

"That's awful," Isabel said with a grimace. "It must have been a terrifying time." All she could think about was how much Frances would love hearing about this. If there was anybody who loved a good serial killer story, it was Frances Spitler.

Tuppence seemed almost to be reliving the events as she spoke. "Some of those poor lasses he did in with a claw hammer. Bludgeoned them to death. The others he stabbed with a butcher knife. Right vicious, he was."

"Why must we talk about this, Tuppence? You know what a fright it gives me."

Tuppence ignored her and continued. "He may have been terrorizing Yorkshire, but we didn't sleep easy here in Cornwall, either, mind you. Who was to say he mightn't have had an appetite for pasties and Cornish lasses?"

"If you don't stop, Tuppence, I shall leave," Matilde announced. Isabel had to hold back a smile, thinking she should probably come up with a threat that was a little more threatening.

Before Tuppence could reply, the front door opened again, and they could hear the clicking of eight corgi paws on the tiled floor of the foyer. Tuppence looked at the clock. "Well, *he's* home early. Anyway, they caught the man. Peter Sutcliffe was his name. Took their sweet time, though, they did. Five years he was out there on the prowl. Claw hammer in one hand, butcher knife in the other."

When Teddy walked into the kitchen, Fred and Ginger went straight to Isabel. He put his briefcase down on the table. "Hello, ladies . . . Tuppence."

"Funny as a crutch you are, Lordship."

"I see we're regaling our guest with warming tales of notorious English serial killers? Lovely teatime chat. I do apologize, Isabel. Tuppence has always been a little bit obsessed with the Yorkshire Ripper. And it does Matilde's head in to even bring it up. She's *still* terrified of him. And the man died in prison not too awfully long ago."

Matilde was clearly irritated. "Because *you* wouldn't stop talking about him the whole time he was out there terrorizing every young woman in England. What did you have to worry about? It wasn't young men he was murdering. I think *you* were the one obsessed with him, Theodore." Matilde's manufactured good mood had crashed and burned. She turned to Isabel. "He talked relentlessly about the Yorkshire Ripper. There was even a time I thought *he* might be the Ripper, the way he went on about him."

"It was newsworthy! I certainly wasn't the only one talking about him," Teddy said, defending himself.

"He took the same pleasure reading old accounts of *Jack* the Ripper to me. I became convinced at a very young age that all of Great Britain was simply crawling with serial killers. I slept with my bedside lamp on until I was well into my twenties."

"Which always puzzled me. All that would do is make it easier for the killer to see what he was doing," Teddy joked as he sat down next to Isabel.

Tuppence brought him his tea. "Don't wind her up, Lordship. You know how she gets. I shouldn't have brought it up."

Matilde had apparently already gotten to how she gets. "I'm glad you can still find humor in it, Theodore. I certainly didn't think it was funny. Not then, and not now. You gave me a serious phobia about being murdered in my sleep." She looked over at Isabel again. "I have that fear to this day. It wasn't as bad in London because I lived in a secured building, but here, who knows what could happen to a woman alone in the Cornish hinterlands? I leave the porch light on all night, a light on in the drawing room, and I leave the upstairs lavatory light on."

"Again, very considerate of you to light the way for your potential murderer. Perhaps you could leave a sandwich out for him too, in case he's worked up an appetite doing you in," Teddy said with a chuckle before having a sip of tea.

"Very funny, Theodore. Ha ha." She turned to Isabel again. "My brother has always had a perverse sense of humor. Had you realized that about him?" There was no way Isabel was getting in the middle of what was obviously a tricky sibling relationship. She said nothing in response, hoping maybe they were moving on. But no such luck. Matilde was not finished. "I also keep a cricket mallet next to me in bed, and a meat cleaver in the drawer of my bedside table."

Teddy directed his next remarks to Isabel. "So, in retaliation for this serial killer phobia my sister has always alleged was caused by *me*, she has refused to read *any* of my books. Not *one*. Can you believe that?"

Isabel wasn't touching that one either. Matilde looked at

her again. This was exhausting. She was beginning to feel like the wall of a racquet ball court. "Why would I read his books? I had more than enough of his dark imagination on the topic of murder while we were growing up! I have never felt the need to revisit that! I detest the whole murder mystery genre. I've never read any of it. Not even Agatha Christie, who has been deemed a national treasure. If I won't make an exception for Agatha, why should I make an exception for my brother?" Isabel was hoping that was Matilde's crescendo. Nope. "I just don't happen to believe murder is anything to make light of."

Teddy nodded. "No, you're right, Matilde. Murder is very serious business. Just ask my publisher. But to be fair, I never wore a dress from your shop, so I suppose we're even. Now, might we change the subject, so Isabel doesn't think we're all complete bloody lunatics around here?"

"That ship may have already sailed," Tuppence injected as she poured more tea for the table.

"*I* didn't broach the subject," Matilde shot back, then looking straight at Tuppence.

Teddy wasn't quite done. "But let me say this before we move on. . . . Matilde, my *dear* sister, I hope you know that anytime you're feeling unsettled, or in any way anxious about being at home alone, you are more than welcome to come and sleep in my guest room. All you have to do is call me, whatever time of day or night, and I'll come over and fetch you."

Matilde seemed to accept the spirit of her brother's invitation. "Thank you, Teddy. I'll keep that in mind."

"But please do not bring your meat cleaver with you, just in case you have a sudden urge to take revenge."

"I can't make any promises." Matilde looked up at Tuppence. "See what you started, Tuppence? You and your serial killers!" She closed her eyes and took a long sip of tea, as if to calm herself down.

Teddy was ready to lighten the mood. "Well, that was

jolly good fun! Moving on . . . Tuppence, I have a bit of news that I think you'll find quite exciting."

"Do tell, Lordship."

"Might I trouble you for one of your rhubarb scones first? I think it's high time I try one, and I see that Isabel has not yet eaten hers, so I'd like to join her. It's only polite." He looked up to see Tuppence glaring at him. "Have I said something wrong?"

"Didn't I ask you kindly to keep the subject of my rhubarb scones under your hat? I don't want it getting back to Hyacinth before the bake-off! She'll steal that recipe off me before you can say Bob's your uncle!"

Isabel made a mental note to ask Teddy what that little phrase was all about. Who in the world was Bob?

Teddy looked genuinely sorry. "I do apologize, Tuppence. Yes, you did. What is it my grandson Josh says? Oh, yes . . . *My bad.* But surely you don't think anybody here would let that information leak."

Tuppence slowly turned her head toward Matilde.

"Don't look at me! Besides, I told you we aren't even on speaking terms right now. And even if I were to become a scone spy, it would only be in *your* favor, Tuppence."

Tuppence nodded. "My only concern was that you might accidentally let it slip. That's all. So if you do happen to see her between now and Saturday, *please* don't say a word."

"My lips are sealed. But I do *not* plan to see her regardless."

Tuppence left the room and came back moments later with a rhubarb scone on a plate and put it down in front of Teddy. "All right, Lordship, now spill it."

"Well, I just heard from a very reliable source, that *this* year, there is a very famous, very special guest who will be presenting the Golden Rolling Pin to the winner of the Mousehole Annual Scone Bake-Off."

"I already know about Raul Bollywood," Tuppence replied.

Teddy shook his head. "Somebody *far* more famous than that chap."

"More famous than Raul Bollywood?" Tuppence asked in earnest.

"I would say so, yes. Exceedingly so. Of course, I wouldn't know Raul Bollywood if he walked into this kitchen right now." Teddy was drawing this out for full effect. He slowly cut his scone in half. "Isabel, will you please pass that tray of cream and jam?"

"I'm going to count to five, and if you're not talking by then, you'll be *wearing* that cream and jam," Tuppence said, even more earnestly.

Teddy chuckled. "Well, it seems we're going to have a *royal* visitor in Mousehole on Saturday," Teddy said with a knowing smirk.

"The queen?" Isabel blurted out before realizing it was not a great guess.

"No, I believe Her Majesty will be in Windsor this weekend. But do you know who *will* be coming?" Tuppence reached for the tray with the cream and the jam. Teddy pulled it away and laughed. "Our very own Camilla, the duchess of Cornwall."

Tuppence looked as if she might faint. She pulled out a chair and slowly sat down. "Go on. You're just having a laugh. The duchess of Cornwall indeed. In Mousehole?"

Teddy nodded. "It's true."

Tuppence could hardly speak. "Blimey. I'm gobsmacked. Absolutely gobsmacked. Are you sure you aren't doing my head in, Lordship?"

"As I said, a very reliable source informed me of this just hours ago. I don't think it's yet common knowledge."

"The duchess of Cornwall coming to Mousehole? Blimey . . . And the winner will get to meet her? And shake her hand?"

Teddy nodded. "Although I don't know if one is allowed to shake hands with the future queen of England. Excuse me, future *queen consort*."

Tuppence was nearly in a daze. "I suppose I'll have to learn how to curtsy, won't I?"

Matilde smiled at her assuredly. "I can teach you how to curtsy, Tuppence. Nothing to it, really."

Tuppence shook her head. "Imagine *me* meeting the duchess of Cornwall. Blimey . . . I'm going to get cracking on another practice batch of scones right now!" Tuppence clapped her hands, then stood up and left the table, still shaking her head in disbelief.

"I hope you aren't having a go at her, Teddy," Matilde said suspiciously after Tuppence was out of earshot.

Teddy scowled. "I would never. No, I heard it from an old friend who works in the press office at Buckingham Palace. He called to tell me he put it on her schedule himself. Apparently she was quite keen on coming."

"Well, that's very exciting, isn't it?" Isabel said before taking a bite of her scone. "I'm sure Camilla will fall in love with these scones too," she added, forgetting her mouth was full, something that did not go unnoticed by Matilde.

"Do you think she'd remember you, Matilde?" Teddy asked.

"Why, of course she would! I dressed the duchess long before she ever *became* the duchess. We got on famously. She was a lovely woman and I'm sure she still is. But I'm certainly not going to have a reunion with her at a village *scone* bake-off."

"Yes, you're far too posh for that. Anyway, my friend from the press office is coming over Friday as part of Camilla's advance team, so I've invited him to dinner. Alistair Piven. He's an old uni friend from Bath. I hope you don't mind, Isabel. I thought it would be a treat for you."

Isabel was ecstatic at the idea of meeting somebody who actually worked in Buckingham Palace, but she played it cool. "Any friend of yours, Teddy, is someone I'm sure I'll find delightful."

Teddy looked at his sister. "You're welcome to join too, Matilde."

"I believe I vaguely remember him."

"I brought him down from uni a couple of times, so I'm sure you met. Lovely man."

Matilde was sold. "Yes, I'll be happy to join. Is he single?"

"As far as I know, he is, but you would be barking up the wrong tree, my dear."

Matilde got the message. "Shame . . . Not many trees left, I'm afraid."

"I have an idea, Teddy," Isabel offered. "How about you giving Tuppence Friday night off so she can prepare for Saturday, and *I'll* make dinner for us."

Teddy loved the idea. "You wouldn't mind, Isabel?"

"I would love it."

"And you can introduce us to some fine American cuisine."

"I didn't know there was one," Matilde said with a sniff.

The real Matilde just stood up. Isabel was trying to come up with a snappy retort when Teddy came to America's defense. "I'm not sure anybody who hails from the kingdom that brought the world kidney pie, haggis, and blood sausage is in any position to question another country's cuisine."

"What is haggis, by the way, Teddy?" Isabel had heard of it but was still unclear on what it was, exactly.

"It's a Scottish dish. . . . And trust me, you don't want to know."

Teddy was determined to get Isabel away from his sister as quickly as possible. It was obvious they were not clicking. But he knew the source of the problem, and it wasn't Isabel. In fact, he anticipated Matilde might well behave in such a way during Isabel's visit. She tended to be very territorial. And she had always been very opinionated about America and Americans, although she had never been to America, and had met very few Americans, so her opinion was fairly meaningless as far as Teddy was concerned. "Do you fancy a walk, Isabel? Absolutely glorious day for it."

"Sounds wonderful. Let me go and get my sweater."

Isabel walked out to the guesthouse feeling a sense of relief that she wasn't going to have to be in Matilde's company any longer this morning. She could take whatever personal digs she had to dish out, but her petty comments about America really got her patriotic dander up. For Teddy's sake, she was going to keep her powder dry, but if Matilde pushed her too far, well, then, as her father used to say, *Katie bar the door.* She never really knew where that expression came from, but she knew what it meant. And Matilde would too, if she kept it up.

Chapter 10

Friday had come, and Isabel was busy in the kitchen when Teddy's friend, Alistair Piven, arrived for dinner promptly at seven. Dressed in a gorgeous charcoal gray pin-striped suit, he was holding a bottle of wine in one hand and flowers in the other when Teddy brought him in to meet her. Alistair was a handsome, dignified-looking gentleman, about Teddy's age, with beautiful black hair, graying at the temples, setting off his bright blue eyes behind his very stylish glasses. Isabel was immediately impressed with his air of refinement and polish, but then he did work in Buckingham Palace, she reminded herself. Not many slouches around there, she didn't suppose. Alistair set the wine down on the counter and handed the flowers to Isabel.

"What a delight to meet you, Isabel. Teddy's told me so much about you." Alistair kissed her European style, on both cheeks. "And thank you for this lovely dinner invitation."

"You're most welcome. And it's lovely to meet you too, Alistair. I've never met anyone who works in Buckingham Palace. Well, that's a ridiculous thing to say, isn't it? I mean, how would I? I only saw it for the first time myself a few days ago! It must be very exciting."

"It's rather a mundane job most of the time, if I'm being honest, Isabel. Or maybe it's just become that for me after thirty years. But to be fair, I do indeed feel honored to have the opportunity to serve my country and the monarchy and, indirectly, the sovereign herself." He looked at Teddy. "Theodore of course is of a different opinion when it comes to the topic of Her Majesty. But he always was rebellious."

"I have no problem with the queen. I think she's perfectly fine. It's her offspring whom I find tedious and rather lacking any purpose or relevance. I mean, they're essentially on the dole, aren't they? And what do they do to earn it? Nothing, as far as I can see. If they paid their own way, I wouldn't care, but I don't know why the rest of us should have to support their lavish lifestyles. Welfare is for the poor, not for people who play polo on the weekends. But let's not get into that, shall we?" He looked at Isabel and winked. "Alistair and I long ago agreed to disagree about our views on the royal family."

"Forgive me Alistair, but I have to ask. . . . Have you ever met the queen?"

"Oh yes, of course. You can't work at the palace for as long as I have and not bump into Her Majesty from time to time. It is her home, after all. Shakespeare wrote, although it's been altered in the past few hundred years, "Heavy is the head that wears the crown." But you wouldn't know it with the queen. For such a demure woman, she has quite a commanding presence and seems quite comfortable with the weight of the crown upon her head. But she's an absolute delight . . . well, most of the time."

"Most of the time?" Isabel was beyond intrigued. So was Teddy, but he was trying not to show it.

Alistair chuckled slightly. "She did get rather cross with me on one occasion. It happened in my very early years at the palace." Isabel was so excited, she could barely stand it. Alistair smiled before continuing. "Of course, we are sworn to a code of confidentiality, so I'm really not at liberty to talk about the sovereign or any members of the royal family, *or* the inner workings of the palace." Isabel's hopes of getting some inside dirt on the queen were suddenly crushed. "But since you're American, perhaps I can make an exception."

"I promise I won't report you to the queen, Alistair," Isabel assured him.

"So, one afternoon Her Majesty popped into the press office unexpectedly while I was entertaining my colleagues by doing an impression of one of her ladies-in-waiting, Lady Clapham, who had quite a peculiar voice. My back was to the door, and when my colleagues facing me all stopped laughing and bowed their heads, I thought they were just playing along. Then I suddenly felt a chill, so I slowly turned around . . . and there stood Queen Elizabeth. And she did not look at all amused. I thought, well, this is it. My career at Buckingham Palace has come to an end before it ever really started."

"Oh, my goodness! What happened?" Isabel could not believe she was talking to someone who actually knew Queen Elizabeth.

"Well, I bowed, of course, and began apologizing profusely while she stared at me for what seemed an eternity, and in a way only the queen of England can stare at you." Alistair then launched into an impression of Her Majesty. "Mr. Piven, Lady Clapham is one of my oldest and dearest friends. I'm rather sure she would *not* appreciate being mocked in such a fashion, nor do I appreciate *hearing* her being mocked in such a fashion."

Isabel cringed. "Oh, dear. You must have been absolutely mortified."

"Horrified! Thankfully I had just used the loo or that would have been an added layer of humiliation. But then she smiled ever so slightly and said, 'But I must say, that *was* rather spot-on.' "

Isabel laughed. "That is a wonderful story. I'm so happy to know she has a sense of humor."

It was time for Teddy to chime in. "With that family of hers, I would think a good sense of humor would be imperative."

Alistair ignored the remark and moved on. "Isabel, I understand you are quite an accomplished cook. I'm most excited about your dinner this evening."

"I do love to cook, but I'll leave it to others to judge how accomplished I am. Would you care to know the menu or would you like to be surprised?"

"I would love to know, if you wouldn't mind, just so I can savor the delicious anticipation."

Teddy had already opened the wine and poured out three glasses. They clinked and toasted Isabel's visit to England. She then took a sip of the most delicious red wine she had ever tasted. "This is just marvelous, Alistair." She took another sip. "What is it?"

"It's a Bordeaux. Château Margaux. It's the only truly decadent purchase I allow myself. Whenever I go to Paris, I come home with a case. I'm very pleased you like it."

Isabel took another sip. "Just marvelous. But I'm not sure my menu is worthy of it. I'm preparing rather simple fare, I'm afraid." Alistair and Teddy both looked at her, anxiously waiting to be wooed. "All right, well, for our soup course I've made corn chowder—my mother's recipe. Then on to a Waldorf salad—that was the Waldorf's recipe. Then I've slow-roasted a lamb shank with mustard and herbs picked fresh from Teddy's garden, and with that, asparagus with hollandaise and mashed parsnips."

"Now I'm afraid the Château Margaux is not worthy of your menu," Alistair said with a smile. "It all sounds sublime."

"Here's something for you boys to nibble on while I attend to my roast." She handed Teddy an artfully composed cheese board. "I'll join you in just a minute."

Matilde was already late for dinner, so Isabel expected her to call at any moment to cancel. Cocktails at seven, dinner at eight Teddy told her. Maybe she was having her cocktails at home and would turn up in time for dinner, which would be quite rude but not unexpected. She had yet to see any indication that Matilde had a gin problem, but maybe, she suddenly dreaded, this would be the night.

And it was . . . By the time Matilde arrived, an hour late, Isabel had put dinner on hold and joined Teddy and Alistair in the living room. The three of them were enjoying some lively conversation about Alistair's life in the palace, drinking that delicious Bordeaux and eating some equally delicious Cornish cheese when Matilde barged in, slurring something about a loose brick along the front walk she claimed to have nearly tripped over. Teddy shook his head, obviously embarrassed, while Isabel and Alistair shared a look indicating both were doubtful a loose brick had anything to do with her nearly tripping. In fact, at the moment it looked as though standing up might be a bit of a challenge for her.

"You didn't drive here, did you, Matilde?" Teddy asked.

"No, brother dear, I rode my bicycle. You know I never drive after I've taken a drink."

"*A* drink? What size glasses are you using now, sister dear?"

"I never tire of your wicked sense of humor, Theodore. Now, are you going to pour me a drink or do I have to do it myself?"

Teddy stood up. "I think you've had enough, Matilde. It's probably best I drive you home." He took her by the elbow and tried to steer her toward the front door.

Matilde snapped her arm away. "Are you retracting your dinner invitation? You're going to deny me the experience of Isabel's culinary genius?" Matilde slurred.

"What's rude is showing up an hour late for a dinner invitation and completely off your trolley."

This was getting way too awkward for Isabel. "I should probably check on my roast," she said, standing up and heading for the kitchen, avoiding eye contact with Matilde.

Alistair was right behind her. "Let me help you, Isabel." He walked into the kitchen and closed the door behind him. Seconds later they were both cringing as Matilde began yelling at poor Teddy. What she was saying, they couldn't quite make out, but she clearly had a lot to get off her chest. Alistair shook his head and turned to Isabel. "Matilde has always been, well, difficult is a nice way of putting it, I suppose. But I had no idea we had added gin to the mix. Rather a tricky combination."

Matilde's voice suddenly erupted from the other room. "Happy?" She forced a laugh. "You don't bloody well care about my *happiness*! Nobody in this family has *ever* cared about my happiness! Nobody in this *world* has ever cared about my happiness!"

Alistair made a face. "Someone's feeling very sorry for herself."

Teddy was speaking softly, obviously trying to calm her down. "It's just very, very sad," Isabel said, opening the oven door and pulling out her roast leg of lamb. "Poor Teddy."

"Poor *us* right now, Isabel! And what about your poor roast? It's being woefully neglected."

Teddy suddenly appeared in the kitchen, looking exasperated. "I'm so sorry. And equally embarrassed. Both for her and for myself."

"You needn't be embarrassed, Theodore," Alistair said, patting him on the back.

"No, of course not. You've got nothing to be embarrassed about," Isabel concurred.

"Other than having a legless sister," Teddy said with a sardonic half smile. "To be fair, this is unusual behavior even for Matilde. I've never seen her quite so deep into her cups. I've convinced her to let me take her home. I'll be back in ten minutes. I hope we haven't ruined your wonderful dinner, Isabel."

"Don't be silly! I'm keeping everything warm. We'll sit down when you get back."

After enjoying a delightfully sumptuous dinner together, despite the rocky start they got off to, Isabel surprised Teddy and Alistair with a surprise pudding, which actually *was* pudding—her grandmother MacGregor's chocolate bread pudding with vanilla sauce, which was an enormous hit. It had been her favorite dessert since childhood, and the first dessert she had ever learned to make.

While they were having their coffee, Tuppence came by to drop off a batch of freshly baked scones and to ask a favor of Teddy. "Would you mind giving me a ride into the village in the morning, Lordship? I need to get all my supplies down to the village first thing and I can't fit everything on my bicycle."

"I'd be happy to. What time shall I pick you up?"

"No, I have everything I need right here. I'll come over and pack it all up and get your tea on. Would anybody care for a scone?"

Teddy and Alistair both thanked her but patted their stomachs and passed. She looked at Isabel. "Would you mind trying just a bite? It's my final practice batch and I've tried something new. Just a wee bit of cardamom. I was hoping you would tell me what you think."

Isabel could tell Tuppence was looking for some validation. "I'd be happy to have a bite."

Once in the kitchen, Tuppence took one of the scones out of the basket she had brought and put it on a plate. Isabel broke the scone in half and then half again before popping it

into her mouth. She closed her eyes and savored the bite before speaking. "I didn't think it was possible, Tuppence, but
they're even more delectable. The cardamom with the rhubarb is a magical combination. I just don't see how you could
possibly lose this bake-off with this scone. I hope Hyacinth is
enjoying her last night as the scone mistress of Mousehole."

"You're very kind. I know this must all seem quite silly to
you, all this codswallop over scones."

Codswallop? That was a keeper. She really needed to
start writing this stuff down. "No, not at all. I understand
that scones are serious business here in Mousehole, but I also
know, as we talked about before, this isn't *just* about scones
for you. I applaud your determination to settle the score with
somebody who treated you so terribly."

"Soon enough it will be in the hands of fate and Raul
Bollywood. And I still can't believe I could actually meet the
duchess of Cornwall."

Isabel wondered if she knew about Alistair's connection
to the duchess, but she thought it best not to bring it up in case
she didn't. "The duchess of Cornwall will be the lucky one
if she gets to try one of your scones."

Tuppence was about to leave when something suddenly
occurred to her. "I thought Matilde was coming for dinner
tonight."

"Matilde was feeling unwell, so she didn't stay for dinner,
I'm afraid."

"Off her trolley again, was she?" Tuppence asked, obviously already knowing the answer.

"And fell off with quite a thud. I almost feel sorry for the
poor woman. She just seems so unhappy."

"I don't imagine having the man who broke her heart
some forty years ago showing up again has done anything to
lift her spirits. But I guess that's what the gin's for."

"Hugo?"

"So, Mr. M. told you about all that, did he?"

"He did . . . But are you saying Hugo is back in Mouse-hole?"

"Yes . . . I had heard from my sister he was back. Then I saw them walking in the village together earlier today. They were deep into it because neither one of them even looked at me when I rode by on my bike. I even rang my bell."

"That may very well explain why Matilde was in the state she was in this evening," Isabel suggested. "She really was a mess. Maybe she's reliving some of that heartbreak seeing him again."

"Could be. Maybe they'll end up together after all. And *maybe* it'll get her off the gin! Well I've got to get home, Isabel. I'll see you at the bake-off tomorrow won't I?"

"Wouldn't miss it for the world!" Isabel yelled as Tuppence slipped out the back door. She walked back into the living room to find Alistair just getting up to leave.

"Alistair is bidding us good night," Teddy said as he stood up. "He and the duchess have a busy day tomorrow." Then to Alistair, "Is Camilla one of the judges?"

"I assume you're referring to Her Royal Highness the Duchess of Cornwall?"

"Yes, that's the one," Teddy replied with a slight eye roll.

"No. She's only there to present the winner with the award. The golden spatula or something."

Teddy corrected him. "I assume you're referring to the Golden *Rolling Pin*?"

"Yes, that's the one." Alistair smiled at Teddy before continuing. "After the bake-off we're on to open a new water-treatment facility in Falmouth, and then off to a spay-and-neuter clinic for cats in Truro. Just another glamour-packed day with the queen consort-in-waiting. Isabel, I cannot thank you enough for that stupendous dinner," Alistair said before kissing her goodnight on both cheeks. "The deliciousness of the food was surpassed only by your charming company."

"I'm so glad you enjoyed it," Isabel replied. She suddenly remembered the basket of scones Tuppence had just brought over. "How would you like to take some scones with you, Alistair? They're the ones Tuppence is entering in the bake-off tomorrow. Rhubarb and orange. They are outstanding."

"I don't believe I've ever had a rhubarb-and-orange scone," Alistair replied. "I'm intrigued. And I do love my scones."

"Well then, you must try these," Isabel said as she turned and walked back into the kitchen. After wrapping a few scones up in foil, she and Teddy walked Alistair out to his car and chatted with him in the drive for a bit before saying their good-nights. "We call that a Michigan goodbye," Isabel told Teddy. "You say your first goodbye in the foyer, again on the porch, and then end up talking in the driveway for thirty minutes before your guests start the car. Abbreviated some-what in the winters, of course."

Back inside, they sat by the fire with Fred and Ginger, and Isabel shared with Teddy what Tuppence had told her about seeing Matilde in the village with Hugo. "Well, *there's* the penny dropping." Teddy seemed relieved to be able to assign *some* excuse to her state of inebriation that evening. "I would bet that's what has her so out of sorts. Well, more than *usual*, I should say. I think you're probably right. Seeing Hugo again has perhaps dredged up some unpleasant memories for her."

Isabel really did feel some sympathy for Matilde despite her unpleasantness toward her, although that sympathy wasn't without limits. Carrying a torch for an old beau was one thing, but it was no excuse for going around and setting fires with it.

Chapter 11

The day of the Mousehole Annual Scone Bake-Off had finally arrived. After Teddy returned from dropping a very nervous Tuppence off at the bake-off venue, he came home and suggested to Isabel that they drive down to the village and have their coffee now, before the throngs of scone lovers descended and made parking impossible. On the drive down, he pointed out Nigel Plumbottom's home and adjoining antique and collectible shop, and noticed Nigel unlocking the front door. "Oh, there he is! Do we have time to stop in for a minute, Teddy?"

"I don't see why not." Teddy turned the Iron Lady around and pulled into Nigel's driveway, tooting his horn to alert him of their arrival. Nigel smiled and waved them inside.

"Nigel, your shop is wonderful!" Isabel was charmed by the place. It was cozy, so there wasn't a lot of room to move around, but it allowed one to take in a beautiful assortment of treasures. There were vintage clothes, furniture, ceramics, nautical collectibles, a glass case filled with antique jewelry, and the walls were filled with paintings of beautiful landscapes and seascapes, all of them reminiscent of Cornwall and its coast. "I'm very impressed," Isabel said, picking up a small ceramic vase for closer inspection.

"Thank you, Isabel. You are clearly a woman with a good eye and exceptionally good taste."

Isabel walked over to take a closer look at a painting that caught her eye. "This seems to have been painted locally," she said to Nigel.

"It was indeed. He was a very well-known early-nineteenth-century artist in London who moved to Cornwall for his health. He ended up right here in Mousehole. The sea air didn't help as much as he had hoped, and his health continued to deteriorate. Consumption, most likely. He died very young, poor man. Thirty-six. His name was Benjamin Prescott."

"It's stunning." Isabel couldn't take her eyes off it.

"I collect him. I have several pieces in my private collection. There's a local woman here named Hyacinth Amesbury. Teddy knows her." He threw Teddy a look and continued. "Anyway, she owns one of his most beautiful paintings. Beauty wasted on her, I might add. But I won't get into all that."

Teddy smiled at Nigel. "Isabel's already had the pleasure of making her acquaintance."

"Oh, dear . . . And lived to tell the tale! Well, I've been trying to negotiate a purchase of that painting for the better part of a year. But the good news is that I understand she's experiencing some financial challenges of late"—Nigel crossed his fingers—"so here's hoping she'll accept my latest and very fair offer before the bank comes for it!"

"What does the painting depict?" Isabel asked, as she examined some of the other artwork.

"It's quite small relative to his other works, which is why it's so rare, but absolutely stunning. It's overlooking Mousehole and the sea at dusk."

Teddy looked over at Isabel. "By the sound of it I wouldn't be surprised if he painted it in the same spot where we go with the dogs to take in the view at sunset."

"Sounds gorgeous," Isabel said. "Well, I hope you get it before the bank does, Nigel."

Teddy looked at his watch. "We'd better get going. Are you coming to the bake-off, Nigel?"

"I think I'm going to pass this year. It's become such a scene these past couple of years, hasn't it? When I was mayor I quite happily served as a judge, but those days are behind me. The truth is I've never liked scones, so it's not a hardship. I'm rather more a crumpet man."

Nigel stood at the door and waved goodbye as they pulled out of the drive. "What a fascinating character," Isabel said as she waved back. "The eccentric English gentleman sent straight from central casting. Love him!"

"We are not short of eccentrics in our little community, as you've no doubt noticed. And, yes, Nigel really is a Mousehole treasure. And he was a fine mayor. Shame he lost that election."

Nigel was right. The Mousehole Annual Scone Bake-Off was a scene and drew quite a crowd. It was a much larger affair than Isabel had expected. The air was deliciously thick with the smell of baking scones. The rules for the bake-off were as follows: The scones had to be prepared from start to finish on-site, and under strict supervision, so Tuppence and the seven other contestants were given two hours to set up their workstations, prepare their dough, and bake their scones. They could bake one batch, and one batch only, so there was no room for error. The event was held at the Mousehole secondary school, so the bakers would have access to their large commercial kitchen, although they had only four ovens, so they would have to pair up when it came time to bake.

The bake-off had started out as a quiet little competition hosted by a local church ten years before as a fundraiser. In those days the scones were baked at home, brought to the church on Sunday, then judged and sold after the service. The first prize was the much-coveted Golden Rolling Pin: a wooden rolling pin spray-painted gold with the winner's name painted on it. Your photo was also on the front page of the *Mousehole Messenger*, so for a week you were a local celebrity.

But when Poppy's Puddings, a well-known British baking supply company, started sponsoring the bake-off, it instantly became an event and moved to the school. And each year it got bigger and bigger. The Golden Rolling Pin was still coveted, but now it was made of brass and sat on a polished wood pedestal with the winner's name engraved on a brass plaque. There was also prize money awarded for first place— five hundred pounds—along with a year's worth of baking supplies.

Soon there were artists and merchants setting up their wares on the playground. There were coffee and tea wagons, homemade jams and clotted cream, homemade pasties, and a farmers' market. For the past few years there had been musical entertainment of some kind, and this year, a Cornish step dance demonstration was the hot ticket. A scone-eating contest sponsored by Sainsbury's—a British grocery store chain, which had its own brand of packaged scones—was also a popular draw. Last year a fourteen-year-old boy who ate twenty-four scones in the span of two minutes was anointed the winner, and then promptly threw up onstage. And then there was a "most unusual ingredient" scone competition, where the only rule was that the ingredients had to be edible, and the contestant who made it had to be the one who ate it. All of it. Last year a sardine scone took first place. The year before, it was a grasshopper scone. And the year before that, it was a scone made of chicken feet. This particular event was also very well attended, but the audience mostly winced and moaned throughout it.

The scone bake-off had become so popular, and had gained so much notoriety, that the BBC recently sent a correspondent to do a story on it. Suffice it to say, it was a big deal for a little village. The actual scone competition had almost become lost in the shuffle, but taking first place was still a great honor. And it gave you bragging rights, which Hyacinth Amesbury had taken full advantage of. But everybody in the village seemed to be hoping it would be Tuppence's turn this year.

Having a celebrity judge like Raul Bollywood, *and* a member of the royal family to present the award, promised to take the event to a whole new level, and Tuppence wanted it more than ever. She had been perfecting her orange-rhubarb scone recipe for months, and now, with the addition of the cardamom, she had taken it to even greater heights. She was certain this was the year the Golden Rolling Pin was going home with Tuppence Pickering! But not if Hyacinth Amesbury had anything to say about it.

After Teddy and Isabel arrived at the bake-off, they had a coffee and strolled around the school playground, enjoying the festive atmosphere. Isabel especially loved the Cornish step dancers but demurred when one tried to pull her from the circle of onlookers to dance. "Nobody wants to see that," she said to Teddy after grabbing hold of him as an anchor.

Isabel suggested to Teddy that they go into the kitchen to check on Tuppence and give her some encouragement. But when they got to the kitchen door they were told by a volunteer that visitors were strictly forbidden. They would have to wait until after the judging ended to see her. Teddy was able to peek in and spot her, but then turned back to Isabel with a slight grimace, "Oh, dear," he said.

"What is it?"

"It looks like Tuppence and Hyacinth got stuck sharing an oven. That's getting the match a little too close to the haystack." Teddy and Isabel walked back outside, over to listen to some Celtic folk singers. "I know it sounds a bit ridiculous," he said, "but I'm worried that if Tuppence loses to Hyacinth again, she may just snap this time."

"I think it's very sweet of you to be pulling for her like this, Teddy. She really is such a lovely woman. Not to mention a gifted baker. But I just don't see how she can possibly lose with those scones."

"Let's not tempt fate. . . . I'm very pleased to see you two getting on so well."

"The way you described her to me, I was a little nervous she was going to eat me alive. But she's been nothing but warm and welcoming."

"You've tamed the beast! I joke. She really is a lovely woman. Heart of gold. And I don't know what I would do without her. But she can be thorny with those who rub her the wrong way. Cornish to the bone."

"She reminds me a little bit of my best friend, Frances, who introduced us at the diner that morning. When she takes a dislike to somebody—and it could be for something as simple as the shoes you have on—she's not shy about sharing her opinion; to your face and to the world."

"I remember Frances well. No, she didn't strike me as a shrinking violet. And while we're on the subject of temperamental personalities, I want you to know that I very much appreciate how patient and gracious you've been with my sister, especially after her performance last night. She can be rather trying."

That's putting it nicely, Isabel said to herself. "Don't give it another thought, Teddy. I just felt bad for you."

"I do love and care about her very much. But Matilde can be, let's see, what would be the most suitable adjectives to describe her?"

"Hmm . . ." Isabel hesitated briefly before continuing, "Well, 'warm and fuzzy' don't immediately pop to mind."

Teddy laughed. "More like cold and prickly?"

Isabel nodded with a smile. "Closer to the mark. But knowing what you told me about what happened with Hugo, and how brokenhearted she was over it, I can understand why she might carry around some bitterness. Even if it did happen a hundred years ago, some people never get over an emotional blow like that. Look at Miss Havisham."

An announcement came over the PA saying the judging was going to be delayed for thirty minutes as both their special guests had been delayed. Raul Bollywood would be arriving by helicopter—which Teddy dismissed as "rather showy for a pastry chef"—and the duchess of Cornwall had also been delayed.

As they were discussing what to do with their extra half hour, they spotted Tuppence storming out of the school building, looking as if she were either already crying or about to start. They immediately went after her but she had disappeared into the crowd. Teddy went back inside, hoping the woman at the kitchen door could tell her what happened. "Her scones didn't rise, love. Flat and hard as a river stone, they were. Dumped her whole tray into the bin and off she went, bless her." Teddy looked back into the kitchen and could see Hyacinth arranging her scones on a platter wearing a smug expression. "She left all her baking supplies. If you'll wait just a minute, Mr. Mansfield, I'll go pack it all up."

Teddy came back outside to where Isabel was waiting with a worried face and carrying a tote bag full of baking supplies. "What's happened?" she asked with alarm.

"I'll explain in the car," he said as he led Isabel toward the parking lot. "We need to find Tuppence. She must be absolutely distraught." After debriefing her on their drive back to Teddy's, Isabel was trying to think of ways they might be able to help Tuppence through what was sure to be a tremendous disappointment, but when they arrived, Tuppence was nowhere to be found.

"Didn't you drive her down here this morning? Do you suppose she's walking home?"

"Unless she got a ride from somebody. Everybody knows Tuppence around here, so that's a safe bet."

Although Tuppence planned to come straight to work after the bake-off—cradling the Golden Rolling Pin—Teddy thought it more likely that in her state she had gone home instead, so they drove to her modest cottage down the road. She wasn't home, and Teddy noticed her bike was gone. "It was there this morning when we passed by. So she's been back to get her bike. It's her only mode of transportation. Tuppence doesn't drive."

"Does she have any family here in Mousehole?" Isabel asked, realizing she had never inquired about Tuppence's personal life. "She mentioned a sister, but was she ever married?"

"Tuppence is widowed. Her husband died before she came to work for us, which was why she needed the job. I never knew him, but I understand he was not very nice to her. And he was rather a ladies' man, with a wife at home taking care of their farm while he was out carousing. So he was visiting one of his lady friends in Penzance one day when Karma paid him a visit, and he was hit by a bus. Apparently, there was some speculation that he may have been pushed in front of that bus, and the person pushing him was one of those lady friends who had just found out he had a wife in Mousehole. But she was never charged. After that, Tuppence sold the farm, bought that little cottage down the lane, and came to work for us. Her only immediate family in Mousehole is her sister, Euphemia. Maybe that's where she's gone."

So off they drove to Euphemia's house, which was a couple miles away, but nobody was at home there either. "This is very, very odd," Teddy said as he got back into the car. "I can't imagine where she's gone off to. I'm getting quite worried."

"Is there any chance she might have gone to Matilde's?" Isabel asked.

"I suppose it's worth checking. I'm sure after last night, Matilde was in no shape to go into the village this morning, so she may be at home in bed."

When they pulled into the drive of the Captain's Cottage, Matilde's car was there, but so was another car parked behind it, one Teddy didn't recognize. "I wonder who that could be. Matilde rarely has company. Do you mind waiting? I'll just be a minute." Isabel was more than happy to wait in the car. At this point, the less time she had to spend with Matilde, the better.

Teddy went to the door and knocked. No answer. He walked around back, and two minutes later came around the other side of the cottage looking even more puzzled. "Her doors are locked, but the curtains are all open. If she's home, they're usually drawn until noon. And to whom does this car belong, I wonder? It has London plates. Looks like a rental."

"Maybe that's Hugo's car? And they've walked into the village for the bake-off?" Isabel suggested, trying to be helpful.

Teddy thought it over. "That would make sense. Anyway, my concern is Tuppence right now. Let's drive around a little more and see if she pops up somewhere."

Eyes peeled, they eventually turned onto the main road that led into the village, just as a motorcade of black SUVs came toward them—two in front and two in back—sandwiching a white Bentley. As the motorcade passed, Isabel actually caught a glimpse of the duchess of Cornwall sitting in the backseat wearing a lavender-colored hat and talking on her phone. Teddy was not impressed. "Well, there goes the future queen consort of England. She's had quite a comeback, that one. Camilla used to be about as popular in this country as the bubonic plague."

Given all that was going on, Isabel didn't want to admit to Teddy that she was thrilled with the sighting. Isabel Puddles from Gull Harbor, Michigan, the former Asparagus Queen of Kentwater County, had just seen the future queen consort of England *in person*. Okay, she was speeding past her at forty miles an hour, but it still counted as a royal sighting.

They drove around a little more, still hoping they might find Tuppence out and about on her bike somewhere, but there was still no sign of her, and nobody they stopped to ask had seen her either. Teddy was looking defeated. "I suppose all we can do is go home and wait for her to turn up. Or *hope* she does."

When they pulled into the driveway at Pembroke Cottage, they were both relieved to see Tuppence's bike leaning up against the willow tree where she always parked it. It was unusually quiet when they entered the foyer. The racket of pots and pans coming from the kitchen accompanied by Tuppence either singing to herself, talking to herself, or arguing with Fred and Ginger was the norm. Even the dogs seemed uncharacteristically low-key when they climbed out of their beds to come over and greet them. When they walked into the kitchen, there was Tuppence sitting at the table with a cup of tea, looking calm as a cucumber. "Oh! There you are. Hello, Lordship. Hello, Isabel."

"Hello, Tuppence," Isabel said cheerfully, relieved to see she appeared to be taking this better than expected.

Tuppence got up from the table. "Would you like some tea? I've got the kettle on."

"Yes, that would be lovely," Teddy answered cautiously, not sure what to make of how composed she was.

Tuppence came back into the dining room with a pot of tea and two cups. "I'm all out of scones. But I suppose that's just as well. I may never bake another scone in my life."

Isabel was quick to reply. "That would be criminal! You

bake the best scones I've ever put in my mouth! You owe it to the world to keep baking scones!"

Tuppence smiled and poured the tea. "You're too kind, Isabel. I suppose you heard what happened? That I quit the contest?"

"We did," Teddy said, patting her on the arm. "I'm terribly sorry, my dear. I know how much it meant to you."

"I guess I've just lost my touch. I wasn't going to serve the likes of what came out of that oven today to Raul Bollywood. Or let the duchess of Cornwall so much as *look* at them. I buggered it up, I did! I don't know how I managed it, but I managed it. Nerves got the better of me, I guess. But I'm not going to go barmy over it. Now, have you two had your breakfast?"

"We had coffee in the village," Isabel told her.

"*That's* not breakfast!" Tuppence looked at the clock. "It's a bit late for it, but how about I make a full English, Lordship? Isabel hasn't had a proper breakfast since she arrived, and I think it's high time she had a full English!"

"I think a full English sounds grand!" he said, keeping things upbeat. He noticed Isabel needed a reference point. "You'll see. But I do hope you're hungry." Teddy looked down at his feet and saw Fred and Ginger patiently waiting for some attention. "How about we take these two out for a quick walk first? A full English takes some time to prepare."

"She seems to be taking it awfully well, Teddy," Isabel said after they stepped outside.

"Yes, that's what concerns me. This is not the Tuppence I know. I'm afraid we may be in the eye of the hurricane right now, so we should keep our rain gear on."

And he was right. When they got back to the cottage fifteen minutes later, Tuppence met them at the front door in a drastically different mood. The eye of the hurricane had apparently passed over them while they were out with the dogs. She was livid. "My sister just called. She won it again! I don't know how she did it, but that woman won the bloody bake-off *again*!" Tuppence took a deep breath and slowly exhaled, trying to compose herself. Teddy and Isabel were grappling for something to say, but both were at a complete loss. Tuppence took another deep breath and slowly released it. "I've got your breakfast almost finished. Go and sit down and I'll bring it out to you."

Two minutes later, Tuppence appeared with two gigantic plates of food and set them down on the table. Teddy looked over at Isabel, whose eyebrows were raised just about as high as they could go. She could barely digest it all with her eyes, so she couldn't imagine how her stomach could ever manage it.

"*This* is what we call a full English. All that's missing is the toast." Tuppence appeared with a plate of toast and set it on the table.

"This all looks wonderful, Tuppence," Isabel said, still trying to take it all in. There were two fried eggs, two sausages—or bangers, as Teddy called them—and two strips of bacon, which looked nothing like American bacon but did look bacon-*ish*. There was also a large spoonful of baked beans, a smaller pile of sautéed mushrooms, and half a grilled tomato. And now toast. It was enough to feed a family of four a hearty breakfast.

"I know it's a rather unreasonable amount of food, which is why I so rarely have it, but once in a while I do crave a full English."

"It all looks quite delicious. But if I ate even half of this, Teddy, you would have a very full American on your hands, and one who would probably have to take to the bed afterward. I don't want to offend her, especially not now, but I just can't eat all this food."

"I don't think I can today either. But let's just eat what

we can, and when she isn't looking, we'll slip the rest to the dogs."

No sooner had they put their napkins in their laps and taken their first bites when they heard Tuppence yell from the kitchen. "*I knew it.*" She stormed back into the dining room and plopped a container of Dr. Oetker, the UK equivalent of Arm & Hammer baking soda, down on the table. She then put down a glass of water, picked a teaspoon up off the table, and dug out a spoonful. "Watch this." She dropped the spoonful of soda into the water and gave it a quick stir. Teddy looked at the glass, then at Tuppence, and then at Isabel. He clearly wasn't sure what he should be watching *for.*

"That's baking soda, I presume?" Isabel asked.

"It's supposed to be!" Tuppence answered trying to once again calm herself. "I just fixed myself a glass of bicarb for the indigestion this has all given me, and look. It's as flat as my scones."

Isabel nodded and looked over at Teddy. "It should be fizzing right now. It's bicarb of soda. An old-fashioned cure for indigestion. Works like Alka-Seltzer." Teddy still wasn't getting it. "It's also what makes baked goods, like *scones*, rise and keeps them from becoming dense."

"So why is this not fizzing?" Teddy asked Tuppence.

"You tell me. I bought this brand-new container last week. Bought another one at the same time to take home. Been using both all week long, baking scones here *and* at home without any problem."

"I'm confused." He still wasn't getting it, which was beginning to annoy Tuppence. Isabel knew where she was headed, though.

"*This* is not the same container! I used this container of Dr. Oetker to make a batch of raisin scones for you day before yesterday and they were just fine. This was in the tote you brought back for me, yes?" Teddy nodded. "So somebody either switched containers on me *or* they mixed something into this one! And I'll let you have one guess at who that would be!" Tuppence was gritting her teeth as her cheeks began to redden even more.

Teddy thought it over for a bit. "You don't really think Hyacinth would do anything as diabolical as *that*, do you?"

"Of course she would! Just as sure as Bob's your uncle! I knew she would figure out a way to cheat! I could just strangle that old cow!" Tuppence stopped and took another deep breath, trying not to overheat. "No, that's too quick. I think I'd like to see her drawn and quartered. Do they still do that?"

Teddy was skeptical of Tuppence's theory. "But how would she have been able to get into our kitchen to manage that? She hasn't been in this house for a very long time. By design, I might add."

Isabel knew exactly how she could have done it with a little help. "Yes, but Alby has been. Remember you had him come over to do a little yard work for you on Friday morning? And when I came home from the market, he was sitting at the table having a cup of tea. He would have had ample opportunity to do it while I was out."

"That cheeky little . . . so and so. How did *he* get in?" Hurricane Tuppence was at about a category three now and gaining velocity.

Teddy hesitated. "I think Alby has a key."

"Since when does Alby Amesbury have a key to Pembroke Cottage?" Tuppence's cheeks were getting even redder.

"He *did* say he had a key, and that he let himself in sometimes if you were out. I didn't think much of it, although he did startle me."

Tuppence turned to Teddy. "You gave that window licker a *key*?"

Teddy was looking contrite. "I don't remember why exactly . . . Oh, I remember now. I had him clean out the fire-places last fall. I gave him a key because I was off for London and you were away at your cousin's in Falmouth, I believe. I wanted it done by the time I got back, so I gave him a key. I don't remember ever asking for it back, or him ever giving it back. And we don't use the term *window licker* to describe the mentally challenged any longer, Tuppence."

"I stand corrected. That *nutter* came in here and switched out my Dr. Oetker's! I'd bet my life on it!"

Teddy shook his head. "We can't just *assume* that."

Isabel was getting on board with Tuppence. Her theory made a lot of sense. "You said the last time you used this container was on Thursday morning, so if he *did* swap out the containers, or somehow sabotaged *this* one, you wouldn't have known before this morning when you took it to the bake-off, correct?"

"That's exactly right! *This* is the container I took to the bake-off this morning. And it was just fine two days before." Tuppence answered conclusively and shook her head. "Boy, you sure lost the plot on this one, Lordship, giving a key to that one."

Teddy was still not completely buying this theory. "It's not out of the realm of possibility, I suppose, but unless or until you have proof, we can't—"

"Ha! My scones are all the proof I need! And you and I both know who was behind it! Alby may have done the dirty work, but it was his mother who put him up to it. And just how are we ever going to prove *that*? You can't stain a black coat!"

"Okay, for the sake of argument," Teddy began slowly, "let's say that Alby *did* swap baking soda containers or tampered with this one. You're certain the end result would be scones that were—"

"Flat!" Tuppence assured him. "And as dense as that boy's head is!"

"All right," Teddy began as diplomatically as possible. "So *if* this happened, then, yes, of course I agree with you that Hyacinth would have had to tell him exactly what to do because Alby doesn't have sense enough to come in out of the rain, but I'll say it again—if we can't prove a crime was committed, we can't accuse either of them of committing a crime."

A look of resolve slowly crept up from Tuppence's tightening lips, passed over her bright red cheeks, and came to rest in her eyes. She looked first at Isabel, then at Teddy, then stood up from the table, took her apron off, and marched toward the front door.

Teddy knew the answer, but he asked anyway, "Where are you going?" Tuppence didn't say a word. "I hope you aren't planning to go over to the Amesburys, Tuppence!" he yelled after her, then looked at Isabel and shook his head. "Tuppence? Are you listening to me?" She answered by slamming the door behind her. Teddy stared at his houseguest for a beat. "Well, Isabel? How are you enjoying Cornwall so far?"

Chapter 12

It had been quite a while since Tuppence stormed out of the house, "mad as a wet hen," as Isabel's grandmother used to say, so now she and Teddy were concerned about her all over again. Naturally Teddy assumed she had gone to the Amesburys to confront Hyacinth and Alby, a choice, both he and Isabel agreed, that was not a good one. To lighten the mood, Isabel suggested they get some air and take Fred and Ginger out for a walk. Why should *their* carefree corgi lives be disrupted by all this human pastry drama? Teddy agreed it was a good idea. He was annoyed with the whole situation anyway. "With all that's going on, and going *wrong* in this world, I find it rather mind-numbing that we have spent several hours of our day trying to find answers to what went wrong with a rhubarb scone recipe, and who's to blame."

After leashing up two very eager corgis, Teddy opened the front door, and to their mutual relief, saw Tuppence coasting in on her bicycle. Wearing an expression that was hard to read, she parked her bike under the tree and came up the walk. "Hello, Lordship. Is there anything I can do for you?" She was eerily calm.

"No, no. I'm fine. We're fine. Just taking these two out for a little stroll," Teddy said casually, studying her face to try to determine what was really going on in her head.

Tuppence looked down at the dogs. "Well, hello there, you two . . . I hope you have a lovely walk." Not only was Teddy confused by her friendly greeting to Fred and Ginger, but so were they. Something definitely wasn't right. She smiled at Isabel as she came into the foyer. "That's a lovely jumper you have on, Isabel. It really suits you."

Teddy could see that Isabel was puzzled by the comment. "She means your sweater."

"Oh. Thank you, Tuppence. I like it too. My daughter picked it out."

Tuppence disappeared into the kitchen without further comment on Isabel's jumper. Teddy handed both leashes to her. "I'll be just a minute. I need to find out what's going on here. We're not in the clear just yet."

Isabel walked out to the front gate and watched Fred and Ginger sniff around for a few minutes until Teddy came back out looking reassured. "Well?" she asked, handing Ginger's leash to him.

"She said she *was* planning to ride over to Hyacinth's, but by the time she got there decided there was no point in having an angry confrontation with her or with Alby, so she decided to just keep riding and blow off some steam. She stopped to have tea with my sister and planned to tell her about what happened at the bake-off, but she said Matilde was acting very strange, so she didn't bring it up. I told her about what happened last night and that my dear sister must be feeling rather ashamed, as well as hungover after that performance, as well she should be." He looked at Isabel with genuine worry in his eyes. "I hope maybe she'll take a closer look at the direction her life's been going of late, which is not what I would call an upward trajectory. Anyway, let's put all this rubbish out of our heads, shall we, and just enjoy a lovely walk. I do apologize. Such spectacle over baked goods, daft conspiracy theories, and my sot of a sister's gin affliction on center stage. . . . You must think us all mad! Your Gull Harbor drama is so much more interesting, Isabel. A murder would be a welcome distraction at this point."

There was no way to avoid walking past Amesbury Acreage if they wanted to take in the sea view at its most magnificent, so they braced themselves and soldiered on, hoping they wouldn't see either of its inhabitants. But no such luck. As they passed by and looked up the drive, there was Hyacinth in her car stopped next to the red Royal Mail truck with the creepy postman, Bobby Blackburn, standing outside it. Even from a distance it was obvious this was not a friendly conversation.

"I wonder what *that's* all about?" Teddy pondered. "Is there nobody in this town that woman *hasn't* had, *isn't* having, or eventually *will* have a falling-out with?"

Just then the red mail truck screeched out onto the main road and headed back toward the village, and Hyacinth proceeded slowly up the drive.

Passing Amesbury Acreage again on their way home, they could see Hyacinth again, this time outside, wearing a floppy, wide-brimmed gardening hat and working in her garden. Teddy stopped for a moment. "I will say, she does keep an immaculate garden. You know what? I'm going to walk up there and just say a casual hello. I'll tell her I saw her arguing with Bobby and wanted to make sure she was all right. Perhaps I can sniff out any potential involvement in this matter of scone sabotage."

They were about halfway up the drive when Hyacinth spotted them, then made a beeline for the house. "That's a bit rude. Well, she's never been accused of having any manners,"

Teddy said with a furled brow. "I get the distinct feeling she doesn't want to see us." But *he* was determined to see *her*, so they continued up the drive with Fred and Ginger eagerly leading the way.

When they reached Hyacinth's front yard, Isabel waited away from the house with the dogs. She really didn't want to become any more embroiled in this possible conspiracy than she already was.

She was suddenly reminded of a near tragic incident involving baked goods that happened years before at a church bake sale back in Gull Harbor. It all began when Irene Gillespie—renowned for her chocolate chip cookies—somehow ended up using two cups of salt and a teaspoon of sugar in her recipe, when obviously it should have been vice versa. Irene sold all three batches of a dozen each to Esther Dolan—her son's fifth-grade teacher. Miss Dolan told Irene that Jimmy had raved about his mom's cookies, so she was going to save them and take them to school Monday morning and share them with the class.

When Irene got home, and to her horror, realized what she had done, she began to panic. With her reputation as the congregation's chocolate chip cookie maven in peril, and possibly her son's education too, she made a fresh batch of cookies, drove to Miss Dolan's house, snuck into her kitchen through the back door—nobody locked their doors back in those days—and swapped out the Tupperware containers. It was just after quietly closing the door behind her when she heard the blast, then the sound of shattering glass. Irene dived to the ground, and when she looked up, there was Miss Dolan, all five feet of her, pointing a rifle at her.

After explaining to Miss Dolan why she had just broken into her house, they made a pact never to speak of it; not Irene's egregious baking faux pas, and not Miss Dolan's almost killing her. Of course her neighbors called the sheriff after hearing the shot, so they ended up having to explain it all to the deputy who arrived on the scene. And he certainly wasn't going to keep a story like that quiet, so it was all over town the next day. A humiliated Irene Gillespie never participated in another church bake sale, and Miss Dolan from that day on became known as Rambo.

Teddy walked up to Hyacinth's front door and knocked, then waited. He knocked again, then waited again. Finally he knocked a third time, and quite loudly this time. He was looking back at Isabel when Alby slowly opened the door looking disheveled and irritated. But that was nothing new. He always looked disheveled and irritated.

"Can I help you with something, Mr. Mansfield?" He looked over Teddy's shoulder at Isabel with an expression that could not be described as friendly.

"I'd like to speak with your mother, Alby."

"Mummy just came in from the garden. She was feeling poorly so she's having a lie-down now. I was just about to call the doctor. You do know about her heart condition."

Teddy nodded. "Oh, yes, that's right. I do remember." He didn't. Or if he did, he had forgotten about it. "All right, well, please do tell her I hope she's feeling better soon. And send her my congratulations on winning the bake-off . . . again."

Alby glared at him for a moment, then looked at Isabel suspiciously. "I'll do that," he said, and closed the door. Teddy walked back and took Ginger's leash. "That one just keeps getting farther and farther round the twist every time I see him, just like his mum."

The walk back to Pembroke Cottage was a quiet one. Teddy obviously had a lot on his mind, and Isabel was feeling her first pangs of homesickness. She missed her friends and family, her dogs, her home, breakfast at the Land's End, and she missed the sense of belonging she was so used to having back in Gull Harbor. Maybe that was another advantage of traveling to faraway places. Hopefully your travels made you realize you were pretty lucky to live where you live, and have the life you were living there. But, homesickness aside, she was still happy to be in Teddy's company, and despite the bake-off drama, and his sister's gin-fueled episode the night before, she was still very much enjoying her visit. She would be home soon enough, and would have plenty to talk about when breakfasts at the Land's End resumed.

Tuppence was sitting at the kitchen table again, staring into her cup of tea, when they walked in with the dogs. Her anger seemed to have subsided, but now she was in a contemplative mood, which was a highly unusual state for her to be in. Although Teddy had admitted that Tuppence often drove him nuts with her endless banter, right now he told Isabel he wished some of her vim and vigor would return. He decided to give her the rest of the day off so that she could go home and rest. Tuppence put up no resistance and was out the door two minutes later. After she closed the door behind her, Teddy turned to his houseguest. "Looks like we're on our own for dinner tonight, Isabel."

"Not a problem. I can whip us up some leftovers from last night, or I can do something else entirely if you prefer."

"No, I won't hear of it. You cooked such a marvelous meal last night. I'm going to take you down to the Lion Pub for a pint and the best fish and chips you've ever had."

Isabel was more than happy with this plan. "I think fish and chips are one of the most wonderful contributions Great Britain has ever made to the world—Jane Austen, Winston Churchill, fish and chips. If it weren't such a delicate topic, I might add scones to the list."

"I'm sure Churchill would be honored to be in such esteemed company. And, yes, I do think the subject of scones will be a sensitive one to broach for some time to come."

Walking into the Lion Pub on a busy Saturday night was like walking onto a movie set. It was, as so many things had been during her visit, exactly how Isabel imagined an English pub would look, feel, and even smell.

"How you goin', guvnor?" came a booming voice from somewhere in the crowd.

Teddy looked around and then waved at a man walking toward them with a broad grin. He was a sturdy-looking fellow about Teddy's age, wearing a bulky, well-worn cable-knit fisherman's sweater and a yellow-and-black plaid kilt, just like the one Teddy had worn to pick her up at the train station. He had a mop of unruly gray hair, a gray beard, and piercing green eyes. Holding his arms out for a hug as he approached Teddy, he abruptly turned and hugged Isabel instead. "And this has to be the one and only Isabel Puddles. Even lovelier than Teddy described." Isabel was not quite sure what to say, since she had no idea who this man was.

"Isabel, meet Kenly Bancroft. The owner of this fine establishment, and one of my oldest and dearest friends."

"I'm absolutely chuffed to meet you, Isabel."

Isabel looked at Teddy. "It means he's happy to meet you."

"Well, I'm chuffed to meet you too, Kenly . . . I just love your pub."

"You are very welcome here. It was my father's and my grandfather's before him. Only Grandad had a funeral parlor attached at the back. He used to say, if you were at the Lion, you were either drunk or you were dead." Kenly laughed and slapped Teddy on the shoulder. "Sometimes it was hard to tell the difference!"

Isabel wasn't sure if Kenly was putting her on or not, and Teddy could tell. "It was not uncommon back in those days for pubs and funeral parlors to be in the same building. In Ireland too. Don't ask me why."

"Convenience, I'd say!" Kenly laughed. "Old John Porter died right there at that table by the window. He was there all night hanging on to his pint with his head down on the table. Old John was a fisherman who came in here every day after he moored his boat, and he always brought Grandad fresh fish he'd trade for pints. Grandad knew the man was up before the crack of dawn every morning, so if after a pint or two he put his head down for a little nap, he'd let him be. Only that last time it turned out to be a longer nap than usual." Kenly had a loud, infectious laugh. "One minute he was sitting at his table in here, the next he was in the back, laid out in his casket. But I can't imagine old John could have wished for a better way to go." Kenly pointed across the room. "Your table's ready for you there, guv. Go and sit down and I'll bring your pint. Isabel, what can I bring you?"

"I'll have whatever Teddy's having."

"I love a woman who drinks beer!" Kenly said as he headed over to the bar.

Teddy guided Isabel to "his" table, which was next to the fireplace. It was a chilly evening, so there was a small fire going, quite a romantic setting if someone were in a romantic mood, which Isabel was not. At least she was trying not to be. But she had to admit that she was starting to have some feelings for Teddy that she thought might be moving slightly beyond the threshold of "just friends," and she got the sense he might be feeling something similar. But it had been so long since Isabel had felt anything vaguely romantic, for all she knew it was a heart murmur.

"Why does he call you *governor*?" Isabel asked as Teddy pulled her chair out.

"For the same reason Tuppence calls me Lordship," he said, sitting down. "Because he knows it annoys me. Governor, or guv, is very old-school slang working-class men and women used to refer to their boss or someone they viewed as their superior. It's an archaic class distinction. And I think you know how I feel about all that nonsense."

Kenly returned with two pints. "One for you, Isabel, and one for you, guv." Kenly pulled up a chair. "I guess I can join for a bit. So how are you enjoying Mousehole, Isabel?"

"I'm enjoying it very much. It's a lovely village. And the people I've met have been just wonderful."

Kenly turned to Teddy and stole a sip of his pint. "So she hasn't met your neighbor Hyacinth, then, I gather?"

Isabel chuckled. "I only met her in passing."

"That's the best way to meet her," Kenly said, then roared with laughter again. "I was fond of her husband. Lovely man. A broken man, but lovely. After thirty-some years with that woman, I'm sure death was a welcome relief when it came to him . . . like slipping into a warm bath." Kenly took another sip of Teddy's pint. "After stepping out of a cold shower!" Another hearty laugh. Isabel already liked Kenly. What a character! After taking another sip of Teddy's beer, he went on. "I won't serve that woman in here anymore. She came in once with that daft son of hers and they each ordered a fish pie. Then she came in the next day throwing one of her wobblers and claiming it made them both sick. Tried to get me to give her a refund. Load of sheep's pucky is what it was."

Teddy smiled at Isabel. "A wobbler is like a temper tantrum. Hyacinth's famous for them."

Kenly continued. "I had the same for my supper that night and it was lovely. So I told her to bugger off. Next thing you know, she starts spreading rumors about my fish pie—my gran's recipe, it was—and nobody ordered it for months! And I hear she won the scone bake-off again. I sure hope she gets what's coming to her one day." Kenly turned to Isabel. "Sorry to spout off, but it still gets me knickers in a twist. So, guv, you want to know who came in here last night?" He didn't wait for Teddy to guess. "Do you remember Hugo Fernsby? Dad was a butcher. Handsome chap. Played cricket."

Teddy nodded. "*And*, speak of the devil, he was once engaged to Hyacinth."

"Was he? Lucky bloke he dodged that bullet."

"Yes, I remember Hugo well. I was just telling Isabel about him. He and my sister, Matilde, dated for a while too."

"So he dodged two bullets!" He slapped Teddy on the shoulder. "I'm just having a go at you, guv. Lovely woman, your sister." Kenly took another sip of Teddy's beer, peering over the glass and looking at Isabel with raised eyebrows and a mischievous glint in his eyes. "Said he hadn't been back to Mousehole in more than forty years. Just retired from driving a bus in London. He's got a niece lives out Sheffield way he's staying with."

"I had heard he was back. And how was he?" Teddy asked. Isabel was curious too.

"Seemed like a right fine chap to me. Says he's thinking about moving back here. He asked about you, guv. How he found out, I have no idea, but he knew you"—Kenly looked around before lowering his voice and continuing—"he knew you and Archie Cavendish were one and the same."

Teddy didn't seem too concerned. He looked over at Isabel. "A lot of folks around here know me just because my family's been here for a few generations now. And a lot of them *do* know I'm an author working under a pen name. But it rarely comes up, mostly because nobody around here gives a monkey's, but also because I don't think Archie has many fans here in Mousehole."

Kenly turned to Isabel. "But there're plenty of folks from everywhere else who are big Archie Cavendish fans. And Detective Waverly is even more famous than the man who invented him. A lot of them know, or suspect, Archie lives in

Mousehole, so I get them coming in every once in a while asking if I know where he lives or where he hangs out. I run cover for him, though." Kenly slapped him on the back again. "Don't I, guv!"

"You're very good at keeping them off my scent, Ken. Don't get me wrong, Isabel, I love my readers. I just don't want Pembroke Cottage to become part of the official Mousehole tour route. I make plenty of public appearances in London and elsewhere, and I very much enjoy meeting fans of my books, but this really is home for me, and I like my privacy."

"I don't blame you in the slightest Teddy . . . I was a nervous wreck during my fifteen minutes of fame. Couldn't wait for it to end! I can't imagine what it must be like for you."

"We have a drink here named after him. Well, named after his famous detective." Kenly looked around again before continuing, "It's called Waverly's Blunt Instrument. It's a secret but a powerful formula. Drink one and you're well on your way. Drink a second, and you're likely to be found on the floor unconscious. Shall I make you one, Isabel?"

"That's very kind of you to offer, but I don't think a blunt instrument is what I need right now, Kenly. I'm only halfway through this pint and I'm feeling tipsy."

Teddy smiled. "We probably should order now, Ken."

Kenly could see that his friend was ready to have his dinner companion to himself. "Sure thing, guv. He looked at Isabel. "I know what *he's* having. Fish and chips for you too, Isabel?"

"Yes, that would be lovely, Kenly, thank you," Isabel answered, afraid she might have just slurred the word *lovely*.

"And will you have another pint, Isabel?"

Isabel raised her hand. "Oh, no . . . Not unless you'd like me to curl up under this table for the night. This beer is delicious, but it's awfully strong. I'd forgotten my cousin Freddie mentioned that to me."

During a delightful dinner of fish and chips, and more of the easy, entertaining conversation they shared, they finally landed back on the topic of Matilde after Teddy remembered Kenly's telling him about Hugo. "Wouldn't it be something if they rekindled what they had all those years ago?"

"Why, Teddy Mansfield! I had no idea you were such a romantic."

Teddy smiled almost bashfully. Isabel loved the idea of Teddy's romantic scenario, but she sure hoped Hugo was up to the challenge, because he was going to have a steep hill to climb dealing with Matilde.

Chapter 13

Isabel fixed breakfast for Teddy on Sunday morning, and afterward he took her out to the garage to show her a hidden treasure. It was a bright yellow Volkswagen Beetle convertible. He told her he bought it as a Christmas gift for Fiona twenty years ago, and said he rarely drove it but just never had the heart to let it go.

"It's adorable!" Isabel said as she looked it over. "And in such beautiful condition. Does it run?"

"Of course it runs! And I do think it's about due for an outing. So how about I take you on a little tour along the coast today?"

Isabel couldn't imagine a nicer way to spend such a gorgeous Sunday afternoon. So for the next few hours, top down, Isabel's hair tied with a scarf, Teddy gave his guest the Cornish grand tour, driving all along the coast of the southernmost tip of Cornwall, from one charming village to the next, and one breathtaking view of the English Channel after another. Isabel was of course partial to the Lake Michigan shoreline, but as beautiful as it was, the coast of Cornwall was something else entirely, and something truly to behold.

Teddy was an endless fount of information and had plenty

of entertaining stories to tell about each village they drove through along the way. They stopped and bought pasties in a picturesque little seaside village on the west coast called St. Ives, which she fell in love with—both the village and the pasties—and had a little picnic on the beach. From there they crossed back to Mousehole through the lush green countryside.

Before returning home, Teddy wanted to stop and check on Matilde. He hadn't seen or heard from her since her regrettable appearance Friday night. After pulling into the driveway, he gave Isabel his blessing to wait in the car. She gladly accepted.

Teddy went to the front door and knocked. It took a few minutes, but Matilde finally opened the door. Isabel noticed all the drapes were drawn even though they were already well into late afternoon. She was wearing her nightgown, which was also odd, given the time of day. A little early for bed, Isabel thought, but maybe she was still recovering from Friday night. Teddy chatted at the door with her for a few minutes before returning to the car. "Matilde is feeling a bit under the weather. She can't say what it is exactly, but she looks awful. I don't think she's sleeping. I'm going to check on her tomorrow, and if she's still unwell, I'll ask the doctor to come over, whether she likes it or not. That's another of her phobias. Doctors. Doctors and serial killers. Oh, and clowns."

After they got home, and with sunset approaching, they decided to top off their day by taking the dogs out for a walk. When they passed Amesbury Acreage, there was Hyacinth again in her garden. "If she puts the same effort into her scones as she does her garden, maybe it's not such a surprise she keeps winning," Isabel suggested. Teddy agreed but warned her off mentioning that observation to Tuppence.

After a light dinner of some warmed-up leftovers from Friday night, they sat by the fire and chatted for a while, but

Teddy had class in the morning, so he went off to bed early. Before retiring he asked if she would mind watching Fred and Ginger for him the next day. "I really only take them to class to get them out of Tuppence's hair. But if you're here, they won't bother her. Or her, them."

"I'd love to! We'll have a nice long walk together."

After Teddy went upstairs, she sat by the fire for a while recounting her experience so far in Cornwall. Touring the coast with Teddy today was one of the loveliest days she could ever remember having. She was overwhelmed by the beauty and the history surrounding her. The trip was already so much more than she imagined it would be. Teddy's hospitality and his delightful company made her feel very welcome. And Tuppence had been a delight as well, so she was very sorry to see her going through this disappointment with the bake-off. But what Isabel could never have imagined she would encounter on this visit was all the *drama*! Lost loves, scone sabotage, a gin-swilling sister—it all made Gull Harbor seem quite tame, if you didn't count the occasional murder.

By the time Isabel was up and around that next morning, Teddy had left for class, and Fred and Ginger were lying outside the front door of the guest cottage waiting for her to appear. She had fallen in love with these two and their quirky personalities. Corgis were not a breed she was familiar with, having never spent any time with any, but now, if she lost her mind and decided to get another dog, she might just look for one to rescue.

Tuppence was busy in the kitchen when Isabel came in, but she was still nothing close to her usual chipper self, so she thought it best to just leave her be and walk down to the village with the dogs and have her coffee and breakfast there. Fred and Ginger seemed quite keen on the idea too, the moment they saw her grab their leashes.

Along the walk, she couldn't help but think how silly this

whole business with the scones really was. Yes, for Hyacinth and Alby to sabotage Tuppence was a deplorable and desperate act—if that is indeed what happened—but at the end of the day, we were still talking about scones. And if Hyacinth had committed such a devious act just to win a bake-off, it said a lot more about her than it did Tuppence's baking prowess.

After having some coffee and a scone that in no way measured up to Tuppence's, Isabel walked around the village for a while with the dogs. At one point she saw a group of people start to cross the street, then step back onto the curb, looking annoyed. A few seconds later she saw Nigel Plumbottom's Rolls-Royce coming down the street with Nigel reading a newspaper in the back and Tiegan behind the wheel as usual. After she passed Isabel, who stayed on the sidewalk, firmly holding the dogs' leashes, Tiegan turned onto a side street. Seconds later she heard a loud scraping sound that caught even the dogs' attention, followed a few seconds later by an irate man yelling a stream of not very nice commentary regarding her driving abilities. Isabel looked down at Fred and Ginger. "Chalk up another one for Mr. Magoo."

It was another dazzling spring day, with billowing clouds, a light breeze blowing, and the sun glistening off the water. She reminded herself that the water she was looking at was the English Channel, and across it, France. Maybe Paris could be her next bucket-list trip. But her daydreaming about Paris ended when she noticed she was walking past Amesbury Acreage again. This time there was no sign of Hyacinth, but Alby was sitting in the car and talking to the postman, who was standing outside his mail truck again. It quickly became obvious that they were not talking but arguing. Why, Isabel asked herself, was there so much strife between these people and their mailman? She had never exchanged so much as a cross word with Barney Sutherland, her mailman of the past twenty-five years, and she didn't know anybody who had. But even if Barney were not the infinitely agreeable letter carrier he was, and someone she always enjoyed having a chat with, who fights with the mailman?

Isabel picked up her pace as they passed the Amesburys' drive. She felt nothing but bad energy coming from that property, so she wanted to get past it as quickly as possible. Then she heard an engine revving up and looked back to see Alby coming down the drive toward the main road, and at a pretty good clip. Cornwall's angriest postman then whipped his truck around and followed right behind. After screeching onto the main road, they both started speeding toward her and the dogs. Taking no chances, she jumped as far off the shoulder as she could, pulling Fred and Ginger with her. But then she lost her balance and fell into a shrub, dropping their leashes while trying to break her fall. By the time she extricated herself from the shrub, they had run off and she watched them heading straight up the drive toward Hyacinth's house, dragging their leashes behind them. Isabel was panic stricken. She needed to get those dogs back, and fast. If anything happened to those two, Teddy would never forgive her. She would never forgive herself!

Fred and Ginger were nowhere to be seen by the time Isabel chugged her way up the drive and reached the house, completely out of breath. She called their names in between breaths, but nothing. She went up to the front door and knocked to see if there was any chance Hyacinth had let them inside, but there was no answer. Then she heard barking coming from behind the house. She rushed around back and was overcome with relief when she saw Fred and Ginger in the garden. Unfortunately, they were up to no good, both digging frantically in a freshly planted flower bed with dirt flying out behind their rumps. She yelled at them to stop as she rushed over, but they were oblivious to her pleas. When she finally grabbed their leashes and tried to pull them away, they refused to budge.

And then she noticed something strange in the flower bed, something the dogs were desperately trying to uncover. They began barking again as they dug, then kept looking back at her as though wanting to bring something to her attention.

Isabel bent down for a closer look. She couldn't quite make it out at first, but when she did, she nearly fainted. An ashen-colored, dirt-covered human hand with painted fingernails was popping out of the sleeve of a sweater, and now, thanks to Fred and Ginger's excavating work, sticking out of the ground. Isabel froze. It took a few seconds for it to sink in that what she was now looking at was a dead body—or at least part of one—buried in a flower bed. Fred continued tugging at the sleeve with his teeth and unraveling it, exposing more of the hand, while Ginger continued digging wildly and exposing more of the arm. Isabel was not only feeling sick to her stomach but was frightened to death.

With all the strength she could muster, she finally dragged the dogs away from their digging and began running as fast as her feet would take her—which was not very—back to Pembroke Cottage. A million things raced through her mind along the way. Who was it? Who put her there? She assumed it was a woman, given the nail polish, but then again, never assume.

Isabel wondered if her life from here on was destined to be intertwined with murder. She couldn't believe her dream trip to the United Kingdom had just taken such a terrible turn. But that was being selfish. It wasn't as terrible as the turn taken by whoever was buried in that flower bed.

Chapter 14

Isabel was relieved almost to the point of tears when she saw Teddy's car parked in the drive after she finally made it back to Pembroke Cottage. After bursting through the front door and startling both Teddy and Tuppence, and in between a series of deep breaths bordering on hyperventilation, a winded and terrified Isabel was eventually able to convey to them what she had just discovered in Hyacinth Amesbury's garden. Teddy immediately picked up the phone and called the police.

After a brief conversation with somebody he seemed well acquainted with, he announced that he was going over to the Amesburys to meet the police. Isabel wasn't exactly anxious to go back, and Teddy wanted her to stay put anyway, but after what she had just seen, and not knowing who was buried in that flower bed or who put her there, she felt safer staying close to him.

Tuppence said nothing. She seemed to have fallen into a state of shock. Teddy asked her to call Matilde, presumably to make sure his sister wasn't the one buried in Hyacinth's garden, so she picked up the phone as instructed. Teddy and Isabel left Fred and Ginger sitting in the foyer, staring at them dejectedly as they headed out the door. They always got treats when they came back from a walk, and they were not at all pleased about being slighted, especially after going to all the trouble of digging up a dead body.

When they pulled up to Hyacinth's house, there were already a few police cars parked around the perimeter, and officers were putting up tape to cordon off the area. As they got out of the car—Isabel doing so very tentatively—Teddy waved to someone who appeared to be the man in charge, given that he was the only one in civilian clothes. He was a tall, thin man, probably in his early forties, with pale skin, a refined nose, and freckles. He was mostly bald, but what hair he did have was ginger, which Isabel had learned was what all redheads were called in the UK. In his sport coat and tie he looked a little overdressed for a murder scene—to Isabel's eye, at least. As soon as he spotted them, he came right over and shook Teddy's hand. "Hello, Teddy. This is quite a puzzling situation. Either foul play or a tragic gardening accident, I suppose."

"Inspector Barclay Carlyle, may I introduce Isabel Puddles."

Inspector Carlyle put out his hand. "Pleasure to meet you, Mrs. Puddles."

"Isabel discovered the body," Teddy informed the inspector.

She was staring back at the garden uneasily. "I was the *human* who discovered the body. Teddy's corgis discovered it."

"And how did that come about, if I might ask." The inspector pulled out a pen and a notepad.

"Well, I was walking them along the main road and they got away from me and ran up here. So I ran after them. By the time I found them, they were already digging frantically in the flower bed."

"Do you have any idea who it is yet, Barclay?" Teddy asked.

"We have not yet exhumed the body. We're waiting for the coroner. So no. All we have to go on right now is what's exposed: the hand and part of the arm. Would you mind walking over there with me, Mrs. Puddles? I'd like you to show me exactly what you saw when you arrived on the scene."

She instinctively reached out and grabbed Teddy's hand, and the three of them walked over to the flower bed. She approached the flower bed slowly and with a grimace. Isabel looked down at the arm and the area around it again closely, then shook her head. "I'm afraid I don't notice anything different than when I was last here, Inspector."

Teddy leaned over to get a closer look at the arm, then looked back at Inspector Carlyle. "I think I might recognize that jumper, Barclay."

Isabel took a closer look at it too, trying to concentrate on the sleeve of the sweater and not the grotesque dead hand poking out of it. All she could make out was that it was sort of a plaid pattern of lavender and a periwinkle blue, but it didn't look familiar to her at all.

"Where do you think you might recognize it from, Teddy?" Inspector Carlyle asked while jotting in his notebook.

Teddy hesitated briefly. "I can't be sure, but I think I saw Hyacinth wearing a jumper in those colors on Saturday at the bake-off. Or one that looked an awful lot like it."

"And when did you last see Mrs. Amesbury?"

"Well, that's the thing. I saw her out in the garden just this morning on my way to school. That was about half eight, so I don't see how that could be her."

"We both saw her working in her garden yesterday too." Isabel hesitated before continuing. "I know it's too early to know when—whoever this is—died, but based on the skin color, it looks like it's been longer than a day."

"I guess the coroner will provide that information, but if this *isn't* Mrs. Amesbury, then where is she?" the inspector asked, not really expecting an answer. Isabel and Teddy looked at each other, both wearing expressions that read "good question."

"Well, I think Isabel is right," Teddy said, clearing his throat. "That hand looks like it's been buried in the dirt longer than a few hours or even a day. And if she was out here this morning when I drove by, that was only five or six hours before Isabel found the body. So I just don't see how it could be her."

Isabel suddenly had a gruesome thought. "Can we even be sure there's a *body* attached? I mean all we can see is the arm, after all."

The inspector and Teddy considered the possibility, although they both looked skeptical.

Isabel winced and shrugged simultaneously. "Just putting it out there."

Teddy thought it over a little more. "True enough that murderers dismember bodies all the time. Whoever she is could be scattered all over this garden. *Or* Hyacinth is walking around somewhere with just the one arm." He immediately regretted what he said. "I'm sorry. That was rather tasteless."

The coroner's van pulled up at that moment, taking the spotlight off Teddy's bad joke.

"I think you should take Mrs. Puddles home, Teddy. We're going to begin exhuming the body soon. If it is just the arm, boy, that would be a real time saver. We could all be home for tea."

Isabel thought Inspector Carlyle had just made an attempt at his own rather tasteless joke in response to Teddy's, someone he obviously held in high esteem, then she realized he was serious.

Inspector Carlyle shook Teddy's hand, then Isabel's. "I'll stop by Pembroke Cottage after I'm done here and read you in. I'll also need to get a statement from you, Mrs. Puddles."

He turned to leave, then turned back. "By the way, have either of you seen Alby?"

Isabel immediately felt foolish for not mentioning this already. "Inspector, I'm so sorry I didn't tell you this before. I guess I'm still in a bit of shock. But while I was walking the dogs past here a little earlier, I saw Alby and the postman—Bobby, I think Teddy told me his name was."

Teddy nodded. "Bobby Blackburn." The name obviously registered for the inspector.

Isabel continued. "I saw them stopped in the drive. The postman was standing outside his red mail truck, but Alby was still in the car. I couldn't hear anything at that distance, of course, but I could definitely make out that they were arguing. The dogs and I kept walking, but then a minute or two later, they both pulled out of the driveway going pretty fast and screeched onto the main road. I don't know if the postman was chasing Alby or what, but they came at us so fast I jumped as far off the road as I could with the dogs. I wasn't taking any chances. That's when I fell into the bushes and dropped their leashes."

The inspector waved one of the officers over and told him to go round up Bobby Blackburn and be on the lookout for Alby Amesbury. He turned back to them. "Thank you both. We'll talk soon."

After they left the crime scene, Teddy wanted to go check on Matilde again before going home. Isabel agreed it was probably a good idea to check in on your neighbors when there's been a murder in the neighborhood, especially if one neighbor happens to be your sister. When they pulled into Matilde's driveway, Tuppence was just riding up on her bicycle, looking panicked. "I've called her a few times like you asked, but no answer! I started getting a bad feeling."

"When did you last see her?" Teddy asked.

"I rode by here yesterday and she was in the front yard talking to Hugo. She didn't look like she was in great shape. Like maybe she'd been crying. And he was looking a bit gutted too. I didn't want to get in the middle of all that, so I just kept going. Do they know who it is yet?" Tuppence asked, catching up to Teddy as he headed for the front door.

"Not confirmed, no, but I have a very strong feeling it *is* Hyacinth. . . . Don't you, Isabel?"

"I feel strongly it's a woman based on the nail polish. And it *is* her garden. But it's the timeline that's confusing. Unless we're both wrong about how long we thought that arm has been in the ground, which is quite possible."

"You really think it's *Hyacinth* that's popped her clogs?" Tuppence asked. "I was thinking it more likely it was her what buried the body. Are there any suspects?"

Teddy took a deep breath. "We don't even know for sure who's dead. But, assuming it *is* Hyacinth, it looks like Alby and Bobby Blackburn were the last to see her alive."

Teddy knocked on the front door, then jangled the old copper bell that hung next to it, but there were no signs of life. Teddy could see Matilde's car in the half-open garage. The drapes were still drawn, and the door was locked. He looked under the mat for a key. Nothing. Tuppence pulled a key chain out of her pocket. "She left it at Pembroke for emergencies. I think this counts." Teddy took the key and unlocked the door, then cautiously entered.

The house was disconcertingly quiet. As they entered the small foyer, Teddy yelled his sister's name. No response. He walked to the base of the stairs and yelled up. Still no response. Teddy turned to Isabel and Tuppence, "You two wait here." He cautiously began to climb the stairs, yelling Matilde's name again. He was no more than five steps up before Isabel and Tuppence were right behind him, afraid to be left behind.

When they reached the top of the stairs, Teddy called Matilde's name one more time, then took a deep breath before slowly opening her bedroom door. It was fairly dark, but a sliver of light coming through the drapes fell on what looked to be a body lying in the bed under a comforter. Teddy ran toward the bed in a panic, mortified by what he feared he might be about to discover. He took another deep breath, braced himself, then lifted up the covers and was met with a groggy, "Will you please just leave me alone, Theodore?" After a collective sigh of relief, Teddy asked Isabel and Tuppence to wait downstairs so he could talk to Matilde privately.

They went downstairs, both feeling quite relieved. Although they didn't say it out loud, they were more certain than not that they were going to fine Matilde dead too. Tuppence headed to the kitchen. "I'll put the kettle on." Isabel joined her and sat down at the kitchen table. "She's always been prone to spells of depression," Tuppence went on as she filled the kettle at the sink, "but I've never seen her not able to get out of bed."

Teddy walked into the kitchen a few minutes later, looking concerned and confused. "She says she's been having migraines. But I know there's more to it than that. I know my sister and I know when she's lying. And she's lying. She looks frightened too."

"Did you tell her what's happened?" Isabel asked.

"Well, we don't *know* exactly what's happened yet. And we don't know for *sure* it's Hyacinth, so no." Teddy took a long pause. "I've never seen her in a state like this, so I don't know how she would handle it, to be honest."

Teddy's phone rang and he lifted it to his ear after one ring. "Hello, Barclay," he said, then listened for a minute or so, nodding the whole time. "You're sure? All right, well, thank you for letting me know. . . . Yes, anytime. I'm sure Isabel will be happy to give you her statement this evening."

He looked over at her for approval. She nodded. "All right . . . we'll be home shortly." Teddy put his phone away and turned to his eager audience. "It's Hyacinth."

"Blimey," Tuppence said softly, "I hope the good Lord knows I was only having a laugh when I wished her dead."

Teddy went on. "They identified her at the scene. Cause of death is not confirmed, but Barclay thinks she was most likely strangled. There was also a contusion to her head, though, and a broken flowerpot nearby. So she may have been knocked unconscious first and then strangled."

The three of them stared at one another for what seemed an eternity until Tuppence spoke up. "Well, somebody wanted to make sure they got the job done, didn't they." She thought things over for a moment before continuing. "Suppose there's another serial killer out there. Another ripper. I guess it's about time for another one to come along."

"That's quite a conclusion to leap to, Tuppence," Teddy said with a slight scowl. "And serial killers don't tend to be seasonal."

"Well, I'll be sleeping at my sister's tonight, I will. She keeps a pistol. And I think you need to go up and tell *your* sister what's happened to her oldest friend. And then take *her* home with you too, just to be safe."

Isabel decided it was time to add her two cents. Or pence, as it were. "Her son and that postman would be who I'd most want to talk to. What are two men doing arguing in the driveway when the mother of one of those men is buried behind the house in a shallow grave? Seems pretty likely those two things are related, wouldn't you say so, Teddy?"

Teddy concurred. "They would certainly be the first two I'd want to talk to."

Tuppence was not in agreement. "I just can't see Alby killing his mother. That woman was the only person he had in the world, as awful as she is, or was. Who's going to support him now? He's as worthless as a chocolate teapot! And Bobby Blackburn? Nobody I want to come across in a dark alley, but why would *he* want to kill Hyacinth? Unless it was just for fun. That I'd believe."

"I'm sure Inspector Carlyle will be looking into Bobby very closely," Teddy said, "And as far as Alby goes . . . We all know he's a very odd bird, so who *knows* what might have set him off?"

Tuppence was stuck on her theory. "Well, I don't think we can rule out having another ripper on our hands. Imagine that. The Cornwall Ripper! Blimey. And Hyacinth may not be the only victim. *Or*, she could be the first." Tuppence seemed to have convinced herself that a serial killer was far and away the most logical explanation for the murder.

They all looked up at once to see Matilde standing in the kitchen doorway, staring at them with a bizarre expression. She was quite a sight wrapped up in an old flannel robe, wearing white athletic socks for slippers, and with hair that looked as if a bird had been nesting in it. Teddy stood up. "Matilde, I have something I have to tell you." He put his arm around her and turned her around gently, then walked her back into the living room. Isabel and Tuppence didn't even pretend they weren't going to eavesdrop on *this* conversation, so they quickly moved closer to the doorway.

"Matilde, dear. I'm afraid I have some very bad news," Teddy said softly. "Hyacinth has been found dead . . . murdered." Matilde said nothing. "Did you hear me, Matilde? Hyacinth has been murdered."

"I heard you, Theodore," she answered without emotion. "Do they know who did it?"

"Not yet. Inspector Carlyle is looking for Alby and Bobby Blackburn for questioning right now." He hesitated slightly before continuing. "There's also the *possibility* it may have been a random killing." Another long silence followed, with

Matilde still not saying a word. "Matilde? Are you hearing what I'm saying?"

"Random murder. I heard you, Theodore. So that's what I heard Tuppence going on about? The Cornwall Ripper?"

"That's just Tuppence being melodramatic. You know how she gets. But it's too early to know who did this, so I'd feel much better if you came to stay with me until we know what we're dealing with here. Why don't you go upstairs and pack a few things."

"Thank you, but I'll be fine here, Theodore."

"Matilde, I'm worried about you, my dear. You are not yourself, and you may be in danger. We all may be. So please pack up a few—"

"I'll be fine. I'm just exhausted. I have not been able to sleep with these migraines. All I need is some rest. I'm going back up to bed now."

Teddy was not happy. "Matilde, please stop being so stubborn. There's a murderer out there somewhere, and who knows who their next victim is going to be? Please just go pack a few—"

Matilde was suddenly annoyed. "Thank you for your concern, Theodore, and I am very sorry to hear about Hyacinth, but if you would all please just go and leave me in peace, I would quite appreciate it."

They could hear Teddy release a heavy sigh, followed soon by the sound of Matilde going back up the creaking staircase. When he came back into the kitchen, Teddy looked discouraged. "I really don't feel good about leaving her here alone. Tuppence, would you mind staying over with her tonight?"

"Not on your life! I'm sorry, but two women here all alone with a killer on the loose? No, thank you! And I don't mean to be selfish, Lordship, but if the Cornwall Ripper breaks in here, it's your sister he's after, not me. I don't want to end up part of some two-for-one deal."

Teddy couldn't really blame her. He excused himself and went upstairs to try one more time to get her to come back with him, but once again she refused. Isabel suggested he could stay there with Matilde, assuring him she would be fine, despite not feeling too wonderful about the prospect of being in that guesthouse alone either. "I have Fred and Ginger to protect me."

Teddy wouldn't hear of it. "And those two will protect you valiantly until somebody throws them a treat, then you'll be on your own."

After they got outside, Isabel could see that Teddy was hesitating. "Are you sure you don't want to stay?"

"I am absolutely sure. You're my houseguest, and I am not leaving you alone. In fact, I'd feel better if you moved into the guest room tonight."

She wasn't going to argue. "I think I would too."

Tuppence got on her bicycle and yelled back as she rode away, "I'll see you two in the morning. Unless the ripper decides my sister and me are next to go!"

As they watched her ride away, Teddy turned and gave Isabel a funny look. "What is it?" she asked.

"Well, I'm just going to say it, because eventually it's going to come up as the investigation ramps up. But if there's one person who we know for certain may well have been angry enough, and had motive enough—at least in her mind—to strangle Hyacinth Amesbury, it's that dear woman riding away on her bicycle right now. I don't believe she did it. Not for a second. I just know that others might."

Isabel slowly nodded her head as she watched Tuppence coasting around the corner. "I wasn't going to say it, but yes, I expect the inspector will want to have a talk with her. But I'm with you. I don't believe she's capable of murder."

When they pulled into the drive back at Pembroke Cottage, Inspector Carlyle was in his car waiting for them, so

Teddy invited him to come in and have a cup of tea. Once inside, he didn't waste any time getting down to business. "We found Mrs. Amesbury's car abandoned out near Trungle's Rock. We assume Alby was driving it but can't be sure. We're bringing in some hounds from Falmouth first thing in the morning to see if they can track him. Of course he or whoever could be in London by then. But since we can't be sure it was Alby who abandoned the car there, we'll be searching the Amesbury property with cadaver dogs, also from Falmouth, to make sure there isn't another body buried around there somewhere." The inspector looked down at Fred and Ginger. "These two seem to have a nose for it. Maybe we could recruit—"

Teddy raised his hand. "You can stop right there, Barclay. I don't want my dogs developing a fondness for digging up dead people or any other dead things. . . . Have you spoken to Bobby Blackburn?"

"Haven't found him yet. Checked his house, his mum and dad's, the pubs where he hangs out. Nothing. I guess if he doesn't show up for work in the morning, we'll have a good idea who our primary person of interest will be."

The inspector's phone rang, so he excused himself and went into the other room. Teddy shook his head slowly. "I just can't figure out how, when she was alive this morning, somebody could have murdered her and then buried her so quickly."

"It is a rather tight timeline," Isabel agreed, "but if you were in a hurry, I think you could probably get the job done."

Inspector Carlyle came back into the room. "That was the coroner's office. We still don't have a time of death, but as I suspected, the *cause* of death does appear to be strangulation. And her garden hose may have been the murder weapon. I've got to get back down to the station." He stood up to leave. "All right if I come back and get that statement from you tomorrow, Mrs. Puddles?" Isabel assured him that would be fine as she and Teddy walked him to the door.

As soon as the inspector said she was *strangled*, Isabel couldn't help flashing back to Tuppence's using that very word to describe what she wanted to do to Hyacinth after she first suspected her of sabotage. But she was certain this was just an unfortunate coincidence. She certainly wasn't going to mention it to the inspector and put her on his list of suspects. She wondered if Teddy remembered. He heard her say it too. He looked at her after the inspector closed the door behind him. "I know what you're thinking. And, yes, it is most unfortunate she chose that particular word while she was venting, but—"

"But I'm still with you. I just don't believe she's capable of such a thing."

"I don't, either," he agreed. "But then life, and *people*, can always surprise you."

Unfortunately Teddy's point was not one Isabel could or would argue.

"Death by garden hose? That's a first," Teddy mused. "But for an avid gardener maybe it's a fitting way to go." He read Isabel's reaction. "Too soon?"

"Do I really need to answer that?"

"You just did. My gallows humor isn't always well received. I stand chastened and rebuked."

Chapter 15

The next morning, Mousehole was abuzz with the news of Hyacinth Amesbury's murder. Even if she was one of the less popular people in the village, most agreed that being strangled with your garden hose and then planted in your own flower bed was a terrible way to go, even for her. But there were a few folks who weren't shy about saying she probably asked for it. What everybody *could* agree on, though, was how disconcerting it was to know that whoever had done this was still out there.

Inspector Carlyle called while they were having breakfast and told Teddy that the bloodhounds had picked up what was most likely Alby's scent at his mother's abandoned car, and were now tracking him. "Well, that can't have been too difficult," Tuppence sniffed, "that one's no friend of soap and water."

Isabel was curious about something, so she decided to ask. "You and the inspector seem to have a very nice rapport, Teddy. He's awfully forthcoming with the details of this case. How did you two get acquainted? Or am I being nosy again?"

Teddy smiled. "Yes, you are being nosy, but we've discussed how well that works for you. . . . Inspector Carlyle was

apparently inspired to become a detective from reading my
Detective Waverly series. So when he moved to Mousehole
several years ago to take a position as a detective constable,
he came over to introduce himself and say thank you. Lovely
gesture. Very nice man. And it never hurts to have a friend
in the police department. Since he's been promoted to chief
inspector, he keeps me up to speed on Mousehole police matters, which amounts to virtually nothing, but it keeps me in
the loop. And sometimes it will trigger an idea or something
I can use. I have four more books to write in the next four
years, so it also doesn't hurt to have fresh ideas in the bank. I
also think he's feeling a bit overwhelmed with this and needs
a sounding board. It's his first murder. They're always special."

While Inspector Carlyle and the bloodhounds on loan
from the Falmouth Constabulary were trying to track down
Alby, Bobby Blackburn had shown up for work as scheduled.
The inspector would no doubt still have plenty of questions
for him, but it wasn't going to be as cut-and-dried as he might
have hoped.

Teddy didn't have class, so he and Isabel had the whole
day to spend together and do whatever they pleased. But what
else could a famous mystery writer and a semi-professional
small-town sleuth do on the day after the murder of somebody they knew—well, somebody Teddy knew and Isabel
was acquainted with—who lived right down the road, other
than ruminate and hypothesize over who might have done it
and why? So that's exactly what they did.

Teddy did go down to check on Matilde after lunch, and
found her still in bed, and still a mess. That was it for him. He
called the doctor and asked him to pay her a visit, whether she
liked it or not. The doctor couldn't come until late afternoon,
so Teddy left her in bed and went home to debrief Isabel and
Tuppence on what he had just learned.

He told them he asked her about Hugo this time, and if

his return to Mousehole had anything to do with her current condition. She said they had seen each other, yes, but there was nothing romantic going on. They were just old friends catching up. So, no, Hugo had nothing to do with anything. Teddy wasn't sure he was buying it, but he had no choice but to take her word for it. He also wondered if it was perhaps her gin affliction that was responsible for her meltdown and told her he was concerned about her drinking. "I was happy to hear her say she hadn't had a drink since the unfortunate Friday-night incident, and that she was off the gin for good." He wasn't sure he was buying that either. Still trying to figure out what was responsible for her very strange behavior of late, Teddy began to wonder out loud with Isabel and Tuppence if maybe his sister was concealing a serious illness. "It would be just like her to do that. I'm going to talk to the doctor about that possibility too."

While Tuppence continued to convince herself that there was a serial killer on the loose, and that she was going to be the Cornwall Ripper's next victim, Isabel and Teddy had both pretty much ruled out any possibility of a serial killer going around strangling women with garden hoses. But there was no convincing Tuppence. So when they decided to take Fred and Ginger for their walk—both enviably oblivious to all the human drama swirling around them—she insisted on going with them, afraid to be alone in the house.

Once they passed through the front gate of Pembroke Cottage, they all looked in the direction of Amesbury Acreage and immediately agreed to go in the opposite direction. Walking away from the water and that magnificent view was nothing they had ever done, but going past a fresh murder scene was just too creepy. As Tuppence continued to theorize about the Cornwall Ripper—her fantasy serial killer—Isabel and Teddy did their best to tune her out while they strolled along the lane, watching the dogs sniffing and enjoying their outing.

Fred and Ginger were the first to hear it, stopping dead in their tracks, perking up their ears, and going on high alert. "What is it?" Teddy asked them, in that casual way dog owners ask questions of their dogs, as if expecting an answer. The faintest sound then began to register for the humans. It was a barking dog. No, it was more than one barking dog. To Isabel it sounded a little like beagles in a fox hunt, although she hoped that barbaric activity was a thing of the past by now. The barking was getting closer, and Fred and Ginger began pulling them back toward Amesbury Acreage. They knew they had no choice but to head in that direction, despite Tuppence's resistance.

As Hyacinth's house came into view, they could see a handful of men running across the field between the main road and the house. Seconds later they could see what the men were running after—two, if not more, large dogs cutting through the tall grass. They couldn't get a good look at the breed, but to Isabel they sounded like bloodhounds. They quickly worked out that these must be the dogs Inspector Carlyle told them he was going to use to track Alby, and apparently track him right back home.

Teddy handed Ginger's leash to Tuppence, while Isabel did the same with Fred's. "Take these two back to the house, please," he said to her. She resisted, still fearful the ripper might be lying in wait in the kitchen, but Teddy and Isabel were already on their way, so she was stuck with them. Fred and Ginger were not happy about being left behind either. They tugged her along for about a hundred feet while she cursed at them until she could finally dig her heels in and get them under control.

Two police cars raced past them on the main road and

turned up the drive onto Hyacinth's property. The next vehicle to pass by was the coroner's van. That was worrisome. Isabel stopped and looked at Teddy. "Maybe those aren't the trackers but the cadaver dogs. Do you suppose they've found another body? Alby's, maybe?"

"Nothing will surprise me at this point, but let's crack on and find out," Teddy said, taking Isabel by the hand and heading up the drive.

By the time they had speed-walked up the long drive, the bloodhounds, three of them, were circling the house, followed by two officers who appeared to be their handlers. Next, they spotted Inspector Carlyle coming out of the field. When he got to the clearing, he bent over with his hands on his knees trying to catch his breath. Dressed in a sport coat and tie again, the inspector looked as if he might have been dragged at least part of the way. His tie was hanging over his shoulder, he had grass stains on his khaki pants—soaking wet below the knee—and his shoes were covered in mud. He raised his head as they walked over and was still breathing quite heavily.

"Do you know how far it is from Trungle's Rock to here?" he asked, taking a handkerchief out of his pocket and wiping the sweat off his brow.

Teddy was working it out in his head. "I would guess five miles?"

"Try seven. And we're right back at the murder scene." The inspector finally caught enough breath to straighten up. "We've already searched the house, so why these bloody dogs led us all the way back here is a mystery. I could have driven here!"

One of the officers that had been following the dogs came over in a rush. "Inspector, the dogs are on point at the back door. They're definitely still on the scent. I know you've already done an inside search, but these three are keen as mustard to get in there."

Keen as mustard? Isabel really did need to start that list. She still hadn't figured out who Uncle Bob or his nephew were.

The inspector looked at his watch. "Warrant's still good and the door's unlocked. Go ahead in." After the officer left, the inspector shook his head and looked at Teddy. "My father was a podiatrist. He and my mum wanted me to go to medical school and take over his practice one day. I don't think you'll find a lot of podiatrists running through the brush chasing bloodhounds and searching for a man suspected of killing his own mother and burying her in the garden. So I'm not sure you did me any favors by introducing me to Detective Waverly after all, Teddy."

Teddy couldn't help but laugh. "Yes, but I'll bet there are plenty of podiatrists who would love to take a break from looking at corns and hammertoes every day to do just that."

Inspector Carlyle excused himself and went inside the house to join the search. Isabel and Teddy looked at each other and could instantly tell what the other was thinking: should they go inside or not? Isabel answered the question out loud. "We probably shouldn't."

Teddy concurred. "You're right. We should just wind our necks back in and go home."

She nodded in agreement. "This is a crime scene. We've really got no business going in there, but . . ."

"But we *are* professionals . . . in a way." Teddy offered.

"That's very true. Maybe they could use our help," Isabel added.

Without saying another word, they headed to the back door leading into the kitchen and went inside. Once inside, they could hear the dogs running around the upstairs and the officers shouting commands. The next thing they knew, the dogs were racing past them and heading down to the cellar, followed by the officers who politely nodded hello as they passed, probably recognizing Teddy, Isabel figured. Inspector Carlyle, now looking even worse for wear, arrived downstairs next. "I think these hounds are just taking the mickey out of us at this point," he said in a tone of sheer exasperation before following them down the stairs.

Now, who was Mickey? Isabel asked herself. Was he related to Bob? Was *he* the nephew? Where did they come up with this stuff?

The sound of frantic barking suddenly rose from the cellar, followed by a commotion that sounded like furniture or some other heavy objects were falling or being hastily moved around. More barking and some yelling followed. Then it went quiet until they heard Inspector Carlyle's voice coming through loud and clear: "Alby Amesbury, I'm arresting you on suspicion of murder. You do not have to say anything, but it may harm your defense if you do not mention when questioned something which you later rely on in court. Anything you do say may be given in evidence."

Isabel looked at Teddy. "The British version of Miranda rights, I assume?"

"Correct."

"You Brits even sound polite when you're arresting somebody for murder." Isabel smiled but quickly realized this was no time for smiling when Inspector Carlyle appeared at the top of the cellar stairs with a handcuffed and distraught-looking Alby in tow. He looked up at Teddy with mournful eyes as he passed by them. "I didn't do it, Mr. Mansfield. I didn't kill my mum." After he was out the door, he yelled back inside. "I swear I didn't!"

"Well, at least he's still alive," Isabel offered, always looking for the bright side. Before they left, they walked through the living room, where she noticed a large rectangular mark

over the fireplace where a painting had obviously once hung
as well as several similar marks on the other walls. It looked
as if Hyacinth had sold off a lot of her artwork. Isabel thought
she'd have a quick look at the few paintings that were left on
the walls. Maybe she could find that painting Nigel was talking about wanting to buy, but there was nothing that came
close to what he had described. None of what remained was
memorable or looked at all valuable. Isabel decided it must be
in another room in the house.

When she got back outside, Teddy was waiting for her and
watching the inspector put Alby into the back of a police car.
After closing the door, he walked back over to them shaking
his head and wearing an odd smile.

"Well, you're never going to believe what we just found
down in the cellar, aside from Alby. This would even have
Waverly scratching his head. But I do think it clears up the
timeline for you, especially since the coroner's report came
back a short while ago saying the time of death was likely
Saturday early afternoon."

Isabel's wheels were starting to turn, but Teddy was a few
strokes behind. "Are you going to let us go down and see for
ourselves, Barclay?" he asked.

"I hope it's no more dead bodies," Isabel pleaded. "*That* I
could do without."

Inspector Carlyle smiled. "Still just the one, Mrs. Puddles.
For now. Please, follow me."

Once they got into the cellar, the inspector led them over
to what appeared to be a hidden doorway. Or was. Pulled out
and away from the doorway was a dusty bookshelf filled with
assorted dusty books. A door handle on the back of the bookshelf allowed whoever was hiding out in there the ability to
pull it flush against the wall behind them and seal themselves
in. This was way beyond creepy, and although Isabel wasn't all
that anxious to go inside, naturally she was going to.

"Well, this is it. This is where Alby's been hiding out since his mother turned up dead under her primrose patch." The inspector smiled. "Well? Shall we go in?"

Inside a dark and dingy room, about fifteen by fifteen feet, was an old sofa, and on it a pillow and a blanket. There was a steel desk against one wall stacked with old magazines, an antique wooden wardrobe on the other wall, and about a dozen empty bags of potato chips strewn across an old rug.

Teddy was appalled by what he was looking at, but also fascinated. "So he's just been holed up in here since killing his mum, eating crisps?"

Inspector Carlyle nodded, then laughed out loud, which to Isabel seemed rather inappropriate, but she had already determined he was an odd one. But then so was Columbo, and he always got the job done. "Yes, so it would appear, assuming he's guilty, which I don't believe to be much of a stretch at this point."

Teddy agreed. "I wouldn't say hiding out in a secret room after your mum's been found planted in the garden smacks of innocence. *But*, that said, for Alby, who is, well, let's be kind and just call him unbalanced, it *would* make sense for him to hide out in here if he knew who *did* murder his mother and was afraid he might be next. Although I wouldn't think taking a month's supply of crisps with you into hiding would be top of mind if that were the case."

Isabel acknowledged to Teddy with a nod that this was a perfectly reasonable alternative theory, but she had a hunch something else was going on here.

"Not a bad theory, Teddy," the inspector agreed. "That's the mystery writer at work. But this is where it gets even more bizarre." He took the lid off a large plastic storage tub next to the sofa and reached inside, looking as if he were about to perform a magic trick. He then pulled out a wide-brimmed gardening hat, a gray wig, and a large pair of sunglasses. Next, he walked over to the wardrobe and opened the doors, again with magician-like flourish, revealing a half dozen of what appeared to be Hyacinth's gardening frocks.

Isabel's hunch was right. After hearing that Hyacinth had been dead since Saturday, and given that both she and Teddy had seen her, or at least assumed they had, from a distance *after* Saturday, she had a strange feeling this might be where things were headed. She had seen *Psycho*. And *Tootsie*!

Teddy looked confused at first, but then the penny dropped. "You don't mean to tell me that when we saw Hyacinth out working in her garden on Sunday, and I saw her again yesterday on my way to class, it was actually Alby dressed *up* like Hyacinth?"

"So it would appear," the inspector answered.

Isabel cringed. "That also means that when we saw Hyacinth out digging in her garden on Saturday, Teddy, it was actually Alby dressed up like her while he was *burying* her. We *saw* him burying his mother! Dear Lord."

Teddy just shook his head in disbelief as he pondered this scenario. "Well, it's all very Hitchcockian, isn't it. And with a little *Tootsie* thrown in for good measure."

Isabel had to smile. For two people from such different worlds and life experiences, she and Teddy always seemed to be on similar wavelengths.

Chapter 16

Inspector Carlyle called first thing in the morning and asked to come by and talk to Teddy and Tuppence. He had some questions about Alby and his relationship with his mother that he hoped they might be able to shed some light on. Going by what Alby had said during his interrogation, the inspector said he was beginning to have some doubts about his guilt. It certainly didn't look good for him, the inspector made clear, but maybe he *was* telling the truth when he laid out his version of events. Teddy invited him to drop by for tea. Turns out he was calling from the driveway, so Teddy went out to the guesthouse and asked Isabel to come in and join them. "My confidence in Inspector Carlyle as a murder investigator is untested," Teddy told her, "but you're an old hand at it, so I'm sure you can provide some useful insights."

"I'm not wild about the term 'old hand,' but I do appreciate your confidence."

"I do apologize. I knew the moment it left my lips it was the wrong thing to say."

"You're forgiven. Let's go hear what the inspector has to say."

When they walked into the kitchen, the inspector was

already sitting down at the table with his tea and getting an earful from Tuppence. "I just told the inspector I thought he should let Alby go, or at most charge him with justifiable homicide."

"Let's not resort to that sort of talk, Tuppence. It's very bad form to speak ill of the dead," Teddy scolded.

"Well, I'm not going to be a hypocrite and start speaking *well* about her, either. What goes around comes around, I always say."

Teddy gave her another look that made it clear he didn't agree. "I think it's safe to stipulate once again that Hyacinth Amesbury was not a person most of us cared for. She was a spiteful, self-centered woman, and a bit of a—"

"Cheater?" Tuppence interrupted.

"Yes, she may well have been a cheater too. Probably was. But just because a person is unpleasant and unpopular, or cheats in a scone bake-off, these are not faults that should be punishable by death." Tuppence's expression implied she wasn't sure she agreed with that at all.

Teddy and Isabel were both anxious to hear what the inspector had to say, or what Alby had to say to the inspector, so Teddy invited him to speak. "Please go ahead, Barclay. Don't mind her."

"All right, well, according to Alby, he came home on Saturday afternoon about four o'clock and found his mother lying dead in the garden." The inspector took a slow sip of tea, which seemed more like he was pausing for effect.

Teddy filled the void. "Most people who found themselves in the unfortunate situation of coming home and finding their mother lying dead in the garden would call an ambulance or the police, I would think. Then perhaps follow up with a call to the local funeral home. Burying her in a flower bed instead is rather an interesting choice."

The inspector agreed. "But, he claims, because he knew

of his mother's heart condition, he assumed she had simply had a heart attack. He saw no indication that she had been murdered and said it never even occurred to him. And, to be fair, the garden hose wasn't found around her neck, so it stands to reason he may well have assumed she died of natural causes."

Now it was Isabel's turn to chime in. "Let's give him the benefit of the doubt and say he did assume she'd had a heart attack. Even so, dragging your mother into the flower bed, whatever her cause of death, and burying her in a shallow grave is certainly not, as Teddy said, a normal *go-to* reaction. Or even legal, I wouldn't think. Or is burying your loved ones in the backyard another Cornish tradition? Like jam first, clotted cream second?"

Teddy laughed. "We aren't animals, Isabel. No, we are not allowed to simply bury our dead in the yard. Well, not since the Iron Age, anyway." He looked back at the inspector. "Did he attempt to explain what possessed him to do this? This home burial project? Or perhaps even more puzzling, why he then began to impersonate her?"

"Actually, he did explain his reasoning, and although it is diabolical, not to mention very illegal, his motives were quite simple and made perfect sense in a horrendously twisted way." Inspector Carlyle took another shamelessly long sip of tea. "Alby intended to keep cashing his mother's state pension checks—five hundred pounds and some change every month—as well as the monthly annuity checks she received from the sale of her late husband's appliance business—about twice that amount—both of which would cease upon her death. Alby explained that they were in dire financial straits, so there was nothing for him to inherit other than debt, and he had no money of his own. So his plan—for as long as he could get away with it, anyway—was to forge his mother's signature on the checks, dress up like her for the sake of the closed-circuit cameras, and then deposit the checks into ATMs at various bank branches outside the village, where his mother wasn't known."

To say the inspector had a captive audience at this point would be an understatement. He knew it too, so he took yet another slow sip of tea. "But even more important than keeping the checks coming in, what he was most fearful of was losing the house. It seems Mrs. Amesbury had taken out a reverse mortgage, and that money had been used up. According to the terms of this agreement with the bank, as long as she was alive, she and Alby could live there."

Isabel wrapped it up for him. "But if and when she *stopped* being alive, and if Alby couldn't pay what was owed, the bank would foreclose."

The inspector, although not pleased about his *story* being foreclosed upon, nodded. "Exactly. Alby was terrified he would be homeless *and* penniless. He needed people to believe she was still alive, so in a panic, he planted Mum amongst the primrose."

Teddy resigned himself to Alby's story with a shrug. "Well, it's just crazy enough to believe, especially given that he's—"

"A complete nutter?" Tuppence offered up to help move the story along.

Teddy ignored her. "But, whatever the case, it doesn't mean he isn't guilty of murdering her in the first place to put his plan into motion."

"That's exactly right. We're waiting for CCTV footage from the bank where he went to do his trial run to at least verify this part of the story is true. And we're still waiting on DNA and fingerprints found on the garden hose."

"But that wouldn't implicate *him*," Isabel offered "I'm sure Alby's used that garden hose any number of times. His prints and his DNA are likely all over it."

"That's very true," the inspector agreed, "but if we find

prints or DNA on that hose that don't belong there, it may help prove he *didn't* kill her."

"Maybe they can get some prints or DNA off the body?" Teddy suggested.

"I'm told by the forensics team that being buried in the dirt may have made that difficult or corrupted any samples they can pull. And even if they did, any solicitor for the defense worth their salt would very likely be able to convince a jury it *was* corrupted."

"And what were these arguments Alby was having with Bobby Blackburn about?" Teddy asked. "How does he fit in? I have a feeling he's up to his eyeballs in this."

"That brings me to my next point, and why Bobby has been brought in for questioning. Alby claims that he and Bobby hatched this plan months ago, right after he discovered his mother's health was so fragile. He offered Bobby a cut to make sure the checks kept coming and that no suspicions were aroused. Bobby initially agreed to it, but when he learned Mrs. Amesbury was dead, he wanted a much bigger cut than had been previously agreed to."

"Have you given any thought to the possibility that Bobby might have been getting impatient and decided Hyacinth needed a little help getting to the grave?" Teddy asked, looking at Isabel for validation of this idea, which she provided with a nod.

"That's what I intend to find out. And thanks to the fact that Bobby was arrested for stealing a bike when he was a teenager, we already have his prints on file. So if they're on that garden hose, and he doesn't have a good explanation for how they got there, we likely have our murderer."

The inspector stood up to leave. "I'm going down to the station to talk to Bobby myself right now. At the very least he and Alby are both guilty of fraud, and I'll have to look up whatever the charge is for burying your mum in the garden.

But if they both end up being cleared of her murder, then we're back at square one, unless, as I said, we get DNA and or prints off that garden hose that point us to another suspect altogether. Thank you for the tea, Tuppence. I'll keep you all posted as to what I find out."

Tuppence nodded at the inspector but said nothing. Isabel noticed she was wearing an odd, slightly pensive expression on her face. She had known her long enough now to know that it was unusual, to say the least, for her ever to be quiet. Did she know something she wasn't sharing?

After Inspector Carlyle left, something odd struck Isabel. "Didn't the inspector say he wanted to ask you and Tuppence about Alby's relationship with his mother, Teddy?"

"That's what he said on the phone, yes," Teddy replied.

"But that never came up. Strange, don't you think?" Isabel was starting to question what the inspector's reason for coming by might really have been. She looked at Tuppence again. Why was she so quiet? Quiet to the point of being disconcerting. Was it possible Inspector Carlyle was looking at her now as a possible suspect, just as she and Teddy had predicted? He surely would have heard about the scone bake-off debacle by now, so he may have decided Tuppence had enough motive to strangle Hyacinth over it. Maybe, Isabel thought, he was here to observe her and test her reaction to these new developments.

"You're right, Isabel. That never came up at all. Well, as I said before, he's no Columbo." Isabel smiled at the reference. Teddy had admitted to Isabel that his famous Detective Waverly had been influenced in part by his favorite American detective, which, funnily enough, was something she had guessed when reading his books long before ever meeting him.

Isabel still didn't believe Tuppence was capable of murder, but she knew if Inspector Carlyle could attach a motive—no matter how far-fetched—he was going to have to follow up on it. But then she had another thought. Was it merely coincidence that Tuppence didn't get quiet and pensive until after the inspector told them they were waiting on forensics testing on the garden hose? If you were somebody who knew you may have left your prints or your DNA on a suspected murder weapon, well, that would certainly make you go a little quiet. And something else just dropped into the potentially suspicious-behavior column. Could Tuppence be concocting this whole notion of a Cornwall Ripper to distract attention from the real killer? Herself? She knew from her criminal psychology classes that it wasn't unusual for a guilty party to create and promote mistruths to distract and sidetrack an investigation. But still . . . Tuppence? A murderer?

Isabel was not at all happy that her mind operated like this now. Since her recent entrée into the realm of solving murders, and attempting to get inside the heads of the people committing them, would everybody become a potential suspect to her anytime somebody around them turned up dead? She suddenly felt awful for even thinking this woman who had been nothing but warm and generous with her, who had defended her when Matilde was assaulting her character, and who made the best scones she had ever eaten in her life, could be the same person who strangled somebody with a garden hose for sabotaging a container of baking soda. But, from an investigative standpoint, to simply dismiss the possibility was naive. And Tuppence did have quite an ample window of opportunity that Saturday afternoon to commit the crime.

No sooner had the inspector left than Matilde walked in. Great. As far as Isabel was concerned, if anybody around here had the temperament to strangle somebody with a hose it was this woman, and although she was the sister of her host, she could have done without seeing her this morning. But at least she didn't look like a patient in an insane asylum anymore. In fact, Matilde was unrecognizable compared with the haggard-looking shell of a woman they had seen shuffling around in an old robe and bed head. Now Matilde was dressed like an English gentlewoman, and one who thankfully had located her brush and some makeup.

Teddy was understandably thrilled to see his sister rise from the nearly dead. "Could this be my sister, Matilde? You look fantastic! Welcome back to the land of the living!"

"Let's not, shall we, Theodore? I just wanted to stop by to let you know that I'm leaving for London today."

Teddy made a face. "Why? What do you have going on in London?"

"I have some private business to attend to," she said in a tone that left no room for a follow-up question from her brother.

"How very mysterious," Teddy teased her. "Is Hugo going with you?"

She stared at him for a moment. "Don't be ridiculous. I told you there is nothing going on between Hugo and me. We're old friends, nothing more. If you *must* know, I have an appointment with my broker. I'm considering selling some stocks and buying myself a little place in Spain. Somewhere along the Costa del Sol, I think would be nice."

Teddy looked perplexed. "But you hate Spain."

"What are you talking about? I never said I hated Spain. It's a beautiful country."

"You don't have to sell me. I love Spain. But I remember specifically your saying—after coming back from a vacation in Spain some years ago—the words 'I hate Spain.' I remember because I thought it was such a ridiculous thing to say about such a beautiful place. I hate Liverpool? Okay. But Spain?"

Matilde was clearly annoyed by her brother's memory. "Well, people change, Theodore. I need some sunshine in my life. This dreary English weather is slowly depleting me of my will to live."

"That's rather dramatic, my dear, don't you think?"

"Life is dramatic, Theodore."

"Yes, it is. But let's be honest. Rainy weather is not what has precipitated this decision. No pun intended."

Isabel wished she could find a graceful way to escape this conversation. None of this was her business, and she didn't care to witness Matilde snapping again. She looked around for Fred and Ginger. Where did they go? And, come to think of it, where had Tuppence gone?

Matilde continued making her case to her brother. "Look, Theodore, one of my oldest friends has been murdered, and the one great love of my life, the one who left me for that murdered friend—a betrayal it has taken me decades to forgive—has returned and, yes, perhaps he has dredged up some painful memories from a time in my life that I've spent the *rest* of my life trying to forget. So, no, this is not a decision based solely on the weather, but I do think introducing more sunshine into a life that has been as overcast as mine has been of late is probably a healthy decision. And I would appreciate your support in that decision."

Wait. What? Had Matilde just become vulnerable before Isabel's very eyes? Now she was glad she stayed for this, because she suddenly felt a pang of sympathy for a woman toward whom she had until this very moment felt nothing but well-controlled animosity. "I'm sorry if I'm interjecting where I shouldn't, but, Matilde, I just want to say that I think this is very brave of you. I admire your decision to take control of your life and open a new chapter."

Matilde looked at her in a way that at first made Isabel think she should not have interjected, but then her face softened. "Thank you, Isabel. And I'm afraid I owe you an apology for allowing my recent personal struggles to affect my behavior toward you and in *any* way make you feel unwelcome."

In every way, Isabel said to herself, but she put that aside for now. "I understand this has been a difficult time for you, Matilde, so please don't be too hard on yourself. We all have bad days."

"You're being more gracious than I deserve, but thank you, Isabel."

Teddy was obviously pleased with his sister's about-face. "I'm proud of you, Matilde. If what you feel you need in your life right now is a place of your own in Spain, I support you wholeheartedly. When you're ready to go look, I'll be happy to come with you."

"Thank you, Theodore. That would be lovely. And you of course will be welcome anytime. As will you, Isabel. Now, where is Tuppence? She must be out somewhere, because she would never miss the opportunity to insert herself into this conversation."

"That's a good question. She didn't say she was leaving but maybe she's popped down to the shops. Or she may be in the garden. I'll check," Teddy said before going out the back door, followed by Matilde.

Isabel looked out the back window and saw no sign of Tuppence, but she did see Teddy open the door to the guest-house and hear him call out her name. He then closed the door and shook his head at Matilde. Isabel did a quick sweep of the house and also called her name a couple of times. Nothing. She opened the front door next and noticed her bike was gone. Oh, dear . . . Here was that nagging suspicion rearing its ugly head again. Tuppence's disappearing act didn't look great coming on the heels of what Inspector Carlyle had just reported about the impending forensics report, but then it was hardly a glaring indication of guilt either. Maybe she and Teddy had underestimated Inspector Carlyle's investigative prowess, though. Perhaps he was baiting her. And perhaps Tuppence had just taken the bait.

Fred and Ginger appeared at Isabel's feet and looked up at

her. It was time for their morning walk and they were obviously growing impatient. She decided she could use some air too, so she opened the back door, where Teddy and Matilde were sitting on the patio, deep in conversation. "Teddy! Sorry to interrupt, but I'm going to take Fred and Ginger for their walk. You two carry on!" Teddy waved and thanked her. Matilde forced a smile.

Once they passed through the front gate of Pembroke Cottage, Fred and Ginger started tugging Isabel toward their usual, pre-murder route past Amesbury Acreage. She gave them a gentle tug on their leashes and turned them around. "No, we're going this way today," she said to them, and began walking them toward the narrow, hedge-trimmed lane that led to Tuppence's cottage. If she had left work so abruptly to go home, Isabel wanted to make sure she was okay.

What she was not looking for, she told herself firmly, were clues that Tuppence might be guilty of Hyacinth's murder. In fact, just the opposite. She wanted to rule her out, in her mind at least. Who knew what was going through Inspector Carlyle's mind, but that wasn't her business anyway.

Tuppence's bike was not parked in its usual spot in front of her cottage, but Isabel decided to knock on the front door anyway. No answer. Before she turned around to leave, Fred and Ginger began to bark at a small car pulling into the driveway. She realized it was the same car that had been parked in front of Matilde's house the other day. She couldn't make out who was driving, but when he got out, Isabel was immediately taken with his appearance. He was a tall, handsome man and quite fit for someone who looked to be around sixtyish. He wore his gray hair short, had on a pair of sporty-looking sunglasses, which he lifted and perched above his forehead when he got out, and was dressed casually in a sweater and blue jeans. She instinctively knew it was Hugo.

Chapter 17

"**Y**ou must be Isabel. Excuse me, Mrs. Puddles?"

"I am. But please call me Isabel. And you must be Hugo. I've heard a lot about you."

He smiled warmly. "As I have you, Isabel. I ran into Tuppence in the village yesterday and she had very nice things to say about you."

Great. Now she felt even *more* guilty for having such evil suspicions about her. They shook hands, and Hugo bent down to say hello to Fred and Ginger. He stood up and looked toward the house. "I thought I might catch Tuppence at home."

"I was hoping the same. But I just knocked and there was no answer. And her bike isn't here."

"I see. Have you perhaps seen Matilde? Nobody's at home at the Captain's Cottage either."

"I saw her just a short while ago at Teddy's. She said she was on her way to London, but I don't know whether she's left or not."

Hugo looked a little lost. "I was hoping to catch her before she left and ask her if she might reconsider."

"Reconsider?"

"Oh . . . I thought you may have heard. Never mind. I guess I'll be on my way. It was lovely to meet you, Isabel."

Isabel stopped herself from saying *Oh, no, you don't* out loud, but she couldn't let him get away after dropping that little morsel. "I'm really not sure what you're talking about, Hugo. I've heard nothing. And I don't mean to be nosy, but maybe if I knew more about what was going on between the two of you, I could be of some help?" Isabel had just surprised herself at what a shameless attempt to extract information *that* was. She knew what was going on between them was none of *her* business, but maybe she could bring some useful intelligence back to Teddy. It was definitely *his* business. And, well, okay, she *might* be just a little bit curious too.

"I wish I knew what was going on between us." Hugo took a deep breath and exhaled with a sad resignation. "I've been in love with that woman since I was sixteen years old. Matilde Mansfield was the sweetest and prettiest girl in Cornwall. Summers were always brighter and warmer when Matilde was here."

Were they talking about the same Matilde Mansfield? She may have been sweet at one time, but all Isabel had ever seen was sour, at least until this morning, when she had seen a gentler side. And her apology did seem sincere. So she was giving her the benefit of the doubt for Teddy's sake, but Matilde's past behavior was a bell that would take some time to unring. Isabel Puddles was a forgiving person by nature, but forgetting was something else. Once her guard went up, it tended to stay up for a while.

"I did hear what happened between you and Matilde when you were kids," she said. "Teddy told me about it. It's very sad when two young people in love are separated by outside forces."

"Between Matilde's mum and dad and Hyacinth, the outside forces were more like an all-out ground offensive." Hugo chuckled slightly in the way people do when something isn't funny.

This was the part that had confused Isabel when she first heard about this love triangle between Hugo, Matilde, and Hyacinth, so now was the time to ask. "Hugo, if you were in love with Matilde, and she was in love with you, how did you ever end up with Hyacinth?"

"Good question. And I wish I had a better answer. I knew Matilde's parents would never approve of me or ever approve of our getting married because they told me so. Matilde said she didn't care, but she did. I really didn't want to be the reason she fell out with her family, but I wasn't going to be bullied by them either. My mum and dad were against it too, by the way. They thought the Mansfields were a bit too posh and snobbish. Her mum and dad *were*—especially her mum. You would have thought that she was to the manor born. But Matilde and Ted weren't. Also, we were Catholic and they were Church of England. That mattered back in those days. I was torn up about it, but I was also angry. So as long as Matilde was willing, I was willing. If I had to fight for the woman I loved, and stand up to her parents, my parents, the Catholic Church, and the Church of England too—I was ready to do it. And I would have, if Hyacinth hadn't gotten into the middle of everything with her evil lies and deception."

Wow . . . Hugo was really spilling his guts here. This was becoming high drama. And Isabel was all ears. "And how did she go about that, Hugo?"

Hugo seemed almost relieved to be talking about this, even to somebody he had met only five minutes before. "When Matilde's mum and dad sent her to Paris—to get her away from me—I was gutted. I was ready to go to Paris to be with her regardless of the fact that I didn't have two pence to rub together. But I made the mistake of telling Hyacinth my plan. Then, lo and behold, a week or two later, she told me she had received a letter from Matilde saying she had fallen in love with some rich French bloke in Paris, and that she was asking her advice on how to tell me it was over."

"Which obviously was a lie," Isabel added.

Hugo nodded. "Yes, but I didn't know it was a lie. I should have asked to see the letter, but it just never occurred to me that anybody could be wicked enough to tell such a lie as that. So I believed her. I was completely shattered, but I was also quite angry at Matilde. And that's when Hyacinth made her next move. She was relentless in trying to convince me that we were meant for each other. She'd always chased after me, even after Matilde and I were together. It was embarrassing. But I was never interested in her in the slightest and told her so *many* times. And that just made her angrier and angrier. Anyway, one night I had a few too many pints with the boys down at the Lion after a cricket match, and Hyacinth showed up . . . and you can probably figure out what happened from there."

Not a real brain teaser, no. Isabel kind of figured this was where the story was going, and she had an idea about where it was going next.

"A month later she tells me she's having a baby. Mine."

Yep. That's exactly where she thought the story was going next.

"My mum and dad were, as I said, not just Catholic but *very* Catholic. They told me I had no choice but to marry Hyacinth. So I proposed. It was one of the worst days of my life, asking a girl I really didn't even like very much to marry me when the woman I loved was in Paris and in love with somebody else. I was eighteen years old and it felt like my life was over."

This was like a Cornish *Romeo and Juliet*! It was all even sadder than Isabel had imagined. "And how long was it before Hyacinth broke off your engagement?"

"Once she knew the damage was done, and she had ruined my relationship with Matilde, she was done with me."

"Why do you think she went to such extremes? I mean that really is just pure evil to do something like that."

"Who knows why she did it? Spite? Jealousy? She was determined to see to it that if she couldn't have me, Matilde couldn't, either. She just couldn't accept me choosing Matilde over her. Which was about as difficult a choice to make as 'Would you like an ice cream or would you rather I knock you in the head with this brick?' And did I mention there was no baby. That was a lie too."

Isabel had seen this coming too. Trapping a man into marriage that way wasn't the most original method, but it did take a special kind of deception and dishonesty and, in her case, wickedness. Poor Hugo.

"I do remember her saying, after all the lies were exposed, that she would never have married the son of a butcher. She planned to find herself a rich husband. But she rather fell short of that. I guess a husband who sold washers and dryers was the best she could do."

"And did you try to talk to Matilde and make her understand what happened?" Isabel couldn't get over how sad this story was. Or how vile and sinister Hyacinth was.

"The next thing I knew, she was engaged to some chap from Oxford. I figured it was the same one she met in Paris and had written to Hyacinth about."

"Apparently that didn't work out very well."

"So I heard. But by then it was too late for Matilde and me." Hugo took a reflective pause. "I had no reason to stay in Mousehole after that. I didn't want to be a butcher, which was my only real option here. So I left and joined the Royal Navy."

"Did you ever get married, Hugo?"

"I did, but that didn't work out very well either. Ten years after that ship sunk, I tried again, but with the same result."

"I'm sorry to hear that. . . . Just curious; when did you find out Hyacinth was lying about the letter?"

Hugo hesitated before answering. "When I saw Matilde for the first time last week, she seemed genuinely happy to see me. And I was thrilled to see her again. We took a walk through the village like we used to. It was as if no time had passed at all. Like we had picked up right where we'd left off. It was lovely. I thought maybe, even after all these years, if I asked her to marry me, she might say yes. But I still needed to know about the letter. So when I went to see her Saturday morning, I finally worked up the nerve to ask her about it. That's when she told me she had never written such a letter. There *was* nobody in Paris. So then I asked her why she never returned any of the letters I sent her in Paris, which all came back to me marked 'return to sender.' I asked her over and over again in those letters who this other man was and did she really love him more than she loved me. If she had just read even one of those letters, we both would have known it was all a lie. But she said after her parents told her I was engaged to Hyacinth, she was too hurt to read them. She just wanted to cut me out of her life for good. And she did. She stayed an extra year in Paris, and by the time she got back, I was long gone, stationed in Hong Kong."

Isabel found this whole story about the letter not only shocking but terribly depressing. "So you and Matilde only learned about this imaginary letter a few *days* ago?"

"Yes. A letter that never existed, invented out of sheer maliciousness by a horrible person, cost us each other. Cost us our lives together. Who knows how different our lives might have been had we just been left alone? I'm sure we would still be married to this day, and have not only kids but grandkids. I confronted Hyacinth about it when I saw her in the village after the bake-off. You know what she said? 'Get over it.' She laughed and told me to get over it. Now, I know what you are very likely thinking, Isabel. But, no, I didn't murder her. Given the opportunity, though, I might have. And I don't mind telling you that I would not have felt an ounce of remorse. And because I was sure people had seen Hyacinth and me having words in the village, I knew I would be the perfect suspect. That's why I called Inspector Carlyle to tell him all about it, so he came out to my niece's farm to ask me a few questions. I offered to cooperate in any way I could. When he asked for my fingerprints and a DNA swab, I was more than happy to oblige. I also told him if and when he caught the killer to please let me know. I might like to bring a cake to them in jail."

Isabel heard a car coming down the lane. She turned around to see it was Teddy. He tooted his horn as he pulled into the drive and parked the Iron Lady next to Hugo's car.

Hugo smiled warmly when he saw Teddy get out of his car. "Hello again, Ted. It's been a while."

Teddy smiled back and walked over to shake Hugo's hand, which turned into a hug. "It has indeed . . . How have you been, Hugo?"

"Oh, you know . . . a few decades older but none the wiser, I'm afraid."

"You just missed Matilde. . . . She's on her way to London."

"And then on to Spain, from what I gather? I knew she would probably turn me down, but I didn't expect her to flee the country."

"You did catch her off guard, but she's not fleeing the country just yet. She'll be back in a day or two. Matilde and I had a chat this morning. I think she just needs to take some time to think about your proposal."

Hugo shrugged his shoulder and looked at the ground. "She already turned me down, so I don't know what there is for her to think about. But I can't say as I blame her."

Teddy shook his head. "I just don't think she's in a great place right now, and I'm not exactly sure what's wrong. Just give her a little time, Hugo. She might come around."

"Well at least we finally know the truth about what really happened. . . . Shame it was forty-something years later, but still better than never knowing. I think, anyway."

Teddy looked puzzled. Whatever the truth about what really happened *was*, she didn't share it with him. He was about to ask Hugo what he meant by that, but he lost his chance. "Isabel, it was lovely to meet you, and lovely to see you again, Ted. But I have to run." Hugo looked at his watch. "I'm picking up my grand-niece and grand-nephew at school and taking them for an ice cream." And with that, Hugo got into his car and drove away with a wave and a friendly toot of the horn.

"What a sweet man," Isabel said to Teddy. "Just so sad what happened between him and Matilde. It doesn't seem as though he's ever gotten over it."

"I always liked Hugo. . . . I think he would have made my sister a fine husband. Now, are you going to tell me what they finally know the truth about that I apparently do *not*?"

She patted him on the back. "I'll tell you when we get back." She looked down at Fred and Ginger. "These two have been very patient, so we need to get them home and get them some treats." That got their stubby little tails wagging. "I'll see you shortly, hon." Did she just call Teddy "hon"?

Tuppence was still out when Isabel and the dogs got back to Pembroke Cottage. Teddy then told Isabel he thought she might have told him she had shopping to do. "She never stops talking, so I'll admit I don't always listen."

But in the spirit of *trust but verify*, Isabel had a suggestion. "How about we call her just to make sure she's all right?"

Teddy laughed. "The woman refuses to carry a mobile

phone. I offered to give her one of mine, but she says she's afraid of the microwave transmissions. Won't let me have a microwave in the kitchen either. If I want to microwave anything, I have to go out to the garage. But I think it's more because she doesn't want me calling her when she's not at work or on her days off. Which I suppose I can't blame her for."

"At some point we all have to drink the Kool-Aid, Teddy," Isabel said with a twinge of defeat in her voice. "I fought valiantly against having a cell phone for as long as I could. But I've gotten used to it now. Begrudgingly. You know what else I miss? Busy signals. Remember when you would call somebody, and if you got a busy signal, it meant they were *busy*. So you hung up and said to yourself, 'Well, I guess I'll try them again later,' easy peasy."

Teddy was on the same page when it came to this topic. "Fiona carried a mobile, but I don't think I ever called her on it. And she never bothered calling me on the home phone when she was out because I always unplugged the phone while I was working and rarely remembered to plug it back in. It used to drive the poor woman bonkers. And please don't get me going on texting . . . that practice is slowly—or maybe not so slowly—chipping away at civilization as we know it. The spoken word will one day cease to exist and humans will be communicating via text messages and emojis only. My grandkids can barely form complete sentences anymore as it is."

Isabel didn't see things quite so apocalyptically, but she agreed in principle. "I would have been very happy to have never owned a cell phone, but when everybody else does, it becomes almost impossible *not* to. I just don't understand why they were invented. After using a regular telephone for roughly half a century, I never once thought to myself, 'You know, if I could only fit this yellow slim-line push button phone into my purse and take it with me everywhere I go so that anybody who wants to call me can do so twenty-four hours a day, seven days a week, my life would be complete.'"

Teddy laughed. "You're a funny lady, Isabel Puddles. My daughter, Elizabeth, finally demanded I get one or she threatened to attach a GPS device to my ankle. It was a bit like finally surrendering to jam first, clotted cream next. At some point you're just too knackered to stay in the fight."

"Sometimes a dignified surrender is your best bet."

"Oh! Forgive me, Isabel. I'm afraid I have, what it is you say? Buried the lede?" Isabel's expression turned quizzical. Teddy smiled and continued. "Barclay called me in the car. There's been an interesting development in our favorite local murder case. Apparently somebody saw Tiegan pulling out of Amesbury Acreage in Nigel's Rolls-Royce sometime on Saturday, after the bake-off. Nigel may or may not have been in the back, they couldn't tell."

This *was* an interesting development. "Hmm. So is Inspector Carlyle thinking they may be involved in Hyacinth's murder?"

"He was on his way to talk to them when he dropped by here. I can't imagine they did her in, but I would certainly be curious to know why they were there. There was no love lost between Nigel and Hyacinth. She had been quite vocal about opposing him in the last election. The one he lost. She wrote a letter to the editor printed in the *Mousehole Messenger* that was scathing. Unnecessarily so."

"Motive enough to murder her? How long has it been since the election?"

"About two years now, I guess."

"They do say revenge is best served cold, but that seems a bit *too* cold, doesn't it to you, Teddy?" This was getting complicated. It might be easier at this point to start identifying who in Mousehole *didn't* have motive to kill this woman.

Isabel was seriously thinking about taking pen to paper and starting a list of suspects and possible motives for murder. It was all becoming very Agatha Christie.

"Nigel's not really the murdering type," Teddy said with confidence. "*Tiegan*, on the other hand . . . She's an assassin behind the wheel of that Rolls. Who knows what she might be capable of on foot? But we shall see what the inspector finds out. All right, now, I want to hear about Hugo and my sister and this recently revealed truth."

After Isabel told him everything Hugo had just shared with her and described how sad and forlorn he had been in retelling the story, Teddy was dumbfounded. He had never heard anything about a letter, or anything about his sister falling in love with someone else in Paris. "That's patently absurd," he said, "she was over the moon for Hugo." Teddy remembered all too well how devastated Matilde was after finding out Hugo and Hyacinth were engaged. And, yes, he also remembered hearing the rumors about Hugo and Hyacinth's engagement having less to do with love and more to do with pregnancy, but he didn't know if Matilde ever had. Teddy couldn't get over what Hyacinth had wrought on this young couple, and for what? "If she's just now finding out about all this deception and duplicity, it's no wonder she's been unraveling these past few days," Teddy said, shaking his head. "I never liked Hyacinth. Never trusted her, as I think I mentioned to you. But I never imagined she could be *so* diabolical. That woman ruined my sister's life." Teddy was fuming. "You know what? After hearing this, I don't care who killed her anymore. In fact, if or when they do catch the person who strangled her, I might like to offer them some tea!"

So now Teddy wanted to offer the murderer tea, and Hugo wanted to bring them a cake in jail. These were not the types of things you typically heard from people familiar with the murder victim. If this was what the village thought collectively about whoever killed Hyacinth Amesbury, there may eventually be a statue in the town center erected in their honor.

Isabel suddenly began to feel her gears clicking into place and Teddy could see it. "What is it, Isabel?"

"Just thinking . . . If Matilde only learned about all this from Hugo after he got back, I can certainly see why that might send her into a spiral." Isabel Puddles the investigator was formulating a theory, but she couldn't let Teddy know what she was thinking, at least not until she had something more to go on than instinct. But even then, how do you tell your host that you think it's very possible his sister is a murderer?

Chapter 18

Teddy had some errands to run, but Isabel wanted to stay behind and wait for Tuppence to get home. So Teddy went on his way, and a few minutes later, Tuppence walked in the door looking and sounding more like herself.

"Hello, Isabel, shall I put the kettle on?" she asked nonchalantly, offering no explanation as to where she had disappeared to for so long. It wasn't as if she owed her an explanation, but Isabel was far too curious not to ask.

"Tea would be lovely, thank you, Tuppence. Not to be nosy"—she had lost track of how many times she had used that line before asking a nosy question—"but where have you been all this time? I was beginning to worry."

"I had a little marketing to do and then I stopped off to see Inspector Carlyle. He was out, but I spoke to one of the detective constables and told her I wanted to give them my fingerprints and a DNA sample."

Isabel wasn't sure she had heard her right. Had Inspector Carlyle asked her to come in or had she volunteered? She was thinking about how to ask her that when Tuppence continued. "After hearing what the inspector said this morning about forensic testing likely determining who the killer was, I figured I would offer, just to take myself out of the running. I know I didn't kill the old bat, so what did I have to be afraid of? But, given how furious I was with her on the very same day she was murdered, I knew I would eventually become a suspect, so why not beat them to the punch?"

"That was very clever of you, Tuppence." Isabel was quite impressed. And the thought that this was something a guilty person who wore gloves when committing the murder might do only flashed in her brain for a nanosecond.

"And I remembered saying to you and Mr. M. that I *wanted* to strangle her. And in that moment, if she had been here, I wouldn't have needed a garden hose. I could have done it with my bare hands. Of course, I knew the two of you would never suspect me, but there was no reason the inspector wouldn't."

Isabel was ashamed of herself, so ashamed in fact that she almost came clean about her previous suspicions, but she decided it would serve no purpose other than to hurt her feelings. "Of course not, Tuppence! Never even crossed my mind. Or Teddy's." Yes, she was lying, and no, she didn't feel great about it, but Isabel firmly believed there were times in life when lying was an absolute necessity if the intention behind the lie was to spare another person's feelings. And, as was the case here, if she could spare herself humiliation at the same time, well, two birds and all . . .

What was weighing on her mind now was how she could surreptitiously gather enough evidence on Matilde to break the news to Teddy that—at the very least—his sister needed to be thoroughly investigated. Maybe the thing to do, albeit the cowardly thing to do, was to take whatever information or evidence she could find straight to Inspector Carlyle and let *him* be the bad guy. But she would decide that later. For now, she was going to compile a mental list of reasons why Matilde had now become her prime suspect, and how she could find the evidence to prove it.

First of all, Matilde had an obvious motive. If, after all these years, she had only just learned from Hugo that Hyacinth had lied to him about her falling in love with somebody else in Paris, and then tricked him into getting engaged to her by lying about being pregnant, she may very well have decided it was time to settle the score. Strangling her with a garden hose probably wasn't the best way to go about it, but it would tick the box. But, as had been mentioned once or twice, the number of people who might want to do harm to Hyacinth Amesbury was practically at take-a-number levels, so motive alone wasn't going to be enough.

The circumstantial evidence was mounting though too. What was this sudden urge to leave the country and go to Spain all about? To decide to do so less than a week after Hyacinth turned up dead was certainly coincidental. *And* she was on record, with her own brother, to not even like the place. Was she thinking she might need a place to hide out if the investigation reached a little too close to home?

And what about her bizarre behavior when they went to see her on the day Hyacinth's body was discovered? To say she was blasé about the news her old friend had been murdered didn't begin to cover it. In Isabel's book, *that* was suspicious enough. Yes, the Brits were well known for their stiff upper lips, but it was hard to imagine anybody could keep their upper lip that stiff under such circumstances. She took it about as hard as hearing from the waiter that they had just run out of the liver and onions special. And, looking back on that conversation she and Tuppence eavesdropped on, why was her first question "Do they know who did it?" Not that this wouldn't be a question you would ask, but would it be the very first? Although she certainly hoped never to find herself in this position, she was pretty sure her first question would be *how*? Maybe followed by *when*? And *then*, do they know who did it? It was a little thing, but it was still a thing that gave her pause.

But then came the real clincher. This was what finally caused the oxygen masks to drop, and she was feeling slightly embarrassed that it took so long for it to finally dawn on her. If Matilde had such a terrible phobia of serial killers, and being murdered in her sleep, then why—after being told Hyacinth's murderer was still on the loose—wouldn't she have immediately moved into Teddy's guest room where she would be safe? Instead, she seemed perfectly fine staying in her house alone, even after learning that a body had just been found buried in a shallow grave only a stone's throw from her house. Isabel could not come up with any explanation for Matilde's sudden conquering of her serial killer phobia other than her knowing there *was* no serial killer, because *she* was the killer! What did she have to be afraid of?

But again, this was all circumstantial, and barely so. She knew what she needed to do next was figure out a way to get Matilde's fingerprints and a DNA sample and get it to Inspector Carlyle. That would be easy enough if she could get into Matilde's house while she was away, but short of breaking and entering, how was she going to manage that? And manage it without Teddy's knowing. Maybe, she thought, Tuppence had put Matilde's house key someplace where she could find it, and she could sneak down later. Surely Matilde had more than the one hairbrush she took with her to London, and a brush would provide a perfect DNA sample, and fingerprints too.

After her chat with Tuppence, Isabel went back to the guest house to find her emergency stash of ibuprofen. She was not someone typically prone to headaches, but if ever there was a situation to cause one, this was it. And it had.

When she walked back into the main house, she planned to do a casual sweep of the kitchen when Tuppence wasn't looking, but she scrapped her mission when she heard Teddy and Inspector Carlyle talking in the living room. When she walked in to say hello, she nearly bumped into Tuppence, who was eavesdropping in the foyer while pretending to dust. Isabel decided not to interrupt the men and hovered there with Tuppence.

"I'm afraid I find myself in an uncomfortable situation, Teddy," the inspector began somewhat timidly. "It's my understanding that there may have been some bad blood between Hyacinth and your sister, and that they recently had a falling-out. I'm sure you understand that I'll need to talk to her, just as a procedural matter."

"Of course, I completely understand, Barclay. But Matilde and Hyacinth fell out with each other constantly. It had been going on since they were girls. They were not speaking to each other one day, and best friends again the next day. But I do recall they had fallen out again recently over something. What it was about, I have no idea. If I'm being honest, I never paid any attention. I'm sure when you do find out, you'll find it very silly."

"I went by your sister's house a little while ago but she was not at home. Do you know where I might find her?"

"I'm afraid she's gone to London. She had some personal business. I expect her back in a few days, though. Would you like me to ask her to call you?"

"No, I'm happy to wait until she gets back. But if you could let her know I would very much like to speak with her, I would appreciate it. It's just procedure, Teddy."

"I understand, Barclay. It's a murder investigation. You need to cross her off your list. I know she will be most cooperative."

Or move her to the top of your list, Isabel said to herself.

"Thank you, Teddy. And thank you for your help."

Tuppence and Isabel both ducked out of the foyer and scooted into the kitchen before they were caught. "Pleasure as always," they heard Teddy say as he opened the front door. After sending the inspector off, he came into the kitchen with a look on his face that was hard to read.

"Tuppence, do you recall what Matilde and Hyacinth's most recent falling-out was about?"

"Impossible to say, Lordship. Those two were like a pair of mountain goats, always locking horns over something."

"That's what I told the inspector. He has apparently learned about their latest." Teddy looked over at Isabel. "Oh, well. I'm not going to worry about it. I'm sure it's nothing. Isabel? Shall we take Fred and Ginger for a walk?"

"That sounds delightful. It's such a beautiful day," she answered. She could see Teddy had something weighing on his mind, and she was pretty sure she knew what it was.

When they returned from their walk, having enjoyed the afternoon sun and some pleasant conversation, Teddy suddenly remembered he had a dinner scheduled with his editor that evening. He invited Isabel to join them, but included fair warning that it was going to be a lot of author-editor business talk, so she would likely be pretty bored. She agreed without saying so and told him she was happy to stay in and relax with Fred and Ginger. In reality, she had another plan . . . something rather covert.

After Tuppence wrapped up her day and went home, and Teddy left for his dinner, Isabel went into the kitchen to look for Matilde's house key again. She spotted a single key in a glass jar in the pantry, and attached to it was a tag with the letter *M.* That *must* be it. She slipped it into her pocket and went back to the guesthouse.

The plan she had devised was to wait until it got dark, then sneak down to Matilde's, go upstairs to her bathroom, and take either a comb or a hairbrush or whatever would provide the forensic evidence she needed or what Inspector Carlyle needed. Isabel hated going behind Teddy's back like this, and she knew he would most likely find out because the inspector seemed happy to share virtually every imaginable detail of the investigation with him. She could probably find a way to deliver the brush or whatever she found to the inspector anonymously, but that was cowardly. It might, however, spare her from a potential burglary charge. She decided she could jump off that bridge when she got to it. The first order of business was to get in, find what she was after, and get out.

When she opened the front door to leave, Fred and Ginger looked quite hurt when they realized she was leaving without them. Ginger even tried to pull her leash off the hook on the back of the door but couldn't quite manage it. "I'll take you out when I get back. I promise," she told them, avoiding eye contact. She was already up to her neck with guilt lately; she didn't need these two adding to it.

When she got to Matilde's house, the Captain's Cottage, Isabel looked around to make sure nobody could see her walking up to the front door. She was feeling quite sneaky. After she put in the key, it was quickly apparent it wasn't the right one. Maybe it was the key to the back door? She slinked around the side of the house and tried the back door. It didn't fit there either, but as she fiddled with the doorknob, the door opened on its own. Turned out it was not even locked. But then Matilde did probably have a lot on her mind when she raced off to London.

The house was dark, but because it was a full moon, there was just enough light coming through the windows to light the way to the staircase. She climbed up the creaking stairs cautiously. It was unnerving enough just knowing she was poking around in someone else's house in the dark when she wasn't supposed to be there, but the creepy factor was heightened even more because, thanks to Tuppence, the possibility that there really was a serial killer on the loose was one she couldn't completely shake. Maybe she was completely wrong about Matilde. Or maybe Matilde was a serial killer! She stopped, took a deep breath, refocused, and continued up the steps.

It was much darker on the second floor, and Isabel wished she had a flashlight, or at least a match. As she rounded the top of the stairs and turned toward Matilde's room, she heard something. She froze for a few seconds and listened for it again. Probably just the wind, she told herself, which was, of course, what people always told themselves when they heard a strange sound they couldn't identify. Isabel had always wondered how many people who thought they had just heard the wind had actually just heard a potential killer coming into their house. She turned and took a few steps back down the stairs until she came to her senses and turned back. Just as she reached Matilde's room, a dark figure jumped out screaming bloody murder. Isabel, paralyzed with fear, screamed bloody murder back. The figure was coming toward her and seemed to be pointing something at her. *Well, this is it,* Isabel said to herself. This is where it ends; strangled to death, or shot, at the hands of the Cornwall Ripper while in the middle of committing a home robbery. Terrific. She could already imagine what the headline on the *Gull Harbor Gazette* would read: "Isabel Puddles Meets Her Maker in Mousehole." They loved alliteration at the *Gazette*.

"Whoever you are, you better run for your life!" a voice yelled from the dark. "I have a gun and I'll be quite happy to put a bullet right through you!"

Isabel finally caught her breath. "Tuppence?"

"Isabel?"

"Yes! Please don't put a bullet through me!" she yelled, while an overwhelming wave of relief coursed through her body. The upstairs hall light suddenly came on, leaving them both squinting. Isabel looked down to see Tuppence holding a hairbrush in a gloved hand. "Is that what you were going to shoot me with?"

"It's not loaded," Tuppence replied as she began to explain not only why she was holding the brush but also what she was doing in Matilde's bedroom in the dark. "I guess I have no choice but to spill it. I began to have a terrible, sinking feeling that our Matilde might have been the one who murdered Hyacinth. I fought it because I felt guilty for even thinking it." Isabel could relate to that feeling. "But I felt like I needed some real evidence before I could take things any further. Hence the brush. Please don't tell Mr. M. you found me here."

"I promise I will not. If you'll do the same."

"Deal. Now, may I ask what *you're* doing here?"

"I'm here for the same reason as you. In fact, I was here to retrieve the same thing you're holding in your hand."

Tuppence let out a sigh. "Fingerprints and DNA? So you think she might have done it too? I'm so relieved I'm not alone in this. I mean, I can't believe she would do it, but on the other hand, I *can* believe she would do it, especially given the strange way she's been acting since Hyacinth was pulled out of her primrose patch the other day. You know, I'm obviously no friend of the deceased, but my concern now is that Alby is going to take the blame for something he didn't do. I'm also, as you know, not an ardent supporter of his, either, but fair is fair."

"What exactly aroused *your* suspicions about Matilde, Tuppence?"

"I've had this nagging question that I just can't get out of my head. . . . Why, with Matilde's phobia about serial killers and being murdered in her sleep, why—"

"Why did she seem perfectly fine staying here alone after learning Hyacinth's murder *might* be the work of a serial killer?"

"Exactly! I have not been able to get it out of my head! I was surprised she didn't get dressed and drive straight to London that night. When she wouldn't accept Mr. M.'s offer to stay in his guest room, I knew something was very fishy. The only way that reaction makes *any* sense to me is that she either killed Hyacinth or she knows who did. So what was there to worry about?"

"Other than worry about being arrested for first-degree murder," Isabel offered.

"Yes, there's that. That would send you under the covers for a few days, that would. And what was all this talk about Spain? I never *once* heard her mention Spain! And she *hates* the sun! Hard to believe she suddenly had a craving for paella and a suntan."

Isabel chuckled but then quickly got serious. "My concern—and I know it's yours as well—is, what do we tell Teddy about our suspicions? Or *do* we tell him?"

"I think he needs to know," Tuppence replied, "but I don't think he needs to hear it from either of us."

Isabel looked down at Tuppence's hand. "I assume you were planning to take that brush to Inspector Carlyle, then?"

"When I heard him say he was waiting to find out if there were fingerprints or DNA on that garden hose, well, like I told you, I wanted to make sure I never became a suspect. You can't unring that bell in a village this size. Tongues would always wag over that. But the next thing I thought was getting him those samples from Matilde. I figured a hairbrush would do the trick, same as you, I guess."

"So do we get that brush to the inspector anonymously? Or do we take it to him and share our suspicions off the record?"

Tuppence was confused and clearly exasperated. "If we're right about this, Mr. M.'s going to be heartbroken. Matilde Mansfield is not an easy one to love, but that man dearly loves his sister." Tuppence took a moment. "How about we sleep on it? I'll take the brush home with me tonight and then let's figure out what we're going to do with it in the morning."

"I think that's a good plan. And, by the way, I have a sneaking suspicion that Mr. M. is beginning to come around to the same conclusion as us."

Isabel hated being in this position, and she knew Tuppence did too, but murder was murder, even if you didn't think much of the murderee.

When she got back to Pembroke Cottage, Isabel took Fred and Ginger out for a walk, just as she had promised. They hadn't gotten much beyond the front gate when she saw headlights coming down the road. She was relieved to see it was Teddy in the Iron Lady. He tooted his horn as he pulled in, and the dogs tugged her over so that they could greet him.

"How was your dinner?" Isabel asked after he got out of the car and leaned down to give Fred and Ginger some love.

"Good. Productive. But you would have been bored to tears."

Isabel sensed a distance with Teddy. He didn't seem himself, which of course led her to believe he had indeed been thinking along the same lines as she and Tuppence had been about Matilde. Isabel didn't have any siblings, but if she did, and she suspected one of them might be a murderer, she imagined it would come as quite a shock, not to mention make for a stressful Thanksgiving dinner, especially when it came time to carve the turkey.

"I have class in the morning and I need to do some reading before bed, so I am going to retire early."

"Please go ahead to bed, Teddy. I'm exhausted, so I'm happy to retire now myself. I'll see you in the morning. Sleep well."

"You too, Isabel. I'll see you in the morning. Sweet dreams."

The next morning at breakfast, Teddy was even more distant. Tuppence and Isabel exchanged a glance as she poured their coffee. "What would you like for breakfast, Lordship? Pancakes? An omelet? Or do you fancy a full English?"

Teddy looked pained. "I think just coffee for me this morning, Tuppence." His cell phone rang, and he grabbed for it a lot faster than he usually did. "Excuse me," he said to Isabel, "I'm just going to pop into the living room to take this."

As soon as he left the room, Tuppence rushed over and got close enough to hear. She turned to look at Isabel as she listened, then, looking alarmed, spun around and ran back into the kitchen, followed only seconds later by Teddy, who was still on the phone. After saying thank you and goodbye to whomever he was talking to, he sat back down at the table, arched his eyebrows, and sighed.

"Anything wrong, Teddy?" Isabel asked, despite it being pretty obvious that something was wrong.

"I can't seem to locate my sister. She doesn't answer her phone. The friend she said she was going to stay with not only hasn't seen her but was never expecting her. I've called a few of her other close friends as well, and *nobody* has seen or heard from her. I'm getting very worried."

Both Isabel and Tuppence were struggling with what to say to him when his phone rang again and he went back into the living room. This time they heard Teddy raise his voice enough for them to hear. "Spain? Are you *sure*? When? Did she say how long she planned to stay?" A long pause followed. "All right, well, thank you, Margaret. I will. I'm sure we'll get it sorted. But if you do hear from her, tell her to, I mean, please ask her to call me." Another long pause followed until they heard Teddy's voice again. "Barclay, hello it's Ted Mansfield. Might you have time this afternoon to meet with me? I have some concerns about my sister, Matilde. She's gone a little bit missing. . . . Yes, I'll call you when my class is over and

I'll come by your office. Cheers, Barclay." Tuppence looked at Isabel and mouthed the words, "A little bit missing?"

When he walked back into the kitchen, Isabel and Tuppence were at a loss for words. He sat down at the table and looked at them with an odd stare. Tuppence was noticeably uncomfortable. So was Isabel, but she felt he might need to talk about what was going on. "Teddy, I don't mean to pry, but I couldn't help overhearing. Did you have any idea Matilde was going to leave for Spain so abruptly? And without telling you?"

"No idea whatsoever. This is just such bizarre behavior for her. Something is going on and I can't help but think it has to do with Hugo's return. At least I *hope* that's the source of all this." Teddy looked at Isabel as if she already knew that he was beginning to suspect what might *really* be behind all this.

Chapter 19

After breakfast, Teddy announced that he was going to London the next morning to see if he could find Matilde or find out why she had bolted to Spain without telling him. He thought he could probably get more information out of her friends if he spoke to them in person.

"What about your classes, Lordship?" Tuppence asked as she cleared his plate.

"I'm going to cancel. I can make them up later in the semester."

"Would you like me to come with you, Teddy?" Isabel offered, if only out of a sense of obligation. She really didn't want to go, so she hoped he would say no. There were things to do here, and things that would be easier to do with Teddy away.

"As long as you feel comfortable staying alone for a couple nights, it's probably best you stay here. I'm going to be terribly preoccupied. When you and I go to London together for the grand tour I promised you, I don't want any distractions."

Isabel was very happy to concur. "I absolutely understand."

Before Teddy left for London the next morning, he

wanted to make sure Isabel was going to be all right staying at Pembroke Cottage alone.

"I'm very comfortable here alone as long as I have Fred and Ginger to keep me company. And Tuppence will be here to keep me company too. So don't worry about me. Go and find out what you can about Matilde and please let us know."

Tuppence walked in at that moment and handed Teddy a bag and a thermos cup. "Here's tea for the journey and a couple of raisin scones I just baked for you."

"Teddy leaned over and gave her a kiss on the cheek. "That's very kind of you, my dear."

Isabel gave Teddy a goodbye hug. "Good luck. I know I can speak for Tuppence when I say we're both very concerned about Matilde too." Concerned she might escape a murder rap, to be more specific.

Teddy finished his tea and stood up to leave. He picked up his small suitcase in the foyer and opened the front door. "I'll be staying at the Dorchester as usual, Tuppence, should either of you need to reach me."

"Yes, sir, Your Lordship. Are you driving or taking the train?"

"I'm catching the train in Penzance and leaving the Iron Lady at the station."

Isabel gave him another a hug. "You'll find her, Teddy. I'm sure of it."

"I do hope you're right, Isabel."

Isabel and Tuppence waved goodbye from the front door. But as soon as the Iron Lady pulled out of the drive, they closed the door and got down to business.

"Okay, so what have we decided about how best to get that brush to Inspector Carlyle?" Isabel asked.

"Do you think he would agree not to tell Mr. M. if we asked him not to? He's such a bootlicker, I'm just not sure we can trust him. And I really don't want Mr. M. to know it was us, or at least know it was me behind it. I'm too old to find another job. He can't fire *you*."

"Well, first of all, I certainly don't think your job would be in jeopardy either way. He adores you! And I don't think he could survive on his own. Here's what I think. Although it feels quite duplicitous, I think if he knew we went to the inspector without telling him first, it would hurt him just that much more if we're right about this. But, as you point out, can we trust the inspector to stay mum if we ask him to?"

A knock at the front door startled them both. Tuppence went to open it to find it was none other than Inspector Carlyle. It was as if he had been listening to their conversation and entered on cue. Had he bugged the place?

"Can I bring you a cuppa, Inspector?" Tuppence asked.

It had taken Isabel a few times hearing the term *cuppa* before she realized it was slang for a cup of tea, and not simply an incomplete sentence.

"Yes, please, Tuppence." He turned to Isabel. "I didn't see Mr. Mansfield's car in the drive. Is he out?"

She looked up at Tuppence as she delivered the inspector's cuppa, sending her a nonverbal cue to take the lead. "Mr. M. has gone into London to see what he can find out about where Matilde has gone off to. He'll be gone a couple days."

"That's rather odd," Inspector Carlyle said as he sat down at the table. "He didn't mention anything about that when we spoke yesterday. Well, hopefully he'll find something out. It's all very troubling, wouldn't you both agree?"

Isabel and Tuppence both nodded. The inspector opened his mouth to talk but stopped and seemed almost to be studying their faces before continuing. "If I share a concern I have with you ladies about Matilde Mansfield, can I trust you not to tell Mr. Mansfield? It's far too premature to bring him into the fold without any hard evidence, but I do have to follow my instincts."

Isabel and Tuppence looked at each other while trying to conceal their surprise. Tuppence took the lead again. "I have no problem keeping my gob shut. How about you, Isabel?"

Isabel made the universal sign for zipping her mouth shut, then looked at him and smiled. "Go right ahead, Inspector. Please tell us what's on your mind."

Inspector Carlyle took a deep breath. "This is probably something you would know more about than Mrs. Puddles would, Tuppence, but what do you know about the friendship between Mrs. Amesbury and Miss Mansfield?"

"What I know is that it's not much of one, if you ask me, but whatever it is, it's been a long one. I would guess that out of the fifty years or so they were friends"—Tuppence inserted air quotes around *friends*—"for twenty of those years they were not speaking to each other."

"Do you think not speaking to each other could possibly have escalated into something a bit more extreme?"

Tuppence looked at Isabel for a sign of approval before continuing. Isabel gave her a nod, but a tentative one. "Extreme, as in strangling-her-to-death-with-a-garden-hose extreme?"

Yes, that was exactly what he meant by *extreme*, but he thought he was going to have to ease into it a bit more than this, so the inspector was surprised they had already arrived. He was quick to add a disclaimer, though. "However, at this point I have absolutely nothing to go on other than a morsel of circumstantial evidence and a hunch."

Isabel was ready to join the conversation now. "Many a murder investigation has been launched and brought to a successful conclusion with a hunch, as you well know, Inspector. So are you saying that if you had some solid, irrefutable evidence, along with a bit more circumstantial evidence, you would be looking at Matilde as a serious person of interest?"

"Yes, regrettably I would," the inspector said, nodding thoughtfully. "And that's what I'd like to keep just between us until we have this sorted."

Tuppence left the room and came back seconds later with the brush from two nights before, sealed up in a ziplock bag. She presented it to the inspector like a cat leaving a dead bird on the porch. "This is one of Matilde's hairbrushes. Should be everything you need for your forensics testing."

"I'm not going to ask you how you happen to have possession of this," the inspector said as he lifted the bag and examined the brush.

"No need to ask, Inspector. I'll tell you. I have a key to Matilde's house, so the other night I let myself in to look for a hairbrush. While I was there, Isabel showed up, also there to retrieve a hairbrush. We had both arrived at the same conclusion—"

"*Tentative* conclusion," Isabel added.

"*Tentative* conclusion," Tuppence agreed.

"And that conclusion was?" the inspector asked, clearly knowing the answer.

"That we have reason to believe, by way of what we consider to be some very telling circumstantial evidence, that Matilde may either be the murderer or at least know who the murderer is."

The inspector was impressed. "Would you care to share this telling circumstantial evidence with me?"

That was the cue they needed, but not before he agreed, just as they had agreed, to keep what they were about to tell him under wraps. And so for the next thirty minutes, Isabel and Tuppence took turns going through what they believed Matilde's likely motive would have been, beginning with her discovering the truth about what Hyacinth did to sabotage her relationship with Hugo many years before, her bizarre behavior since the day the body was discovered, her nonchalance about the possibility of a serial killer on the loose when she had a phobia of serial killers, and, finally, her sudden and rather suspicious desire to not just visit Spain but buy a home there. The inspector was soaking it all in and taking notes. When they had laid out all their evidence, he put his notebook away in his breast pocket and looked up at them with a smile. "That was quite a Sherlockian deduction, ladies."

"But all *circumstantial* deductions, which is why Tuppence and I both knew her hairbrush could provide you with all the hard evidence you're looking for," Isabel said, then added, "or prove her innocence if we've just been pounding sand here. Either way, the truth is likely inside that ziplock bag."

The inspector finished his tea and got up from the table. "All right, well, thank you, ladies. This has been quite informational. I'll have this brush sent in to the lab today and ask for a rush. We're still waiting on results from the initial testing. Apparently a woman found strangled to death and buried in her garden is not a terribly high priority with their current workload. Murder is quite a popular pastime in the United Kingdom this spring. I even mentioned the victim was the winner of the Mousehole Annual Scone Bake-Off, but that didn't carry as much weight as I thought it might."

Isabel looked at Tuppence for a reaction to that last bit but got nothing. "Do you still have Alby in custody?" she asked.

"We do. And I'm holding him for now. At the very least he's guilty of fraud, and of burying his mother in the garden, whether he's the one who killed her or not."

"And I suppose there's nobody who could put up the money for bail now," Isabel added.

"Bail in the UK is not a moneymaking industry like it is in the States. It's purely up to the discretion of the police, in this case me, after the defendant is charged, or by the court as a defendant waits to go to trial. But given that Alby's legged it from us once already, until I can officially clear him of the murder, he's going to continue serving at Her Majesty's pleasure." He looked at Isabel and made sure to clarify. "I know serving at Her Majesty's pleasure sounds more like having tea with the sovereign, but it's actually the same as what you call *serving time* in the States."

"I see," Isabel said with a nod. "Well, it does sound a lot more pleasant. I'll add it to my growing collection of British-isms. Is he allowed visitors, Inspector?" Both Tuppence and the inspector seemed puzzled by the question.

"If he *agrees* to have visitors, I don't see why not," he replied, "but there hasn't exactly been a waiting list. And he's currently our only prisoner, so I'm sure he wouldn't mind some company."

"Would it be all right if Tuppence and I went to see him?"

Tuppence looked at Isabel and shook her head. "I'm sorry but I'm not signing up for that, Isabel. He still gives me the willies. And what for? Aren't we pretty sure we know who did his mum in at this point?"

"All we have now are our strong suspicions. If Matilde's prints or DNA are not found on that garden hose, there's nothing connecting her to the murder other than some flimsy circumstantial evidence, and that's not enough to charge her. Isn't that right, Inspector?"

"That is correct. We'll be right back to square one."

"And I feel like we owe it to Teddy to explore other possi-bilities. I would love nothing more than to help prove Matilde *isn't* guilty of this murder by proving somebody else is. I think Alby might know more than he even realizes."

Tuppence agreed with Isabel's point. "I suppose you're right. But I still don't want to go see him."

Isabel looked at the inspector and gave him an innocent shrug. "You never know. I may be able to get something out of him that he hasn't shared with you, Inspector. A friendly conversation with somebody only concerned with his well-being, as opposed to an interrogation, may prove fruitful."

"He hasn't had much to say to me, Mrs. Puddles, so please feel free. If he'll agree to see you, that is."

"And Bobby Blackburn?" Tuppence asked. "What about him?

"What *about* him? We only have Alby pointing the finger at Bobby for now, so I can't formally charge him with murder *or* with fraud. I do believe him when he says Bobby was involved in their warped little scam, but unfortunately there's just no evidence of that, at least not yet, so my hands are tied for the time being."

After the inspector left, Isabel thought about what Alby might divulge to her if he agreed to see her. First of all, she wanted to get to the bottom of this whole scone sabotage mystery. Whether it had anything to do with the murder or not, that storyline needed an ending. And although she still thought Matilde was most likely the one who had killed Hyacinth, she had another idea percolating in her head that she wanted to explore. She just needed to figure out how best to go about it.

After getting ready to walk down to the village, hopefully to talk with Alby, she went back inside to let Tuppence know she was leaving, and was presented with a large Tupperware container. "I know I haven't always been very sympathetic toward Alby, or very tolerant of him. But with a mother like the one he had, is it any wonder he's such a barmy lad?" She slipped the Tupperware into a shopping bag and handed it to Isabel. "These are some Hobnobs, they're biscuits—sorry, cookies—I baked for him. I figured he was probably as tired of scones, as I am." Tuppence was reading Isabel's mind and smiled. "Don't worry, I've set aside another dozen for you and Mr. M."

"That's very kind of you, Tuppence, thank you. Okay, well, I'm off! Wish me luck!" With that, Isabel headed out the door, not noticing two corgis in the foyer staring at her dejectedly as she left without them.

Isabel was happy to see that Inspector Carlyle was in when she walked into the Mousehole police headquarters. The place was old and a bit run down but it had character. The inspector spotted her from his office and came out to greet her. "Hello, Mrs. Puddles. Welcome!" He looked down at the bag. "May I inquire as to what you have in the bag?"

"Hello, Inspector," Isabel said as she reached into the bag and pulled out the Tupperware. "They're cookies—sorry, biscuits. Tuppence made them for Alby." She popped the lid so the inspector could inspect.

"Are those Hobnobs? I do love a Hobnob." He looked at Isabel, hoping she got the message.

"You should probably try one just to make sure they're safe."

"I do believe that's the protocol. Thank you." He reached into the Tupperware, took a cookie out, and immediately bit into it. "Absolutely delicious," he said with his mouth still full.

"Take another, Inspector. Can't be too safe."

"Thoroughness is important. Thank you." He slipped the second cookie into his shirt pocket, as if that were the natural place to store an extra cookie, then finished the first cookie with his second bite. "Tuppence sure knows her Hobnobs. Please, come into my office, Mrs. Puddles." The inspector closed the door behind them. "Please have a seat, won't you?"

Isabel sat down as invited, saying nothing, but quite curious. Inspector Carlyle obviously had something on his mind. "May I call you Isabel, Mrs. Puddles?"

"I wish you would," she replied with a smile.

"Now, Isabel, I do hope anything we say to each other here remains confidential."

"Of course, Inspector. You have my word."

"Please call me Barclay."

"If it's all right with you, I'm going to stick with Inspector. It just feels more official." It also sounded more British, which Isabel had to admit she liked.

"As you wish. Well, I have to admit that Mr. Mansfield told me about your rather sterling reputation in your home state—Michigan, correct?" He held up his right hand to acknowledge he knew the shape of her home state. Isabel smiled and nodded. "I was not aware of your famous sleuthing prowess until then."

"That doesn't surprise me, Inspector. I can't imagine whatever that reputation may be would warrant it traveling all the way over here. And as far as famous? That may be overstating it just a bit. But I do seem to have developed a flair for *sleuthing*, as you say, later in life. Whether it's a blessing or a curse is yet to be decided."

"A curse for Michigan's murdering population, I should think. And now here you are on the Cornish coast embroiled in yet another murder investigation!"

"Just my luck! Heaven forbid too much time passes between homicides! But to clarify, I don't see myself as necessarily *embroiled* in this investigation, Inspector," Isabel said with a half smile. "I just feel a commitment to do whatever I can with *what*ever sleuthing talents I may have, to hold people accountable for their crimes. And on the flipside, do what I can to help ensure innocent people are not prosecuted for murders they didn't commit. Maybe I should stay out of it while a guest in another country, but I can't seem to help myself."

"A noble endeavor indeed. And please don't stay out of it! Stay in it. I need all the help I can get. I'll deny ever saying it, but I'm at sixes and sevens with this, Isabel. It's my first murder."

"Yes, Teddy mentioned that to me. Well, I'm happy to

help in any way I can. But I'm in a rather terrible position here. When you're the houseguest of a dear friend, and you have a growing suspicion that this dear friend's sister may very well have committed a murder, or knows who did, it's rather awkward. So if there is somebody responsible for this murder other than Matilde, I would be thrilled to help you find them."

The inspector smiled and nodded. "Fair enough. But I agree with you, Isabel. Matilde Mansfield is our most likely suspect at this point. All roads lead to Rome! Or I guess in this case, Spain. But I still see this investigation as quite fluid. Until I have solid physical evidence directly implicating her, there is no way I can or would arrest her. The Mansfield family is far too established and well regarded in this community. Especially Mr. Mansfield, aka, Archie Cavendish. People would be outraged if I arrested his sister without sufficient evidence. Matilde does have a reputation for being a bit too posh, and she's not nearly as beloved as her brother, but she's still a Mansfield. And she's a far sight more popular than Hyacinth Amesbury. But then so is the stomach flu. At any rate, we'll just have to wait and see what the forensics lab turns up."

"Might I ask who you were leaning toward before Matilde was on your radar?" Isabel asked, not expecting to be surprised by his answer, if he would even give her one.

"Confidentially, I will tell you that I had a very strong hunch from the start that Alby was telling the truth about finding his mum already dead. Why? Well, not to be unkind, but I just think he's too simpleminded to make up a story as complex as the one he told me. But I still had to arrest him. Not surprisingly, I looked at Bobby Blackburn—our dodgy postman—as quite a strong possibility, but I have zero evidence to go on. That could change, however. *Then*, having heard about the whole scone kerfuffle between Tuppence and Mrs. Amesbury, I must admit I began to look at *her* as a viable candidate. Seems absolutely mad to imagine anybody would commit murder over a scone, but people have killed for less."

"I understand putting clotted cream on your scone before your jam is taking your life into your hands around here," Isabel quipped.

Inspector Carlyle laughed out loud. "Absolutely sufficient grounds for murder! And no jury would convict. I grew up in Devon, but my nan was Cornish through and through. She cut me off from her scones until I agreed to cream and jam my scones the Cornish way. I still prefer cream first, jam next, but it just feels like a betrayal of her memory now."

Isabel smiled. She was still kind of amazed that this whole Cornwall versus Devon scone controversy was taken so seriously, but she didn't want to get into it again.

"I'm ashamed to admit that I suspected Tuppence myself for a little while. I tried to fight it because I think she is absolutely incapable of murder. I still feel guilty over it."

"I don't believe anybody is incapable of murder. Give the queen reason enough to kill someone, and I have no doubt she would be happy to oblige. Or perhaps have a footman do it."

Isabel laughed. Inspector Carlyle had grown on her over the past few days. He was quirky and a little befuddled, but it was all part of his charm. "Now, about Alby, Inspector. Has he agreed to see me?"

"He wanted to think about it, but now I will insist on it. I'm quite anxious to learn what he might tell you that he hasn't told me. I'll mention you've brought him some of Tuppence's Hobnobs as enticement. I'm sure he'll bite."

After the inspector left his office, Isabel popped open the Tupperware, grabbed a cookie, and took a healthy bite before she even realized what she was doing. These cookies were not hers to eat! Giving a couple to the inspector was merely a harmless form of bribery, what *this* amounted to was stealing a cookie. She decided to chalk it up to the stress. But it *was* a delicious cookie. She would have to add Hobnobs to her list of recipes she would ask Tuppence to give her once they got all this murder business behind them.

The inspector walked back into his office. "The prisoner will see you now, Isabel."

The prisoner? That sounded a bit harsh to Isabel's ears. She wasn't here to see Hannibal Lecter. Alby only *buried* his mother, he didn't eat her with fava beans and a nice Chianti. Then she noticed Inspector Carlyle was smiling. Oh, he was being ironic. She smiled back. "That's wonderful. Thank you, Inspector." Isabel slipped him another cookie and gave him a wink as she left his office.

Chapter 20

When Isabel walked into the interrogation room, she was not the least bit surprised to find it dreary and depressing, but she knew this was the whole point of an interrogation room. They were not designed for comfort. Throw pillows and scented candles were not going to do anything to get you the answers you were looking for from a suspected criminal.

She was sitting down at the table when one of the constables brought Alby into the room, holding him by the arm. She stood up to greet him. "Hello, Alby. I'm Isabel Puddles. Do you remember me?" Alby said nothing. He wouldn't even look at her. Okay, not a great start. "Thank you for agreeing to see me." Still nothing.

His demeanor was a little bit unsettling, but he looked harmless enough.

As opposed to jail togs, Alby was dressed in jeans and a dark blue sweater, his hair was neatly combed, he was clean-shaven, and he was holding a cup of steaming hot tea. He looked more like a librarian on his lunch break than he did a jail inmate . . . or a murderer.

"I'll be just outside the door, ma'am. If he gives you any

trouble, just yell," the constable said with assurance before leaving the room.

"I'm sure we'll be fine, but thank you, Officer—I mean, Constable."

Alby was still not making eye contact with her as he walked over and sat down across from her at the table. His eyes were trained on the Tupperware, and that's where they stayed. "Are those the Hobnobs Tuppence baked?"

Isabel sat back down. "Yes, they are. And they're divine. Here, try one." She popped the lid off and slid the Tupperware across the table.

Alby wasted no time grabbing a cookie and taking a bite. He chewed thoughtfully before speaking. "I've had Tuppence's Hobnobs before. Dog's bollocks they are. She's a proper baker. I felt bad about what happened to her at the bake-off."

Well, there was an opening if ever there was one. These cookies already seemed to be working their magic. "What exactly *did* happen that day, Alby? I've been so curious about it, because we clearly both agree Tuppence is a wonderful baker. Do you have any idea what could have gone wrong?" She posed the question as if she were just making friendly conversation.

"You're Mrs. Piddles, you said?"

"Close. Puddles. Piddles is something your dog does on the floor." Isabel thought that was a pretty clever line, but it was lost on her new acquaintance.

"My mum says you're Mr. Mansfield's girlfriend."

Okay, well that had nothing to do with anything, nor was it any of his business. Now she had no choice but to address the comment. "Your mum is, sorry, *was* mistaken. We're just very good friends, Mr. Mansfield and I. . . . So you were talking about what happened with Tuppence at the bake-off."

Alby was looking up at the ceiling now. "I wasn't there,

but from what Mum told me, her scones didn't rise or fluff or puff or something," he said while reaching for another cookie.

Alby's unwillingness to make eye contact with her was becoming increasingly disconcerting. His eyes were darting around the room, as if he were following a trapped bird. She didn't know if this was normal behavior for him or if she was just making him very uncomfortable. But then why wouldn't he be uncomfortable with her? She was a perfect stranger, an American at that, who he most likely agreed to meet with just to get his hands on some homemade Hobnobs. "So was that it? They wouldn't rise?" Isabel asked, playing dumb. "Such a shame, because Tuppence baked the best scones I've ever had in my life. Sounds to me like there was something wrong with her baking soda. Or bicarb, I guess you call it here? That would definitely prevent anybody's scones from rising. Or fluffing or puffing, if you like."

This time he looked her straight in the eye and held his gaze, but there was something menacing about the way he was looking at her. Now she was the one feeling uncomfortable, so she reached for a cookie. More stress eating. Alby was not happy about it. "Aren't those Hobnobs for me?"

Isabel was determined not to allow him to see how uneasy he was suddenly making her. If there was one thing she had learned in her criminal justice studies, it was that an investigator could never show fear in the presence of a suspect. "That remains to be seen, Alby. I have a few questions I'd like you to answer, and if you do, I'll leave you the whole batch." Alby's unnerving stare indicated that he was not overjoyed about this sudden quid pro quo situation, but given his obvious obsession with the Hobnobs, she knew she had leverage now.

"What do you want to know? I didn't kill my mum, if that's what you're thinking. I did dress up like her, but that's not a crime."

"I think it was burying her in the garden that raised a red flag, Alby, but we'll get to that," Isabel said, shaking the Tupperware ever so slightly as if making the cookies whisper at him to say more.

"I know that was daft, burying her, that is. But Mum did love her garden." He said this as if it were a perfectly adequate explanation; simply a loving tribute to Mum. He was looking down at the cookies again.

"Do you think it's possible somebody tampered with Tuppence's bicarb, Alby? All water under the bridge at this point, I know, but it's just so curious. She said it was a brand-new container."

Alby shrugged his shoulders and said nothing, but his eyes were still trained on the cookies. She had seen Labrador retrievers less focused on a tennis ball. Isabel decided to try a new approach. "Do you think your mom might have tampered with Tuppence's bicarb?"

With that, Alby's demeanor abruptly switched to almost animated. "It was Mum's idea! But it was me what pulled it off!" he bragged, either unaware that he had just confessed to sabotaging Tuppence in the bake-off—which was nothing compared to the crimes he was currently facing—or else he didn't place a lot of importance on the matter. He reached for his third cookie. "Mum promised me she'd take me to the sea park if I done it for her. I think she *would* have done, if she didn't, well, you know, get murdered and everything." His face flushed with disappointment. "I bet I'll never get to go to the sea park now."

"Never give up on your dreams, Alby. So when exactly did you manage to do that? 'Pull it off,' as you said."

"I let myself in with the key Mr. Mansfield gave me a while back, and then I just swapped out Tuppence's new container of Dr. Oetker with the one Mum gave me. I don't know what she did to it. I didn't ask."

"Do you think it was fair to do that to Tuppence, Alby?" Isabel was now sounding like a schoolteacher scolding a sixth-grader.

"I just wanted to go to the sea park. And Mum said we needed the prize money from the bake-off or we couldn't afford to go."

How shameless was this woman? Isabel said to herself. "How were you able to get in and out without anybody knowing? And when exactly did you do it?"

"It was the day Mr. Mansfield asked me to do some yard work for him, so I guess it was on the Friday. I had the container of Dr. Oetker Mum gave me to swap out, so I was just waiting for the opportunity. I knew Mr. Mansfield and Tuppence weren't there, so when I saw you leave, I finished up my yard work, then let myself in and made the swap. I even had time for a cuppa. That's when you came back."

Alby seemed quite pleased with his achievement and was eyeing a fourth cookie, but his smug attitude had really rubbed Isabel the wrong way, although she was doing a good job of hiding it. She put the lid back on the Tupperware just as he reached for that next cookie. How dare he sit there gorging on poor Tuppence's Hobnobs after just admitting what he had done to her? Shameless must run in the family! Isabel took a breath and tried to channel the anger she was feeling on behalf of poor Tuppence into some compassion for this young man who really did appear to be, as everybody seemed to agree, *thick as a brick*, or some variation of that.

So now the riddle of the tainted bicarb had been solved. Tuppence might feel better knowing for certain she had been sabotaged. Now Isabel could focus on a few questions she had about the murder. Could the baking soda debacle somehow be related? Not likely, but given all the twists and turns in this case so far, it could very well be. What she was still really hoping for now was to turn up something, anything, that might point *away* from Matilde as the killer. And Alby might just know something that could help.

"Who do *you* think killed your mom, Alby?" she began fiddling with the Tupperware lid again to lure him into answering. "By the way, I don't believe *you* did it. I never have. But you must have some suspicions as to who's responsible, don't you? I'm sure you would want to honor your mother's life by helping find the person responsible for her death."

Alby looked at Isabel, then at the cookies, then back at Isabel. She met his look this time with a coy smile. She fiddled a little more with the lid but could see it was beginning to agitate him. Given the icy stare he had given her before, maybe agitating him was not such a great idea. But she was a pro, kind of, so she remained calm and composed. She did stop fiddling with the Tupperware lid, though. "Where does the postman fit into all this? Do you think he had anything to do with your mom's murder?"

Alby lit up. "I told the inspector that's who I thought done it. I'd bet my own life it's Bobby what done it. He's mean, he is! Meaner than Mum, and that's saying something."

Well, *that* was an interesting little nugget. "Your mom was mean to you, was she, Alby? I'm very sorry to hear that." Now she was feeling sorry for him again. She popped the lid off the Tupperware and slid it across the table. He reached in quickly to grab another cookie before this strange American lady put the lid back on.

Isabel composed her thoughts for a moment while Alby chewed. She then put her blinker on and turned down an avenue of inquiry she had begun to entertain as a possible motive for murder. Solving the murder of someone who had no shortage of enemies did on the one hand provide a wealth of possibilities when putting together a list of possible suspects and their motives. But on the other hand, solving the murder of someone who had no shortage of enemies also created a lot more work to cull the herd of those who may have wanted to do it, and even had motive to do it, but didn't do it.

"What can you tell me about a deal Mr. Plumbottom had with your mom to buy a painting she owned?"

"That little painting of the village, you mean?"

"I do believe that's the one, yes."

"That was my nan's, and her nan's before her. I guess she knew the artist. In the biblical sense."

That was a lot of information Isabel didn't need or ask for. "And did that deal ever go through?"

"Not sure. All I know is Mum said he called after the bake-off to say congratulations, and I thought she said he was coming out with the money that day. Or Tiegan was. Two thousand quid, I think he wanted to pay for it. She held out a while to try to get him to go up, but he never would. So she finally agreed to sell it. Two thousand quid for some dinky little painting. That's just bonkers. But I never knew what happened, and never thought to look for any money after Mum, well, you know, died and everything. I checked her pockets before I buried her too."

Isabel was starting to feel slightly nauseous. She could not believe what she had just heard. It was difficult enough to find the right adjectives to describe what Alby did with his mother after she died, but the adjectives one would need to describe this act—actually going through your dead mother's pockets before you buried her in her own garden—those words simply did not exist. And shouldn't.

Inspector Carlyle knocked on the door as he was walking in. "How're we going here, you two?" He didn't wait for an answer. "Mrs. Puddles, may I have a quick word with you?"

"Of course, Inspector."

"Alby, if you'll excuse us, please?"

Isabel hesitated for a moment before leaving, wondering what to do about the cookies. They seemed to be doing the trick as incentive for him to talk, but she decided to take them with her so he didn't just fill his pockets and clam up. Isabel could feel him glaring at her as she left the room.

The inspector motioned to Isabel to come back to his office, then closed the door behind her. "Forensics are back from the initial examination of the garden hose. Not what I sent in today obviously, but what I sent the day of the murder."

"And?" Isabel had the feeling he was burying the lead.

"*And* I just sent two of my men over to bring Bobby Blackburn in. His prints were all over that garden hose."

Isabel felt a crashing wave of relief. So Matilde wasn't a murderer after all. It had just begun to seem so probable, but she had never been so happy to be wrong about anything. She wasn't alone in that assessment; Tuppence and the inspector were right there with her, but now she could breathe easy knowing Teddy would not have to deal with anything as horrific as discovering his only sister was a killer. Unless maybe Bobby and Matilde had somehow teamed up, which seemed highly unlikely.

"Do you think you can wrap things up in the next fifteen minutes with Alby?" the inspector asked. "I'll need that room to interrogate Bobby. By the way, and don't tell him this, but I think I might send Alby home, if I can get my division chief to approve a new ankle bracelet. We only have two; one doesn't work too well since Angus Flaley took a hammer to his. He didn't manage to get it off, but it did buy him a month in jail and a fine of two hundred quid for destroying government property. And the other bracelet's with Maeda Morrison. She's the wife of a vicar who also happens to be a compulsive shoplifter. Stickiest fingers in all of Cornwall, that one's got. We just let her keep her bracelet in between arrests now. Saves time."

Isabel laughed. "I'll go back in and finish up with Alby. Won't take long. I'm exploring a new theory, but I'll share it with you later. Maybe Tuppence could bake up another batch of Hobnobs to help you with your interrogation of the postman. They do seem to grease the wheels nicely."

The inspector nodded. "Not a bad idea, although I myself might consider confessing to a crime I didn't commit to get my hands on a batch of those Hobnobs."

Isabel went back into the interrogation room and gave Alby another cookie. "Alby, can you think of any reason your postman's fingerprints would be on that garden hose?"

"Sure I can. Because he used it to strangle my mum."

"Okay, forget about how his prints got there. Why do you think he would want to kill your mom?"

"Because he's greedy. He didn't want to wait. We made a deal, but I reckon he thought the sooner Mum was gone, the sooner I could start cashing her checks and the sooner he could get his cut. I would never have killed her. She was tough as an old boot, but she was still my mum. People can't just go around killing their mums anytime they take a fancy. I could wait until God wanted her to die. But I guess Bobby decided to give Him some help."

"Do you have any *proof* to support this theory?" Isabel asked.

It was a motive for murder that certainly made sense. Sadly, it had been Isabel's experience since she got into the murder business that craven greed was usually a good starting point when you were looking for a motive and a murderer. Although it was beyond her how anybody could find their mother dead in the garden and casually drag her into a flower bed and bury her like a dog burying a bone—after patting her down—but in Alby's case, it seemed to be less about greed and more about fear and survival. Isabel had heard all she needed for now, so she stood up to leave. "Thank you for agreeing to see me, Alby. And I'm very sorry for your loss."

"What loss? Aren't you leaving those biscuits with me?" Alby obviously had his priorities sorted out.

"Yes, I am," she said, sliding the Tupperware across the table to him. "And I hope you'll enjoy them." Isabel popped her head out the door to let the constable know they were done. She thanked Alby again as the constable led him out of the room and then down the hall. When they got a few steps away, the constable had a question for his prisoner. "Are those Hobnobs you've got in there, Alby? I haven't had a Hobnob since my own mum died." Isabel didn't hear Alby reply, but she did see him reach in and hand a Hobnob over to him. Apparently you could make a lot of friends in this village with the right cookie.

Just as she opened the front door to leave, two constables were bringing Bobby Blackburn up the steps, still in his postal uniform and wearing handcuffs. Isabel stepped back and held the door for them, then saw Inspector Carlyle come out of his office to greet him. "Thanks for coming in, Bobby."

"Didn't have much of a choice, did I, Inspector."

"Fair point. You did not." The inspector looked at the constables. "Put him in the interrogation room, please." Then back at Bobby, "I'll be in momentarily. Don't go anywhere." He laughed at his own joke, then spotted Isabel at the front door and gave her a smile and a wave. "I'll be in touch soon, Isabel!"

On her walk back to Pembroke Cottage, Isabel was deep in thought, trying to make sense of everything that had happened since Fred and Ginger first discovered Hyacinth's body. She was feeling somewhat relieved to know they had likely found her killer now. Yes, she and Tuppence had been wrong about Matilde, and for that she was very grateful, and she knew Tuppence would be as well. It must have been revisiting the whole Hugo affair that had caused Matilde to unravel the way she did, as opposed to simply having a bad reaction to strangling an old friend.

Bobby Blackburn murdering Hyacinth made a lot more

sense, anyway. And he certainly looked the part of somebody who would strangle an old woman for a few bucks. But was it too predictable? For whatever reason, she wasn't entirely convinced the postman did it, not without help anyway. She then recalled the inspector saying early on in his investigation that if Bobby Blackburn's fingerprints *were* on that garden hose, he better have a good explanation for how they got there. So what if he did?

Chapter 21

The next morning, Teddy called Isabel to let her know he was staying in London another night, then got her up to speed with where he was in his search for Matilde. First of all, it turned out her friend was mistaken about her having gone to Spain, although it may have been her intention to at the time. And, thanks to Teddy having an old friend in the passport office, he learned that her passport had not been used, so she hadn't fled the country, after all. Teddy then asked Isabel if she had seen Hugo around lately, to which she replied that she had not. Teddy had apparently been trying to reach Hugo for the past couple of days and had left messages, but he hadn't returned any of his calls. They couldn't help but wonder now if Hugo and Matilde might be somewhere together. Maybe they had finally run off together? But, whatever the case, Teddy intended to find his sister, so he was going to meet with a private investigator in the morning—another old friend—to see what they could "dig up."

Isabel had a suggestion. "Let's maybe not use that phrase for a while, Teddy."

Teddy chuckled. "Duly noted."

Tuppence had not yet arrived for work, so Isabel leashed

up Fred and Ginger and took them out for their walk. As they were about to turn onto the trail that led to their favorite view of the water, she heard a car horn and turned to see Inspector Carlyle pulling up. He parked off to the side of the road and got out of his car with a spring in his step. "Good morning, Isabel! Another gorgeous day in Cornwall!"

"I'm beginning to think your country's reputation for rain and fog is all a hoax. I've seen a lot more sunshine than I have any of the notoriously dreary weather you're famous for," she said as Fred and Ginger tugged her over to greet the inspector.

"You're on to us! It's a misinformation strategy designed to discourage tourism. Doesn't really work very well, though. Have you got a moment? There's something I'd like to run by you."

"Sure, Inspector. Would you like to walk with us?"

He looked back at his car. "I guess I could leave my car here. If I get a violation, I'm fairly certain I can have it taken care of."

"So what's on your mind, Inspector?" she asked as her team of corgis pulled her along. She handed Fred's leash to the inspector. "Will you take one, please? For having such stumpy little legs, they're powerful little buggers."

The inspector took the leash and his arm was immediately stretched to its limits. After finally reeling Fred in, he got to the point. "Do you recall my saying that if Bobby Blackburn's fingerprints were on the garden hose used to strangle Mrs. Amesbury, he would need to have a very good explanation for how they got there?"

"I do. In fact, I was thinking about that yesterday. And I gather he does?"

"Of course I would never take his word for it. Bobby Blackburn wouldn't know the truth if it bit him in the"—he corrected course—"if it landed in his lap. How he's trusted with the Royal Mail is a mystery to me. But I spoke with

Alby, who has corroborated his explanation. So I have nothing to hold him on now."

"Are you able to share this information with me, Inspector?" Isabel was playing it cool, but she was dying to know.

"I am, and I will, because I'm quite interested in your take. So, according to Bobby, and again, confirmed by Alby, a few days prior to the murder, he had just delivered Mrs. Amesbury's mail and was standing next to his Royal Mail truck having a chat with her. Then they heard a loud splat. They looked up to a seagull flying off after delivering a commentary on the Royal Mail service with a special delivery of seagull guano on his truck. Evidently Mrs. Amesbury laughed and said something along the lines of her not being the only one who thinks the mail service is crap."

Isabel considered this for a moment. "I see where this is going."

"I thought you might. Yes, according to Bobby, at Mrs. Amesbury's suggestion, he pulled his truck over closer to the garden, close enough for the garden hose to reach. She then went over and turned the water on so he could spray off his truck. He told me he just couldn't allow Her Majesty's mail truck to be dishonored in such a way."

Isabel had to agree it was a pretty solid explanation. "So now what?"

"It doesn't clear him completely, but since Alby corroborated his story, the fingerprint evidence is useless. So, in answer to your question, we are back to looking at Miss Mansfield as our most likely suspect. If her prints come back on that garden hose—as much as it pains me—I'm going to have no choice but to arrest her. Assuming we can find her. If she's gone off to Spain, that could be problematic."

"Funny you should mention that, because I spoke to Teddy less than an hour ago, and he told me that Matilde has *not* gone to Spain, after all. According to his friend in the passport office, she has not left the country as of this morning, but Teddy still doesn't know where she is."

"Well, that's still rather troubling," the inspector said with a scowl. "But I am happy to know she has not run away to the Continent."

"He also told me he's been trying to reach Hugo for the past couple of days to see if he might know her whereabouts, but he's not answering his phone or returning messages. So that's curiously coincidental too, don't you think?"

"Coincidental? Yes, I would agree with that. But not answering your phone or returning messages for a couple of days is nothing too alarming. At any rate, there's nothing to do but wait until the forensics are sorted. Until then, I'm afraid we remain in a holding pattern."

"And what about Alby, Inspector? Do you still plan to release him?"

"If I ever get approval for the additional ankle bracelet, yes, I intend to send him home. I asked Maeda Morrison if I could take hers, but she said she couldn't find it. My guess is that she's nicked *it* now too. The Eighth Commandment evidently doesn't carry a lot of weight in the Vicar and Mrs. Morrison household."

The inspector's phone rang. But it wasn't a ring, it was the opening theme from *Law & Order*, which had been one of Isabel's favorite shows. She liked the inspector more and more every day. "Excuse me, Isabel, I do need to take this call."

"Go right ahead, Inspector. We're going to keep walking."

The inspector gave her back Fred's leash, waved goodbye, and took his call. With the corgis clearly in charge, Isabel's mind was free to wander back to the brief conversation she had just had with him. She couldn't believe that in the past twenty-four hours she had gone from believing Tuppence *might* be guilty of murder to thinking Matilde *was* guilty of murder to believing she *wasn't* guilty of murder and that the creepy postman was the guilty party. And now Matilde was the prime suspect again. *And* she was missing. This roller-coaster ride was exhausting. And frustrating.

While taking in the gorgeous view of the English Channel with her canine companions, Isabel was distracted by their turning and wagging their stumpy little tails. Inspector Carlyle was rejoining them. He crouched down to say hello to them again before standing up and looking at Isabel with the slightest smile but saying nothing. She raised her eyebrows to signal to him that she was ready to hear what he had to say. But she had already learned that Inspector Carlyle enjoyed milking the moment, so she stayed quiet. "Forensics on the brush are back."

"And?"

"And Miss Mansfield's prints *and* her DNA are a match."

Isabel's stomach sunk. "Well, I guess you have your answer, then, Inspector. . . . Poor Teddy."

"But they were not found on the garden hose."

What kind of game was he playing here? Now she was getting slightly annoyed. Isabel knew he was waiting for her to ask, but she was determined to wait him out. She counted to five in her head. Okay, he won. "So? Where *were* they found?"

"Remember the broken flowerpot? Well, I sent that in for testing too, when I sent in the garden hose, and there was only one set of prints on it."

"Matilde's?"

He nodded. "Bingo."

"Well, what do you suppose *that* means?"

"Don't know yet. But unless she had the wherewithal to wear gloves, she was nowhere near that garden hose. But then maybe she did have the wherewithal to wear gloves."

"So back to square one?"

"I have no idea what square we're on now, Isabel. There are so *many* squares. I'm reminded of *The Brady Bunch*. Did Jan do it? Did Bobby do it? Or was it Alice?"

Isabel laughed. "You appear to be quite a fan of American television, Inspector."

"I lived for it as a lad. My Homer and Marge Simpson impersonations drove my poor mum and dad bonkers. They finally offered me money to stop." The inspector's phone rang again. He looked down at the number before answering. "Yes, Constable Hilliard . . . Who? Just came in off the street? Hmm. All right . . . well, have him wait in my office and I'll be right there." He looked back at Isabel with an odd expression. "Hugo Fernsby just came into the station and asked to talk to me."

"Really? Yet *another* square, Inspector. Maybe Cindy did it."

"I never bought that innocent-little-girl act . . . Would you care to accompany me to headquarters and hear what he has to say?"

"Of course I would, but what about these two?"

"They can come. They are the ones who dragged us into this mess, after all. If it weren't for their obsessive digging, Mrs. Amesbury would probably still be resting comfortably under a lovely bed of primrose."

They all loaded into the inspector's car and drove down to headquarters to meet Hugo. Isabel's mind was racing over what this could be about, but at this point, she was no longer speculating. Why bother?

Hugo was sitting in the inspector's office, casually flipping through a copy of the *Daily Mail* when they walked in. He stood up and shook both their hands.

"I hope you don't mind Mrs. Puddles being here. She's a private investigator held in very high regard back in the States and has been kind enough to serve as a consultant on this case."

"Fine by me. She's going to hear about this soon enough." Hugo looked over at Isabel. "You may as well hear it from me."

Isabel sat down next to Hugo, while Inspector Carlyle took his seat behind his desk. "Please, tell us what's on your mind, Hugo."

Hugo took a deep breath. "No point dragging this out any longer than necessary. *I* killed Hyacinth Amesbury."

No, you didn't, was Isabel's immediate reaction, but using her inside voice. Inspector Carlyle waited a moment to see if Hugo had anything else to add after launching that grenade. Apparently not. He gave Isabel a look of bewilderment before turning his attention back to Hugo. "So let me ask you this, Hugo. Were you aware of what the coroner's report said about Mrs. Amesbury's cause of death?"

"No, I was not aware of it, but I don't need his report to know how it happened because I was there. I did it."

The inspector let that hang in the air for a moment before continuing. "And how *did* you do it, Hugo?" He reached for a round tin on his desk and gave it a shake before opening it up and holding it out for his guests. "Would anybody care for a Simpkins?" Hugo passed, but Isabel was happy to reach in. "Now, where were we? Oh, you were about to tell us how you committed the murder."

"I hit her over the head with a flowerpot," Hugo said, anxious to get back to his confession.

"Ouch. And then what?" The inspector reached into his mouth, took out a red candy, examined it, then popped it back in and rolled it around. "I just love these. Strawberry-and-cream flavor. All right, so you hit her over the head with a flowerpot. Then what happened?"

"And then she fell to the ground. I checked for a pulse, couldn't feel one, so I panicked and ran off."

Isabel looked over at the inspector and raised her eyebrows slightly. He winked back. It was now pretty obvious who did, given that Matilde's prints were the only ones found on the broken pot fragments. But that was good news! It meant Matilde *didn't* kill Hyacinth, she just bonked her on the head. That is, unless the coroner's report was wrong, and what actually killed her *was* a blow to the head. And it had been her experience that this sort of thing *did* happen from time to time. The coroner wasn't always right.

Inspector Carlyle continued. "Do you recall what was in the flowerpot? What kind of flowers, I mean. Could they have been geraniums?"

Hugo shrugged his shoulders. "I'm not very good with flowers. I couldn't tell you what they were."

The inspector looked through some notes on his desk, or pretended to. "Oh. There *were* no flowers in that flowerpot. Just some dirt."

"You're right. It *was* empty." Hugo was not great at making false confessions.

The inspector stared at Hugo for a beat. "There were geraniums in that flowerpot, Hugo."

"Well, there were a few flowerpots out on her patio. I don't remember which one I grabbed. I was in a rage!"

"I've never had very good luck with geraniums. We don't seem to get along," the inspector added for no apparent reason. "How about you, Isabel?"

"I've been planting them on my deck every summer for years now. We get along just fine."

Hugo was suddenly annoyed. "Why are we talking about geraniums? Shouldn't you be handcuffing me or something, Inspector? Or is murder no longer a crime in Mousehole?"

"Was Matilde Mansfield with you when you hit Mrs. Amesbury over the head with that flowerpot" the inspector asked, "or were you there alone?"

Hugo quickly took a defensive posture. "Why are you dragging her into this, Inspector? Matilde had nothing to do with any of this."

Inspector Carlyle nodded thoughtfully. "And what if I told you that the forensics lab found Matilde's fingerprints on that broken flowerpot? Not yours."

Hugo fumbled for an answer. "I would say they got it wrong. Or maybe Matilde picked up that flowerpot one time when she was visiting Hyacinth. They *were* friends, you know."

Inspector Carlyle took another dramatic pause before speaking. "It wasn't you who hit Hyacinth over the head with that flowerpot full of geraniums, was it, Hugo? It couldn't have been."

"I was wearing gloves," he quickly replied, but he seemed pretty aware that his plan to martyr himself to spare Matilde from a murder rap was unraveling rather quickly.

The time had come for the inspector to drop the mic. "Here's the good news, Hugo. According to the coroner—and that's all we have to go on—Hyacinth Amesbury did *not* die as a result of a head injury. She died of strangulation."

Hugo's entire body seemed to react to this news, and he slumped in his chair. "Are you saying she—I—didn't kill her?"

"No, you did not," the inspector said with a smile. "Nor did those geraniums."

"I can't tell you how relieved I am to hear that, Inspector," Hugo said as the stress continued leaving his body like a deflating raft.

"You're relieved to hear you didn't kill Mrs. Amesbury, are you, Hugo?" The inspector could barely stop himself from laughing. "I would think so!"

Hugo looked at him with a deadpan stare for a moment, then at Isabel. "I'm just relieved, that's all. Can we just leave it at that, please?"

A knock on the inspector's door ended that conversation. "Come in," he yelled, keeping his eyes trained on Hugo as if trying to decipher a secret code.

One of the constables poked his head in the door. "Chief, there's somebody here to see you."

"Well, let's not turn this into a guessing game, shall we, Constable? Who is it?"

"It's Matilde Mansfield, sir, and her solicitor, Mr. Fitzsimmons, I believe he said his name was."

Hugo stood up in a state of shock. "Matilde's here?"

"Well, I'll be gobsmacked!" The inspector slammed his hand on his desk, startling Isabel and Hugo both. "By all means send them in!" He stood up and prepared to greet them as if they were surprise guests on his talk show.

Hugo was still dumbfounded. But then so was Isabel. She had a fair amount of difficulty following the plot turns in *The Mousetrap* when she saw it in London the week before, but the twists and turns in this real-life drama were even more theatrical, and almost as complicated. The inspector looked at Isabel with a beaming grin, quickly wiped clean when Matilde and her solicitor—a finely dressed older gentleman carrying a briefcase—entered the room. Matilde's eyes instantly locked on Hugo's, and vice versa as they walked to each other and embraced, whispering into each other's ears.

The inspector continued playing host. "Please, Miss Mansfield, have a seat. And you too, Mr. Fitzsimmons, is it?" He reached out to shake his hand.

"Preston Fitzsimmons. My pleasure, Inspector." He reached into his vest pocket, "And here's my card." He placed the card at the edge of the inspector's desk and sat down next to his client. Matilde had yet to say a word to anybody or even

make eye contact with anybody other than Hugo. She sat
down next to him and they took each other's hands. Fred and
Ginger were still lying in the corner, napping. They hadn't
bothered to get up to greet anybody. Even *they* were getting
tired of all these twists and turns.

"Well! Where shall we begin?" The inspector reached for
his tin of candy. "Would anybody care for a Simpkins? I just
love these. Absolutely *addicted*."

Chapter 22

"My client is here to confess to the murder of Hyacinth Amesbury," Preston Fitzsimmons stated, as if he had been rehearsing his opening line.

"Well, isn't that a funny coincidence? Because Hugo—Mr. Fernsby—is here for the very same reason. Shall we draw straws to decide who the real murderer is?"

Isabel could plainly see that Matilde was both surprised and touched at hearing this. She looked at Hugo and slowly shook her head. He looked away. Despite his game face, Mr. Fitzsimmons was obviously taken aback by this piece of news, but he shook it off and got down to solicitor business. "May I please have a look at the police report, as well as the coroner's report, Inspector?"

"You certainly may." Inspector Carlyle shuffled through the papers and folders on his desk. "Let's see . . . Okay, here's the police report, and"—he shuffled some more—"and here's the coroner's report." He handed both files across the desk to Mr. Fitzsimmons. "I know you're probably used to receiving things via electronic file transfers, or email, or whatever, but we're rather old-school here. And when I say 'rather,' I mean 'quite.' I have twelve constables in my department and I'll bet ten of them have never sent an email in their lives, nor do they intend to. So I content myself with legible handwriting, which I do even get on occasion."

Mr. Fitzsimmons was not listening to anything the inspector was saying as he leafed through the reports. He pulled out a document for closer examination, then looked across the desk incredulously. "It says here that the victim died of strangulation." He then looked over at his client, who was suddenly paying very close attention.

"Strangulation?" Matilde was mystified.

Mr. Fitzsimmons continued reading and was again left perplexed. "And the murder weapon was determined to be a garden hose?" He looked back at his client, then at the inspector again. "What about the flowerpot full of geraniums?"

Inspector Carlyle answered the question with a question. "What about it?"

Mr. Fitzsimmons was even more baffled now. "So you're saying it was *not* blunt-force trauma to the head that killed her?"

"I don't believe I ever *did* say that? Nor did anybody else. What we *did* find was a broken flowerpot at the murder scene, so I sent the fragments into the forensics lab to see what they might find."

Isabel knew the inspector was definitely going to milk this pause for ultimate dramatic effect, so she began counting down from five in her head. When she reached one, he took her subliminal cue. . . . "And what they *found* was your client's fingerprints all over those fragments."

Mr. Fitzsimmons was now officially indignant. "And just how may I ask did you acquire my client's fingerprints?"

Inspector Carlyle reached for his tin of candy again. "I'm telling you, I just can't *stop* with these!" He popped another Simpkins into his mouth and offered his guests another. There were no takers. "That's a very astute question, Mr. Fitzsimmons," he replied, rolling his candy around in his mouth, "but I'm afraid I can't answer that."

Isabel was barely listening to the back-and-forth between the inspector and the solicitor. She was too busy watching Matilde's reaction to this breaking news. Discovering you weren't guilty of murder—only a violent assault—had clearly come as a relief. She was also watching the looks she and Hugo were exchanging, which seemed to run the whole gamut of emotions. Matilde suddenly broke eye contact with Hugo and put herself in the game, despite her solicitor's putting his finger to his lips and shaking his head. "My fingerprints were on that flowerpot, Inspector, because I—well, we—after all these years, had finally learned the truth about what that horrible, mean-minded little ogre of a woman did to Hugo—the first, and only love of my life—and the deceptiveness and deceit she used to sabotage our future together."

"I think you've said quite enough, Matilde," her defeated-looking solicitor said to his recalcitrant client.

Matilde looked at Hugo and her eyes went from strong and stoic to wounded and tearful. Hugo looked as if he were fighting back tears himself. Isabel was feeling bad for them both, especially now that she had witnessed the bond they obviously still shared after so many years apart. The lingering heartbreak in their eyes from being denied a life together—thanks to one woman's malice—was palpable. It really was an unbelievably heartless thing Hyacinth had done to them. Even Inspector Carlyle seemed moved and handed her a box of tissues. "Would you care for some tea, Miss Mansfield? Water? A Simpkins, perhaps?"

"No, thank you, Inspector," she answered softly as she pulled out a tissue and dried her eyes, "I'm fine." Matilde then took a breath, pulled herself together, and continued confessing, once again ignoring Mr. Fitzsimmons. "So when I finally learned how diabolical and cruel she had been, I went straight over to her house and confronted her. And you know what she did? She laughed in my face. She laughed in my face and called me an old, unloved spinster, then turned around and went back to her gardening." Matilde paused briefly as if she were reliving the moment. "And out of nowhere this blind rage rather overwhelmed me. It was like nothing I had ever felt before, and I hope never to again. Before I even realized what I was doing, I was reaching for that pot of geraniums sitting there on the table. So I picked it up, came up behind her, and smashed her over the head with it." Matilde paused again to compose herself while Isabel, the inspector, Hugo, and her exasperated solicitor all looked at her in silence for a moment. "And let me just add—as long as I'm being completely honest—in that moment, the only remorse I felt was for the geraniums."

The room remained silent until Mr. Fitzsimmons finally cleared his throat and offered some professional advice to his client. "I really do not think it wise for you to say anything more, Matilde. As your solicitor, I simply cannot allow you to—"

"So after I broke the pot of geraniums over her head, she turned around and looked at me with an absolutely bewildered expression on her face. But I can imagine she *was* quite surprised, as anybody would be. Then she raised her arms up and grabbed her head. Her eyes fluttered a little and I saw a trickle of blood running down her forehead . . . and then she just crumpled. You know when you see footage on the news where they've intentionally set explosives inside an old building to make it implode? That's what she reminded me of; a crumpling old building." Mr. Fitzsimmons put his head in his hands as Matilde continued, "It took me a minute to comprehend the enormity of what I had just done, then I crouched down beside her, shook her a little, but got no response. I took her wrist to see if I could find a pulse, but I felt nothing. So rather than call nine-nine-nine, I panicked and raced home across the field to my house. As far as I knew, I had killed her. When I got home and came to my senses, naturally I was mortified—although if I may say so, if anybody deserved to have their skull cracked open with a pot of geraniums, it was Hyacinth Amesbury. But obviously I knew it was still murder whether she deserved it, or whether I intended to murder her or not. I was afraid that somebody had either seen me do it or seen me racing home, so I was terrified that I was going to be arrested at any time. It's funny, after all those years refusing to read my brother's books, it was as though I had unwittingly been transported into the world of Archie Cavendish and one of his Detective Waverly's murder investigations."

Isabel thought Matilde's definition of *unwitting* was a pretty liberal one. Once you've knocked somebody unconscious with a flowerpot and left them for dead, it seemed to her it made her pretty *witting*.

Isabel thought she heard a vague whimper come from Mr. Fitzsimmons as his client kept on going.

"When Hugo told me she had been murdered—without my knowing it was a result of her being *strangled*, of course— I naturally assumed I was the one who murdered her. Who else? But I couldn't let Hugo know, so, although it broke my heart, I had to tell him I couldn't accept his marriage proposal, as much as I wanted to. I just couldn't let him marry a murderess or become an *accomplice* to murder." She turned to Hugo with a sad smile. "But I couldn't leave him wondering what happened, either, not after the last time, so I finally called him from London and confessed to him what I had done." She held his hand to her cheek and looked into his eyes. "And now here you are trying to take the blame for me." Matilde began to cry again, so the inspector passed the box of tissues back. She thanked him and continued. "But I had a sneaking suspicion he would do just that, so that's why I had to come back and own up to my crime." She turned back to

Hugo. "I just couldn't let you . . . But I do love you for it."
Hugo just stared back into her eyes. He had no words.

A few moments of silence followed, and Isabel was, in
a word, astonished at what she had just heard come out of
Matilde's mouth. Either she had been doing a remarkable
job of hiding a badly wounded heart—like a Russian nesting doll—or she had just turned in an Oscar-worthy performance.

"And what was this business about Spain?" the inspector
asked her.

"You don't have to answer that, Matilde. But by all means,
go right ahead." Mr. Fitzsimmons had clearly given up.

"That was my escape plan if and when I needed to imple-
ment it." Matilde was turning somewhat haughty again and
more like the woman Isabel had come to know. "I'm not trying to convince anybody that I'm being noble or virtuous by
confessing to what I did, but I will say that I am relieved to
learn I wasn't the one who killed her. I assume I am still guilty
of *some* criminal act, though, am I not, Inspector?" She then
looked at her solicitor. "Preston?"

Mr. Fitzsimmons shook his head. "That will be for the
inspector to decide, Matilde. The crime you absolutely *are*
guilty of though is utterly ignoring every piece of advice your
solicitor has given you, and doing everything he has told you
not to do instead. If I could put you in jail for that, I would do
so immediately."

Isabel couldn't help but giggle a little at that. Mr. Fitzsimmons had more gumption than she had presumed him to have.

"What in the world is going *on* in here!" Fred and Ginger
got up and raced to the door, where Teddy had suddenly appeared. "Matilde! I have been worried sick about you! I've
been all over London *looking* for you! I did everything but
drag the Thames!"

Matilde stood up and gave her brother a hug. "I'm so very,

very sorry, Theodore. It was absolutely inexcusable of me to go missing like that and worry you so." Teddy was hovering somewhere between angry and confused, but leaning toward angry, so he did not respond in kind to her hug.

Mr. Fitzsimmons stood up and offered his chair to Teddy. "Please, Theodore. Have a seat. I'm going to the loo. I may or may not return."

"Thank you, Preston. And nice to see you again by the way," he said to Preston as he left the office. "And hello, Isabel. Always lovely to see you of course." He reached down and gave her a hug, then pulled over a chair and sat down next to her. "Now, is somebody going to tell me what's going on here? Barclay? Anybody? And why is Preston here? And why are *you* here, Matilde?" he asked while trying to give Fred and Ginger the attention they were demanding. "And what are *these* two doing here?"

"Preston is here because he's my solicitor, Theodore, as well as yours, and I needed some legal advice. I'm not certain if I'll need a criminal solicitor yet or not."

"This doesn't sound good," Teddy said, taking a deep breath.

Matilde sat back down and took Hugo's hand again, a gesture that was not lost on Teddy. "Actually, it *is* good, Theodore. Quite good. Now, would you like the *very* good news first, or the even *better* news first?"

"I don't care, Matilde. Whatever the case, I have the distinct impression there is going to be *bad* news to follow at some point." This comment he directed at Inspector Carlyle, who remained deadpan.

"Don't be a killjoy, Theodore. All right, let's get the *very* good news out of the way. I did *not* murder Hyacinth Amesbury. Isn't that wonderful? I thought I did, and I probably intended to in the moment, but in fact I did not. At any rate, this was why I—what is it you say in the States, Isabel?—skipped town?"

Isabel replied with one of those tight-lipped smiles, which were always tricky to decipher. There was no way she was wading into this quicksand.

Matilde went on. "But ultimately I decided the life of a fugitive hiding out in Spain waiting for a visit from Interpol was not for me, so I came back to confess to a murder that it turns out I didn't commit!"

Teddy looked the very definition of *befuddled*. "I'm going to need some more information. So the *very* good news is that you aren't a murderer? That's comforting to know. Now, can we discuss how we reached that conclusion?"

Getting Teddy up to speed took a while, but between Matilde, Hugo, Isabel, Inspector Carlyle, and Mr. Fitzsimmons, Teddy had been fully debriefed. He sat quietly for a moment and looked around the room before speaking. "That's a lot to take in. It's rather like a plot I might devise for a book of mine and then ultimately abandon because it was too convoluted to follow." He looked at Isabel and smiled. "So has Cornwall lived up to your expectations, Isabel? Wouldn't the Brontë sisters be proud?"

Isabel smiled and patted him on the arm. "The scones have been very nice. And of course the company has been delightful. But I could have done nicely without the murder. I get enough of that at home."

Teddy laughed heartily, as if he were releasing days of pent-up angst. He looked over at his sister. "I would certainly not disagree that your not being a killer is very good news indeed, Matilde; for you and me both. Finding out your only sister has not committed murder certainly falls into the *very good news* category. It would have been great publicity for my books, though. I'm sure my publishers would have been thrilled. And in all honesty—and I say this with brotherly love—I had begun to think perhaps you *had* done Hyacinth in. The circumstantial evidence was piling up. But let's move on. She's still quite dead either way, isn't she? *Isn't* she? Or is this going to be the surprise ending?"

"Dead as a doornail," the inspector confirmed, "and properly buried this time."

"All right, good. So that's Hyacinth Amesbury done," Teddy said with some measure of relief in his voice. "Now, what was this even *better* news you were referring to, Matilde?"

Matilde looked at Hugo and smiled. "Hugo proposed to me. But it was on the day of the *incident*, so I had to refuse him because I still thought I was a murderer. Now that I'm *not* a murderer, I'm going to accept. That is, if he'll still have me."

Hugo leaned over to kiss her on the cheek. "I think you know the answer to that, my dear. However, I think we'll do without geraniums in our garden. And I'll make sure the flowerpots are well out of reach in case you should ever get cross with me."

"So, Barclay," Teddy began, "this all begs the question as to whether or not there will be charges filed against my sister. Or perhaps *you* would know, Preston?"

"I must defer to Inspector Carlyle on this matter," Mr. Fitzsimmons replied. "Criminal law, as you know, is not where my proficiency lies, and for that, I might add, I'm quite grateful."

The inspector was staring vacantly at nothing in particular until he finally snapped out of it and addressed his guests, who were all eagerly waiting to hear what he had to say. "I have no idea. One would assume that knocking somebody unconscious with a flowerpot is a fairly serious infraction of the law, when the person being knocked unconscious ends up dead through other means shortly thereafter or not. It's rather tricky. Tricky and sticky. There are no witnesses to the assault—living, anyway—other than you, Miss Mansfield, and you've just made this confession without me giving you warning, so not a word of it is admissible as evidence. So I really don't think I have a case even if I wanted to bring one. I must, however, strongly suggest that you refrain from making any future assaults."

"That's *it*?" Teddy asked.

Matilde shot her brother a look. "Would you *like* for me to be arrested and charged with a crime, Theodore?" Teddy was taking his time to respond. "I'm waiting for an answer, Theodore!"

"I'm thinking!" he finally answered, looking as if he were considering the matter seriously. "You can't just go around hitting people over the head with flowerpots, Matilde. It's not only illegal but it's terribly bad form."

"For heaven's sake! It's not as if there's been a pattern of assaults in the past, has there, Theodore?"

Teddy pulled up his right sleeve and pointed to a barely visible scar on his forearm. "You see this? Do you recall how I got this scar?"

"You aren't really going to dredge that up again, are you? You cannot *still* believe that I *intended* to cut off your arm!"

"Oh, no? Even though you came at me with a kitchen knife and said you were going to cut off my arm?"

"I was ten years old! Just turned! And what business did you have eating the very *last* piece of *my* birthday cake?"

"Yes, you're right. A completely measured response."

Inspector Carlyle was being signaled from a colleague outside his office and looked slightly relieved for it. "I'm afraid I need to veer off this trip down the Mansfields' memory lane," he told his visitors as he stood up. "So, unless or until there are any new developments with this case, I do believe we can wrap things up here. *My* job, however, is far from over. Let's not forget there is still a killer on the loose, and we cannot be certain that he, or she, is finished killing just yet." So on that cheerful note, the inspector grabbed his tin of Simpkins, gave it a shake, and left his guests behind to mull that over.

Chapter 23

After their group meeting with Inspector Carlyle ended, Matilde and Hugo took Preston to the train station so he could catch his train back to London, and Teddy, Isabel, Fred, and Ginger returned to Pembroke Cottage. It was a quiet ride, as Teddy obviously had a lot to think about. He finally turned to Isabel as if she had been following the conversation he had going on in his head. "I really am trying to be happy for Matilde and Hugo. But this is a less than ideal way to start a new life together, wouldn't you agree? And after all these years, do you think it will work? It's a little like finding an old car that's been sitting in a garage for forty years, then jumping in and expecting it to start."

"It looked to me like that old car *did* start right up. And, by the way, what happened to Teddy Mansfield the romantic?"

Teddy really didn't have an answer to Isabel's question, so he continued voicing his concerns. "And I can already hear Mousehole's gossip mill churning. If the real killer isn't found, those two will remain the prime suspects forever."

"Except, given who the victim was, they may end up with the keys to the city," Isabel offered.

Teddy abruptly pulled over to the side of the road. "I can't face going over all this again with Tuppence right now. She'll have a thousand questions. What do you say we go down to the Lion for a pint and some fish and chips?"

"I say that's an excellent idea." She wasn't anxious to relive the whole thing either.

"We can tell her when she gets to work in the morning. Or you can. I have class." Teddy smiled.

"Knowing what I know of Tuppence *and* the Mousehole gossip mill, I'm guessing she'll be fully up to speed by then," Isabel predicted as Teddy turned the Iron Lady around and headed back into the village.

When they walked into the pub, Fred and Ginger made a bee line for the kitchen, where the cooks always treated them to a few snacks. Kenly was there to greet them with his booming voice coming from across the room. It was crowded, and Teddy's usual table by the fireplace was occupied, but there were two stools at the bar, so they saddled up there after Teddy stopped to say some hellos, make some introductions, and shake a few hands. Kenly came around behind the bar and put two pints down in front of them. "Lovely to see you both, especially you, Isabel. So nice that you could make it for our annual scone bake-off *and* our murder season. Have you picked up a T-shirt yet?"

Isabel laughed, but quietly. Teddy shook his head. "That's in very poor taste, Ken."

"I pride myself on it, guv! And before you ask, no, I didn't do it and, yes, I have an airtight alibi!"

A voice came from down the bar alerting Kenly that he had a phone call. "Excuse me. Will you be ordering the usual?" Isabel and Teddy both nodded. Kenly yelled to somebody as he walked back down the bar, "Two fish and chips for the guv and the lovely Mrs. Puddles!"

"What a character that one is. But you have no shortage

of eccentric characters in your little village, Teddy. You put Gull Harbor to shame!"

Teddy raised his pint for a toast. "Cheers, Isabel. I think your charming little hamlet can hold its own, but it's going to be up to you to host the next murder."

"Cheers to that." She clinked her pint to his. "I'll put a list of potential victims together."

Kenly appeared again. "That was Tuppence, guv. Says she's been trying to track you down. Poor woman sounded quite frantic."

"What now?" Teddy said with a sigh. "Is she still on the line?"

"No. She's on her way here. And she gave me strict instructions not to let either of you leave."

Isabel took a sip of her beer. "Well, this should be interesting."

Tuppence must have ridden her bike at the pace of a Tour de France rider, because less than ten minutes later, she rushed into the pub huffing and puffing, then went straight to the bar where Teddy and Isabel were sitting. "You aren't going to believe this. You just aren't going to believe this!" Kenly held an empty pint glass up to her. "No, thank you, love. Not for me." Teddy started to get up to give her his seat but she stopped him. "Thank you, Lordship, but I'm too excited to sit."

"You sure you wouldn't care for a pint? Might calm your nerves a bit," Teddy suggested.

"I couldn't possibly."

Isabel had never seen Tuppence in such a state. Teddy seemed quite surprised as well. "Well, are you going to let us in on this fantastical happening or are you going to leave us in wonder?"

Tuppence finally composed herself. "Your friend, Mr.

Piven, called the house. I told him you were out, but he said it was me he wanted to talk to."

"That's rather curious," Teddy had to acknowledge. "Whatever for?"

"Maybe I'd better sit down. And maybe I'd better have a pint too. Might calm my nerves." Teddy chuckled. She really was working herself into a lather. He stood up, pulled the stool out for her, and signaled Kenly to bring her a pint.

"You're just not going to believe this!"

"Yes, Tuppence, you've mentioned that. Why don't you give us a try. Perhaps we will."

"Your friend Mr. Piven called—oh, I told you that part."

Teddy widened his eyes and looked over at Isabel, who was holding in a laugh.

"I do remember you saying you had a mate who worked in the palace. But you never told me he worked for the duchess!"

"To which duchess are you referring? There seems to be no shortage of them in our United Kingdom," Teddy teased her, and winked at Isabel.

"Stop doing my head in, Lordship! You know exactly to which duchess I'm referring!"

Isabel was being thoroughly entertained by these two. It was very nice to have the mood lightened after so many dark days in a row. Kenly came back and set Tuppence's beer down in front of her. "Here you go, love." She immediately raised it to her lips and chugged it halfway before plopping it back down on the bar.

"Tuppence, are you going to reveal this great mystery to us sometime this evening?" Teddy pleaded.

Isabel was also on the edge of her barstool waiting for the big reveal.

Tuppence leaned over and gave her a hug. "It's you I have to thank, Isabel, for sending Mr. Piven home with my orange-rhubarb scones the night he came for dinner." Isabel and Teddy were both thoroughly confused, so Tuppence tried to clarify. "The kitchen staff of the estate where the duchess was staying that night—Lord and Lady Something or Other's estate—burned the scones they baked for her breakfast the next morning. And the duchess begins every morning with tea and a scone, so this was quite a serious matter, because there was no time to bake a new batch in time for her breakfast. But luckily, Mr. Piven remembered he had the scones you sent back with him, so he had the maid put those on the duchess's breakfast tray." Tuppence reached for her pint and took another healthy glug. "And she told him—the duchess of *Cornwall*—told Mr. Piven that they were the best scones she had ever had in her life! But that's not all. She asked him to invite whoever baked them, me, to come to the kitchen at Buckingham Palace to show *her* pastry chef how to bake *my* scones for the duchess, *and* for His Royal Highness, the prince of Wales!"

Isabel screamed and gave Tuppence a huge hug. "This is *so* exciting! Baking scones for the duchess of Cornwall? How incredible is that?"

Kenly reached across and high-fived her. "Well done, you!"

"*And* he also said she wants to come down to the kitchen and meet me in person! *And* she was going to make sure Her Majesty tried them too!" Tuppence finished her pint.

Isabel screamed and hugged her again, then realized the beer was making her slightly more excitable than usual.

Tuppence was still on cloud nine. "I can't stop pinching myself. I just can't believe this is happening to me! Things like this don't happen to me!" And now she moved into panic mode. "But what am I going to wear? What do I call her? What if I bugger up my recipe? And I still don't know how to curtsy! I'll need to learn to curtsy! I have such terrible

balance. What if I fall flat on my face in front of the duchess of Cornwall mid-curtsy?" Tuppence was then struck with
another daunting thought. "What will I do if I run into the
sovereign herself? I think I'd faint right there in front of her.
They'd have to take me out on a stretcher."

Teddy put his arm around her. "I'm very proud of you,
Tuppence. Very well done, and very well deserved. And I expect if you're offered a position in the palace, you'll drop me
like a bad habit."

"Don't be silly, Lordship. A Cornish farm girl like me
working in Buckingham Palace? I'm already a bloody wreck
just thinking about being inside there for a day! What if I
throw up? Sometimes I throw up when I get too nervous.
Oh, dear."

Teddy winced. "Can we put the vomiting talk away for
a bit? Now, did Alistair give you a date? And where will you
stay? At the palace?"

"I wouldn't sleep a wink. No, he told me the name of a
hotel. And he said he'll arrange my train ticket and have a car
and driver to meet me at Paddington Station. Can you imagine? A car and a driver for *me*? To take me to Buckingham
Palace? I'm still just completely gobsmacked. My head is fully
done in, it is. I think I might throw up right now."

"Please don't," Teddy requested as Tuppence took a few
deep breaths. "And what are the dates of this royal adventure
of yours?" he asked as he pulled up the calendar on his phone.

"June eighteenth at ten a.m. But I'll need to travel to London the afternoon of the seventeenth, and if I'm unable to
make the last train back to Penzance on the eighteenth, I'll
have to spend another night and come back the morning of
the nineteenth."

"So you're going to need all three of those days off?"
Teddy took a moment and shook his head. "I'm afraid that's
quite impossible. I'm having houseguests for those same dates.

I'll need you baking scones right here." He took a long drink of beer. "But I'm sure the duchess can find alternative dates. I'll talk to Alistair for you."

Tuppence was speechless, while Isabel and Kenly looked at Teddy incredulously. Teddy played it off for as long as he could before he started laughing. Isabel and Kenly then joined in, but it took Tuppence a minute to compose herself. Teddy put his arm around her again. "Do you think I would ever stand in the way of you baking scones for the duchess of Cornwall and the future king of England? I'd be sure to hide the garden hose if I did!" They all went silent again. Teddy looked around. "Still too soon?" Isabel answered him with raised eyebrows and a dip of the chin while Kenly laughed and went to pour three more pints.

Tuppence had finally come back to earth. "Oh, my goodness! I almost forgot about all that! You have to tell me what's happened!"

"We absolutely are *not* going to raise *that* unpleasant topic tonight! Ken, scrap those pints and bring us a bottle of your best champagne! We're going to celebrate!"

"What are we celebrating?" came a familiar voice from behind them. It was Matilde. "Hugo's parking the car. I hope we aren't intruding."

Teddy stood up and hugged his sister. "Of course not . . . Now we have two happy occasions to celebrate!" He yelled down the bar, "Make it two bottles, Ken! And five glasses. No, six! One for you too!"

After sitting down together, ordering dinner, and drinking even more champagne, they all enjoyed a wonderful, lighthearted evening together, with Kenly popping in and out to make six. Tuppence shared her news about her upcoming trip to the palace, and Matilde and Hugo shared their plans for their wedding, which they decided would be held at the Captain's Cottage. The actual ceremony would be under the elm tree where they had their first kiss. "We're thinking the week of June eighteenth," Matilde announced, and was promptly met by a collective "No!" followed by more laughs.

For Isabel, it was an unforgettable evening. She saw a side of Matilde she had never seen before and didn't imagine even existed: soft, kind, romantic, and unmistakably in love. And Hugo turned out to be quite an interesting character too. He had become quite animated now that he wasn't re-living a traumatic tale of a lost love or trying to confess to a murder he didn't commit. Or maybe it was the champagne. Whatever the case, he was excited to share their plans for their retirement together, which included cruising the Greek Islands in his recently purchased sailboat. Upon hearing that, Teddy leaned over and whispered to Isabel, "I wish him luck and a bon voyage. Trapped on a thirty-five-foot sailboat with my sister? Not even the *QE2* would provide enough room to make that experience bearable." Matilde, the only one at the table not drinking champagne—which Teddy and Isabel both agreed was a very encouraging sign—did her best to teach Tuppence to curtsy. But because she *had* imbibed in a few glasses of champagne, it looked more as if she were practicing Cornish folk dancing moves, and not very well.

They had all forgotten, at least for a few hours, about all the depressing murder business that had consumed them for so many days. But they had also forgotten another related matter: somewhere out there, lurking in or around this quaint seaside village, a killer was still on the loose.

Chapter 24

Isabel's visit to Cornwall was finally nearing an end. In two more days, she would be taking the train back to London to catch her flight home. Although she had made Teddy promise to give her a rain check for the grand London tour he planned to give her, she was letting him off the hook. She had seen all the major tourist attractions on her double-decker bus tour; enjoyed high tea and a lovely stroll through Hyde Park and Kensington Gardens with her new friend, Runa; had been to see a play in the West End; and had stayed in an exquisite hotel, thanks to her kids. But the real reason she wanted to go straight home was that she was terribly homesick. Isabel Puddles was ready to get home to Poplar Bluff; to her home, her lake, her friends and family, her dogs, her breakfasts with Frances at the Land's End, and her job at the hardware store. Plus, it was springtime in western Michigan, a time of year she loved. It was a different kind of magic from springtime in Cornwall, but for her, no place was more magical than the shores of Lake Michigan during springtime.

When Teddy got home from class, he and Isabel took Fred and Ginger on a nice, long walk to take in the view and then down to the village to have lunch at an outdoor café on the harbor. They talked about Teddy's plans to come to the States to see Elizabeth and his grandkids in the summer, and to get settled in his new "tiny house" in Gull Harbor. And they talked about Isabel's Fourth of July barbecue and going back to the Old Cottage Inn to have the duck. What they didn't talk about was their friendship turning into anything more than just that. And that was fine by Isabel. She knew she had feelings for Teddy that could potentially turn into something more romantic, but she wasn't quite there yet. At least she didn't think she was. And if Teddy had been, this would have been the time to bring it up. But he didn't. And that was fine by her too. Had their feelings for each other been lopsided, continuing what had become a wonderful friendship would have been difficult. And cultivating a romance in the midst of a murder investigation also had its drawbacks. Isabel wasn't somebody who believed everything happened for a reason, but she liked to believe that maybe some things did, and maybe this would turn out to be one of them. Who could know what the future might bring for them, but she was perfectly happy to let things unfold naturally.

They had been sitting down at the café for less than five minutes when they saw Nigel Plumbottom's Rolls-Royce coming toward them. Teddy secured the dogs' leashes, and the other locals at the café went on high alert, looking around to identify exit paths. But when the Rolls passed them, and without any casualties or causing any property damage, two things stood out as very peculiar. For one, Nigel was not sitting in the backseat. But even stranger was that Tiegan was not wearing her uniform or her chauffeur's cap. Instead, she had on what appeared to be an American baseball cap, worn backward. She also had the driver's-side window down with her arm out and her elbow resting on the door, *and* she was listening to the Spice Girls—a group Isabel recognized only because Carly and Charlie played them incessantly as kids.

She couldn't forget the Spice Girls even if she had tried. And she had tried.

"Something very strange is afoot," Teddy declared as they watched the Rolls disappear around the corner. The locals were also abuzz, looking around at one another in disbelief. Not since Nessie's last sighting in Loch Ness had there been so much bewilderment. Teddy's phone rang. It was Inspector Carlyle. "Hello, Barclay . . . I'm in the village right now, as a matter of fact. . . . Yes, she's still here, sitting across the table from me as we speak. She leaves tomorrow. . . . All right, we'll come by shortly." Teddy had a peculiar look on his face as he slipped his phone back into his pocket. "Well, as you gathered, that was Mousehole's own Columbo. He was afraid he'd missed you. Evidently, he has some big news regarding the Amesbury case. He'd like to share it with us before it becomes public knowledge. Which in this village means we have about fifteen minutes. Shall we head over?"

"Absolutely!" Isabel stood up, alerting Fred and Ginger that it was time to go. "Do you think there's any chance he's made an arrest? I would love to leave here knowing this case has been solved."

"Wouldn't that be wonderful? Let's go." Teddy stopped and tugged the dogs away from the curb after he spotted the Rolls-Royce again rounding the corner. There was still no Nigel in the back, and this time Tiegan waved at them as she passed. Teddy was flummoxed. "Something is *very* much out of order. Where could Nigel possibly be?" He thought it over for a moment, then turned to Isabel with a slightly panicked expression. "Please don't tell me we've got another murder on our hands."

Mousehole's police headquarters were very active this afternoon. Inspector Carlyle had just come out of his office when he spotted Isabel and Teddy coming in with Fred and Ginger. "Well, if it isn't McMillan and wife!" They looked at each other, both somewhat puzzled by the reference. The inspector continued after shaking their hands, then leaned down to say hello to Fred and Ginger. "And my two favorite canine investigators. Please come into my office!" He yelled at somebody in the outer office to bring in some tea and biscuits. "I'm so glad not to have missed you, Isabel. It's been such a pleasure trying to solve this murder with you. You've made my first homicide a very special one, and your insights have been most helpful."

"That's very nice of you to say. Thank you, Inspector. I'm glad I could be of some help. But I'd feel much better about leaving if we actually *had* solved this murder!"

"Funny you should mention that, Isabel. Please have a seat and I'll bring you both up to speed."

"So, Barclay, is it safe for us to assume from your rather upbeat mood that you've finally got the Amesbury murder sorted out? Or is this magical thinking on my part?"

"I'm happy to say—well, *happy* is perhaps the wrong word, because I take no joy in this. Let's say I'm pleased to—no, *pleased* isn't right, either. . . . I'm both sorry and relieved—that's better, let's go with that. I'm both sorry and relieved to tell you that only hours ago, I arrested a member of our community— someone widely respected, I hasten to add—for the murder of Hyacinth Amesbury. *And* I now have an eyewitness to the murder." He reached for his tin of candy. "Would anybody care for a Simpkins?" The deadpan stares coming from across his desk were a strong indicator that candy was not what his guests wanted right now. "I won't keep you in suspense any longer. Nigel Plumbottom is in custody and awaiting arraignment, where he will be charged with murder."

Isabel and Teddy looked at each other in pure astonishment and their jaws dropped simultaneously, before they exclaimed in unison, "You're *kidding!*"

Inspector Carlyle popped a Simpkins and waited for his guests to recover from the shock of the news before he picked up his story. "I'll explain. It seems Nigel and Hyacinth had recently made a financial arrangement for him to purchase a painting she owned. Two thousand pounds, they had apparently settled on. Must have been some painting."

Isabel looked at Teddy. "Remember Nigel telling us he had been trying to negotiate a deal with her for one of her paintings? What was the artist's name?"

"Benjamin Prescott?" the inspector offered.

"Yes, that's it," Isabel answered, "Nigel said he collects him."

Teddy nodded and appeared to be trying to say something, but, still in a state of disbelief, he was at a loss for words, so the inspector started up again.

"Well, out of the blue, Tiegan called and asked to meet with me privately. She was afraid to come into the station, so I went to her apartment. That was an experience I do not care to share with you or with anybody. All I'll say is, if Andrew Lloyd Webber had experienced what I did last night, the world would have been spared his musical."

Teddy had recovered from the shock and now seemed to be growing impatient. "We get it, Barclay. Please get to the point. This is agonizing."

The inspector smiled. He really did enjoy drawing things out. "Well, Tiegan had quite a story to tell, and went on to share with me what happened that Saturday afternoon at Amesbury Acreage when they went to pay Hyacinth the two thousand quid and pick up the painting. It was a rather gripping account, I must say."

A constable knocked, then entered the office with the tea and biscuits, giving the inspector another opportunity for a dramatic pause. Isabel wondered for a moment if he might be trying to impress Teddy with his storytelling abilities. If he was, it was lost on him. Teddy was getting even more impatient. "Can we please get on with this gripping tale, Barclay?"

"Tiegan told me everything seemed perfectly fine when she pulled up to the Amesbury home. She parked in the drive and waited in the car while Nigel went to the front door and knocked, but nobody answered."

"Did she say whether or not Alby was there?" Teddy asked.

"According to Tiegan, he was not. But he may well have been in his secret room in the basement eating crisps. Who knows?"

"Continue, please," Teddy said, almost pleading.

"Apparently Nigel then went around the side of the house, presumably to see if Hyacinth was out in her garden. But after a few minutes Tiegan realized Nigel had forgotten the envelope with the money in it. She had been holding it for him since they took it from the safe in the shop. So she walked around back to give it to him and found Nigel talking to Hyacinth, who was sitting in a chair, looking rather unwell, she said, and holding an ice pack to her head. Of course, now we know what the ice pack was all about, but no need to revisit that. So Tiegan walked over, handed Nigel the envelope, said nothing, and went back to the car. She didn't ask what the ice pack was for because she said, quite candidly, that she didn't care. So she went back to the Rolls and began dusting off the exterior—part of her job—and after a few minutes she began to hear arguing. She said she didn't think anything of it because, again, she didn't care, *and* because it was Hyacinth Amesbury, who, as we all know, was a notorious arguer. But she said the argument didn't last long, maybe two minutes, and then it went quiet. It was Saturday and Tiegan said she had to get home and feed her cats and then get ready because she had plans with her boyfriend—" Teddy and Isabel were in shock all over again. "I know, I know. It was a stunner for me too!" the inspector was quick to add.

"Who *is* it?" Teddy asked incredulously.

"She wouldn't say. But I got the impression he wasn't a local." The inspector was interrupted by a knock at the door. "Come in!"

"Chief, Mr. Plumbottom's solicitor is here."

"Set him up in the interrogation room and then bring Mr. Plumbottom around to meet with him."

"Sure thing, Chief."

"Nigel's already been arrested?" Teddy's utter disbelief in this perplexing scenario was growing by the second.

"Yes, and you'll see why in a minute. Now, where was I?" The inspector reached for his candy tin again. "Would anybody—"

"Barclay, if you offer us another Simpkins right now, I cannot be responsible for what I might do," Teddy told the inspector quite emphatically.

"Point taken, Teddy. Right. So Tiegan walked back to the garden to tell Nigel she needed to go, and found him struggling to get up off the ground. He's a rather rotund man, as you know, so I can't imagine it was a graceful performance. When he finally righted himself, there was Hyacinth lying on the ground looking rather deceased, according to Tiegan."

Teddy's jaw dropped open again. "Nigel Plumbottom strangling someone to death? Even if it *was* Hyacinth, it just doesn't make sense."

Isabel agreed with that last part. "No, that's the problem. It *doesn't* make sense," she said to both Teddy and the inspector.

"So, Barclay? Can you make it make sense to us?" Teddy was also waiting to be convinced.

"Just bear with me Teddy, please. I think it will all become clear after you've heard the whole story. So, Tiegan said she ran back to the car before Nigel could see her, although she was afraid he might have, but I'll get to that bit. A few minutes later Nigel came out the front door with the painting and put it in the boot of the car. And when he got back into the car, she could see the top of the envelope the money had been in, sticking out of his coat pocket."

Teddy was skeptical. "So you're saying Nigel's motive for killing Hyacinth was so he could acquire this painting without having to pay her for it? I don't know, Barclay. Doesn't seem like motive enough to me. Nigel's hardly a pauper."

Isabel agreed with Teddy, but then had a question for the inspector that was slightly off track. "What took her so long to report this?"

"That was my very first question, Isabel: 'Why did you wait until now to report this?'"

"And her response was what?" Teddy asked.

"Her exact words were, 'I wasn't angry enough until now.' So, of course, that begged the question: 'What made you angry enough to turn your brother in for murder?'"

"Whatever that reason may be, Barclay, doesn't her admitting she was angry make her story rather questionable?" Teddy looked at Isabel, who gave him an approving nod. She was nowhere close to being convinced Tiegan's story was true.

"How do you know her story hasn't been completely fabricated, Inspector? Isn't it possible she's throwing *him* under the bus because *she* strangled Hyacinth?"

"My thoughts exactly. And normally I would dismiss an account such as hers as simply one angry sibling taking revenge on the sibling who made them angry. Especially if I was lacking any physical evidence . . . but I'm not."

Isabel and Teddy shifted and straightened up in their chairs, then shared a look. Okay, this was suddenly getting more interesting. Naturally Inspector Carlyle was going to let that little teaser hover in the air for as long as his audience would allow. Just as he sensed they were about to let him know his time was up, he picked up where he left off. "So after Nigel strangled her, *allegedly*, for some inexplicable reason he picked up the ice pack Hyacinth had been holding on her head, and was *still* holding it when he got back to the car with the painting. So apparently he threw it into the boot along with the painting. When they got home, Tiegan took the painting into the shop as Nigel had instructed, and then she put the ice pack under the sink in the loo and forgot about it until yesterday."

Isabel thought this last part over for a moment. "What sort of ice pack was it, Inspector?"

"The old-fashioned kind, with a fabric bag that expands, you know, with a cap on top."

"Yes, I know the kind you mean," Isabel replied. "And you can use it as an ice pack or a hot-water bottle." Now it was time for a follow-up question. "How do we—excuse me—how do *you* know it even belonged to Hyacinth?"

"I drove out and showed a photo of it to Alby. He identified it as belonging to his mother. He also remembered it had a burn mark somewhere from her getting it too close to the stove one time. And it does have a burn mark on it. The lab found Nigel's prints on the lid, which is metal, and his DNA was found on the bag itself. It even had a spot of Hyacinth's blood on it from the head injury. I got the forensics results back this morning, so I went to his shop and arrested him. I really had no choice in the matter."

"How did you get Nigel's prints and a DNA sample?" Teddy asked.

"The same way—" The inspector caught himself and stole a look at Isabel. "Well, I asked Tiegan to bring in one of Nigel's hairbrushes along with the ice pack. The brush provided what we needed."

"Isn't *she* guilty of a serious crime here, Inspector?" Isabel asked as her skepticism of Tiegan's story gained steam. "That is, allegedly witnessing a murder, not reporting it, and then withholding evidence implicating the killer? That's a felony in the States."

"Indeed it is! A very serious crime here too. We're not a banana republic, Isabel!" Inspector Carlyle laughed before getting serious again. "*Unless* you were afraid for your own life if the alleged murderer knows, or suspects, you were a witness to the crime. And to that point, as I think I mentioned, Tiegan was afraid Nigel may have seen *her* see *him* strangle Mrs. Amesbury, or suspected she had."

The inspector seemed perfectly satisfied with that as an explanation, but for Isabel it was dubious at best and she said so. "She *claims* she was afraid. With all due respect, Inspector, that's a rather flimsy explanation, if you ask me. And awfully convenient too, isn't it."

Teddy couldn't seem to make up his mind about Nigel's culpability. "Incriminating evidence, I would agree, but you still haven't told us what she was so angry about. And I think that may very well matter here."

"I absolutely agree," Isabel added. "And was it something that angered her *enough* to frame her brother for murder? One she in fact committed?" Isabel waited for the inspector to interject. He did not, so she continued. "But, all right, let's give her the benefit of the doubt. Don't you find it strange that for all this time, she was willing to overlook her brother committing murder *and* live with the fear, her *alleged* fear, that he might eliminate her? Then only decide to report any of this to you when it suited her?"

"So what put the bee in her bonnet, Barclay?" Teddy was getting impatient. "I could have written a book in the time it's taking you to tell this story."

Inspector Carlyle laughed. "I could tell it faster were I not being peppered with questions. Now, Tiegan, as you may or may not know, lives in an apartment her brother owns in the village. Her salary as his chauffeur is only a hundred quid a week, but she lives rent free in that apartment as part of their arrangement. She's also, as I may have mentioned, a cat lover, so Nigel allowed her to have two cats. Tenants in his building could have either one small dog or two cats. Those were the rules. After talking to Tiegan, I then spoke to her neighbors next door. Lovely couple. They complained to Nigel about a stench coming from his sister's apartment that exceeded anything two cats could ever produce. So Nigel popped in for a visit and discovered she had more like ten. I didn't count, but I think that's probably a conservative estimate. The smell was horrendous. Nigel was apparently very displeased and told her she had to get rid of all but two. If she refused, he would call the authorities and have them *all* removed. Her only other choice was to move out. Well, with a hundred cats and a hundred quid a week, where was she going to go?"

Isabel had been listening attentively. "So that's when she decided her brother was the one who needed to go, not the cats."

Teddy was suddenly aggravated. "Not that I'm siding with Nigel. He may very *well* be a murderer. Who knows these days? But even still, Tiegan is no hero here. As Isabel has pointed out, what kind of person sits on evidence that could potentially solve a murder and says nothing about it until her cats are in jeopardy? It doesn't add up."

Isabel circled back to what, for her, was the most nagging question: "What I'm still unclear about, Inspector, is what you believe Nigel's motive for murdering Hyacinth would have been. It can't have been about the money. We know he was not a poor man. Two thousand pounds is a hefty sum of money, but is it worth killing for?"

The inspector was quick to answer. "For those inclined to murder, I would argue it is more than sufficient."

Isabel couldn't argue that sad reality, so she changed course. "And what about the painting in question? Have you found it in Nigel's art collection?"

"Not yet. I have men over there doing a search of both his home and his shop."

Teddy straightened up in his chair. He clearly had something to say. "I'm still not convinced he's guilty, but if he did strangle Hyacinth, it wouldn't have been over two thousand quid. What might have overtaken him, though, was some lingering rage over Hyacinth's role in him losing the election. Nigel loved being the mayor of Mousehole. He hasn't been the same man since he lost. And Hyacinth did everything she could to destroy him with a rather aggressive smear campaign. Who knows what she had against him? And it doesn't matter, because she had something against everybody. I do know he had considerable animosity toward her. But again, take a number."

"Does Nigel know it's Tiegan who turned him in?" Isabel asked.

"If what she's told me is true—"

"That's a big if." Isabel immediately apologized for letting her inside voice speak out loud.

Barclay forced a smile and continued. "Again, *if* what she has told me is true about Nigel suspecting she may have witnessed or *suspected* she witnessed what he did—*allegedly* did—I can't imagine he wouldn't assume it *was* her."

"And do you intend to carry on with your investigation while Nigel is serving at Her Majesty's pleasure, Barclay?"

"Of course, Teddy. I'm keeping an open mind. But my gut tells me Tiegan is telling the truth. In the meantime, and until I'm presented with evidence that can exculpate Mr. Plumbottom, Tiegan and her thousand and one cats can sleep easy for now."

Isabel looked at the inspector for a second or two, then

decided it was time to speak her mind. "I'm sorry, but don't you think this is all just a little bit too easy, Inspector? I mean everything seems to have worked out quite nicely for Tiegan and her cats, but not at all well for Nigel. I have to go back to what I said before—how do we know *she* isn't the one who strangled Hyacinth, stole the money, and then framed her brother for murder so he would no longer pose a threat to her cats? And put a little money in her pocket at the same time. And as far as your evidence goes, wouldn't it have been quite simple for her to have been the one to take the ice pack after she killed Hyacinth, and then find a reason to hand it to her brother later for the sole purpose of getting his prints on it? He would think nothing of it other than wonder why his sister was handing him an ice pack. Or maybe she left it on the counter in the shop so he would have to move it and leave behind his prints and some DNA on it that way. She wears driving gloves for her job, as I recall. Her prints would be nowhere to be found—not on the ice pack *and* not on the garden hose."

"The gloves don't help much," Teddy inserted as he reached down to pet Fred and Ginger, asleep at his feet.

Isabel continued to build her case against Tiegan. "And why would he have picked up the ice pack after he had just strangled her anyway? Then go inside and take the painting, still carrying the ice pack, and *then* go put the painting *and* the ice pack in the trunk of his car? It makes absolutely no sense."

Teddy and Inspector Carlyle looked at each other while mulling over Isabel's very reasonable questions. Teddy spoke first. "Why *would* you strangle somebody and pick up their ice pack to take with you?"

"Unless you were planning to present it as evidence after making sure the person you were trying to frame had his fingerprints on it," Isabel added. "And here's another thing that doesn't smell right. If Tiegan's job as Nigel's chauffeur included handling his cell phone, holding on to his money, those sorts of assistant-like things, why would *he* be the one to go in to make a simple cash transaction for a painting with a woman he held in such contempt? Wouldn't it have been much easier, and completely in character for him, to send Tiegan in to do it while he waited in the car? Assuming he was there at all?"

Inspector Carlyle didn't disagree, but how could he? Isabel was making a very convincing argument. And he was well aware, as was Teddy, that her instincts and sleuthing skills were usually pretty spot-on. The inspector looked slightly defeated. "I do suppose we would be remiss if we didn't at least explore the possibility that she's more of a criminal mastermind than I would *ever* have given her credit for."

"Inspector, I'm prepared to accept that I may be completely off the mark here," Isabel assured him, "but if all you have is a cat lady afraid of losing her cats, who has a reputation for being, well, not quite all there, and an ice pack with some fingerprints and DNA—evidence with a chain of custody that is highly questionable—I think there is every possibility I'm right. It seems to me that if Tiegan's motive for the murder— two thousand pounds—and her motive to frame her brother for the crime to eliminate the threat of losing her cats or possibly become homeless, then she is far more likely to be your killer than Nigel." Isabel suddenly stood up, and the corgis scrambled up to join her. "It's all just food for thought, Inspector. Teddy, would you mind if we went over and had a talk with Alby? He is home now, correct, Inspector?"

"I sent him home yesterday. Never did get that ankle bracelet approved, but I let him out anyway."

"With your blessing, Inspector, I'd like to see if Teddy and I might be able to bring you enough evidence to convince you of Nigel's innocence. There's something that's just not adding up with this whole business about the painting. I have a feeling this is where the key to this whole case lies." She stopped and smiled at the inspector. "I do hope I haven't overstepped here, Inspector."

"Not at all, Isabel," he replied somewhat unconvincingly. "I asked for your insights and you have given them freely. I *am* taking some solace in knowing that at least we have narrowed it down to two suspects. One, I'm still leaning toward as our likely killer, but I'm open to other possibilities. Now, if you'll excuse me I'm going to see if Mr. Plumbottom is ready to answer a few questions for me now that his solicitor is present."

Teddy stood up and handed Fred's leash to Isabel. "Any hunch of yours, Isabel Puddles, is worth following up. Let's go see Alby. Barclay, we'll call you if this leads us anywhere. And you'll let us know what Nigel has to say?"

"I will indeed. But I'll have no choice but to proceed with the evidence I do have unless you bring me something that supports this alternate theory. He's going to be arraigned tomorrow afternoon, so consider this investigation open and active until then."

As they left the police station, Isabel told Teddy she felt bad about poking so many holes in his case. Teddy laughed. "If it were a lifeboat, he'd be swimming right now. But, as you said, Tiegan's story is flimsy, at best, and a man's life is at stake. And don't forget, this is Barclay's first murder. You've ridden in this parade before."

Chapter 25

After Teddy and Isabel dropped the dogs off at home, they were too tired to walk anymore, so they got into the Iron Lady to drive over to Amesbury Acreage to talk to Alby about the painting. But then Isabel had an idea. "How about we go by Nigel's shop first to see what's going on there? Maybe we can have a chat with Tiegan if she's around."

"I think that's a grand idea," Teddy concurred as he turned onto the road that would take them back into the village. As they approached Nigel's shop, they could see his Rolls-Royce parked in the driveway along with a couple of police cars. Isabel looked over at Teddy and smiled. "Well? Shall we go inside and have a look around?"

"This should be interesting," Teddy said with a smile as he killed the engine.

Before they even got out of the car, Tiegan had come out of the shop looking irritated and a little bit confused. She was dressed sloppily in a pair of jean shorts, flip-flops, an over-sized Garfield the Cat sweatshirt that said something about Mondays and lasagna, and she was wearing the same ball cap they had seen her in earlier. Isabel got out of the car first and smiled. Having no idea who she was, Tiegan was rather curt.

"May I help you?" But when she saw Teddy get out, she got slightly friendlier. "Oh, hello, Mr. Mansfield."

"Hello, Tiegan. I'd like you to meet my dear friend, Isabel Puddles."

"Lovely to meet you, Tiegan. I've been annoying Teddy for days about coming into your shop."

"It's not the best day, as you have probably heard, Mr. Mansfield. The police have ransacked the shop and now they're searching Nigel's house. I'm not even sure what they're looking for. I thought they had all the evidence they needed. Anyway, I was just about to close up. I've got somewhere to be." She looked back at Isabel. "You're American."

Isabel couldn't tell if that was a question or an observation. "I am indeed. But my great-grandfather was English. He came from Yorkshire."

Tiegan could not have cared less. "So what is it I can do for you? Like I said, I was just about to close up."

"That's a shame. I'm leaving tomorrow, so this really is my last opportunity. I talked to the owner of this shop. Nigel, I believe his name was. Teddy introduced us."

"He's my brother."

"Such a lovely man." Tiegan had no reaction to that. "Well, your brother told me about a painting he was in the process of purchasing from, oh, who was it, Teddy?"

"Hyacinth Amesbury," Teddy answered. "You know her of course, Tiegan." The cat lady had no reaction to that either. "Apparently they made the deal shortly before she was— before she died."

"Such a shame," Isabel said, shaking her head. "Well, it comes for us all in time, doesn't it? Now, your brother described it to me as a painting of your charming village with the water beyond it. I'd be very interested in seeing it, assuming you have it here. I've fallen in love with Mousehole and I'd love to preserve that memory with an original piece of art.

The way your brother described the work to me, it sounded just exquisite. I'm prepared to pay whatever you're asking. I'm really not much of a haggler."

Tiegan stared at her for a moment, then at Teddy, almost as if she were looking for reassurance that this lady was legit. "I'll go in and get it. You can look at it out here."

"That would be lovely. Thank you, Tiegan." Isabel waited until she was inside before turning to Teddy. "Why do you suppose she doesn't want us to come inside the store?"

Teddy shrugged his shoulders. "Don't know. Maybe she's got more cats in there?"

Tiegan came out the door moments later carrying a large oil painting. It was indeed similar to what Nigel described as far as what the painting depicted—an overview of Mousehole and the sea beyond it—but artistically it was, in a word, dreadful. One of her cats could have painted it. And it couldn't have been more than twenty or thirty years old if the frame was any indication of its age. "Isn't it just exquisite, Teddy? I'm getting chills! What are you asking for it, Tiegan?"

"What are you offering for it?"

"I hope you won't be insulted if I were to offer you, say four thousand American for it? I'm afraid that's all I have left in my budget for this trip. I don't think it's worth quite that much, if I'm being honest, but it's worth that much to me."

Tiegan was feeling nothing close to insulted. "I suppose I could let it go for that. Cash?"

"Of course. But would it be imposing of me to ask you to wait here while Teddy drives me back to my cottage to get you the money? I know you said you have someplace to be."

"I can be late. Sure, I'll wait for you."

"Thank you, Tiegan. You're a doll! Teddy, would you please take a quick photo on your phone so I can send it to my decorator back in the States?" She turned back to Tiegan.

"She's doing my new living room, and I want this to go right above the fireplace. You don't mind, do you?"

Tiegan shrugged her shoulders, so Teddy pulled his phone out and took a few shots of the painting. "And do you happen to have a tape measure so I can send her the measurements too?"

"I think there's one inside. I'll go look." Tiegan was suddenly in a very cheerful mood.

The minute the door closed behind her, Teddy looked at Isabel with wide-eyed amazement. "I haven't a clue as to what you're up to here, but it's a pleasure to watch the master at work. And, by the way, your well-heeled American art collector character is quite impressive."

"Why, thank you, Teddy. I've been listening to the summer ladies in Gull Harbor for years. I suppose I must have picked it up through osmosis."

"But why do you need to measure it?" Teddy asked. "Just curious."

"Well, I thought we might be able to sneak the measurements of the trunk—sorry, the boot—of Nigel's car, but there's no need to now. I can see from here there's no way that monstrosity could ever fit. So that's the first hiccup in her version of events. Did she not tell the inspector that Nigel put the painting in the boot and threw the ice pack in with it?"

"Right you are."

"But that's the least of it. What completely torpedoes her story is that it is absurd to believe that Nigel would ever have paid one pound, let alone two thousand for this abomination in oil. He knew exactly what he was trying to buy from Hyacinth, and it certainly wasn't this! So it wasn't him who carried it out of the house. In fact, he could not have been there at all."

Tiegan reappeared with the tape measure and Isabel

quickly measured. "Four feet wide by three feet high. I think it's going to be a perfect fit. All right, we will see you back here very shortly, dear."

"Do you want me to wrap it?" Tiegan asked, now with an even friendlier tone.

"Don't bother, dear. I'll need to have it crated and shipped," Isabel yelled back as she walked to the car. After Teddy opened the door for her, she turned and waved before getting in. "Ta-ta!"

As they backed out of the drive, Isabel smiled at Teddy. "I wouldn't have that painting hanging in my *garage*. I'm looking forward to our chat with Alby. I think I've almost got this figured out."

Teddy looked over at her admiringly. "I get the feeling this does not bode well for our village cat enthusiast. But I'm going to just sit back and enjoy watching it all unfold."

Alby was sitting on the front porch when they pulled up to the house. Teddy got out of the car first and yelled up to him, "Hello, Alby! Just wanted to come over and check in on you. You all right?"

"I'm all right," he replied without much commitment.

Isabel got out next. "Hello, Alby! Nice to see you again! And in such a lovely setting this time!"

"Did you bring any more Hobnobs?"

"I'm sorry, I did not, but I'll talk to Tuppence. Maybe she can bake you up a fresh batch!" Isabel and Teddy walked up to the edge of the porch. "Alby, I wanted to ask you again about that painting your mom sold to Mr. Plumbottom. Teddy, would you mind showing Alby the picture we took of the painting we saw in that shop?" Teddy pulled up the photo and walked over to show it to Alby. "You recognize this?"

Alby leaned in and squinted a bit, then started to laugh. "Who's going to buy *that*? That's one of my dad's paintings. Mum hated it, but my dad insisted it go above the fireplace. My poor dad loved to paint, but he was just terrible at it. We didn't have nothing else big enough to hang there, though, so it just stayed. I didn't even notice it was gone. Guess Mum sold *it* too. Where did you find it?"

Teddy jumped in and answered for her. "Just some junk shop outside the village."

"Well, that's a good place for it. But that's definitely not the painting Nigel wanted to buy."

That much she knew. What Isabel really wanted to know was the whereabouts of the painting he *did* want to buy. "Do you still have that painting here? The small one of the village we talked about? Or did that deal go through, after all?"

"That painting you're talking about disappeared. It used to hang in my mum's dressing room. After we talked about it when I was in jail, I went up and looked for it first thing when I got home. It wasn't there. So either she sold it to Nigel and hid the money someplace where I can't find it—and believe me I've looked—or somebody came in here while I was away and either stole *it* or the money. Either way, I'm high and dry, as usual. I don't suppose you've got any work for me over there at Pembroke, do you, Mr. Mansfield?"

"I wish I could help you out, Alby, but after that situation with Tuppence's bicarb it really wouldn't be safe for you right now."

"My mum put me up to that. It weren't my idea. I just wanted to go to the sea park." Alby stared off into the distance for a moment. "You want to buy *this* place? The bank's going to be auctioning it off here at the end of the month. If I'm lucky, I'll make a few quid if they get a halfway decent price. Then maybe I can take myself to the sea park."

"I wish you all the best, Alby. I really do. Isabel, are we ready?"

Isabel nodded and looked at Alby with a sympathetic smile. She was suddenly feeling only compassion for this poor soul. What a sad life he must have had. And what a bleak future he had ahead of him. Frisking his dead mother before he buried her in the garden was an unfortunate choice, but it was obvious Alby was dealing with some formidable demons, so she preferred to blame *them* for those horrendously gruesome acts. She was sure that trapped in there somewhere was a very lonely and troubled boy, and she really hoped he did make it to the sea park. "Best of luck, Alby," Isabel said to him, feeling her voice crack slightly. "You take care of yourself."

Alby said nothing in return. He just stared at them blankly as they left. When they got back into the car, they were both quiet as they drove away from Amesbury Acreage. Isabel looked back before they pulled out onto the main road. "It really is a lovely property. All it needs is a little TLC."

Teddy agreed. "But I would certainly be hesitant to do any gardening."

"You could always bring Fred and Ginger over to do a sweep of the grounds before you plant," Isabel suggested.

"Mrs. Puddles, I have a question. What are we doing and where are we going?"

"I think those are two very good questions, Teddy. Here's what I'm thinking and let's see what you think. . . . We need to find a way to smoke Tiegan out, right? It's obvious she was lying about the painting, so it stands to reason she's lying about everything else, including, most importantly, who really killed Hyacinth. Would you agree?"

"I would have to agree with that, yes."

"What I haven't quite figured out is: how do we gather the evidence necessary for Inspector Carlyle to drop the charges against Nigel and charge Tiegan? *But* what if we go back to the shop and I break the news to Tiegan that my decorator told me the painting is too big? Of course she's going to be furious because she knows the painting is worthless now. She thought she found a real live one with this American lady who she could unload it on and pay her four thousand dollars for it. But before she can grab the garden hose, I'll tell her that her brother also told me about *another* painting he was trying to buy from Hyacinth, which is also a depiction of Mousehole, but a much smaller work. And it's by a famous artist named . . ."

"Benjamin Prescott."

"That's the one! I'll tell her I've done a little research on Mr. Prescott and discovered his work is quite valuable, so it would not only be a thing of beauty but also a good investment. *And* I could take it home with me on the plane. Are you still following me?"

"I'm still with you. I think."

"Then, to really entice her, I'll tell her I'd be willing to go as high as—I don't know, pick a number—seventy-five hundred American for it?"

"That would buy a lot of cat food."

"I do think that when she left Hyacinth's with the other painting that day, she thought it was the one Nigel wanted. She doesn't strike me as a connoisseur of fine art. He would have described it as a painting of the village and a sea view, and since she couldn't ask Hyacinth to confirm that it *was* the right one—because she had just killed her—she assumed the painting of the village and a sea view that was hanging over the fireplace was the right one. So she brought it back to Nigel and kept the money."

"But Nigel would have been irate if she came back without the money *and* without the right painting."

"Yes, of course. But maybe she *didn't* come back that day, or not until late. Remember she said she had plans to see her boyfriend that evening. But whenever it was that Nigel discovered it was the wrong painting, it was too late to rectify anything because Hyacinth's body had already been found. So what could he do then?"

"Excellent point. Do you suppose he suspected Tiegan of being the one who murdered her?" Teddy was connecting the dots.

"I would bet my life on it. And I would also bet that if anybody was afraid of anybody, it was Nigel who was afraid of his sister. If he believed she had killed once, why wouldn't she be prepared to kill again? Especially if she feared he might turn her in?"

"So she framed *him* instead," Teddy added.

"Eventually, yes."

"And what about this business with the cats?" Teddy wondered.

"I have no doubt that's all true. I think Nigel probably did give her an ultimatum regarding the cats. But if you're afraid your cat-lady sister has just committed a murder, that is *not* the time you're going to choose to threaten to take her cats or kick her out of her apartment."

"A catastrophically bad idea!" Teddy winced at Isabel slightly. "Sorry."

"But what she *did* need to come up with was something to justify to the inspector what took her so long to turn Nigel in. So she went with the cat story."

"Okay, this all makes very good sense. But what I'm most shocked about at this point, is that Tiegan had the where-withal to come up with a plan as complicated as this."

"What if she had help? What if her *boyfriend*—whoever that might be—is also her *accomplice*?"

"It's the only thing that makes sense. She had to have help. But how do we prove it?" Teddy was starting to get excited. After solving crimes in his books for so many years, he might finally have the chance to help solve a real-life murder.

"We need to find out where that little painting went. I have a hunch that once Tiegan learned that it was the small painting that was so valuable, either she or her boyfriend, or both of them, went back to Hyacinth's house and stole it when Alby was in jail."

"And what does your hunch tell you about where the painting may be now?" Teddy asked.

"She wouldn't have stashed it at Nigel's and risked him finding it. And she wouldn't risk having it at home around all those cats. So I would think it's most likely with the boyfriend slash accomplice. But once she learns there's seventy-five hundred dollars in cash on the line, I don't imagine she's going to waste any time going to fetch it."

"I'm following you now. So after we drop this little bombshell on her about the big painting, we'll tell her we'll be back first thing in the morning with the cash for the little one. Then we'll stealthily follow her when she goes to get it. I think it's a brilliant plan, Isabel. It feels very *Hart to Hart!*"

Isabel laughed. "I loved that show! And, yes, that's the plan. I'm glad you approve."

"Might I suggest one little tweak in your plan?"

"Please do, Teddy."

"Rather than go back to the shop right now, maybe it's better that we drive over and get within striking distance, then I'll call her from the car and tell her everything you planned to tell her in person. Don't take this the wrong way, but I think she'll be more likely to trust me. Then, if your hunch is correct—and I have no doubt it is—we'll follow her and let her lead us to the Benjamin Prescott."

"I do think that's a better plan, Teddy. Now, let's go catch a murderer!"

Chapter 26

Teddy parked the Iron Lady far enough down the road so that he and Isabel could see Tiegan pulling out, but he also made sure whichever way she went, they were hidden from view. Teddy made the call and followed the script perfectly, and very convincingly. When he hung up, he looked at Isabel and winked. "And now we wait." But they didn't have to wait long! No more than five minutes had passed before they saw Nigel's Rolls pull out of the drive and turn the opposite direction of where they were parked. Teddy smiled at Isabel mischievously. "It's go time."

Teddy stayed far enough behind the Rolls so as not to arouse suspicion or risk Tiegan recognizing the Iron Lady. A red vintage Jaguar was probably not an ideal car to tail somebody with. But then the Harts drove a canary-yellow Mercedes convertible with vanity plates, and they tailed people all the time without being spotted.

After Tiegan wound her way through several narrow, hedge-lined lanes, consistently scraping the Rolls against most of the hedges along the way, she finally turned into the driveway of a run-down-looking cottage with a front yard badly in need of weeding. And with a Rolls-Royce parked in front, it now looked even more run down. Teddy pulled off to the side of the road, well away from the cottage, and they watched Tiegan get out and march with purpose up to the front door and knock. They couldn't make out who came to the door, but she went in as if it were a home invasion robbery. Isabel and Teddy shared a look, then got out of the car and walked slowly toward the cottage.

There were two windows facing the road, but they both had heavy curtains drawn, so they didn't see much risk of being seen from the inside. "Do you happen to know who lives here, Teddy?"

"I have no idea. But I can see the mailbox on the porch. I'll run up and see if there's anything in there with a name."

"Let me go, Teddy. You're too easy to recognize if somebody comes out."

"I think I'd better go, Isabel. It's too"—she was already on her way—"dangerous."

She looked inside the mailbox, then turned back to Teddy and shook her head. Nothing in there. As she was turning around to leave, she heard a crash followed by some yelling. It was loud enough to alert Teddy, who was with her at the front door five seconds later. It was unmistakably Tiegan who was doing the shouting, but all they could make out from her verbal assault against whomever it was she was attacking were variations of "Where is it?" followed by threats of physical violence. There was no doubt in their minds that it was the painting she was demanding. Then they heard another loud crash, followed by a man's low, whimpering voice. They could barely make out what he was saying, but it sounded as if he were pleading for his life. "I'm calling Barclay," Teddy whispered, then took out his phone and dialed, looking up at the house numbers so he could give him their location. He whispered briefly into the phone, then put it back in his pocket. "He's on his way. Shouldn't be more than five minutes."

"Let's hope this guy *has* five minutes," Isabel said. "I think we need to find a way to distract her and buy some time for whoever she's thinking about killing in there until the inspector gets here." The question was *how* to distract her without her knowing *who* was doing the distracting. Then they heard another crash; a much louder one this time. Tiegan's yelling had turned to screaming, and the man's pleading sounded even more desperate. The situation was clearly escalating. They needed to do something *now*.

Isabel spotted a pile of bricks next to the house. She signaled Teddy to follow her, then picked up one of the bricks. "Go hide behind that hedge over there and I'll join you in two seconds." It was obvious what she planning to do, but Teddy wasn't sure it was such a great idea. He also knew it was too late to talk her out of it. Isabel held the brick up and waited for Teddy to go hide. He hesitated, but then did as she had instructed. As soon as Teddy was safely out of sight, Isabel wound up and launched the brick through the larger of the two windows with the strength of a Russian shot putter. An enormous shattering sound followed as she ran over and ducked behind the hedge with Teddy. "That felt almost therapeutic," she said to Teddy.

"I think we need a better place to hide," Teddy said, looking around for where that better place might be. He saw a garden shed beside the cottage next door, then took Isabel's hand, and they ran over to it. The door was locked, so they hid behind it instead. Isabel peeked around the corner and saw an angry Tiegan standing out in the driveway looking around the yard and up and down the street. Isabel hoped maybe this would give whomever she was terrorizing inside enough time to slip out the back and run for his life.

Just as Tiegan was about to go back inside, a man came stumbling out of the house with a thick rope wound tightly around his neck and his face turning a light shade of blue.

Isabel signaled Teddy to come and see if he could make out who it was, but before he could get a good look, Tiegan had grabbed him and started dragging him back inside. He continued to plead and put up as much resistance as he could muster, but then he seemed to surrender to his fate and went limp. Or he may have passed out. Whatever the case, she finally got him back inside and slammed the door.

At that very moment, Isabel and Teddy were elated to see Inspector Carlyle pulling up in his unmarked car and screech to a halt, followed by two patrol cars with their sirens blaring. They rushed out from behind the shed, startling the inspector. "Tiegan's in there right now trying to strangle a man with a rope!" Isabel yelled to him. "You better hurry!"

Isabel and Teddy then stood in the drive and waited anxiously while the inspector and his men broke down the door and rushed inside. They heard more yelling as the inspector and his men barked orders, presumably at Tiegan, but they could hear her barking back. Suddenly the same terrified man came running out of the house, trying desperately but unsuccessfully to unwrap the rope from around his neck, then passed out no more than twenty feet away from them. They walked over cautiously to take a closer look at him, then looked at each other in disbelief. . . . It was Bobby Blackburn.

An ambulance was next to arrive on the scene. The paramedics jumped out, pulled out a stretcher, and went into action. Within a minute they had completely unwound the rope from Bobby's neck, revived him with a shot of some kind, and put an oxygen mask over his face. After lifting him onto the stretcher, they wheeled him past Isabel and Teddy. Bobby looked up at them, first with bewilderment, and then with what seemed to be an expression of gratitude, probably figuring they were the ones who called the police and saved his life.

After the ambulance pulled away, Inspector Carlyle came

out the front door ahead of two uniformed constables, each holding an arm of the handcuffed and snarling Tiegan. The look she gave Isabel and Teddy as she passed was anything but grateful. In fact, she looked like she would have loved nothing more than to have the chance to strangle them both. The officers put her in the back of one of the police cars, then went back inside. The inspector joined Isabel and Teddy, but nobody had anything to say until he reached into his pocket. "Would either of you care for a Simpkins?" Isabel and Teddy both reached into the tin and took a piece of candy.

"Well done, Mrs. Puddles," Inspector Carlyle said, shaking Isabel's hand. "You have once again proven that murderers—no matter how clever they are, or *think* they are—do not stand a chance once you're on their scent. No matter which side of the Atlantic you're on. Agatha and Sherlock would be most impressed."

"And Detective Waverly would be even more impressed," Teddy was quick to add.

"Thank you for the crash course in how to conduct a proper murder investigation, Isabel," the inspector said humbly.

"You're both too kind. But I'm sure you would have un-raveled the mystery eventually, Inspector."

"I'd like to think so, but it may not have happened until after an innocent man was already—"

Isabel said it with him in unison, "Serving at Her Majesty's pleasure."

The inspector laughed. "Well, I'm off. I've got a murder suspect to book in, and a former murder suspect to release. After profusely apologizing to him. I hope we'll have the chance to say goodbye before you leave us, Isabel."

"I'd like that very much, Barclay."

Chapter 27

It was Isabel's last night in Cornwall. She would take the train back to London in the morning and then to Heathrow to catch an afternoon flight home. She had never been away from home this long in her entire life, and although she was feeling very excited to get back to Gull Harbor, she was also starting to feel a little melancholy about leaving Teddy and Tuppence and the cast of characters she had met during her visit. And she was going to miss Fred and Ginger too. They seemed to sense, just as Jackpot and Corky had, that she was getting ready to leave.

She was in the guest cottage and had just finished her packing when Teddy called for her to come in for tea. As soon as she walked in the door, there was a roomful of smiling people clapping for her. Teddy and Tuppence had put together a surprise bon voyage party for her. Isabel was completely overwhelmed and immediately felt tears running down her cheeks. Hugo and Matilde were there, and so was Kenly from the Lion Pub. After a round of hugs—even one from Matilde—two more guests arrived: Inspector Carlyle and with him none other than Nigel Plumbottom, who came right over and gave her a bear hug.

"I understand I have you to thank for my freedom, Isabel. I had just about given up hope when Barclay told me about everything that happened, and how it was your dogged determination that brought the real killer to justice. Shame it turned out to be my sister, but one less gift I have to buy at Christmas, I suppose." Everybody laughed at Nigel's remark, including Isabel, despite its being slightly inappropriate. "I owe you my life, Isabel. How can I ever repay you?"

"Seeing you here is payment enough for me, Nigel. I never believed for a second you were guilty. Not for a second."

The sound of a champagne cork exploding startled the room. Tuppence distributed flutes, while Teddy came behind and poured. Tuppence had prepared another Cornish feast in Isabel's honor and made another banoffee pie, which Isabel was determined to learn how to make and introduce to her friends and family back home.

The conversation flowed easily and the mood was jovial. Isabel was touched beyond words to have been given such a thoughtful, heartfelt send-off. It was going to make it just that much harder to say goodbye, though. Throughout the meal, Teddy and Isabel exchanged glances, a few that even bordered on flirtatious. This trip had been quite a bonding experience for the two of them, and Isabel was already looking forward to seeing Teddy this summer. Where things went from here, who could know, but whether or not anything romantic was in the cards, she knew she had made an amazing friend in Teddy Mansfield, and she hoped he felt the same about her.

After the pie was served, Matilde and Hugo stood up to say their good-nights. "We still have packing to do," Hugo told the table.

Matilde then chimed in with excitement. "We are off to Greece first thing in the morning!"

Isabel still couldn't get over the change she had seen in Matilde since Hugo came back into her life. Yes, the two of them had gotten off to a rocky start, but it was obvious to Isabel that Matilde's less than friendly welcome was merely a sign of how lonely and unhappy she was, so all was forgiven, as far as she was concerned. Now they had become, if not friends, at least much friendlier. She hugged them both and wished them well in their new life together.

"Are you going to start your cruise through the Greek islands already?" Teddy asked.

"No, we're looking at properties," Matilde announced.

Teddy looked confused. "What happened to Spain, Matilde?"

"I hate Spain! You know that, Theodore."

Matilde and Hugo made sure Isabel knew she was invited to their wedding. And Isabel made sure they knew they were invited to visit her in Gull Harbor. "Maybe it *is* time for me to finally visit the colonies," Matilde teased. "Although I've heard mixed reviews."

After the soon to be newlyweds left, Teddy suggested the remaining guests come into the living room and have a brandy. Tuppence excused herself to clean up, but Teddy insisted she join them. "I'll help you with those dishes later."

"I will too!" Isabel said. "Please come and sit down, Tuppence."

Once Teddy poured the brandy, it didn't take long for Isabel to get around to asking Inspector Carlyle and Nigel about the Benjamin Prescott painting that had created such drama.

"Bobby took it to a pawnshop in Penzance and pawned it for two hundred quid. When he finally admitted that to Tiegan, that's when she got out the rope."

"And I went to that same pawnshop with Bobby's pawn ticket and got it back!" Nigel added with pride.

"Did we ever find out whether it was Tiegan or Bobby who stole it from Hyacinth's house, Barclay?" Teddy asked.

"Bobby said it was Tiegan and Tiegan said it was Bobby.

In this case I *do* believe Tiegan. Alby has agreed not to press charges, but I insisted that be conditional upon Bobby paying Alby the two thousand quid."

"And are you charging Alby with anything, Inspector?" Isabel asked.

"I really don't want to. He's got enough problems, mental and otherwise, but we'll have to see what the magistrate has to say. I'm going to suggest probation, however."

"I think that would be the right thing to do. But he's still got a tough road ahead, and it sounds like pretty soon, homeless to boot." Isabel shook her head sadly. "Poor thing."

Tuppence was not feeling quite as sympathetic. "Well, that poor thing sabotaged any chance I had at winning the bake-off this year, and he buried his mother in the garden and then impersonated her! I do believe in forgiveness, but let's see if he earns it. As far as being homeless . . ." Tuppence looked over at Teddy and raised her eyebrows. "Go ahead and tell them, Lordship."

"I thought we agreed to keep that confidential," Teddy scolded.

"Like my scone recipe! That's right . . . My bad!"

Teddy's guests were all waiting for their host to come clean about whatever it was Tuppence was on about. "All right, well, I talked to the bank today and I put in an offer on Hyacinth's property."

"Go on, Lordship."

Teddy shot Tuppence a look. He was clearly annoyed. "And I told Alby he could live there rent free for one year, contingent upon his getting a job and also seeing a therapist. If he can afford the rent after his year is up, he can stay, if not, he'll need to move on."

Isabel smiled at Teddy and her eyes welled up. "That's just about the sweetest, most generous thing I've ever heard, Teddy Mansfield. You really are something, you know that?"

"Yes, he's something all right! Now I have to have that window licker for a neighbor for at least another year!"

"'To err is human, to forgive, divine.' Alexander Pope," Teddy said to Tuppence with a smile.

"I never claimed to be divine. Too late for me to catch *that* train!"

"Wait a minute, Tuppence . . . Aren't you the one who sent me down to see Alby in jail with a Tupperware full of Hobnobs? I'd say that was pretty divine."

Teddy clapped his hands together. "Cover blown! You old softie! You're all bark."

"You know what *was* divine? Those Hobnobs! I'd love that recipe, along with your scone recipe *and* your recipe for banoffee pie."

"I'll write them down for you, Isabel."

"And remember, my dear," Teddy added, "If things had gone any differently than they did with that bake-off, you may never have been given your once-in-a-lifetime chance to go to Buckingham Palace and bake scones for the future king and queen consort of England! Alby and Hyacinth may have done you quite a favor. Rather beats a golden rolling pin *any* day, I'd say!"

"All right, all right . . . you've made your point, Lordship. I suppose I can try to drum up a little forgiveness for that barmy boy."

Inspector Carlyle got up to leave. "Thank you again, Isabel, for all your help and for saving my reputation. May I call on you for our next murder?"

"Absolutely, Barclay. I'm just an ocean away."

Next it was Nigel's turn to say good night. "You're my hero, Isabel. If it weren't for you, this one would have had me shackled in a dungeon serving at Her Majesty's pleasure for the rest of my life. I'll never forget what you've done for me." He grabbed her in another bear hug. "Please come back and see us."

"I may just do that, Nigel. I still want to see that Benjamin Prescott painting!"

"And so you shall." Nigel followed Inspector Carlyle through the foyer and out the door. "And Teddy, see if Alby's interested in adopting some cats, will you, please? That's quite a large property. And probably crawling with mice!"

The next morning, Tuppence arrived early for work and made a fresh batch of orange-rhubarb scones to send with Isabel. "You have no idea how happy this makes me, Tuppence. Thank you!" Isabel hugged her and put the scones into her tote bag.

"I wrote down those recipes you asked for too." Tuppence handed her some folded sheets of paper.

"You're the best. I can't wait to try them!"

"I'm not very good at goodbyes. They sound too final"—Tuppence's eyes were filling with tears—"so I'll just say, see you again soon." She gave Isabel a hug and quickly composed herself. "Now I need to tend to the wash. You have a safe trip, Isabel. And promise to come back and see us. Even with all the madness these past few weeks, I haven't seen Mr. M. as happy as he's been with you here in some time."

"That's lovely to hear. And remember you promised to write and tell me all about your visit to the palace! I'm so excited for you!"

"I'm a nervous wreck, but I promise to write."

Teddy walked in with Isabel's suitcases. "I'll go put these in the car. Then we should get going. Don't want you to miss your train."

Isabel looked down at her feet and saw Fred and Ginger looking up at her with those beautiful corgi eyes. She nearly broke into tears when she noticed they had both managed to pull their leashes off the door hook and drag them over to her.

Teddy came back inside. "Are you ready, Mrs. Puddles?"

"As I'll ever be," Isabel answered. She looked back to say

a final goodbye to Tuppence, but she had disappeared. What Isabel couldn't know was that she was in the garage loading up the washer and wiping away tears with the laundry.

"Come on, you two," Teddy said to his faithful corgis. "It's back to school for you!"

Teddy had to get to class, so he and Isabel only had time for a quick goodbye at the train station. Fred and Ginger slathered her with kisses before she got out of the car, and Teddy carried her suitcases up to the platform. "I can't thank you enough for coming to visit, Isabel. I don't remember the last time I ever enjoyed anyone's company as much as I have yours." He put his arms around her and they had a long hug.

Isabel looked up at him. Her eyes were welling up again, and so were Teddy's. "I can't thank *you* enough for inviting me to visit. Not only have I had the experience of a lifetime seeing a country I've been dreaming about since I was a girl, but I also got to spend time with somebody whose company I've enjoyed more than I have anyone else's in a very long time either."

They hugged again, and this time—as they went to kiss each other on the cheek—they veered off course a bit and ended up giving each other a little peck on the lips. Teddy then presented her with his latest book, which he had been hiding under his jacket, the same book her new friend Runa was reading at the airport in Chicago. "As promised . . . a little something for you to read on your flight home. If you feel like it. No pressure."

Isabel was thrilled. "I will relish every word. Thank you, Mr. Cavendish." Isabel slipped the book into her tote. "Between your book and Tuppence's scones, this is going to be a very enjoyable trip home."

Teddy looked down the tracks and saw the train coming. "All right, my dear. Have a safe trip, and I will see you in Gull Harbor this summer. I already can't wait to see you again."

"Likewise," Isabel said.

When the train came to a stop, Teddy quickly boarded with Isabel's bags, put them in the luggage rack, and before he got off, gave her another hug. "I'll see you soon. And do see if you can make it home without being dragged into another murder."

Isabel laughed. "Don't jinx me." Once on board, she found her seat next to the window and looked out to see Teddy smiling and waving goodbye as the train pulled away. She waved back, and although she felt a little bit like crying, she decided instead that there was nothing to cry about. In fact, she had everything to smile about. Isabel could already sense that her life after the UK, and especially after Cornwall, was going to be even richer than it was before.

Once she arrived in London, Isabel caught another train from Paddington Station to Heathrow with plenty of time to spare before her flight home. She had already emailed Ginny and Grady to give them her flight information, and they assured her they would be at the airport to pick her up. It was comforting to know they would be on the other end to meet her. She had just gotten herself settled and seated at the gate, then took Teddy's book out of her tote. She opened it to find that Teddy had inscribed something in it.

For Isabel . . . With many thanks and humble gratitude for your friendship and your inspiration. Love, Teddy (aka Archie)

Isabel was about to get choked up all over again when she heard a voice. "Don't you just love his work?"

Wait. Isabel knew that voice. She looked up from her book. "Runa!"

"Isabel! What are the chances? How lovely to see you again." Isabel stood up and they gave each other a hug. Runa was looking as elegant as ever, wearing another gorgeous sari, this one in blues and greens. "How was your trip to Cornwall? I must tell you, I read about a murder in some little Cornish village—I've forgotten the name—but of course I thought of you. Some poor old woman was strangled to death with a garden hose and buried in her garden! In a primrose patch! I don't know if they ever caught the murderer. But can you imagine?"

Isabel was caught off guard, but quickly recovered. There was no way she was going down this road. "What is this world coming to when a woman isn't safe in her own garden?" She shook her head sadly. "But I suppose these are the times we're living in." Maybe she would fill Runa in this summer if she came to her barbecue and met Teddy, but in the meantime, she'd had just about enough talk of murder. Isabel was looking forward to a nice, long chat with her new friend about something far more pleasant. "Now, I want to hear all about the wedding. Oh, and you must try one of these scones!"

Tuppence's Orange-Rhubarb Scones with Cardamom (aka "Duchess of Cornwall Scones")

Ingredients

- ½ cup granulated sugar
- 2¼ cups all-purpose flour
- 1 tablespoon baking powder
- 1 tablespoon orange zest
- 1 teaspoon ground cardamom
- ½ teaspoon salt
- 8 tablespoons cold unsalted butter, cut in pieces
- ½ cup, possibly a little bit more, cold buttermilk or half-and-half
- 1 teaspoon vanilla extract
- 1 cup chopped rhubarb, about 1 to 3 stalks, depending on size

Icing

- 2 or 3 tablespoons fresh orange juice
- 1 teaspoon orange zest
- 1 cup confectioners' sugar

Instructions

Preheat oven to 375 degrees F. Line a baking sheet with parchment paper.

1. To the bowl of a food processor, add the sugar, flour, baking powder, orange zest, cardamom, and salt, and pulse to combine.

2. Drop in the pieces of cold butter and pulse about 20 to 25 times, until the mixture resembles coarse crumbs. Or mix to same consistency with your hands.

3. Transfer the mixture to a large mixing bowl and add in the buttermilk or half-and-half, and vanilla extract. Mix gently with a large spoon until the dough is crumbly. If it's too dry, add a little more buttermilk or half-and-half. Carefully fold in the chopped rhubarb.

4. Turn the mixture onto a floured surface and knead a few times until the dough becomes one piece, without too much dry flour left. Pat it out into a rectangular shape and use a 3-inch biscuit cutter to cut out the scones. You can also cut the dough into squares or triangles if you prefer.

5. On the lined baking sheet, arrange the scones a couple of inches apart and bake for about 20 minutes, until scones just start to turn golden. Don't overbake!

6. To make the icing, simply mix together the fresh orange juice, orange zest, and confectioners' sugar to a consistency that will allow you to drizzle over your scones after they've cooled.

Acknowledgments

I would like to extend my sincerest thanks and gratitude to John S. at Kensington who has been a delight to work with. I couldn't ask for a more gracious, supportive, or patient editor . . . And thank you to Larissa, publicist extraordinaire, and the rest of the Kensington team for keeping the pages turning . . . Special thanks to my friend and fellow Michigander, Mark L., for his loyalty and encouragement and for so warmly embracing Isabel and her world. Thank you to Mitchell B., my oldest friend, for his ongoing support and friendship and for lobbying his suburban Detroit librarian to order my books . . . Thanks to my friend Michael M., yet another Michigander, for his devotion to Isabel and company and for his real-time updates on his favorite lines . . . Love and deep appreciation, as always, to my dear friends Rick C. and Rob S. for their many, *many* years of loyal friendship, never-ending laughs— appropriate and inappropriate—and for showing a fair amount of tolerance when required . . . Thank you to Alicia G. for her friendship, her generosity, and her entertaining quirkiness . . . Of course I could never forget my dear friends George S. and Alex S.—I know this because I've tried. Love and thanks to my former neighbor but always my friend Rachel M., and to my other Palmerston Place neighbors and friends: J.J., Carey, and Carlos. Finally, a heartfelt thank-you to my *Brit Whisperer*, Jonah H., for his consult, his humor (sorry, humour), and for enhancing both this book and my life.